Thren snapped up his short sword and blocked the first two blows from the man's dagger. He tried to counter, but his vision was still blurred and his speed a pathetic remnant of his finely honed reflexes. A savage chop knocked the sword from his hand. Thren fell back, using his chair to force a stumble out of his pursuer. The best he could do was limp, though, and when a heel kicked his knee, he fell. He spun, refusing to die with a dagger in his back.

"Leon sends his greetings," the man said, his dagger pulled back for a final, lethal blow.

He suddenly jerked forward, his eyes widening. The dagger fell from his limp hand as the would-be assassin collapsed. Behind him stood Aaron, holding a bloody short sword. Thren's eyes widened as his younger son knelt. The flat edge rested on his palms, blood running down his wrists.

"Your sword," Aaron said, presenting the blade.

"How... why did you return?" Thren asked.

"The man was hiding," the boy said, his voice still quiet. He didn't sound the least bit upset. "Waiting for us to go. So I waited for him."

Thren felt the corners of his mouth twitch. He took the sword from a boy who spent his days reading underneath his bed and skulking within closets, often mocked by his older brother for being too soft. A boy who never threw a punch when forced into a fight, never dared raise his voice in anger.

A boy

BY DAVID DALGLISH

Shadowdance

A Dance of Cloaks

A Dance of Blades

A Dance of Mirrors

A Dance of Shadows

A Dance of Ghosts

A Dance of Chaos

Cloak and Spider (*novella*)

Seraphim

Skyborn

Fireborn

Shadowborn

A DANCE OF CLOAKS

SHADOWDANCE: BOOK 1

DAVID DALGLISH

www.orbitbooks.net

ORBIT

First published in Great Britain in 2013 by Orbit

11 12

All characters and events in this publication, other than those clearly in the public domain, are fictitious and any resemblance to real persons, living or dead, is purely coincidental.

A CIP catalogue record for this book is available from the British Library.

ISBN 978-0-356-50278-6

Printed and bound by Clays Ltd, Elcograf S.p.A

Papers used by Orbit are from well-managed forests and other responsible sources.

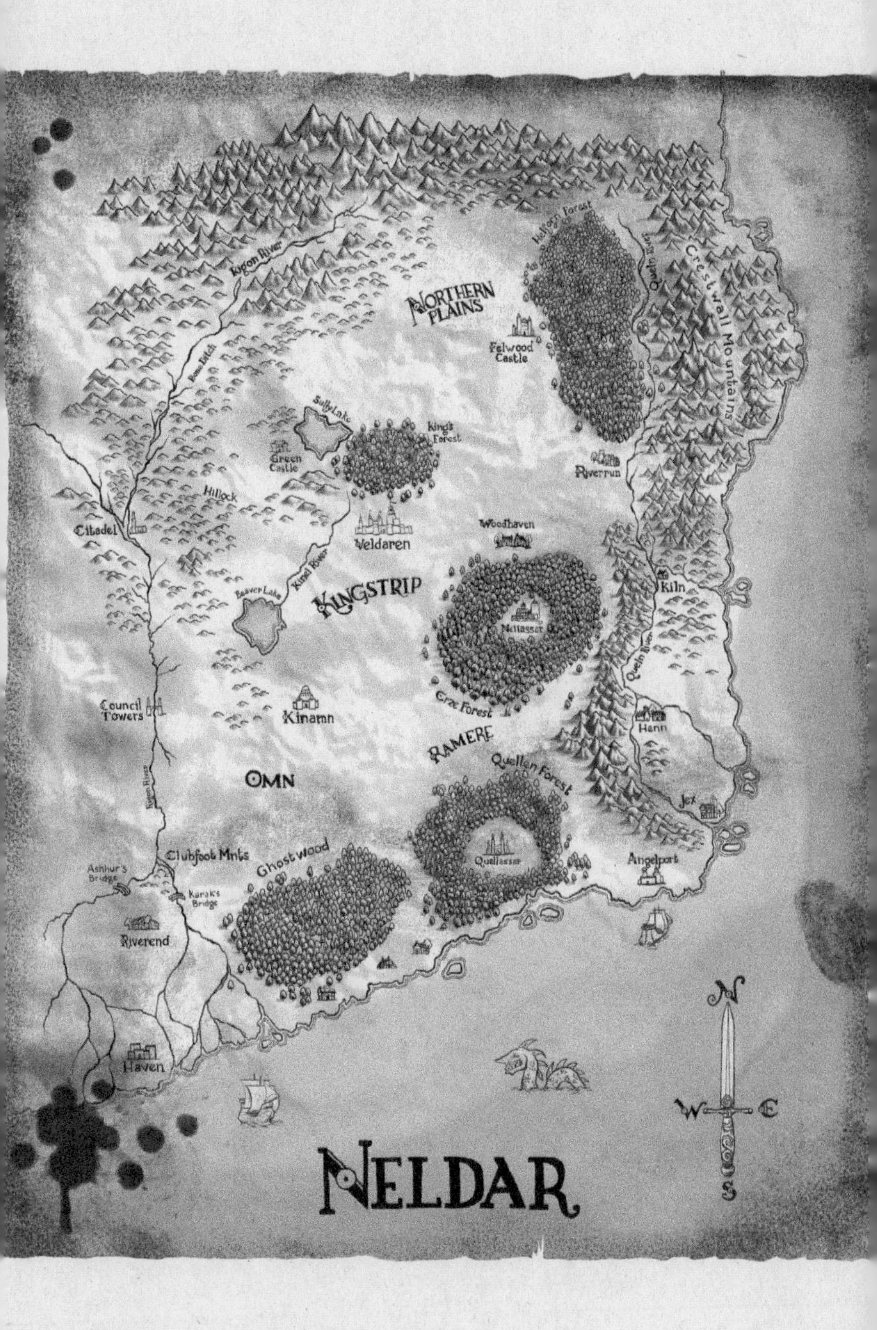

NORTHERN PLAINS
Felwood Forest
Felwood Castle
Crestwall Mountains
Rygon River
Sally Lake
King's Forest
Green Castle
Riverrun
Hillock
Citadel
Weldaren
Woodhaven
Beaver Lake
KINGSTRIP
Kiln
Nellassar
Council Towers
Kinamn
Erze Forest
RAMERE
Hann
Quellen Forest
OMN
Jex
Clubfoot Mnts
Ghostwood
Quellassar
Angelport
Ashhur's Bridge
Karak's Bridge
Riverend
Haven
N
W
E
S
NELDAR

PROLOGUE

For the past two weeks the simple building had been his safe house, but now Thren Felhorn distrusted its protection as he limped through the door. He clutched his right arm to his body, fighting to halt its trembling. Blood ran from his shoulder to his elbow, the arm cut by a poisoned blade.

"Damn you, Leon," he said as he staggered across the wood floor, through a sparsely decorated room, and up to a wall made of plaster and oak. Even with his blurred vision he located the slight groove with his fingers. He pressed down, detaching an iron lock on the other side of the wall. A small door swung inward.

The master of the Spider Guild collapsed in a chair and removed his gray hood and cloak. He sat in a much larger room painted silver and decorated with pictures of mountains and fields. Removing his shirt, he gritted his teeth while pulling it over his wounded arm. The toxin had been meant to paralyze him, not kill him, but the fact was little comfort. Most likely Leon Connington had wanted him alive so he could sit in his padded chair and watch his "gentle touchers" bleed Thren drop by drop. The fat man's treacherous words from their meeting ignited a fire in his gut that refused to die.

"We will not cower to rats that live off our shit," Leon had said while brushing his thin mustache. "Do you really think you stand a chance against the wealth of the Trifect? We could buy your soul from the gods."

Such arrogance. Such pride. Thren had fought down his initial impulse to bury a short sword in the fat man's throat upon hearing such mockery. For centuries the three families of the Trifect, the Conningtons, the Keenans, and the Gemcrofts, had ruled in the shadows. Over that time they'd certainly bought enough priests and kings to believe that the gods wouldn't be beyond the reach of their gilded fingers either.

It had been a mistake to deny his original impulse, Thren knew. Leon should have bled out then and there, his guards be damned. They'd met inside Leon's extravagant mansion, another mistake. Thren vowed to correct his carelessness in the coming months. For three years he'd done his best to stop the war from erupting, but it appeared everyone in the city of Veldaren desired chaos.

If the city wants blood, it can have it, Thren thought. *But it won't be mine.*

"Is that you, Father?" he heard his elder son ask from an adjacent room.

"It is," Thren said, holding his anger in check. "But if it were not, what would you do, having given away your presence?"

His son Randith entered from the other room. He looked much like his father, having the same sharp features, thin nose, and grim smile. His hair was brown like his mother's, and that alone endeared him to Thren. They both wore the gray trousers of their guild, and from Randith's shoulders hung a gray cloak similar to Thren's. A long rapier hung from one side of

Randith's belt, a dagger from the other. His blue eyes met his father's.

"I'd kill you," Randith said, a cocky grin pulling up the left side of his face. "As if I need surprise to do it."

"Shut the damn door," Thren said, ignoring the bravado. "Where's our mage? Connington's men cut me with a toxin, and its effect is . . . troublesome."

Troublesome hardly described it, but Thren wouldn't let his son know that. His flight from the mansion was a blur in his memory. The toxin had numbed his arm and made his entire side sting with pain. His neck muscles had fired off at random, and one of his knees kept locking up during his run. Like a cripple he'd fled through the alleyways of Veldaren, but the moon was waning and the streets empty, so none had seen his pathetic stumbling.

"Not here," Randith said as he leaned toward his father's exposed shoulder and examined the cut.

"Then go find him," Thren said. "How did events go at the Gemcroft mansion?"

"Maynard Gemcroft's men fired arrows from their windows as we approached," Randith said. He turned his back to his father and opened a few cupboards until he found a small black bottle. He popped the cork, but when he moved to pour the liquid on his father's cut, Thren yanked the bottle out of his hand. Dripping the brown liquid across the cut, he let out a hiss through clenched teeth. It burned like fire, but already he felt the tingle of the toxin beginning to fade. When finished, he accepted some strips of cloth from his son and tied them tight around the wound.

"Where is Aaron?" Thren asked when the pain subsided. "If you won't fetch the mage, at least he will."

"Lurking as always," Randith said. "Reading too. I tell him mercenaries may soon storm in with orders to eradicate all thief guilds, and he looks at me like I'm a lowly fishmonger mumbling about the weather."

Thren held in a grimace.

"You're too impatient with him," he said. "Aaron understands more than you think."

"He's soft, and a coward. This life will never suit him."

Thren reached out with his good hand, grabbed Randith by the front of his shirt, and yanked him close so they might stare face-to-face.

"Listen well," he said. "Aaron is my son, as are you. Whatever contempt you have, you swallow it down. Even the wealthiest king is still dirt in my eyes compared to my own flesh and blood, and I expect the same respect from you."

He shoved Randith away, then called out farther into the hideout.

"Aaron! Your family needs you, now come in here."

A short child of eight stepped into the room, clutching a worn book to his chest. His features were soft and curved, and he would no doubt grow up to be a comely man. He had his father's hair, though, a soft blond that curled around his ears and hung low to his deep blue eyes. He fell to one knee and bowed his head without saying a word, all while still holding the book.

"Do you know where Cregon is?" Thren asked, referring to the mage in their employ. Aaron nodded. "Good. Where?"

Aaron said nothing. Thren, tired and wounded, had no time for his younger son's nonsense. While other children grew up babbling nonstop, a good day for Aaron involved nine words, and rarely would they be used in one sentence.

"Tell me where he is, or you'll taste blood on your tongue," Randith said, sensing his father's exasperation.

"He went away," Aaron said, his voice barely above a whisper. "He's a fool."

"A fool or not, he's my fool, and damn good at keeping us alive," Thren said. "Go bring him here. If he argues, slash your finger across your neck. He'll understand."

Aaron bowed and did as he was told.

"I wonder if he's practicing for a vow of silence," Randith said as he watched his brother leave without any hurry.

"Did he lock the outer door?" Thren asked.

"Shut and latched," Randith said after checking.

"Then he's smarter than you."

Randith smirked.

"If you say so. But right now, I think we have bigger concerns. The Gemcrofts firing at my men, Leon setting up a trap... this means war, doesn't it?"

Thren swallowed hard, then nodded.

"The Trifect have turned their backs on peace. They want blood, our blood, and unless we act fast they are going to get it."

"Perhaps if we offer even more in bribes?" Randith suggested.

Thren shook his head.

"They've tired of the game. We rob them until they are red with rage, then pay bribes with their own wealth. You've seen how much they've invested in mercenaries over the past few months. Their minds are set. They want us exterminated."

"That's ludicrous," Randith insisted. "You've united nearly every guild in the city. Between our assassins, our spies, our thugs... what makes them think they can withstand all-out war?"

Thren frowned as Randith's fingers drummed the hilt of his rapier.

"Give me a few of our best men," his son said. "When Leon Connington bleeds out in his giant bed, the rest will learn that accepting our bribes is far better than accepting our mercy."

"You are still a young man," Thren said. "You are not ready for what Leon has prepared."

"I am seventeen," Randith said. "A man grown, and I have more kills to my name than years."

"And I've more than you've drawn breaths," Thren said, a hard edge entering his voice. "But even I will not return to that mansion. They are *eager* for this, can't you see that? Entire guilds will be wiped out in days. Those who survive will inherit this city, and I will not have my heir run off and die in the opening hours."

Thren placed one of his short swords on the table with his uninjured hand. Holding it there, he met Randith's gaze, challenging him, looking to see just what sort of man his son truly was.

"I'll leave the mansion be, as you suggest," Randith said. "But I will not cower and hide. You are right, Father. These are the opening hours. Our actions here will decide the course of months of fighting. Let the merchants and nobles hide. *We* rule the night."

He pulled his gray cloak over his head and turned to the hidden door. Thren watched him go, his hands shaking, but not from the toxin.

"Be wary," Thren said, careful to keep his face a mask. "Everything you do has consequences."

If Randith sensed the threat, he didn't let it show.

"I'll go get Senke," said Randith. "He'll watch over you until Aaron returns with the mage."

Then he was gone. Thren struck the table with his palm and swore. He thought of the countless hours he'd invested in Randith, the training, the sparring, and the many lectures, all in an attempt to cultivate a worthy heir for the Spider Guild.

Wasted, Thren thought. *Wasted.*

He heard the click of the latch, and then the door creaked open. Thren expected the mage, or perhaps his son returning to smooth over his abrupt exit, but instead a short man with a black cloth wrapped around his face stepped inside.

"Don't run," the intruder said. Thren snapped up his short sword and blocked the first two blows from the man's dagger. He tried to counter, but his vision was still blurred and his speed a pathetic remnant of his finely honed reflexes. A savage chop knocked the sword from his hand. Thren fell back, using his chair to force a stumble out of his pursuer. The best he could do was limp, though, and when a heel kicked his knee, he fell. He spun, refusing to die with a dagger in his back.

"Leon sends his greetings," the man said, his dagger pulled back for a final, lethal blow.

He suddenly jerked forward, his eyes widening. The dagger fell from his limp hand as the would-be assassin collapsed. Behind him stood Aaron, holding a bloody short sword. Thren's eyes widened as his younger son knelt. The flat edge rested on his palms, blood running down his wrists.

"Your sword," Aaron said, presenting the blade.

"How...why did you return?" Thren asked.

"The man was hiding," the boy said, his voice still quiet. He didn't sound the least bit upset. "Waiting for us to go. So I waited for him."

Thren felt the corners of his mouth twitch. He took the sword from a boy who spent his days reading underneath his bed and skulking within closets, often mocked by his older brother for being too soft. A boy who never threw a punch when forced into a fight, never dared raise his voice in anger.

A boy who had killed a man at the age of eight.

"I know you're bright," Thren said. "But the life we live is twisted, and we are forever surrounded by liars and betrayers. You must trust your instincts, and learn to listen to not just what is said, but what is not. Can you do this? Can you view men and women as if they are pieces to a game, and understand what must be done, my son?"

Aaron looked up at him. If he was bothered by the blood on him, it didn't show.

"I can," Aaron said.

"Good," said Thren. "Wait with me. Randith will return soon."

Ten minutes later the door crept open.

"Father?" Randith asked as he stepped inside. Senke, Thren's right-hand man, was with him. He looked slightly older than Randith, with a trimmed blond beard and a thick mace held in hand. They both startled at the dead body lying on the floor, a gaping wound in its back.

"He waited until you left," Thren said from his chair, which he'd positioned to face the entrance.

"Where?" Randith asked. He pointed to Aaron. "And why is he here?"

Thren shook his head.

"You don't understand, Randith. You disobey me, not out of wisdom, but out of arrogance and pride. You treat our enemies with contempt instead of respect worthy of their danger. Worst of all, you put my life at risk."

He looked to Aaron, back to Randith.

"Too many mistakes," he said. "Far too many."

Then he waited. And hoped.

Aaron stepped toward his older brother. His blue eyes were calm, unworried. In a single smooth motion, he yanked Randith's dagger from his belt, flipped it around, and thrust it to the hilt in his brother's chest. Senke stepped back, jaw hanging open, but he wisely held his tongue. Aaron withdrew the dagger, spun around, and presented it as a gift to his father.

Thren rose from his seat and placed a hand on Aaron's shoulder.

"You did well, my son," he said. "My heir."

"Thank you," Aaron whispered, tears in his eyes. He bowed low as behind him the body of his brother bled out on the floor.

FIVE YEARS LATER…

CHAPTER

1

Aaron sat alone. The walls were bare wood. The floor had no carpet. There were no windows and only a single door, locked and barred from the outside. The silence was heavy, broken only by his occasional cough. In the far corner was a pail full of his waste. Thankfully, he had gotten used to the smell after the first day.

His new teacher had given him only one instruction: wait. He had been given a waterskin, but no food, no timetable, and worst of all, nothing to read. The boredom was far worse than his previous instructor's constant beatings and shouts. Gus the Gruff he had called himself. The other members of the guild whispered that Thren had lashed Gus thirty times after his son's training was finished. Aaron hoped his new teacher would be outright killed. Of all his teachers over the past five years, he was starting to think Robert Haern was the cruelest.

That was all he knew, the man's name. He was a wiry old

man with a gray beard curled around his neck and tied behind his head. When he'd led Aaron to the room, he had walked with a cane. Aaron had never minded isolation, so at first the idea of a few hours in the dark sounded rather enjoyable. He had always stayed in corners and shadows, greatly preferring to watch people talk than take part in their conversation.

But now? After spending untold hours, perhaps even days, locked in darkness? Even with his love of isolation and quiet, this was . . .

And then Aaron felt certain of what was going on. Walking over to the door, he knelt before it and pushed his fingers into the crack beneath. For a little while light had crept in underneath the frame, but then someone had stuffed a rag across it, completing the darkness. Using his slender fingers he pushed the rag back, letting in a bit of light. He had not done so earlier for fear of angering his new master. Now he couldn't care less. They wanted him to speak. They wanted him to crave conversation with others. Whoever this Robert Haern was, his father had surely hired him for that purpose.

"Let me out."

The words came out as a raspy whisper, yet the volume startled him. He had meant to boom the command at the top of his lungs. Was he really so timid?

"I said let me out," he shouted, raising the volume tremendously.

The door opened. The light hurt his eyes, and during the brief blindness, his teacher slipped inside and shut the door. He held a torch in one hand and a book in the other. His smile was partially hidden behind his beard.

"Excellent," Robert said. "I've only had two students last longer, both with more muscle than sense." His voice was firm but grainy, and it seemed to thunder in the small dark room.

"I know what you're doing," Aaron said.

"Come now, what's that?" the old man asked. "My ears haven't been youthful for thirty years. Speak up, lad!"

"I said I know what you're doing."

Robert laughed.

"Is that so? Well, knowing and preventing are two different things. You may know a punch is coming, but does that mean you can stop it? Well, your father has told me of your training, so perhaps you could, yes, perhaps."

As his eyes adjusted to the torchlight, Aaron slowly backed into a corner. With the darkness gone he felt naked. His eyes flicked to the pail in the corner, and he suddenly felt embarrassed. If the old man was bothered by the smell, he didn't seem to show it.

"Who are you?" Aaron asked after the silence had stretched longer than a minute.

"My name is Robert Haern. I told you that when I first brought you in here."

"That tells me nothing," Aaron said. "Who are you?"

Robert smiled, just a flash of amusement on his wrinkled face, but Aaron caught it and wondered what it meant.

"Very well, Aaron. At one point I was the tutor of King Edwin Vaelor, but he has since gotten older and tired of my... corrections."

"Corrections," Aaron said, and it all confirmed what he'd guessed. "Was this my correction for not talking enough?"

To Aaron's own surprise, Robert looked shocked.

"Correction? Dear lord, boy, no, no. I was told of your quiet nature, but that is not what your father has paid me for. This dark room is a lesson that I hope you will soon understand. You have learned how to wield a sword and sneak through shadows. I, however, walk with a cane and make loud popping noises. So tell me, what purpose might I have with you?"

Aaron shifted his arms tighter about himself. He had no idea whether it was day or night, but the room felt cold and he had nothing but his thin clothing for warmth.

"You're to teach me," Aaron said.

"That's stating the bloody obvious. What is it I will teach you?"

He sat down in the middle of the room while still holding the torch aloft. He grunted, and true to his word his back popped when he stretched.

"I don't know," the boy said.

"A good start," Robert said. "If you don't know an answer, just say so and save everyone the embarrassment. Uninformed guesses only stall the conversation. However, you should have known the answer. I tutored a king, remember? Mind my words. You will always know the answer to every question I ask you."

"A tutor," said Aaron. "I can already read and write. What else can an old man teach me?"

Robert smiled in the flickering torchlight.

"There are men trying to kill you, Aaron. Did you know that?"

At first Aaron opened his mouth to deny it, then stopped. The look in his teacher's eye suggested Aaron think carefully before answering.

"Yes," he finally said. "Though I convinced myself otherwise. The Trifect want all the thief guilds destroyed, their members dead. I am no different."

"Oh, but you are different," Robert said as he put his book down and shifted the torch to his other hand. "You're the heir to Thren Felhorn, one of the most feared men in all of Veldaren. Some say you'll find no finer a thief even if you searched every corner of Dezrel."

Such worship of his father was hardly foreign to Aaron, and something he always took for granted. For once, he dared ask something he'd never had the courage to ask.

"Is he the finest?" Aaron asked.

"I don't know enough of such matters to have a worthwhile opinion," Robert said. "Though I know he has lived a long time, and the wealth he amassed in his younger years is legendary."

Silence came over them. Aaron looked about the room, but it was bare and covered with shadows. He sensed his teacher waiting for him to speak, but he knew not what to say. His gaze lingered on the torchlight as Robert spat to the side.

"There are many questions you should ask, though one is the most obvious and most important. Think, boy."

Aaron's eyes flitted from the torchlight to the old man.

"Who are the Trifect?" he asked.

"Who is what? Speak up, I'm a flea's jump away from deaf."

"The Trifect," Aaron nearly shouted. "Who are they?"

"That is an excellent question," Robert said. "The lords of the Trifect have a saying: 'After the gods, us.' When the Gods' War ended, and Karak and Ashhur were banished by the goddess, the land was a devastated mess. Countries fractured, people rebelled, and pillagers marched up and down the coasts. Three wealthy men formed an alliance to protect their assets. Five hundred years ago they adopted their sigil, that of an eagle perched on a golden branch. They've been loyal to it ever since."

He paused and rubbed his beard. The torch switched hands.

"A question for you, boy: why do they want the thief guilds dead?"

The question was not difficult. The sigil was the answer.

"They never let go of their gold," Aaron said. "Yet we take it from them."

"Precisely," Robert said. "To be sure, they'll spend their gold, sometimes frivolously and without good reason. But even in giving away their coin, they are still master of it. But to have it taken? That is unacceptable to them. The Trifect tolerated the various thief guilds for many centuries while focusing on growing their power. And grow it did. Nearly the entire nation of Neldar is under their control in some way. For the longest of times they viewed the guilds as a nuisance, nothing more. That changed. Tell me why, boy; that is your next question."

This one was tougher. Aaron went over the words of his master. His memory was sharp, and at last he remembered a comment that seemed appropriate.

"My father amassed a legendary amount of wealth," he said. He smiled, proud of deducing the answer. "He must have taken too much from the Trifect, and they no longer considered him a nuisance."

"He was now a threat," Robert agreed. "And he was wealthy. Worse, though, was that his prestige was uniting the other guilds. Mostly your father tempted the stronger members and brought them into his fold, but about eight years ago he started making promises, threats, bribes, and even assassinations to bring about the leaders he needed. As a united presence, he thought even the Trifect would be reluctant to challenge their strength."

The old man opened his book, which turned out to not be a book at all. The inside was hollow, containing some hard cheese and dried meat. It took all of Aaron's willpower to keep from lunging for the food. From his short time with his teacher, he knew such a rash, discourteous action would be rebuked.

"Take it," Robert said. "You have honored me well with your attention."

Aaron didn't need to be told twice. The old man rose to his feet and walked to the door.

"I will return," he said. His fingers brushed over a slot in the wall, too fast for Aaron to see. He heard a soft pop, and then a tiny jut of metal sprung outward. Robert slid the torch through the metal, fastening it to the wall.

"Thank you," Aaron said, thrilled to know the torchlight would remain.

"Think on this," Robert said. "Eight years ago, your father united the guilds. Five years ago, war broke out between them and the Trifect. What caused your father's failure?"

The door opened, bright light flooded in, and then the old man was gone.

Thren was waiting for Robert not far from the door. They were inside a large and tastefully decorated home. Thren leaned against the wall, positioned so he could see both entrances to the living room.

"You told me the first session was the most important," Thren said, his arms crossed over his chest. "How did my son perform?"

"Admirably," Robert said. "And I do not say so out of fear. I've told kings their princes were brats with more snot than brains."

"I can hurt you worse than any king," Thren said, but his comment lacked teeth.

"You should see Vaelor's dungeon sometime," Robert said. "But yes, your son was intelligent and receptive, and most importantly, he let go of his anger for being subjected to the room's darkness once I told him it wasn't a punishment. A few more torches and I'll give him some books to read."

"The smoke won't kill him, will it?" Thren asked as he glanced at the door.

"There are tiny vents in the ceiling," Robert said as he hobbled toward a chair. "I have done this a hundred times, guildmaster, so do not worry. Due to the isolation, his mind will be craving knowledge. He'll learn to master his mind, which I'll hone sharper than any dagger of yours. Hopefully when his time with me is done, he will remember this level of focus and mimic it in more chaotic environments."

Thren pulled his hood over his face and bowed.

"You were expensive," he said. "As the Trifect grows poorer, so do we."

"Whether coin, gem, or food, a thief will always have something to steal."

Thren's eyes seemed to twinkle at that.

"Well worth the coin," he said.

The guildmaster bowed, turned, and then vanished into the dark streets of Veldaren. Robert tossed his cane aside and walked without a limp to the far side of the room. After pouring himself a drink, he sat down in his chair with a grunt of pleasure.

He expected more time to pass, but it seemed people had gotten more impatient as Robert grew older. Barely halfway into his glass, he heard two thumps against the outside of his door. They were his only warning before the plainly dressed man with only the barest hints of gray in his hair entered the living room. His simple face was marred by a scar curling from his left eye to his ear. He did his best to hide it with the hood of his cloak, but Robert had seen it many times before. The man was Gerand Crold, who had replaced Robert as the king's most trusted teacher and advisor.

"Did Thren leave pleased?" Gerand asked as he sat down opposite Robert.

"Indeed," Robert said, letting a bit of his irritation bleed into his voice. "Though I think that pleasure would have faded had he seen the king's advisor sneaking into my home."

"I was not spotted," the man said with an indignant sniff. "Of that, I am certain."

"With Thren Felhorn you can never be certain," Robert said with a dismissive wave of his hand. "Now what brings you here?"

The advisor nodded toward a door. Beyond it was the room Aaron remained within.

"He can't hear us, can he?" Gerand asked.

"Of course not. Now answer my question."

Gerand wiped a hand over his clean-shaven face and let his tone harden.

"For a man living by the king's grace alone, you seem rather rude to his servants. Should I whisper in his ear how uncooperative you're being in this endeavor?"

"Whisper all you want," Robert said. "I am not afraid of that little whelp. He sees spooks in the shadows and jumps with every clap of thunder."

Gerand's eyes narrowed.

"Dangerous words, old man. Your life won't last much longer carrying on with such recklessness."

"My life is nearing its end whether I am reckless or not," Robert said before finishing his drink. "I whisper and plot behind Thren Felhorn's back. I may as well act like the dead man I am."

Gerand let out a laugh.

"You put too much stock in that man's abilities. He's getting older, and he is far from the demigod the laymen whisper about when drunk. But if my presence here scares you so, then I will hurry along. Besides, my wife is waiting for me, and she promised a young redhead for us to play with to celebrate my thirtieth birthday."

Robert rolled his eyes. The boorish advisor was always bragging about his exploits, a third of which were probably true. They were Gerand's favorite stalling tactic when he wanted to linger, observe, and distract his companions. What he was stalling for, Robert didn't have a clue.

"We Haerns have no carnal interests," Robert said, rising from his chair with an exaggerated wince of pain. Gerand saw this and immediately took the cup, offering to fill it for him.

"We just pop right out of our mud fields," Robert continued. "Ever hear that slurp when your boot gets stuck and you have to force it out? That's us, making another Haern."

"Amusing," Gerand said as he handed Robert the glass. "So did you come from a nobleman's cloak, or perhaps a wise man's discarded sock?"

"Neither," Robert said. "Someone pissed in a gopher hole, and out I came, wet and angry. Now tell me why you're here, or I'll go to King Vaelor myself and let him know how displeased I am with *your* cooperation in this endeavor."

If Gerand was upset by the threat, he didn't show it.

"Love redheads," he said. "You know what they say about them? Oh, of course you don't, mud-birth and all. So feisty. But you want me to hurry, so hurry I shall. I've come for the boy."

"Aaron?"

Gerand poured himself a glass of liquor and toasted the old man from the other side of the room.

"The king has decided so, and I agree with his brilliant wisdom. With the boy in hand, we can force Thren to end this annoying little war of his."

"Have you lost your senses?" asked Robert. "You want to take Aaron hostage? Thren is trying to end this war, not prolong it."

He thought of Gerand's stalling, of the way his eyes had

swept every corner of the room and peered through all the doorways. A stone dropped into his gut.

"You have troops surrounding my home," Robert said.

"We watched Thren leave," Gerand said. He downed his drink and licked his lips. "Trust me when I say you're alone. You can play your little game all you want, Robert, but you're still a Haern, and lack any true understanding of these matters. You say Thren wants this war of his to end? You're wrong. He doesn't want to lose, and therefore he won't *let it* end. But the Trifect won't bow to him, not now, not ever. This will only end when one side is dead. Veldaren can live without the thief guilds. Can we live without the food, wealth, and pleasures of the Trifect?"

"I live off mud," Robert said. "Can you?"

He flung his cane. The flat bottom smacked through the glass and struck Gerand's forehead. The man slumped to the floor, blood dripping from his hand. The old man rushed through the doorway as shouts came from the entrance to his home, followed by a loud crack as the door smashed open.

Robert burst into Aaron's training room. The boy winced at the sudden invasion of light. He jumped to his feet, immediately quiet and attentive. The old man felt a bit of sadness, realizing he would never have a chance to continue training such a gifted student.

"You must run," Robert said. "The soldiers will kill you. There's a window out back, now go!"

No hesitation. No questions. Aaron did as he was told.

The floor was cold when Robert sat down in the center. He thought about grabbing the dying torch to use as a weapon, but against armored men, it would be a laughable ploy. A burly man stepped inside as others rushed past, no doubt searching for Aaron. He held manacles in one hand and a naked sword in the other.

"Does the king request my tutelage?" Robert asked, chuckling darkly.

Gerand stepped in beside him, hand wrapped in a cloth to soak up the blood. A bruise was already growing on his forehead.

"Stupid old man," the advisor muttered, and he nodded to the soldier.

Robert closed his eyes, not wanting to see the butt of the sword as it came crashing down on his forehead, knocking him out cold.

CHAPTER

2

Information meant wealth, and Kayla loved both. She was not the quietest thief, and unlike many in her line of work, she did not take to the shadows as fish took to water. Her fingers lacked the dexterity for caressing locks into opening. But her ears were always listening, and her eyes sharp. Throughout her rough life she had learned that dealing with information could net her coin and safety... although it could just as easily earn her death. Sometimes secrets were too dangerous to sell.

Watching the soldiers surround the home, Kayla debated the value of what she saw. Clearly the king, or at least one of his minions, was interfering with the shadowy war being waged between the Trifect and the guilds. She shifted her weight from leg to leg, trying to make sure neither fell asleep. She lay atop a nearby home, having stalked the troops ever since they left the castle grounds by following along the rooftops.

She could barely see the front door, but she had long learned to analyze everything about a man. What a man wore, and the way he walked, could identify him no matter how dark the night, no matter how well he hid his face. Kayla needed little of that skill, though, for when the man stepped out of the door, his hood flapped in the wind, revealing the scarred face of Gerand Crold. He held a hand against his forehead as if he had been wounded. Suddenly he realized the mishap with his cloak, glanced about as if worried, and then pulled it back over his face.

Good luck finding me, she thought.

Kayla smiled. Now this was something she could sell. Every week she met with a squat little man named Undry who ran a shop specializing in perfumes. She would whisper to him what she knew, and then he would give her a garish oversize bottle of what looked like perfume, except filled with silver and gold coin. From there the information traveled upward until it reached Laurie Keenan, the wealthiest of the three lords of the Trifect.

Kayla heard shouting. Shifting her weight, she watched as a boy leaped through a window, hit the ground with a roll, and then darted away. A single soldier was in sight, startled by the broken glass and sudden burst of movement mere feet away.

Before she knew she had reached a decision, Kayla was already moving. Her hand slipped into her belt, where dozens of slender daggers were clipped tight, designed more for throwing than for wielding in melee. Based on the shouts and frantic searching of the soldiers, they clearly wanted the boy. Whoever he was, he was valuable, and Kayla would not let such easy money slip through her fingers. If Undry would pay for rumors of newly hired mercenaries and extra-large shipments, how much might he pay for the blood relative of a Trifect, or perhaps one of the many guildleaders?

She threw her dagger. The shadows might not be a second skin to her, and silence only a loose friend, but when it came to throwing the blade, she knew of no one better. Before the soldier could give chase, a wickedly sharp point pierced the side of his neck and ruptured his windpipe. He collapsed, unable to cry out to the others. Sheathing the second dagger she had grabbed in case she missed, she looked for the boy.

Damn, he's fast, she thought, sprinting after. If the boy hadn't been so panicked, he easily would have heard her clattering across the rooftops. He darted through alleys, cutting back and forth as if to lose a pursuer. His path remained steadily eastward, regardless of how crooked and curved. Once she realized this, Kayla began to shrink the distance by taking a more direct route.

Where are you taking me? she wondered. A great cry rose up all around her. She stopped and crouched, feeling a bit of worry crawl up her chest. It seemed the soldiers had given chase after all, but not just the few that had surrounded the home. Hundreds rushed up and down the streets in small groups.

"The boy!" they shouted. "Hand us over the boy!"

They pressed into homes, swarmed over alleyways, and pushed aside any they wished. Slowly, systematically, they were sealing off the entire eastern district.

"Shit," she muttered.

Kayla wasn't exactly the most wanted lady of Veldaren, but she was no friend of the law, either. A guard in a pissy mood could easily take away her daggers, and if any should make the connection between her and the guard she'd just killed...

"Fuck me up, down, and sideways," she said, wondering how she'd gotten herself so messed up. She hurried from one side of her current rooftop to the other, taking in the positions of the soldiers. Frantic, she ran back to the north edge, realizing she had taken her eyes off the boy. If he'd made a sudden turn, or jumped through a window, then it would be the soldiers who found him, not her.

She did know this: Undry would not be the one paying her for capturing the child. Anyone worth having the entire city guard chase after deserved a far better ransom. A king's ransom, in fact. When she spotted the boy, she let out a sigh. He was a walking bag of gold, and she'd never have forgiven herself for letting him slip away.

He was limping now, though she wasn't sure the reason. He was also veering off the road, and she felt a mix of feelings when she realized why. Before him was an old abandoned temple to Ashhur, which had been stripped of all its valuables when the elegant white-marble temple farther north was completed. The grand double doors had been boarded shut, but those boards were long broken. Kayla smiled when he slipped inside, for she knew there was no way out. At the same time, she wanted to strangle the boy. If the guards searched inside, well... there'd be no way out.

She looked down the street, seeing no nearby patrols. She shimmied down the side of a home. Without pause she ran across the street, kicked one of the doors open, and rushed inside.

Where there had once been painted glass were now thick boards with even thicker nails. Where there had once been rows of benches were now splinters and ruts in the floor. The entire place stank of feces and urine. She paused just inside the door to look for the boy, and that was when he struck her.

She felt a fist smash her temple, followed by a swift kick to her groin. As she staggered to one knee, she couldn't help but smile knowing the boy had assumed a man chased after. Another punch struck her nose, but she caught his wrist before he could pull his fist back. She was not prepared for the sudden maneuver he made. His fingers wrapped around her own wrist, his body twisted, and then she was down on both knees, wincing as the bones of her arm protested in pain.

Any delusions she had of his being a normal boy vanished with her shriek of pain. Her fingernails clawed his skin, but he didn't seem to care. Face-to-face they stared, and if she'd expected to find fear or desperation, she was badly mistaken. His blue eyes seemed to sparkle, and as the boy let go of her wrist and tried to kick her chest, she realized he was enjoying himself.

She ducked under the kick, spun around him, and then jabbed his throat with her elbow. When he collapsed, he rolled his body, avoiding the next two blows from her foot. He caught her heel on her third kick and then shoved it upward. She somersaulted with the push, snapping his chin with her other foot. As he staggered back, she landed lightly on her feet, drew two daggers from her belt, and hurled them across the room.

They stabbed into the floor barely an inch to either side of his feet.

"Soldiers give chase, you stupid boy," Kayla said. "Do you want to get us both killed?"

He opened his mouth, then closed it. Kayla drew two more daggers, twirling them in her fingers. The boy was smart, she could see that. He had to know he was beaten, yet she'd held back her killing blow. Surely that would earn her some measure of trust.

"Your name," she said. "Tell me, and I'll hide you from them."

"My name..." He was not at all winded from the run or their tussle, though he spoke low, as if embarrassed by the sound of his own voice. "My name is Haern."

"The Haerns are simple farmers," Kayla said. "Stop lying to me. We both know you've never bent your back in a field or soiled your clothes in pig shit."

"Haern is my first name," the boy said, and he looked insulted she'd found out the lie so easily. "You haven't asked for my last name yet."

She glanced toward the door, expecting soldiers to come barging in at any moment.

"And what might that be?" she asked.

The doors opened, a pair of guards with swords drawn standing at the entrance.

"Here!" one shouted, the last word he ever spoke. A throwing dagger speared his left eye. The other guard swore, and then another dagger sailed through his open mouth and jabbed into the back of his throat.

"Follow me," Kayla shouted as she grabbed Haern's shirt. He did his best to follow, but she noticed his limp had returned.

"The door," he said, nodding to where the dead guards lay.

"No time," she said. "They'll be there soon."

On the opposite side of the temple was a boarded window. Kayla reached up and yanked on the boards. The wood was old and weather-beaten, but she was not the strongest of women. She tugged and pulled, but the wood refused to break.

"Give me a dagger," Haern said.

Kayla at first thought to refuse, then decided it couldn't possibly make things worse. She gave him one.

"Keep the pointy end away from me," she said.

Three more guards poured through the door and shouted for them to surrender.

"Damn it," Kayla muttered.

"You handle them," Haern said. "I'll get us out."

As if completely oblivious to the danger, the boy used his

dagger to slice into the wood surrounding the nails. Kayla thought him crazy, but he worked the wood like an expert. In a handful of seconds, the first nail popped into his palm.

Still, many nails and boards remained. Kayla drew two more daggers and faced the guards. Remaining in the corner defending Haern was counter to her methods of combat, so she ran to the side, hurling dagger after dagger to keep the guards' attention. A couple glanced off their mail, another ricocheted off the flat edge of a blade, but one sank deep into the flesh of a soldier's thigh. He swore and pulled it out while the other two rushed closer.

Kayla dodged and rolled, her lithe body narrowly avoiding the swings of the guards' swords. Once she was on the far side of the temple, she turned and sprinted, rolling past the two nearer soldiers and straight for the wounded man. Down on one knee clutching his wound, he only had time enough to look up and curse again before she stabbed a dagger in his eye. She yanked it out as she passed, wincing at the eyeball lodged halfway up the slender blade.

When she reached Haern, she leaped into the air and spun, her hands a blur as daggers flew. The two guards crossed their arms to block their faces, but she had anticipated such a basic defense. Sharp points dug into their legs, hands, and feet. Blood poured across the faded floor.

"Hurry," she heard Haern shout. She turned to see him toss her dagger back, hilt first. Three boards lay by his feet. He climbed up and out the window, not pausing to see if she followed. Kayla blew the wounded soldiers a kiss, then sprang after him.

"How fast can you run?" she asked Haern when she landed outside. The drop from the temple was longer than it looked, and she felt her knees ache.

"Not fast enough."

"Limp if you have to," Kayla said, grabbing his arm. "But we're still going to run, even if it's on one foot."

He hesitated only a brief moment before looping his arm around her neck and running alongside. Shouts echoed behind them, and Kayla felt her heart thud in her ears. She had killed four soldiers now, as well as wounded two more. There would be no jail cell waiting for her if they were caught, just a thick stone and an ax.

They hobbled down the road, Kayla desperate to add distance between them and the guards. She asked questions in a rapid-fire manner as they ran, hoping against hope for a plan to emerge in her mind.

"You said Haern's your first name. What's your last?"

Haern refused to answer at first, but then she cuffed him on the side of his head.

"I'm trying to save your life, and mine, so talk."

"I . . . I'm the son of a guildmaster."

Kayla rolled her eyes. Well, that matched one of her earlier theories.

"A thief guildmaster, I take it?" she said, and he confirmed it with a nod. "That's what I thought. I'm sure you have a hideout, so where is it?"

"The western district," Haern said, elaborating no further.

"That's too far," Kayla said. Not that it mattered. She couldn't take Haern there until they lost their pursuers. Leading half the city's soldiers to a thief guild's secret hideout was another good way to end up dead, regardless of her somewhat noble intentions.

"Any other safe houses?" she asked.

"None I know of."

"Friends that can hide us?"

"Friends are dangerous."

Kayla rolled her eyes.

"Are you useful in any way?"

Haern shocked her by blushing.

"Not yet. But I will be. One day I'll kill as well as you, milady."

She laughed, even as a pair of soldiers turned into the alley ahead of them. She wished she hadn't killed earlier; then she might have been able to turn Haern over and save her own life. Daggers twirling, she accepted her only recourse. Haern let go of her to free her movements.

"Keep your eyes open for a place to hide," she said.

Two more guards stepped out behind them, shouting for them to surrender. Haern grabbed a dagger from Kayla's belt and kissed the blade.

"Your name?" he asked.

"Kayla," she replied.

"If we separate, I'll find you. As long as I draw breath, I'll ensure my father rewards you well."

Back to back they faced the approaching guards. At first it seemed they would wait for more to arrive, but when Kayla flung several daggers through the air, one sinking into the flesh above a man's knee, the soldiers decided subduing the unarmored woman and the hapless boy would be easier than dodging an angry barrage of steel. Kayla felt worried knowing Haern faced two, but she remembered how well he had fought back at the temple. Maybe he could survive long enough for her to finish her own and switch over to help him…

The first soldier slashed his sword at her chest. She parried it with the dagger in her left hand, stepped in closer, and then cut across his face with her right. Blood splashed her arm, and he howled as the tip hooked the underside of his eye. His companion lunged, forcing Kayla back and preventing a killing blow. The wounded man clutched his face with his free hand, glaring with his good eye. The other man struck again, a weak thrust that revealed just how green he was. She batted his sword aside, slashed his wrist, and then hurled her dagger. Kayla could kill a man from a rooftop. Standing mere feet away, the man had no chance. The dagger struck just above his gorget, and he gargled out a few unintelligible words as he collapsed.

Kayla heard shouts behind her, followed by a cry of pain. Knowing her time was short, she pressed an attack on the wounded soldier. He parried a couple of her stabs, his movements awkward from clutching his face with his other hand. Kayla curled about him, always drifting to his wounded side, until one of his blocks came in too early. Her daggers sank into the flesh of his throat and stomach. Gasping, he fell and died.

Feeling certain the boy was dead, she spun around and brought her daggers up to defend herself. Instead she saw Haern dancing between the two soldiers, his dagger a blur of steel. Both soldiers were bleeding, and one in particular was soaked with blood from a gash underneath his arm. She watched as the boy ducked a sideways slash, spun on his heels, and then lunged to the side of a thrust. The sword pierced the air inches from his face, but Haern seemed not to care how close he came to death. His dagger punched underneath the breastplate, slicing open the flesh and spilling intestines to the cold dirt of the alley.

He never hesitated, not even after such a cruel killing. The other soldier's strike would have severed his spine, but instead it clacked against the ground. Haern slashed his wrist, danced about, stabbed his side, and then as the guard turned he continued dancing, continued twirling. His dagger buried itself in flesh, finding two more exposed slits in the armor. Blood ran freely, and when the boy kicked out his knees, the guard fell without the strength to stand.

Kayla shook her head in amazement. Learn one day to kill as well as she? Nonsense, she thought. He already did.

Haern sheathed the dagger and joined her side.

"Your limp," she said, realizing he had shown no hint of the injury during battle.

"I hurt it worse," he said, wrapping his arm around hers. "But I've been taught how to ignore such things. Better to live torn and in pain than die in perfect health."

He spoke as if the saying were memorized, and the gasps of pain he made with each step seemed to mock him.

"We'll never escape," she said as they turned down a small alley between rows of houses that stank more like a sewer. "Not with us leaving a trail of bodies behind us."

"We just need to keep going," he said. "It doesn't matter where."

"Why not?" she asked.

"Because my father's eyes are in all places. Once we're seen, he'll come for us."

Kayla smirked.

"I don't care who your father is, Haern, he's not the Reaper. The night is deep, the soldiers are about, and if we're to see the dawn we'll need to hide."

Haern looked upset at her dismissal of his father, but he refused to argue the point.

Kayla scanned the houses she passed, hoping to recognize one. Considering how she prided herself on having information, she realized just how little she knew her surroundings. She was friends with the scum of the streets, but the eastern district was home to the rich and influential. She might know her way around, and be able to list many names useful for blackmail, but not one person she could count as a friend. In all of Veldaren, this was most definitely farthest from home.

"Wait," Haern said as they passed by a wide mansion surrounded by a thick fence. Its bars were made of dark iron, their spiked tops over ten feet above the ground. Behind them, oak trees with interlocking branches surrounded the building, giving privacy to the mansion with their beauty.

Haern pointed. "We can hide here."

It took a moment for Kayla to realize where they were, but when she did her eyes widened.

"Are you daft, boy? This is Keenan's estate."

"Exactly," Haern said, a bit of a smile curling his lips. "The one place no one would dare look for us."

The reasoning was sound, but looking at those enchanted bars, she was baffled as to how they would cross them.

"Follow me," Haern said. Instead of climbing the bars, though, he turned and shimmied up the wall of a much more modest dwelling on the opposite side of the road. He clearly favored his right leg, bracing his weight on the left as often as he could. It seemed there was no way up, but his feet and hands found crevices, windowsills, and indents in the plaster. He made it seem so easy, as if a pathway were there, waiting hidden just for him.

Kayla knew she was good at climbing, but she doubted her ability to follow. Not that she had a choice, given the constant shouts of guards hunting after them. Trying not to think about it, and therefore worry, she began climbing in a reckless rush. She made it halfway up before her foot slipped. The windowsill cracked and broke. Her hands flailing wildly, she grabbed the first thing she could: Haern's wounded leg. The boy hung from the roof by his hands, and though his grip seemed like iron, she could hear his grunts of pain. She swung her foot farther to the side, onto what remained of the windowsill. When she let go of his leg, she heard him exhale slowly, as if he fought to control his pain. A moment later he was atop the roof and gone from her sight.

The rest of the way up was easy, and when she got there she found Haern lying on his back, tears running down the sides of his face.

"I'm sorry," she said. "We can hide here, surely the guards won't see..."

"They will," Haern said. "They can see us from the street. Even if it takes all night, they'll find us."

Kayla sighed. He was right, of course. The roof was not perfectly flat, but instead sharply angled, with triangles rising up to make a space for windows. If they hunkered down they might go unnoticed for a while, but any searching eyes would eventually spot them. Slowly Haern shifted all his weight to his left leg and tried to stand. Kayla gently put her hands underneath his elbows and helped him.

"I'll scream when I jump," he said. "Ignore it. I'll be fine."

And then he was off, showing no sign of his injury. The roof, while angled, was still wide and offered plenty of room for a running start. In between the spikes of the gate were thick strips of the dark iron, and it was for them he dove like a swan. With both hands he latched on, and when his body swung downward, he kicked off the bars with his good leg. Feet in the air, he vaulted over the spikes and landed on the smooth carpet of grass on the other side.

Kayla felt her lips tremble at the display. Perhaps it would be better to remain on the rooftop, hoping the guards would miss her. They weren't searching for her, after all, just the strange, incredibly trained teenage boy who fought like an assassin. She couldn't possibly mimic his act, could she?

She made her decision. With her longer legs, perhaps there was another way...

In a single quick motion she unbuckled her belt, counted to three, and then ran off the side of the house. When the fence neared, she looped the belt around one of the spikes and then did her best to hold in a shout of pain as her body rammed into the bars. She started to fall, but then the belt tightened. Using a technique similar to Haern's, she kicked off the bars and somersaulted. Her breath caught in her throat as she passed over the incredibly sharp tips. She pictured herself impaled, her corpse upside down like some grotesque ornament, and then closed her eyes to banish the image.

Then she was over, and blessed ground met her feet. She rolled along, then scrambled toward the nearest tree. Compared to the house, it made easy climbing with its many shoots and branches. Haern was waiting for her among the leaves.

"Keep quiet," he whispered. Tears ran down his face, but he kept the sobs out of his voice. With a slender hand he pointed through a gap in the leaves where the street was visible to them both. Soldiers ran past, torches in hand. They scoured the area, but not once did they inspect the land behind the walls.

"Laurie Keenan's property might as well be a foreign nation," Kayla whispered. "No city guard will dare trespass onto property of a lord of the Trifect, not in the middle of the night for a whelp like you. A smart call, though you have the courage of a lion to leap like you did. If your knee had buckled..."

"It didn't," Haern said. "Not until I landed."

She pulled up his pant leg and looked. His knee had already turned a shade of blue, with the very center an ugly brown. When she touched it with her fingers, she could tell it was badly swollen.

"We need it wrapped and iced," she whispered. "And you need to give it rest."

Haern nodded. "How long can we hide here?" he asked.

Kayla shrugged. "We're pressing our luck as is, but if we stay away from the mansion we should be safe. I hear all his traps are within its halls."

Haern leaned his head against a branch and closed his eyes. "Don't let me fall," he said. "Please?"

"Sleep if you must," she said, reattaching her belt. "I'll keep us safe."

CHAPTER

3

Maynard Gemcroft paced the halls, his bare feet cushioned by the thick carpet. He paced far from the windows. Even though he had paid handsomely for thick glass, he did not trust it. A heavy stone followed by a single arrow was all it'd take to lay him out on the carpet, bleeding red on the blue weave. A thin, wiry man, he lived amid constant protection with over a hundred guards. One of the three lords of the Trifect, he controlled the Gemcroft empire from within his fortress-mansion, hiring mercenaries, plotting guard routes, and approving a dozen trades a day. Only the king was as well protected.

Yet two days prior, Maynard had nearly died.

A guard opened a door and stepped inside. His teeth were crooked, and when he talked the sight of them disgusted Maynard. He wore chain armor, with a dark sash wrapped around his waist signifying his allegiance to the Gemcroft family line.

"Your daughter is here to see you."

"Send her in," Maynard said as he checked his robes and smoothed his hair. He always prided himself on his appearance, but lately he found less and less time to primp and preen. It seemed as if every other night he awoke to alarms and cries of trespassers. Come the morning, somewhere on the grounds, yet another guard would lie dead. It made keeping their ranks full a nightmare.

The guard stepped out, and his daughter entered.

"Alyssa," said Maynard as he approached with open arms. "You've returned early. Were the men in the north too boring for you?"

She was short for a lady, but her slender body was supple and strong. Maynard had never seen a man best his Alyssa in any feats of dexterity, and he knew she could outdrink many as well. Her mother had been a wild one, he remembered. A shame she had slept with another man. Leon Connington's gentle touchers had never been given a woman so fine.

Alyssa brushed a hand over the red hair cropped around her shoulders and woven into tight braids. Her fingers pulled aside an errant strand and tucked it behind an ear. Her green eyes twinkled with mild amusement.

"*Boring* does not go far enough to describe them," she said in a husky voice. "The women there preen and prattle like they've never heard of a cock, and so the men oblige by never pulling it out to teach them otherwise."

She snickered as Maynard felt his neck flush. He knew she was just trying to embarrass him. John Gandrem ruled the Northern Plains from Felwood Castle. The lord had, through his letters, kept him painfully aware of whom Alyssa had slept with. When any one of them could produce a potential heir to the Gemcroft fortune, even the most private details had to be known.

"Must you use such... such... *common* language?" Maynard asked.

"You sent me to live with common women. Fosters and sitters whose entire wealth couldn't buy the privilege to clean the... filth from my bottom."

She winked at her father.

"I did so for your own safety," Maynard said. He caught her nearing the windows and put himself in the way. When he opened his mouth to explain she pressed a finger against his lips and kissed his forehead.

Servants arrived to inform them that the evening meal was ready. Maynard took his daughter's hand and led her through the mansion to the extravagant dining room. Suits of armor lined the walls, holding erect lances decorated with silken flags of kings, nobles, and ancient members of the family. Over a hundred chairs waited at the giant table, their dark wood upholstered in purple. Decorating the top were twelve roses, each in a ruby-encrusted vase.

Twenty servants stood ready, although only the two leaders of the family would eat first. Maynard took a seat at the head of the table as Alyssa sat to his left.

"Don't worry about the food," he told her. "I have everything tasted."

"You're the worrier, not me."

Maynard thought she might have reacted differently if she'd known seven tasters had died over the past five years, including one only two days ago.

The first course was steamed mushrooms smothered with gravy. Servants flitted in and out of sight, always bustling, always hurrying. Alyssa closed her eyes and sighed as she bit into one of the mushrooms.

"You have your quirks, but at least you ensure quality meals," she said. "The servants in Felwood seemed to think a skinned cat was a delicacy. Every other meal I spent the evening pulling hair out of my teeth."

Maynard shuddered.

"They have always been fair when dealing with me, so I felt them a safe home for you, especially so far away from Veldaren. Please, don't jest about such crude things while we eat."

"You're right," Alyssa said. "We should talk business instead."

The next course arrived, an unknown meat smothered with so much gravy and seasoning that she could barely see it. The smell made her mouth water.

"Business is exhausting," Maynard said. "And in more ways than one. I would prefer we not discuss it while we relax."

"You would prefer we not discuss it at all. I went away a young girl, but I've had plenty of time to learn. Years, in fact." There was no hiding her resentment. "How many years has this embarrassing war with the thief guilds lasted?"

"Five years," Maynard said, frowning. "Five long years. Don't be bitter with me for sending you away. I just wanted you safe."

"Safe?" Alyssa said. She put down her fork, pushed away the plate. "Is that what you think? You wanted me out of your way, you always have. Easier to plot murder and money when your little girl isn't underfoot."

"I have missed you dearly," Maynard insisted.

"You showed it poorly," she said. The words stung him like a needle to the chest. "But enough of this. I am a Gemcroft, same as you, and this pathetic conflict shames both our names. Gutter vermin and lowborn cutthroats defeating the entire wealth and power of the Trifect? Pathetic."

"I would hardly say we are being defeated."

She laughed in his face. "We control every gold and gem

mine north of the Kingstrip. They have bastards and whoresons robbing caravans and peasant workers. Leon Connington keeps Lord Sully and the rest of the Hillock in his pocket. They have lice and fleas in theirs. And what about Laurie Keenan? Half the boats on the Thulon Ocean are his, yet I worry his sea dogs will start thinking those boats better protected in their hands instead of his."

"You forget your place!" Maynard said. "It is true we have much more than they, but therein lies our danger. We pay a fortune for mercenaries and guards while they bring in men off the street. We have our mansions and they have their hovels, and you tell me which is easier to hide? They are like worms. We cut off a head only to have two worms grow from the parts."

"They don't fear you," Alyssa said. "None of you. Spineless men, you will lose everything but what you hold in your hands, hands that shrink with each passing day. Do you know how many of your own mercenaries give a portion of their coin to the guilds?"

"I know more than you could possibly dream," Maynard snapped. He leaned back in his chair. His shoulders felt heavy and his arms made of stone. So many times he had heard this same argument from reckless fools. It saddened him to realize his daughter was now one of them. Still... if Alyssa had such thoughts, he doubted they were originally her own. She had been out of the city for far too long to be so aware. Who was feeding her this information? Who was twisting his daughter for their own gain?

"Tell me, O wise daughter of mine," Maynard said, "tell me how *you* know all these little details?"

"How I know doesn't matter," Alyssa said a bit too quickly.

"It is all that matters," Maynard said. He rose from his chair and clapped for his servants. "Yoren Kull has been whispering in your ear, hasn't he? I forbade Lord Gandrem from allowing him contact with you, but where there's walls there's rats, isn't that right?"

"He's not a rat." Her voice was losing a bit of its certainty. She did fine when on the offensive. Now that his eye was on her, she faltered. "And what does it matter? I stayed with Lord Kull during the winter months. His castle is closer to the ocean where it's warm."

"*Lord* Kull?" Maynard laughed, reminding himself to reprimand Lord Gandrem for such a lapse in judgment. "He and his father collect taxes from Riverrun. My servants live in a better home. Tell me, did he seduce you with whispers of power and a glass of wine?"

"You're avoiding my..."

"No," Maynard said, his voice growing stern. "You've been tainted with lies. We are still feared, but the guilds are feared even more. They are desperate. However long you felt those five years drag, I assure you, they've moved at far more brutal pace here. These thugs, these vermin, they kill with abandon. Worse, someone whispers in the ear of King Vaelor, always blaming us for the violence. The crown refuses to help us, as do his soldiers. The nobles who do publicly side with us gag on their food or have their children vanish from their bedchambers."

He slammed his palms against the table, holding himself up with quivering arms.

"We may have all our wealth," he said, his soft voice penetrating the sudden quiet. "But they have Thren Felhorn. And right now, our wealth means nothing compared to that."

He clapped again. Servants crowded around them. Alyssa felt uncomfortable in their presence, and then the guards arrived.

"Take her," Maynard said.

"You can't!" she shouted as rough hands grabbed her arms and pulled her flailing from the table.

Maynard forced himself to watch as they dragged her away. He said nothing. There was too much chance he'd reveal his pain.

"What do you want us to do with her?" asked his keeper of the guard, a simpleminded man made useful by his muscles and sheer devotion to his work.

"Put her in one of the cells," Maynard said as he sat at the table and picked up a fork.

"The gentle touchers would make her talk sooner," said the guard. Maynard looked up, appalled.

"Never," he said. "She is my daughter. Give her time to cool underneath the stone. Once she's ready to open her eyes to how things truly are, I can show her just how bloody this war has gotten. It was my fault to leave her away too long. No idea, the stupid girl, she has no idea how terrible things have been. She says she is a woman grown, and of that I have no doubt. Let us hope her cunning surpasses even my own, and she sees Yoren for the liar he is. I will not have my wealth stolen from me by the pathetic son of a *tax collector*."

CHAPTER

4

Several hours passed. If Kayla had had any doubt as to the boy's importance, the tenacity of the soldiers' search erased it. Carefully she pushed the blond hair off his face and looked at his soft features. He was cute for his age, just barely entering the transition into manhood. With his baby blue eyes, he'd no doubt break a few hearts...and with his skill, a few bones as well. But who was he? She rarely forgot a face, and she doubted she'd have ever forgotten his, but so far she had come up empty.

With the sun finally beginning to creep above the city walls, Kayla nudged him awake. He snapped his eyes open and stared at her without a word. It was as if he had grown inward and shy now the danger was past. She thought to ask him of his father, then decided against it. No matter who he was, she'd been careful to foster no enemies among the thief guilds.

"Should we head west?" she asked. He nodded. "I thought so, but we have a slight problem. How do we get over the gate?"

He didn't know. It seemed that when the hounds were at his heel, he was a fountain of ideas, but when things quieted down, the fountain ran dry. She almost smacked him upside the head and threatened to cut his throat if he didn't produce an idea, but the thought was so absurd she laughed.

"I guess we wait," Kayla said. Her stomach was rumbling, and she badly wanted someone to look at Haern's knee. When she glanced about, she had little faith in the tree's cover once the sun reached its fullest. If discovered, she would probably wish for the comfort of the noose. Inside Laurie Keenan's compound, he ruled, not the king.

"What if someone else opens the gate?" Haern whispered. "Maybe we can run through."

"Maybe," she said absently. But even *maybe* was pushing their luck. They needed someone to open the gate without noticing them hiding first, and then they'd have to escape the guards on their frantic dash to the street, all while hoping no archers in the windows feathered them dead. But if they were to do something, they needed to do it before the rest of the estate began its daily routines. Even though Laurie and his family lived in a second home south in Angelport, Kayla knew they still kept guards and a skeleton crew of servants to keep the place safe and clean. If any one of them spotted the two, they didn't have a beggar's chance of convincing anyone they weren't pawns of the thief guilds, sent to kill yet another lackey of the Trifect.

Kayla looked to Haern and held in a smile. Maybe if they were found, the boy might reveal another amazing skill. The kid could pull out nails with a thin knife and vault over fences like a mummer's monkey. What could he do when cornered behind a locked gate?

Locked?

"Haern, look at me," she said. "Can you pick a lock? Not

some apprentice's crap, I mean a true smith's lock. I've never had the fingers for it, but do you?"

He looked away from her, angling his head so the rising sun no longer reached through the leaves to light his face. In the shade, he seemed to grow more confident.

"Your daggers are thin, and I could try. I'd need something else, though, something even thinner."

She handed him a dagger, then reached into her belt and pulled out a small spyglass. She used it when she needed to be absolutely certain who a person was, when guesswork and reliance on body structure and clothing were not enough... or when naming the wrong name could get her killed by all parties involved. The spyglass wasn't what she wanted, though. What she wanted was the length of wire wrapped around the middle to reinforce the fragile creation. Haern saw and nodded happily. He snatched the spyglass from her hands, unwound the wire, and handed the spyglass back.

"How long?" she asked.

"Master Jyr was my teacher," he said. "When he left, he said I was his fastest student ever."

Kayla shook her head.

"Not good enough. Tell me, how fast?"

Haern shrugged.

"A minute? Two if it's expertly made."

"Expect three minutes," she said. Her blue-green eyes darted about. It wouldn't be long before a servant or two headed out for the market to fetch fresh eggs and warm bread for breakfast. The sun was low... perhaps they could go unnoticed. She had seen no guards, but that meant nothing. After five years of warfare, there were always guards.

"Pick the lock as fast as you can," she told him. "If anyone tries to stop us, I'll kill them."

Haern nodded.

"I'll do my best."

The ground wasn't far, but Kayla worried about Haern's leg. Once they made it to the streets, they could lose themselves in the sea of merchants, tradesmen, and common folk that always swelled in the morning hours. Until then, they'd be horribly vulnerable.

"I'll help you down," she said. "Hurry, but don't injure your knee any further. An open gate does us no good if you can't walk through it."

She guided him down to the grass. Limping like an old man, Haern approached the closed and barred front gate. Kayla remained hidden in the tree. She was close enough to intercept any guards who might spot him, and she hoped to surprise the first few who tried to stop the boy.

When Haern reached the gate, he knelt down on his good knee, cupped the lock in his hands, and examined it. After a moment he glanced back to the tree and held up two fingers.

Two minutes, she thought. *The gods are kind.*

She began counting in her head. At seventeen she heard a cry of alarm. By twenty-nine she'd seen several men run around the side of the estate, all wearing brightly polished chain mail and brandishing curved swords. They were five in all, and glumly Kayla checked the daggers at her belt. She had only three left. There would be no whittling them down before they reached her, and she knew veteran killers were underneath that armor.

Not good, she thought.

"Up, down, sideways, and every way between..." she muttered. If Haern knew of their approach, he obeyed Kayla's request and kept his back turned and his eyes focused. Twirling one of her few daggers in her fingers, the woman silently dropped to the grass. One good throw, and she could make it four to one.

Her speed was good, so she might blind or wound another before they realized she was there. After that, she might distract them long enough for Haern to open the gates. Would he escape, limping on a busted knee with angry guards chasing after?

"Should have just let you run," Kayla whispered as she began her sprint. "Easy money is never easy."

The whole while, she had never stopped her counting.

...thirty-seven, thirty-eight, thirty-nine...

She chose not to throw her extra dagger. An errant throw might alert them to her presence, and surprise was the only advantage she had. Her heart pounding in her ears, she angled toward them. If she was right, she'd slam into the pack only ten feet away from Haern.

...forty, forty-one, forty-two...

She cut one across the eyes as he turned toward the sound of her charge. Another screamed and fell back, blood pouring out from underneath his arm. *Better than expected*, Kayla thought as she tried to twirl away. A hand latched onto her short raven hair. Now it was her turn to scream as she felt her scalp tug painfully, her momentum far too great for her to stop. The guard swore and tossed a handful of hair to the ground.

...fifty-five, fifty-six, fifty-seven...

The blinded man staggered back toward the mansion, screaming like a stuck pig the whole time. Two chased after her, slashing the air before her chest and waist with their curved swords. The other man she had stabbed collapsed to the ground, only an occasional moan escaping his pale lips. That left only one to make for Haern.

Their lives depending on it, Kayla hurled a dagger between the two guards chasing her. End over end it twirled, and when it stuck true, Kayla let out an excited cry. The man rushing for Haern collapsed, a blade embedded in his neck.

. . . sixty-two, sixty-three, sixty-four . . .

Now able to focus solely on the two guards, she went purely defensive. Her daggers could never compete with the reach of their swords, but they had seen her throw, and that fear was strong enough for her to work with. As she twirled and dropped, she would randomly pump a hand as if to throw. Each time, one of the guards would back away and hunker down, trying to protect his exposed parts with the bulk of his armor. She never let one go, and she knew it wouldn't be long before they stopped falling for such a simple trick.

. . . seventy, seventy-one . . .

More shouts came from the house. The first five had only been a quick roundup of the outside guard. They'd expected only a young boy picking a lock. Now that they saw their own dying, the doors were flung open, and a group of at least twenty approached in an impressive collection of swords, armor, and shields.

Kayla laughed, her situation so dire she found it somehow amusing.

"Fuck, seventy-seven, me, seventy-eight, up, seventy-nine, down, eighty . . ."

Now her opponents stepped back, clearly knowing numbers and time were on their side. They also blocked her way to Haern. Fear clawed at her throat. Accompanying a thief guildmaster's son into the grounds of Keenan's estate? She might as well have spit in the Reaper's face. They would be tortured, killed, and sent as gifts into the underworld in many different-size containers. After five years, the Trifect was desperate for any sort of victory.

. . . eighty-five, eighty-six . . .

She heard Haern shout her name. The guards must have seen her own shocked look, and they spared a quick glance.

Haern stood before the gates, lock in hand. Men charged after him from the estate, murder on their minds, yet the boy only smiled and hurled the heavy metal contraption toward Kayla's attackers. When they glanced back, she had already thrown her daggers.

She didn't wait to see how badly she'd hurt them. At full run she dropped to one leg, sliding between the group, rolling to preserve her momentum coming out on the other side. And then she was on her feet, heart pounding, legs churning. Haern had pushed open the gate for her by the time she arrived. She grabbed his arm as she passed, never slowing. He cried out in pain, but his leg moved as fast as it could go, which was not fast enough.

The guards poured out of the gate, sure to catch them.

For a moment she thought of ditching the boy to save her own skin. In the end she laughed the thought away. They'd made it this far. To run like a coward now just felt pathetic. Besides, she could count at least three times now she'd thought them doomed and they had survived. Why not try for four? Kayla had hoped to lose herself in the crowd, but the crowd gave way instead, wanting no part of the bloody affair. Swearing, Kayla spun to face the guards, determined to die fighting rather than in the torture cells of Laurie Keenan's mansion.

A small quarrel shot into the nearest guard's throat. Several others fell back as more crossbow bolts whizzed through the air. Kayla grabbed Haern and pulled him down, cradling his head against her breast as she held him tight. Another volley of bolts tore into the guards. The common folk screamed and fled, even the few who had desired a bit of spectacle. A single errant shot was all it'd take to change their role from spectator to dead participant.

Men wearing tattered green cloaks and wielding crossbows

surrounded Kayla and Haern. Several others held long dirks, and grinning feral grins they dared the remaining guards to attack. In their indecision, more crossbow bolts shot at gaps in the guards' armor. Whoever remained their leader, for a good many were dead, raised his arm and shouted a command. The guards turned tail and fled back to the Keenan mansion.

"Stand up, girl," one of the green cloaks said to her.

Kayla glanced up to see a bearded ruffian smiling at her. His eyes were green, and covering both cheeks were tattoos of snakes, one red, one emerald. When she tried to pull Haern along, they closed ranks, blocking the way with their dirks.

"We have no business with the Serpents," she told the man, doing her best to add a hard edge to her voice. It was the voice she used when someone offered to pay far less than her information was worth, or even worse, refused to pay at all.

"The Serpent Guild chooses its business. Now move your ass. We have places to go."

There were eight of the Serpents, and with their crossbows loaded they searched up and down the street, which was slowly returning to its normal hum of voices and trade. Kayla started to ask where they were to go, but then the bearded man struck her with his fist. Rough hands grabbed her wrists. Another pinned Haern's arms behind him and pushed him along.

"Hope he's worth it," another of the Serpents said.

"Someone both the king and Laurie Keenan wants?" the bearded man said. "He's worth it." He turned to his two captives. "Keep your mouths shut and your feet moving, or you'll find out just how much venom a Serpent can spit."

Kayla was in no shape to argue. Through the street they marched, the green cloaks encircling and protecting their recent acquisition. They took a winding path through the streets, but the general direction was west. When she realized this, Kayla perked up, her eyes searching the blur of faces they passed. Haern had said his guild's hideout was in the west. Perhaps, just perhaps, one of those blurs might be reporting their location...

The bearded man led them on an abrupt turn to their left, passing between two vendors selling apples and pears. The Serpents' crossbows fidgeted in their hands, and their eyes seemed to be more alert. They hurried along, jabbing Kayla harder in the back, one helping Haern due to his obvious limp. She assumed they passed through enemy territory. Whose, she did not know, considering she wasn't affiliated with any of the guilds. She'd rather sell information in her own quiet way and avoid the death warrant that joining one almost always entailed. No intelligent person could say the Trifect was winning its little war, but it certainly had eliminated a large portion of Veldaren's underworld. The thieves recruited with promises of wealth and murder, while the wealthy nobles handed over real coin. Kayla knew which one she preferred to accept as payment.

A shrill whistle rang out above them. To either side of the group were giant homes, four stories tall, each one crammed tight with families barely able to scrape together a living. A few of the green cloaks looked up, but saw nothing.

Kayla, however, had much sharper eyes than they, and what she saw was the barest hint of a gray cloak leaping across a building. She felt her heart race, and though it was a gamble, she had to take it. The men looked far too worried. If there was to be a rescue, it'd be now.

"Keep going," the bearded man said. Kayla let her body slacken, and she acted as if a fainting spell were coming over her.

"What is your—Aw shit, someone grab her," she heard one of them say. Acting weak wasn't a tough chore. After a night spent fighting guards, leaping over gates, climbing trees, and running for her life, she was plenty exhausted. Someone grabbed her arms and another her neck, but a clever twist of her body pulled her free. Like a dead fish she flopped to the dirt, biting down hard on her tongue upon landing. When she coughed, blood flecked across her lips.

"Get her up," the bearded man ordered. "Quick, I said get her up!"

Another whistle from above. Now all the Serpents looked up, and a few saw the gray cloaks. Hands reached underneath her armpits to yank her to her feet. She thought she might resist, but then two sharp whistles stopped them.

"Let her go, Galren," a voice shouted from down the street. Kayla felt a slight gasp escape her throat. She had heard that voice once before, only once, but that was enough for her to forever remember its hard tone.

"This is no concern of yours," said the bearded man, apparently Galren.

A man stepped out from an alley, his face hidden by the hood of his cloak.

"It is my concern," he said. "And you're a damn fool if you think otherwise. Veldaren is my city, Serpent, *mine*, and I know more of your guild than you do. Did you think you could kidnap and sell my son without my knowing?"

"Your *son*?" Galren sounded like he might wet himself.

Kayla contained her shock no better. The boy, the strange boy she'd thought to capture and sell...was Aaron Felhorn, Thren's son? She felt caught between horror and hysterics. The moment she'd tried to demand a ransom, Thren would have hunted her down and executed her in as brutal a manner as possible. But then again, everything she'd done had kept the boy alive. That would protect her. Galren and his Serpents, however, were dead men. It was that simple.

Thren had come for what was his.

"Yes," Thren said, approaching with his bare hands hovering just above his short swords. His next words came out almost a whisper. "My son."

Gray cloaks descended from the rooftops. Arrows shot from windows. Death came upon them swiftly, and only Galren remained standing after the sudden assault, his arms pinned behind him, a waiting present for Thren as he approached. Without a word the guildmaster slashed open the bearded man's throat, then quickly stepped aside to avoid blood splashing across his clothes. A little stained his hands, but he wiped them clean on a cloth provided by one of his men.

Haern stood and bowed to his father.

"You have much to tell me," Thren said, motioning for him to stand. He then pointed to Kayla, who had gotten to her knees and lowered her eyes in respect. "But first I must know what her role was in all of this."

Haern answered without hesitation, and to his father's surprise he did not whisper.

"She saved my life," he said. "And not just once, but many times."

Thren sheathed his sword and offered a hand to Kayla. She took it, her mouth hanging slack.

"I do not know your name, nor who you might have sworn your life to," he said. "But I offer you a place at my side, so that I might one day repay you for the kindness you have shown my son."

She thought of the coin rattling inside the perfume jars and how it was a pittance compared to Thren's wealth. Accepting might mean death, but the position was an incredible honor... as well as potentially lucrative in a way she could only have dreamed of.

"I accept," she said while bowing. "Humbly, and undeserving, I accept."

Thren's hideout was not far, and though she needed rest, and though Thren insisted they talk soon, she had one matter she had to handle first. For years she'd indirectly sold information to Laurie Keenan. Should anyone find out—more important, should Thren find out...

After grabbing what few things of hers she had at her old rented home in the deep south of the city, Kayla hurried back to the merchant district. She walked by Undry's perfume shop, opened the door, and then continued without even slowing. Undry collapsed on the counter, scattering bottles of perfume and raising a horrendous stench. Deep in his fat breast lodged a dagger.

When she returned to her room in Thren's hideaway, she found a yellow rose lying on her pillow. Below it, formed out of twelve stones arranged just so, was the letter *H*.

CHAPTER

5

It seemed the nights had grown darker and silent over the past years, as the war between the thieves and the Trifect claimed more than its share of innocent casualties. Moonlit revelries had lost their allure, and most kept their drink and their women inside. No one wanted to be mistaken for either a member of the thief guilds or a turntail for the Trifect. Daggers and poison floated through the streets when the sun was set, and only those prepared to deal with them dared walk in the open.

Yoren Kull was competent with a blade, but that was not why he walked with his head held high. It was because of the man who traveled with him, dressed in the black robes and silver sash of a priest of Karak. Officially, their kind was banned from the city. Unofficially, they made sure every king knew of their presence, and of the immediate death that would follow should he try to remove them. Yoren felt quite confident no one would dare harass him with a priest at his side.

"When will we arrive at the temple?" Yoren asked. The priest responded in a soft voice honed by years of practiced control.

"I am not taking you to the temple. If I were, you'd be blindfolded."

Yoren chuckled. He stood a bit straighter, as if insulted by the very notion. His left hand clutched his sword while his right straightened a few errant hairs hovering over his forehead. He was a handsome man, his skin smooth and bronze while his hair was a healthy blond. When he smiled, his golden teeth gleamed in the light of the torch the priest carried.

"Forgive me for my false assumption," he said, trying to lighten the mood. "I assumed meeting disciples of Karak would involve Karak's actual temple."

"Our hallowed walls are sacred," the priest said. "Discipleship to Karak involves a life combating this sinful world, and we do not tolerate weakness. Those whom you seek are not worthy of staying within the temple, despite their . . . insistence to their faith. You've asked for the most unruly of Karak, and so to them I bring you. Whatever you need them for, I pray it is worth it. Keep your sword sheathed. My presence may keep us safe, but if you draw steel, you alone will deal with the consequences."

Yoren had never been to Veldaren before, but so far he was hugely unimpressed. The enormous wall surrounding the city had seemed ominous, and the towering castle doubly so. The god Karak was rumored to have built them, and it seemed few argued otherwise. What was inside, however, seemed to almost mock the great walls and castle. Much of the southern district had slowly died off. King Vaelor had ordered all trading caravans to enter through the west gate, where the guards were thicker and the road easier to watch. Poor slums and weather-beaten homes had greeted Yoren when he entered from the south.

The city improved near the center, but it was all wood-and-plaster buildings. Other than the sheer size, and a population of three hundred thousand men and women crammed together just begging to be exploited, Yoren saw little that would make him wish to live within the walls.

"Where are we now?" he asked.

"It is better you not know," the priest said. "It would be dangerous for you to come again without my assistance."

After meeting him in the center of the city beside some ancient fountain of an even more ancient king, the priest had led Yoren through a winding crisscross of roads and back alleys. Yoren had long lost track of which direction he was headed in, though he guessed they'd traversed back into the southern slums.

"I am not the weakling babe you treat me as," Yoren said.

"You are young. Young men are often hotheaded, foolish, and governed by their loins more than their wits. Forgive me if I treat you like all other men of Dezrel."

Yoren felt his face flush but bit his tongue. His father, Theo Kull, had insisted he treat the priests better than he would the king. If that meant enduring a few false comments about his nature, so be it. Yoren stood to gain much from his father's plan. His pride could withstand a few barbs.

"Here," the priest said, stopping before a house that looked just as dilapidated as any other. "Enter through the window, not the door."

Perhaps it was a trick of the eye, but when Yoren pushed his fingers up against the glass of the window his fingers slid through, and he realized no glass was there at all. He lifted his foot and climbed the rest of the way inside. He turned, expecting the priest to follow, but his guide had already vanished.

"Such wonderful hospitality," Yoren muttered before turning

and taking stock of his surroundings. The walls and floor had been stripped bare. Stairs led higher up, the steps rotted and broken. Through the single doorway farther in, he saw shelves coated with mold. Massive piles of rat droppings covered the floor.

He took a step, and then the room darkened. He heard whispers in his ears, but every time he turned there was no one there. The words kept changing, his mind unable to lock down a meaning. Yoren reached for his sword before remembering the priest's words. Shadows swirling all around him, the young man released his blade and stood up straight. He would not be afraid of cantrips and echoing whispers.

"You are brave, for a coward," a serpentine voice whispered from just inches behind his neck. Yoren jumped but refused to turn around.

"That seems a contradiction," he managed to say.

"Just as there are skinny sows and smart dogs, there are brave cowards," said another voice, eerily similar in sound and tone. Instead of behind his head, this one seemed to come from under his feet.

"I have done as asked," Yoren said as the shadows thickened before him. "My sword is sheathed, and I came through the window instead of the door."

The shadows coalesced before him into a shrouded figure. Every inch of its skin was wrapped in purple and black cloth. Even the eyes were hidden behind a single strip of thin white material, obscuring the features just enough while still allowing sight. From her shoulders hung a pale gray cloak. Despite the tight wrapping and modified voice, Yoren could tell by the slenderness of body and the curve of chest that he dealt with a woman.

"Doing Karak's will involves more than following orders,"

the woman said, wisps of shadow floating off her like smoke. "You ask for aid from the faceless. For us to interfere in the squabbles of lesser men we must be certain of your heart, as well as whatever sacrifice Karak may receive for his blessing."

A serrated dagger curled around his throat and pressed against his flesh.

"Sacrifice," whispered another faceless shadow behind him.

"I come with the promise of my father," Yoren said, for once glad of his infallible sense of ego. It was the only thing that kept him from stammering. "We have no temple in Riverrun, though the priests of Ashhur have begun building one on land loaned to them by Maynard Gemcroft."

"Is that so?" asked the woman before him.

"If you help me, then that land becomes my own," Yoren said. "You may no longer war, but I know Karak and Ashhur's followers are far from, uh, friendly. If you do as I say, I will cast out the priests. Karak may have the temple and the land on which it was built. Will that suffice?"

The faceless woman's ragged cloak pooled on the floor as if it were liquid darkness, yet when she stepped back, it immediately snapped erect and wrapped about her sides.

"It is a start," she said. "Yet how does land owned by a Gemcroft end up in the hands of a Kull?"

"Because Alyssa is my betrothed," Yoren said. "And everything that is hers will become mine."

The faceless woman glanced to one behind him, and Yoren felt a conversation passing unspoken between them.

"What is it you need from Karak's most zealous servants?" one asked at last.

Yoren licked his lips.

"They say you can handle even the most impossible task," he said. "So let's see how good you really are. As for what I need, it is rather simple. For the daughter to inherit, the father must go first."

He grinned at them.

"I need you to kill Maynard Gemcroft."

At least she had a blanket. For that, Alyssa was grateful. The cells underneath the Gemcroft estate hadn't been built with comfort in mind, and it had been ages since the light of the sun touched the gray stone. While growing up, she had heard one of her father's men brag about how the stone walls had been cut just the right way to ensure a draft always blew to every corner of every cell. Soaked in moisture that dripped from the ceiling and unable to avoid the constant, chilling blow of air, many prisoners had broken down in desperate clamoring for warmth. While the deep cold of snow and ice eventually numbed the skin, the Gemcroft cells chilled relentlessly.

With that draft in mind, her father's head guardsman had given her a thick blanket. Still, no matter how tightly she wrapped it around her body, she always felt a draft sneaking up her leg or down the small of her back. She trembled, remembering tales of men who had been imprisoned naked. Growing up, Alyssa had always thought such a simple chill merely uncomfortable. After all, how could a bit of cold air really break a man? But now, given just a taste of the drafts, she understood its potential for torture, especially over the course of months, if not years.

And that wasn't even counting the actual torture that went on, something she was obviously spared.

Alyssa wasn't sure how long she'd been in her cell, though judging by her meals it hadn't even been two days. The first day she'd shouted and threatened and demanded her release. When she finally crumpled into a corner, huddled underneath her blanket, most of her anger had subsided. A deep core remained in her breast, but she did her best to keep it contained. She had more important things to deal with.

There was only one thing that could have rankled Maynard so, and that was any mention of the Kulls. Along the eastern coast, the Kulls were in charge of acquiring the king's taxes, among many other responsibilities. That alone had caused strife between them and her father, strife Alyssa thought childish. Her father often prattled on about how the Kulls were using the tax money to build their own trading empire along the coast, slowly pushing Maynard out, and that it was only his superior number of guards that kept Theo Kull, the elder and ruler of the family, from seizing his lands. But that was business, all business, and Alyssa had seen no proof of any such claims in her time with Yoren.

Alyssa pulled the blanket tighter, scrunching her knees against her chest to preserve every shred of warmth.

He'll come for me, she thought. Her father would have to. He just wanted to show her how seriously he took her words. When the door opened, and he appeared holding a torch in one hand and another blanket in the other, she'd forgive him for this punishment. She'd wrap her arms around him, kiss his cheek, and willingly tell him everything. Theo and Yoren had no sinister plans. They had no ulterior motives. The Kull family was only trying to protect its interests, for if the Trifect fell, then the scum of the underworld would turn its hungry maw upon the Kulls next.

"You know how you stop a raging bull?" Yoren had asked her. "Kill it before it starts running. It has already gored the Trifect. It needs to die before it turns its horns to us."

Maynard did not come that second day.

On the third morning he appeared with two guards. One

held another blanket, while the other carried her food. Maynard stood between them, his arms crossed. He wore no cloak or vest, as if the sweeping chill meant nothing to him.

"Believe me, my daughter, when I say I have no ill will toward you for this foolishness," he said. Alyssa fought down an urge to stand and fling her arms around him. "But you must tell me what the Kulls are planning. They are liars, girl, liars and thieves and conniving men, so tell me what it is they want."

She shook her head. Her anger lashed out, temporarily uncontrolled.

"They're mad at your incompetence, same as me," she said. "And if they plan a move against you, it is your own doing, but I swear I know nothing."

Maynard Gemcroft nodded, and the sides of his mouth drooped a little.

"You have your mother's wisdom," he said, "but sometimes you are such a stupid girl." He turned to one of the guards. "Take her blanket."

She felt panic bubble up in her throat as she watched the second blanket leave, and she felt even worse when her first blanket was ripped from her arms. She clawed at it frantically, screaming that it was hers, hers, they couldn't take it. But they did, and she was cold now, very cold, and it was only day three, and she still knew nothing.

On the fourth night she was cold, miserable, and suddenly not alone.

"Do not be frightened," a voice whispered into the cell. Alyssa jumped like a startled rabbit. Her lips were blue, and her skin a sickly pale color, wrinkled from the moisture that hung thick in the air and clung to the stone walls. She felt wet and disgusting, and her mind leaped to the darkest conclusions about why someone might come calling in the deep of night.

"My father will find out," she said from her crouched position on the far side from the cell bars. "He'll punish you if he..."

Her voice caught in her throat, for there was no one at her cell. Again she heard the voice, echoing from wall to wall like a magician's trick. This time she clearly realized that a woman was doing the whispering, a fact that should have calmed her but strangely did not.

"We are Karak's outcast children," said the whisperer. "We are his most fervent, his most faithful, for we have much to atone for. Are you a sinner, girl? Will you lift your arms to us and accept our mercy?"

Shadows danced around her cell, not cast from the torch flickering outside the bars. Alyssa put her hands atop her head and buried her face in her knees.

"I want to be warm," she said. "Please, my father, he's not bad, he isn't. I just want to be warm."

When Alyssa peered over her knees, she saw the shadows swarm together, grow volume and mass, and then finally fill with color, becoming a woman shrouded in black with a thin white cloth covering the gap left for her eyes.

"There is warmth in the Abyss," the woman said as she drew a serrated dagger. "Would you like me to send you there? Careful of what you ask, little girl. Be clear with your demands, or accept the cruel gifts fools and selfish men may give."

Alyssa forced herself to stand. She felt skinny and naked before the strange woman, and it took all her willpower to suppress the shaking of her hands and keep them at her sides.

"I want out of this prison," she said. "I have done nothing to deserve its cold. Now tell me, who sent you here?"

"Who else would send us?" the woman asked. "Do not ask questions you should already know the answer to. Remain quiet. We are few, and some things must be done in silence."

She wrapped her cloak around her body, its fabric seemingly made of liquid shadow. A sudden jerk and she was gone, her body exploding into dark fragments that splashed across the walls and faded like smoke.

"You have accepted the help of the faceless," echoed a whisper throughout her cell. "Remember, the cost you pay is always dearer once it has left your hand."

Alyssa sat back down, curled her knees to her chin, and began to cry. She wondered what Yoren would say if he saw her like that. He was so beautiful, and she knew she could be too, but not here, not cold and wet and crying like a pathetic street urchin. Her tears did not stop as she hoped. Instead she cried louder.

Far away she heard a door open, the sound thick with bolts and metal. Her eyes lifted, and with detached curiosity she watched and waited.

A hefty man lumbered into view, his thumbs tucked into his belt. His eyes were beady and close together, and his long mustache dripped with grease. Alyssa had never met him before returning home to Veldaren, though she had quickly learned his name. Jorel Tule, master of the cold cells.

"I got dogs howling up a storm," Jorel said. "Figure I'd make sure you're nice and cozy."

"A blanket," she said. Her teeth chattered, and it was no act.

"Maynard says to wait until you can't stand no more," the man said, hoisting up his belt. "I think he means to have me wait until you're close to dead before warming you up."

A hard edge entered his eye. Alyssa recognized it as perverse joy in seeing one of noble birth sunk to his level and then put at his mercy. When shadows began coalescing behind his back, she openly smiled.

"I think you can wait a bit longer," Jorel said.

"A blanket might have saved your life," Alyssa replied. Jorel gave her a funny look but did not respond. When he turned to leave, a serrated dagger awaited him. It sliced his throat and splattered blood across the floor. The blood slid off the faceless woman's robes like water.

"He never would have served you," the woman said. "But there are others that will, and we must spare them if we can. Otherwise, your rule will be disputed and last as long as a sputtering candle in a storm."

"My rule?"

Alyssa waited until the faceless woman opened her cell, then grasped the door with one hand and held it firm.

"Tell me your name," she said.

"I have no name," the woman replied.

"You said you are faceless, not nameless, now tell me."

Alyssa could not see the woman's eyes through the white cloth, but she had a feeling that behind it and the wrappings hid an amused smile.

"A strong candle," the woman said. "My name is Eliora."

"Then listen well, Eliora," Alyssa said. "I will not accept rule of my household over the murdered body of my father. Whatever you were paid or promised, I can match it. All I ask is that Maynard be captured, not killed."

"You assume much. How do you know we have been sent to kill your father?"

"Why else would you mutter nonsense about candles and my rule?"

Eliora let go of the door and stepped back so Alyssa could exit.

"You are clever, child, and you are also correct. This world is chaos, but I will do what I can. Be warned: your father may already be dead. If that is the case, turn your anger on who hired us. Do not blame the sword for the blood spilled, only the hand that wielded it."

The faceless woman led her up the winding stairs out of the dungeon. They encountered no guards, dead or living. As they ascended, Alyssa heard the ruckus the dogs were making. Eliora must have noticed the look on her face, for the hounds sounded as if they were ravenous for blood.

"They are frightened and angry," she explained. "It is a simple spell we cast upon them to draw the guards out of the estate. My sisters are all inside, I assure you."

Alyssa nodded but said nothing.

The stairs ended in a cramped room with bare walls and a lone door, the outside of which was normally bolted. Eliora gently pushed it open; Jorel must have gone down without alerting anyone, otherwise they would have locked it behind him.

"How many are with you?" Alyssa asked. Eliora shot her a glare.

"We are three," she said. "Though we may be less if you continue braying louder than a mule."

With so little time between her arrival and subsequent imprisonment, Alyssa had not taken stock of her father's defenses. She knew they could not be light. No matter how much she might belittle the thief guilds, she was not an idiot. Without adequate protection, cloaked men with daggers would be lurking under every bed and within every closet.

Of course, those defenses seemed to have meant little to the faceless woman, and that thought gave Alyssa a chill. Surely the Kulls were behind their hiring, but what if it had been Thren Felhorn handing over the coin instead? Suddenly her father's difficulties in dealing with the guilds didn't seem quite so pathetic. Clearly the Kulls meant for her to take over the Gemcroft estate. Once in a position to rule, she would keep all that in mind when deciding how to deal with her father.

Men shouted in the far distance, their voices muffled through the walls.

"That would be Nava," Eliora whispered. "She is looping the compound, killing guards foolish enough to leave themselves vulnerable. Hurry now. We go to your father's room."

The plush carpet felt wonderful to her bare feet. Even better was the warm burst of air blowing across her skin. She remembered how warm her father kept the mansion, and how she used to stretch out before the large fires roaring in the multitude of hearths throughout its halls. Winter still approached, but already Maynard had begun fighting the chill. Alyssa almost stole away from Eliora for such a fire, desiring nothing more than to huddle close and burn away the deep frost that had settled into her bones. The biting words the faceless woman might say kept her from doing so.

They hurried down a long hall. Over twenty windows stretched along the right, their glass covered by violet curtains. On the left hung paintings of former masters of the Gemcroft estate. A hysterical laugh died in her throat as she wondered if her own painting would someday hang on that wall. She also wondered if she'd live long enough for someone to paint it.

I come for my crown, she thought. *What the bloody Abyss has come over me?*

She wanted none of this. When she'd returned to Veldaren, she'd meant to berate her father, show him his cowardice and hesitance and by doing so spur him into harsher dealings with the guilds. Once that business was done, she'd hoped to breach the subject of Yoren Kull, and of how they'd spent many nights together, and amid whispers atop pillows, murmured promises of marriage. But to usurp her father before the waning of the moon? To have strange women slaughtering guards loyal to her own flesh and blood? No, this was a dream, a nightmare. She tried to tell herself she would be a better ruler. She tried to tell herself she was ready.

She didn't believe a word of it.

They reached the end of the hall. Eliora slipped through the empty doorway, silent as a ghost. A guard stood to the right of it, and he died with a dagger in his throat and a hand wrapped over his mouth. As she watched the blood spill across the floor, Alyssa remembered the questions her father had asked. What did the Kull household plan? Nothing, she'd insisted.

Nothing but your elimination, she thought. Dimly she wondered if her own eyes were as covered as Eliora's with her thin white cloth.

Once certain no more guards were about, Eliora waved Alyssa on through.

"Is there anyone who might help supervise the Gemcroft estate?" the faceless woman asked as they passed through a series of bedrooms. "An advisor or a wise man, perhaps?"

"My father does have an advisor," Alyssa said. She remembered Eliora's earlier warning and lowered her voice. "Though I cannot recall his name."

"Do you remember his face?"

She nodded.

"Describe him."

A face flashed before her eyes, that of an older man with a short white beard and a shaved head. His eyebrows she especially remembered. He had shaven them regularly, and as a little girl she had been fascinated by the strange way it made his face look.

Eliora bobbed her head up and down, looking like a doll with its head off balance as Alyssa described the man.

"Will you hurt him?" she asked when done.

"No," Eliora said. "Now I know, I will let him live. The elder man is the key to your take-over. To the common worker and guard, there is little difference when the figurehead changes names, so long as their immediate master stays the same."

The faceless woman stopped at another hallway and glanced in both directions.

"Which way to your father's bedroom?" she asked.

Alyssa thought for a moment.

"Left," she said. "Not far from my own."

"Stay here, and stay silent," Eliora said. "There will be guards."

The shadow cloak swirled about her body, her limbs and head fading away into a shapeless blob of black and gray. Only the serrated dagger shone bright and true in her violet hand. Alyssa glanced behind her every few moments, feeling almost certain a guard would find her alone and helpless. She had turned down numerous offers of training, and had been taught only rudimentary self-defense while living with John Gandrem at Felwood Castle. As she stood there, she wished she had taken those offers. She'd have given up anything if it meant holding a blade without fear of the shouts she heard throughout the mansion.

The core of anger hidden in her breast flared. She had stridden into her father's house as cocksure as any man might have. Had the chill of the cells stolen that away from her? She was the rightful heir, and after the embarrassment of five years of secret warfare against an inferior opponent, most members of her household would welcome a stronger, smarter leader. If any guard appeared, she would *demand* the loyalty of his sword.

The sounds of a scuffle reached her ears, coupled with a single pained scream that was cut off halfway through. She was nervous about looking around the corner to see, but did so anyway. She saw several bodies lying in a bloody path that ended at another corner. She thought to give chase when a dagger pressed against her neck.

"Where is my sister?" she heard a voice ask.

"Are you Nava?" Alyssa asked, trying her hardest not to sound afraid. Her voice came out sounding weak but annoyed. Given the circumstances, she thought that was acceptable. The dagger shifted against her skin, and from the brief pause, she figured the woman was surprised.

"Not Nava," she whispered. "Zusa. Now where is my sister?"

"Eliora went ahead," Alyssa said, telling no more than what was asked for. She tried to remind herself that this was *her* home, and that she should be the one asking the questions, but her logic was weak against the serrated edge pressed against her soft skin.

"I hope you're not lying," Zusa said. "False tongues are often split."

The dagger scraped across her neck. Alyssa was certain blood would run down her chest, but none did.

"It's not a lie," she said. "Now remove that blade. I am Alyssa Gemcroft, and it was your task to free me from my prison. Threaten harm upon me, and you risk the boon you were promised for this affair."

The dagger left her neck, and Alyssa felt proud of how she'd handled the situation. When she turned, she was surprised to see another of the faceless women had joined them. Disguised as she was in her black and purple cloth, Alyssa had not a clue who it might be, but then she heard the soft whisper and knew.

"Maynard is not in his room," Eliora said. "Something is amiss."

"Find him," Zusa said. "Time is our enemy."

The dogs howled louder as both faceless women turned to Alyssa.

"Where is your father?" they demanded.

"I don't know," she said, taken aback. "The hour is late; he should be in bed. Maybe something needed his attention, or his sleep was troubled and he took to wandering..."

"Or he was waiting for us," Eliora said. "May Karak damn them all. Move, while Nava still buys us time outside."

They hurried down the hall, Alyssa's mind racing. She wondered if her father had any hidden rooms or safe places tucked away in corners of the estate, but she remembered none. She had been a rambunctious girl, and curious too. If there had been any, she would have known.

Unless Father added them recently, she thought. With five years of secret war, he would have had plenty of time to build and remodel.

Their path led them to the dining hall, which looked naked with the empty chairs, covered table, and unlit chandeliers. The shouts of the guards grew louder. The faceless women tilted their heads toward each other, as if sharing a thought. Guards were pouring into the mansion.

"Alerted," Zusa said. "But how?"

Alyssa knew of no other way to describe it: the bare wall to her left dissolved. What should have been solid stone crumpled and curled, red smoke wafting off it. Inside was a room of which she had no memory. The walls were gray plaster, undecorated and leading farther into the mansion. Filling that room were more than twenty guards, armored in steel and armed with swords. Tabards emblazoned with the Gemcroft sigil covered their tunics.

"Sister, with me!" Zusa shouted, drawing her dagger and lunging toward the soldiers. Eliora was quickly behind her. The guards attempted to flood into the room, but they were held back at the narrow exit. Those in the front battled with the faceless women, but their movements seemed slow compared to the grace of their opponents'. Alyssa thought they'd struggle against the guards' heavy armor, but the faceless women's serrated daggers sliced through the mail as if it were butter. The metal melted and smoked purple after each cut, helpless before a powerful magic.

The women held strong, but they were pushing back a river with only daggers. Five died at their feet, but the rest pressed forward, shoving aside their dying comrades. As the guards spread out to surround them, the two assassins flipped back and away, their bodies curling around sword strikes as if their bones were water.

"Run, girl!" Eliora shouted. Alyssa sprinted down the hall and into a long corridor. She glanced out the rows of windows, her heart shuddering at the sight. Pouring through the front gates in frightening numbers were various mercenaries wearing the Gemcroft standard. Whatever her punishment would have been in the cell, Alyssa realized that her attempt to escape and supplant her father would increase it tenfold.

Screams chased her down the hall. Escape was all that mattered now, she realized. There would be no grab for power, no careful bartering of life for rule. The thought of returning to her cold, drafty cell spurred her on. When she reached a door, she glanced behind. None of the faceless had come yet.

Glass shattered, and Alyssa cried out as shards of it cut across her face. A figure crashed in through the window. She felt arms wrap around her body.

"Worry not for my sisters," said a deep-voiced woman who could only be Nava. "Your life is precious. Follow me into the night."

Alyssa's breathing was ragged, frightened gasps. Her pulse was a war drum in her ears. With trembling fingers she took

Nava's hand. A painful lurch later, they tumbled through the broken window and onto the cool grass of the lawn.

"Stay silent," Nava said, pressing a wrapped finger across Alyssa's lips. "Not a word until we leave the gate. Understand?"

Alyssa nodded.

"Good. Come."

They were on the western side of the complex. The main gates were to the south, but instead of going there, Nava pulled her north. The stars were hidden behind clouds, and in the dim light Alyssa stumbled as she ran. Only the strong grip on her wrist kept her moving. More mercenaries spread around the house, and she heard their shouts behind her. They had not yet been spotted, but how long until they were?

The tall gate loomed high to her left. She felt the tug on her wrist lead her closer and closer, until suddenly a hand was clasped over her mouth, holding in her startled cry as they halted all movement.

"Shhh," Nava hissed into Alyssa's ear.

The faceless woman removed her cloak, the fabric making a soft sigh as it slipped through her fingers. A single word of magic and it snapped erect. Nava flung it upon the bars, where it stuck like honey. The woman rolled through it as if the bars no longer existed, spun on her heels, and then reached back. Her hand pressed through the cloak as if it were darkness, only darkness. Alyssa swallowed her fear and took her hand. A hard jerk forward, and then she was on the other side.

Nava snapped her fingers. The cloak returned to cloth, glinting as if a thousand stars were woven into its fabric. She wrapped it across her shoulders and took Alyssa's hand. Together they fled from the shouts of soldiers and mercenaries. Alyssa gave one last look at the mansion, knowing in her heart that it would never be hers.

* * *

Deep within, Maynard stepped out from the gray tunnels winding throughout his estate. His advisor, the gray-bearded man with shaved eyebrows, stood beside him. His name was Bertram Sully.

"I knew the Kulls were desperate," Bertram said, frowning at the mess the mercenaries were making as they stamped throughout the place. "But to hire faceless women? Have they gone mad?"

"Perhaps," Maynard said. "And I wonder what they could have offered as payment. However, that's not important, not now. The priests of Karak swore to us they would remain out of our war. It would seem that promise has finally been broken."

Bertram stroked his beard.

"Perhaps not. The left hand does not always know the actions of the right. If this is true, then we might have an opportunity here."

"And what is that?" Maynard asked. He kicked a nearby chair, knocking it to the floor. He had known the Kulls would try to rescue Alyssa, and he had hoped to capture a few of their kind in the attempt. How he would have loved to shave the head of that pompous Yoren and then hang him with his own golden locks. Instead his daughter had escaped, and over twenty of his guards were dead. From what he had seen, his own men had not scored a single cut.

"Think on this," Bertram said. "Should we confront the priests about the actions of the faceless, they will have few recourses. They can punish the faceless for disobedience, thereby removing the only weapon the Kulls have against us. The priests may also try to atone for the broken promise by allying with us, perhaps even giving *us* the service of the faceless. We can smite the Kulls with their own weapon."

"You forgot a third option," Maynard said. "The priests deny any involvement while secretly accepting whatever bribe the Kulls offered, and nothing changes."

"The priests would not be so foolish as to betray the Trifect," Bertram insisted.

"This war has made fools of everyone," Maynard said. "But it will not happen to me again. Set up a meeting with high priest Pelarak tomorrow night. We will force the servants of Karak to break their neutrality, one way or another."

"And if they refuse?"

Maynard Gemcroft's eyes glinted with danger.

"Then we reveal their existence, all while flooding the city with rumors of human sacrifice and murdered children. Let the mobs burn their temple and tear them limb from limb. We shall see if they remain neutral when *that* is the fate I offer."

CHAPTER 6

Kayla wasn't sure what she'd expected of Thren's safe house upon first arriving there, but the elegant mansion surrounded by steel bars was certainly not it. She spent the day scouting the place, meeting new members, committing faces to memory. All throughout, Haern made excuses to see her, not that she minded. Having Thren's son with her seemed to make everyone treat her with more respect.

When her tour of the place was done, she returned to the room, Haern in tow like a lovesick puppy.

"Can't have asked for a nicer room," she said as she plopped down onto the bed. At the door, Haern remained, as if embarrassed to come farther inside. "So how did your father get such an... impressive building to be his safe house?"

"Some rich merchant fled the city with his family," Haern said, his voice much quieter than it had been during their flight from the soldiers. "The Kanes, I think they were called. All his helpers stayed to keep the mansion clean, warm, and safe. My father moved in shortly after. I've even heard he keeps a few business contracts with various men about the city while pretending to be a friend of the real owner."

"What happens when the merchant returns to his home?" she asked.

"He will not return until our war is done," Haern said. "By then, we will need this place no longer."

Kayla thought the logic sound, but in the back of her mind she wondered what might happen if the merchant showed up with his possessions and servants and the rest of his guards. She doubted it would be Thren who ended up looking for a new home.

"Wait," she said when the boy made to leave.

"Your name," she said when he stopped halfway through the door. "I suppose I should start calling you Aaron now?"

He looked away, and his neck flushed red.

"I suppose you should," he said. "But..."

"But...?" she pressed when his voice trailed off.

"But I like not being myself," he said, unable to meet her eye. His fingers tugged at loose splinters in the door. "I liked you not knowing who I was. That meant I could be anyone. So you can call me Haern if you want. Just not... just not around my father. I don't think he'd like that."

And then he was gone. Kayla shook her head, deciding she was more confused now than before she'd asked the question.

"Kayla?"

She looked up, saw one of the younger members of the Spider Guild standing at the door.

"Yes?" she asked.

"Thren wants to see you."

She let out a sigh, then waved him away. At last she'd find

out just what the man wanted from her. Sitting in her room with nothing to do would drive her insane.

As she walked through the estate, marveling at various paintings of the faraway lands of Omn, Ker, and Mordan, she let her mind wander to her own situation. She had avoided guilds, instead relying on her information and her contacts to keep herself warm, fed, and safe. Now she had allied herself with the most dangerous man in Veldaren, and for what? A vague promise of wealth, the same vague promise that she had mocked hundreds of others for following?

No, it wasn't the wealth. It was the power, she realized. He had offered her a role at his side, the highest reward he could bestow. If the entire city quaked in fear at the name of Felhorn, might not the same one day happen for Kayla? A foolish fantasy, perhaps, but she could not shake it away. It sucked wisdom from her heart like a leech. She distantly hoped that her reward for such folly would not be too severe.

The hall of paintings ended at Thren's room. She knocked twice, then waited patiently. A moment later the door crept open, and a mailed hand waved her in. She entered, passing between two guards with their dirks drawn. Inside was a plush room of velvet reds and silky yellows. An enormous bed, its wood painted silver and its knobs carved into pairs of wings, was in the far corner. In the center of the room was a rectangular table with six chairs, seeming like a strange joke with its dull finish and undecorated nature amid a sea of decadence.

Thren sat in the middle seat facing the door. He waved her to him. Two other men sat with him, one on each side. She recognized neither.

"Kayla, I would like you to meet two of my most trusted friends," Thren said. The man on his left stood and outstretched his hand. She took it and accepted his kiss on her wrist.

"My name is Senke," he said. "I am honored to be in the presence of such beauty."

He was a handsome man, although some of that was hidden by the numerous scars along his cheeks and neck, like fleshy pale crosses.

"Senke is, to put it bluntly, my enforcer," Thren said. "He ensures my orders are obeyed, without any troublesome deviations."

As Senke sat down, the other man stood. His skin was dark, and his eyes were darker. He had thin lips and wide eyes, and his clothes seemed about twenty years out of fashion. His enormous frame seemed to dwarf the table.

"My name is Will," he said. He did not offer his hand.

"Will trusts no one," Thren said as the giant man returned to his seat. "And I may be partly to blame. He has been with me since the very beginning, and every turncoat and sellsword knows that if he deals with me dishonestly, he will find Will beating down his door."

"I don't like liars," Will said, as if that explained everything.

"Neither may be the smartest counsel," Thren said, smiling a little at Senke's feigned offense, "but they are honest with me. Too many quiver at the notion of the word *no* when in my presence. However, you are braver than that. I looked into you, Kayla. Twice you have turned down recruiters seeking to add you to my guild."

Kayla shifted her weight from one foot to the other, trying to hide any discomfort.

"Guilds aren't for me," she said. "At least, not at the time."

"You're skilled," Thren continued. "I've gone over the events several times with my son, heard everything you have done. You once made a living selling information. No, don't tell me to who, for I do not care. But you operated within my territory, refusing to join my guild, yet you not just survived, but thrived. Four years ago you turned down the first recruiter. Four years. Yet now you aided my son. Why?"

Kayla wished she had a better answer, but she gave the honest one.

"I thought I could make a profit," she said.

She expected him to be angry, but instead he laughed.

"As I hoped," he said. "You do not lie, do not hide, do not waste my time. Your skill is undeniable, Kayla, and your motives are as pure as I might hope for. If it is money you want, I can give it to you. If it is power, I have that as well. Already I owe you greatly for saving the life of my son, and if you are willing, I will give you a chance others could only dream of."

Kayla glanced at Will and Senke, wishing at least one of them might give a hint as to what exactly was being offered.

"And what is that?" she asked.

"Join me as part of my council," Thren said.

"Sink or swim, to put it most simply," Senke chimed in. "You've got potential, and given this whole fight against the Trifect, we're not much for wasting time. You're good. Are you good enough?"

"I want you to aid Will and Senke tonight in an endeavor," Thren said.

Kayla took a seat before them and crossed her legs.

"What might that be?" she asked.

"Those who betray me must be punished," Thren said. "Loyalty until death. Death to the disloyal. I have based my entire life around those two laws, and I will not break them now. The king has imprisoned Aaron's former tutor, an elderly man named Robert Haern."

Kayla's cheek twitched at the name, and Thren misinterpreted this as a sign of recognition.

"Indeed, the king's former tutor was also my son's. When the soldiers stormed his home, Aaron insists Robert helped him escape. I must know if this is true. I must know what part Robert played in that fiasco. If he saved my son's life, then I owe him as dearly as I owe you. If he was a willing member of the attempt..."

Will cracked his knuckles.

"You want us to break him out of prison," Kayla said. "I've never once heard stories of you doing so for any of your other members. Why risk all this for one old man?"

Senke nudged Thren's elbow, clearly amused. Thren was not.

"Someone was behind the attempt on my son," he said. "Someone with the power of the castle. I must know who. I will not assassinate a king until I am certain of his guilt."

His tone made it perfectly clear he was not joking. Kayla felt a knot swelling in her throat, and she swallowed it down.

"What do you want of me?" she asked.

"I will be leading this endeavor," Senke said. "Will is coming too. We need a third, but it's possible the attack on Aaron was orchestrated with the help of someone within our organization. We need someone clean. So what do you say? Want to help break into the dark dungeons of King Edwin Vaelor's castle?"

Insane, Kayla thought. *Absolutely insane. We will be caught, and killed, all for an old man who may know nothing, nothing at all...*

Thren was watching her, they all were. She knew what saying no would mean. She would never join their private talks again. There would be no seat for her there on Thren's council, not when her cowardice could win out over her loyalty. All hopes of wealth and power and fear would be lost forever.

"I'll go," she said. "I'll most likely die, but I'll go."

"That's my girl," Senke said with a wink. Will only grunted.

Knowing the dungeon could be the death of the old man at any time, they made their plans for that night. Many hours later, a new collection of daggers clipped to her belt, Kayla met the others in the deep recesses of the safe house.

"Thren's built tunnels leading out to a couple different homes and alleys," Senke said as he adjusted his gray cloak, cinching it tighter about his body. Kayla caught sight of a long dirk tucked into his belt, the sides of its hilt painted red. The blade curved up and down like waves of the ocean, and she shuddered at the thought of its piercing her flesh.

"There are times when no one, not even of our guild, can see us," Will said. "Not going. Not coming. This is one of those times, you understand?"

"I'm no child," Kayla said. Will had painted his face gray to match the color of his cloak, and when he smiled at her he seemed like a graveyard wight come to feed.

"Maybe," Will said. "But when blood gets spilled, we'll see if you cry like one."

"A most impressive silver tongue you have, my friend," Senke said, slapping Will on the back. "It is a wonder you must pay the ladies to stay in your presence. I would think they would be paying you."

"After they see what I have, they do," Will said. He glanced at Kayla, as if expecting her to blush, but she only rolled her eyes and gestured for them to move on ahead.

"The tunnels are waiting," she said.

"Be serious if you must," Senke said, "but remember to smile. It lights your face up so beautifully when you do."

This time she did blush, and when she noticed the begrudging annoyance on Will's face, she let her cheeks bloom full red.

Senke pulled up a few boards underneath a painting of a broken castle. Cut into the packed dirt was a hole curving deeper underneath the house, like some oversize rabbit hole.

"There will be no light," Senke said. "I'll go first. Try to crawl slow and steady, and under no circumstances panic. If you get too close to me, I might kick you in the face, and I'd feel just horrible. It might feel tight at times, but keep crawling, and remember that if Will can fit, you surely can."

"I've never had a problem with enclosed spaces," Kayla said.

"What about the dark?" Will asked.

"I said I'll be fine."

Senke winked at her.

"I hope you are. Count to five, then follow."

Headfirst, the rogue climbed into the hole and was gone. After a count of five Kayla followed. At first she could see, but when the tunnel curled lower the light of the mansion faded, and she stared into what looked like the gullet of some enormous monster. Her heart fluttered, but she imagined the jokes Senke might make about her, as well as what would happen when Will bumped into her from behind. Most likely push her on, she realized. Hand after hand, she crawled into the darkness.

Gradually the tunnel narrowed. Instead of crawling on her hands and knees, she fell to her stomach and pulled herself along. *So much work just to keep our mission secret*, she thought with some annoyance.

"How long did it take?" she asked, and was startled by how loud her voice sounded. Some part of her seemed to think the darkness would swallow her words, smothering them in the void.

"Take to do what?" she heard Will ask from farther back in the tunnel. His deep voice rumbled in the dark, and she held in a curse as her head thumped the roof of the tunnel. She felt like a skittish rabbit.

"To dig all this," she said, hoping her nervousness wasn't too obvious in her voice.

"Two weeks," Will said. "All day. All night. Two died in this tunnel alone."

Kayla shuddered. She decided not to ask how many had died digging the rest of the tunnels that no doubt snaked out in all directions from the mansion. Occasionally her fingers would brush against wooden supports, and each time her heart was thankful. Any sense of humanity in the darkness, however remote, was a blessing.

The tunnel veered upward sharply. Kayla wasn't sure how long she had crawled, though the pain in her back insisted it had been at least half an hour. Her mind guessed a more reasonable ten minutes. Soon dim light lit the tunnel, but to her eyes it was a blazing beacon, and seeing it, she smiled. Her head emerged in the middle of a sparsely decorated home. Senke helped her out of the tunnel, his hands a bit too friendly around her waist as he did. She was so glad to be out of the tunnel, she let it slide.

Will was not far behind her. A bit of dirt had joined the gray paint on his face and hands, only reinforcing the wight image she had of him.

"Where are we?" Kayla asked. With only darkness visible outside the lone window, she had nothing to go on but a vague sense of the direction in which she'd crawled.

"A home Thren's bought and hollowed out," Senke explained. "We swing by occasionally to make sure no vagabonds take up residence. There's also a few friends of mine that have the dreadfully difficult duty of pretending to live here every couple of days so no neighbors get curious."

"Night's moving," Will said. "Shut up and move, Senke."

Senke laughed. "Yes, milord."

They slipped out and hurried north. Attached to the castle like an extra foot, the prison was a giant cube made of thick stone bricks. Only the top floor poked half above the ground, the rest stuck deep into the earth. Barred windows lined both sides, marking the cells of the lesser offenders. Kayla highly doubted they would find Robert Haern in one of them. She could only dream of their plan being so easy.

Anxious, she ran the plan over in her mind. With just the three of them, brute force would not do, not with so many guards stationed throughout the dungeon. Even worse, it could provoke a far greater retaliation if they left a massive trail of bodies. They needed stealth, they needed quiet...and they needed a tiny bit of magic.

"I thought the castle was warded against magic," she had said when they explained the plan.

"The castle is," Thren had said. "But the prison is not the castle."

Kayla wondered how such stupidity could have come to pass. Most certainly it involved money. Whatever the reason, the weakness was their boon. They had procured a simple spellscroll, which Senke kept hidden in his cloak. When they reached the prison they would sneak around to the back, slip past any guards, and then use the scroll to enter the prison. Once inside they would have about ten minutes before their exit vanished into the ether. The three had worked out a few strategies to distract, disable, and render unconscious any guards they might encounter. Picking Robert's lock would be child's play to someone like Senke. After that, it was a quick trip out of the prison and back to the safe house.

"Why are we bringing Will?" Kayla had asked once she

could pull Senke aside. "With his size, he cannot be an expert at silence and shadow."

"That big lug?" Senke had laughed and then grinned at the giant man. "He's coming with us in case stealth isn't enough."

As they neared the prison, she hoped that Will would be of no use to them whatsoever. Of course, she was in a doubtful mood. By night's end, Will would crack a few heads. She had little doubt of *that* fact.

"I count only six," Senke whispered as he and Kayla hunched around the corner of a home and watched the guards make their rounds. Will hung back, either not wanting to crowd the others or not caring how many they faced.

"Three at the gates," Kayla said, tracking their movements. "Two more traveling around in a circle. Another is stationary at the southeast corner. We should assume another guard is out of sight at the northwest corner."

"Seven, then. Still, far less than I was worried about."

"The soldiers are inside," said Will. When he first spoke, Kayla instinctively tensed, expecting his booming voice to alert guards for miles, but instead out came a controlled whisper, deep and quiet. She chastised herself for such naïveté. Will had not risen to such high ranks within the Spider Guild by being foolish or unskilled. Despite his size, she now wondered if he would be better at stealth and hiding than she was. Her pride said no, but a nagging voice of reason in her mind insisted otherwise.

"Far more men within," Senke agreed. "Mostly bunched at entrances to all three of the lower floors. They're far more afraid of people breaking out than breaking in. We must use that to our advantage, but also remember, the escaping may be much more difficult."

They waited a few more minutes, counting how long it took the roving patrol to loop around.

"We'll have maybe thirty seconds," Kayla said. "Unless you want to take out the two guards."

"Take them out, we gain another minute to get in," Will said. "But then we lose the rest of the night in getting out."

Senke nodded. If they could sneak in, their entrance would be unnoticed. Dead or unconscious guards, however, tended to attract attention.

"What about the guard at the northwest corner?" Kayla asked.

"We don't know for sure he's even there," Senke argued.

"Then let's go find out."

They climbed up to the roof of the home they'd hidden beside. As they prepared to move west along the rooftops for a better view, Kayla wondered at Will's dexterity. He climbed as well as she, and although he weighed more, the boards and plaster made no extra groans or creaks when he crossed.

Lady Luck was not with them. Leaning against the corner, whistling a tune, was their unknown guard.

"Damn," Senke whispered as he lay on his belly peering off the roof. "That complicates things tremendously."

"We need him diverted," Kayla said. "But that may mean only two of us going inside."

"We go as three, or not at all," Will said.

The woman spun at him and glared.

"Then give us an idea, ox."

As if this were a serious request, Will nodded and crossed his arms.

"Fine. Wait for me."

Will climbed down, his giant girth looking comical as he hung from slender handholds. Once on the ground, he strode up to the guard without any attempt to hide his presence.

"What is he doing?" Kayla asked.

"Calm yourself," Senke said. He put a hand on her shoulder,

and this time she did pull away. If he was offended, he didn't show it. "Will knows what he's doing. And if he doesn't, well, we're up here and he's down there, right?"

She didn't reply. Silent, they watched as Will waved at the guard, a noticeable drunken gait suddenly overcoming him. He said something, but they could not hear what. The guard pointed away, as if shooing a mutt. Will turned, as if considering, and then spun around, his massive fist clobbering the guard. His beefy arms wrapped around the guard's neck as he fell, tightening, twisting, and then the guard went still.

Kayla counted in her head, tracking how long until the patrol would find them. Will had thirty seconds, forty at most.

If Will was worried, he didn't show it. Calmly, he picked up the body and propped it against the wall. He crossed the guard's arms, adjusted his legs a tiny bit, and tilted his helmet so that it appeared he had nodded off. He kicked the legs a couple of times until they locked.

A moment later and Will was climbing up the house, rejoining them on their rooftop perch.

"Surely they will wake their friend," Kayla said, not impressed with the ploy. "Once he's awake, they will search for us."

"You don't know guards," Will said. A crude smile spread across his lips. "Why is he in back and alone? Because he's not liked. You will see, but for now, hurry. Our chance approaches."

They skirted the light of the various torches hanging from large brass rings off the sides of the prison roof. They were nearing the giant wall surrounding the city, and therefore were out of homes to climb across and use to hide their presence. Only their cloaks and the shadows offered them protection, but they used them with the calm skill of experienced thieves.

When the two patrolling guards walked around the corner, Kayla felt a bit of vindication at how quickly they noticed the guard sleeping. One yanked the helmet off him, while the other prodded him in the stomach with the hilt of his sword. When he did not wake, the first guard slapped him across the face, and then finally the man startled. She listened as the guards mocked him, grabbed his arm, and then marched him toward the front.

"He's to be punished," Kayla whispered, suddenly feeling very foolish.

"Go, now," Will said.

The three of them ran behind the soldiers and to the back of the now-unguarded prison. They made not a sound. Senke knelt beside the center of the wall and unrolled the scroll from the pocket in his cloak. He pressed it against the stone and whispered the activation word. The scroll sank inward, dissolved, and then, with an audible pop that made all of them wince, it vanished.

Senke slowly pressed his hands against the bare stone, a grin spreading across his face as it passed as through a desert mirage. His arm sank in farther, and after a wink to the others he dove headfirst inside.

After a deep breath to collect her courage, Kayla followed.

CHAPTER

7

Robert Haern remembered his comment to Thren Felhorn about the cruelty of King Vaelor's dungeon, and his dry, bleeding lips cracked a smile. How prophetic those words seemed now. His arms were chained above his head, each shoulder pulled out of its socket. The tips of his toes brushed the ground. Every few hours a guard came in and raised him higher, so that despite the stretching of his skin and his dislocated joints, he never supported himself with them.

He'd come to fantasize about those toes. He wanted to feel the weight of his body on them, to flex and curl them in grass while his back lay comfortably supported on solid ground. Robert sipped soup from a spoon at midday, which was held by a small boy who went from cell to cell carrying a little wooden stool.

What madman lets such a young child work in this pit? he had wondered the first time the door opened and the dirty-haired boy stepped in. Now he didn't wonder. Instead he tilted his head back, opened his lips, and waited for the soothing liquid.

Dreams came and went. They did so easily enough with old men, and the boredom only increased their vividness and frequency. There were times when he thought he stood at the king's bedside, telling humorous stories to scare away the nightmares that pierced his mind. Other times he was with his wife, Darla, who had passed away of dysentery a decade ago. She hovered before him with startling brightness, looking as she had when they first met. Light streamed through her blond hair, and when she touched his face he pushed against her hand, only to have soup spill across his cheek.

"Stop it and hold still," the boy told him, the only time he'd spoken.

Robert drank the soup while tears trickled down the sides of his wrinkled face.

Now it was night again, although he only knew because of the changing of the guards. The bars were thick around him, and there were no windows. He remembered men Edwin had sentenced to ten, twenty, even thirty years. Often the punishments had little to do with the crime and more with the look of the man and his inability to grovel convincingly. Robert wondered what his own punishment might be. No matter how much he hoped, he knew his imprisonment would last until death. He was old; it wouldn't be long.

The bars rattled, and he heard a soft bang on the door. His head tilted backward almost instinctively. Part of his mind thought it was too early for soup, but perhaps he had dreamed, or maybe he was just too hungry and thirsty to care about the time of day.

Just don't let it be time for another stretching, he pleaded. *No more, please, no more...*

Arms wrapped around his waist. When he opened his mouth to scream, a hand rammed over it to stifle the noise.

"Silence, old man," a deep voice rumbled in his ear. Robert opened his eyes to look, but they were full of tears. Through blurred vision he saw three strangers, cloaked and almost invisible in the darkness.

"This will hurt," said another voice, this one feminine. Then fire erupted through every joint in his body. His shoulders felt like the center of the inferno. He might have screamed again, but if he did he wasn't aware. All he knew was that the giant hand across his mouth pressed tighter. The chains rattled above his head. He heard a click. A sudden lurch followed, and though his whole body flushed with pain, he felt a wonderful, delirious satisfaction in the sudden feel of his weight resting no longer on his dislocated arms but instead on the chest of another.

"We don't have much time," said a new voice, male and not as deep as the first. "We need to go, and quick."

"We've killed too many," said the deep voice. "Thren will not be pleased."

"As long as we've got Robert, he'll keep his displeasure in check. Now hurry!"

The ache in Robert's shoulders had begun to fade, and a dim part of his mind was aware that they were no longer dislocated. That knowledge was little comfort when he felt himself thrown over the shoulder of what must have been a giant man. The sudden movement churned his stomach, and he vomited all over the man's back.

"Lovely," he heard his rescuer say.

Robert clamped his teeth tight as his body bounced up and down with each hurried step. Someone was rescuing him, so screaming was bad, screaming was dangerous. Silence was golden. His muscles were aflame, his joints throbbed, but the only sound he made was a soft, quiet sob.

To take his mind off the pain, he tried to visualize the prison in his mind. He had been there plenty of times, usually accompanying Edwin on some morbid jaunt past all the cells. The king had always been doubtful of his commands being carried out, so seeing men he'd sentenced actually being punished put a smile on his face. Those trips had given Robert ample opportunity to memorize the layout.

From what he remembered, he was on the third level built below the ground. Beneath were two more floors, where the punishment was far more active and brutal. To get out, they'd need to pass upward two floors to the entrance. Each stairway was locked and guarded. But if he was being rescued, perhaps they had killed the guards, or rendered them . . .

He moaned as the man carrying him skidded to an abrupt halt. The woman cursed. When Robert opened his eyes, his awkward position disoriented his vision, and he closed them to prevent another wave of vomit. The smell of it was still strong from the first time, although when he compared it to the stench of his cell, he figured he could endure it. Sounds of drawn weapons met his ears.

"Who?" he asked. His voice seemed meek compared to the rest of the sounds around him. "Who sent you?"

"Thren," said the big man. "Now shut your mouth."

Robert wasn't sure he could have spoken even if he'd wanted to. Steel rang against steel. He heard a man scream. Then they were running, his head bobbing up and down with each step. Stairs, Robert realized. They were going up a flight of stairs.

More sounds of battle. It was so strange hearing the fight without a visual accompaniment. The sound of a sword striking armor could be good or bad. Each cry of death could be one of his rescuers, or a man blocking their exit. He found that his mind was too exhausted to hope one way or another. Honestly, he hoped they failed in their attempt, and he was killed along with the rest. Because if Thren Felhorn wanted him, then the only place safer than the Golden Eternity was back in his cell.

A sound of trumpets flooded the prison. The big man carrying him swore long and loud. Robert was gently placed on the ground, ground that felt beautifully firm underneath his tucked knees. The stone was cold, but he didn't mind. He shivered, and absently he wondered if he had a fever. No longer upside down, Robert slowly opened his eyes and watched the battle to save his life rage around him.

A beautiful woman with raven hair twirled by a doorway leading deeper into the prison. Daggers flew from her hands, unable to score killing blows through the thick armor of the guards but stalling them nonetheless. Robert glanced the other way. Down past rows of cells made of thick stone and sealed wooden doors was the final set of stairs. Ten guards pressed their way down, but only four made it off the steps. Two men held them back, wielding long daggers with such precision that Robert knew they were men of Felhorn. One was a thin, wiry man with blond hair while the other looked like a dark-skinned giant. All three of his rescuers wore the gray cloaks of the Spider Guild.

Robert closed his eyes as guard after guard died. With the trumpet sounded, they would come endlessly. Three against a multitude; Robert didn't need all his wits to know the likelihood of escape. He waited for rough hands to grab his soiled clothes, or perhaps for a blade to pierce his chest. Death after death he heard, the cries a chorus of blood and skill. And then rough hands did grab him, but instead of hauling him back to his cell they flung him over the shoulder of the giant.

"Run!" boomed the man.

Up the stairs they went. When they reached the top, Robert dared open his eyes. The big man had swung around to check behind him, and as he did, Robert saw ten more soldiers blocking the way. They were not in a frantic hurry, nor did they look overly worried. They were arrayed in a diamond shape, with those at the back wielding long pole-arms while the front men carried shields and maces.

"Give 'im up," one of the macemen shouted.

"Where's the gate?" the woman asked.

"Follow me," the smaller man said. "As long as they don't know..."

The three rushed down the hall toward the defensive formation, then swung right. Robert was baffled. They approached a dead end of solid stone. The shadows across it were thick. The smaller man jumped at the wall, and just as Robert wondered what gymnastic trick he planned to perform, he slipped right through as if the wall were air. The girl followed next. Hope dared kindle in the old man's breast.

As the guards shouted behind them, Robert and his giant leaped through the shadows of the wall. Cool fresh air blew across Robert's skin, and feeling it, he gasped.

"Aaaand done," said the smaller man, clapping his hands twice before the wall of the prison behind him. Something black and watery ran off to the ground, leaving a disgusting-looking stain.

"Let's take him home," the woman said. Robert tried to smile at her, but the comfort of clean lungs was too much for him.

He fell asleep, still slung across the giant's shoulder.

When they approached the guards, Nava brushed back her cloak and stood to her full height. With her dark clothing and the white cloth over her face, there was no doubt as to what she was.

"We see nothing," one of the guards said, repeating the line he had been instructed to say when one of the faceless sought exit from or entrance into the city, lest he and his superiors incur the wrath of the temple.

Alyssa followed, still clutching Nava's hand. She had no idea why they were leaving the safety of the walls, and the faceless woman had given her no explanation. They'd stayed one day in a dilapidated inn, just her and Nava. The faceless woman had sneaked in through the window, letting Alyssa be the one to pay using money Nava gave her. Yet come nightfall, with Alyssa still exhausted and wearing her torn clothing, Nava told her it was not safe and brought her back out into the streets. Alyssa could only guess why. Even with her father hunting for her, there had to be safe places in the city to hide, places like that inn.

But why hide? The thought slapped her like a wet cloth. Her claim to the Gemcroft line was most certainly severed. Perhaps she could flee to safety with one of the foster families she had stayed with for the past few years. John Gandrem would surely welcome her, though he might also report her whereabouts to Maynard. And of course there were the Kulls...

They exited the western gate. The road leading southwest was packed tight from all the daily wagons and caravans of trade. Off the path, the tall grass was a deep green and grew as high as Alyssa's knees. The tug on her wrist giving her little choice, Alyssa followed Nava into the wide fields. They traveled north, curling around the walls and toward the King's Forest. As they neared the forest, the grass grew shorter, and by the time they walked through the rows of thick trunks, it had given way to carpets of fallen leaves.

"Why are we here?" Alyssa asked, rubbing her shoulder with her free hand as if she were cold. She had spent many nights listening to her maids tell ghost stories of the King's Forest, with its faithless maidens lost for eternity, chivalrous knights who had wandered astray, and scores of evil robbers and rogues eagerly awaiting a man foolish enough to enter alone. Of course the stories were just to keep the children away from the forest, where poaching was a serious enough offense to warrant death. Knowing this did little to fight back the ghostly chill that gave her goose bumps.

"Do not ask questions when you should know the answer," Nava said. "Why else would we enter the forest?"

They would kill her, Alyssa realized. Cut her throat and hide her body so when Yoren asked what happened, they could tell him she was already dead when they found her, her blood spilled across the floor and rats gnawing on her insides...

Alyssa waited until Nava tugged on her wrist, and then after her initial stumble forward, she jerked her entire arm to the side. The sudden pull back surprised the faceless woman, and Alyssa's thin hand slipped free. She bolted in the opposite direction, praying she had not gotten turned around inside the forest. Branches lashed at her face, and bushes they had easily walked around seemed to suddenly spring up and claw at her legs and ankles. Her attire was silky and thin, a poor guard against the grasping fingers of the forest.

She heard no shout behind her, but she knew the woman would give chase. She imagined Nava holding a serrated dagger in her left hand, her right reaching for Alyssa's hair or the neck of her dress. One tug, just one tug, and she'd stumble and fall.

Her heart soared when she saw the forest's edge. The trees were spaced farther and farther apart, and she ran more easily. When she dared look behind her, the faceless woman was gone.

Then she looked forward again, and a large, masculine shape stepped directly in her path.

Alyssa cried out, and as rough hands grabbed her arms, she felt her legs weaken at the thought of being raped by a lowborn ruffian.

"Alyssa?" she heard the man shout, and for a moment she ceased her thrashing. Her eyes opened (she'd never realized she shut them) and then she saw who it was who held her: Yoren Kull, sporting a fresh set of scratch marks on his face.

Relief broke her tension. She flung her arms around his neck and sobbed against his chest, all the while mumbling incoherently about robbers and ghosts and faceless women.

"She'll kill me," Alyssa shouted once she regained a bit of her wits. She spun and pointed to where Nava approached from the forest, no longer running but instead flowing around the bushes and trees as if her muscles were liquid.

"Kill you? Why?" Yoren glanced over to the faceless woman, and his right hand drifted to his sword hilt.

"Don't be a fool," Nava said. She pointed to Alyssa. "I was taking her to your camp, but she fled like a child."

"Your camp?" asked Alyssa. Her cheeks flushed.

"Yes, my camp," Yoren said. He smiled at her, and she felt her flush grow bolder. Gingerly, she touched the scratches she had made, and when she felt no blood she kissed them.

"Forgive me," she said. She disentangled herself from his arms and curtseyed in her dirty, torn dress. Her hair was a mess, and no quick wipe from the back of her hand could hide her tears.

"There is nothing to forgive," Yoren said, pulling her close and kissing her forehead. "All is safe now. All is safe."

Her sobbing began anew. After her time in the cells, shivering in the cold and desperate for conversation, to hear comfort and concern in his voice was more than she could bear. If he was embarrassed, he did not show it. She felt his arms tighten around her. With her face buried against his neck, she did not see the cold glare he shot to Nava, who only sheathed her dagger and glided back into the woods.

"I expected all three of you back last night," Yoren explained once they were deep in the woods. Alyssa sat next to him, the warmth of the fire divine on her cold flesh. Nava sat opposite them, keeping her distance from the flame.

"There were complications," Nava explained.

"If Alyssa is hiding here with me, I can imagine so," Yoren said. "She should be the ruler of the Gemcroft estate, not a runaway outcast. How did you fail so spectacularly?"

"They were ready," Nava said. "When Eliora and Zusa return, they will tell you the same thing. Hundreds of mercenaries hid within the walls. You fooled no one with your attempt to use Alyssa, and surprised them only in your choice of aid. We should all be dead."

"I was told you never failed," Yoren said. He had tied his blond hair behind his head, giving his face a stretched, dangerous look. "I was told even Thren Felhorn would quake if he knew you came for him; so how did some fool-headed merchant defeat you so easily?"

"If you had come," Nava said, her voice cold enough to freeze water, "then you might have seen for yourself. You'd have died, but at least you'd have your answer."

Alyssa thought he might reach for his sword, but before he could, the rest of the faceless women arrived. Nava greeted the others with curt nods. They sat side by side near the fire, facing Yoren and Alyssa.

"Why are you alone out here?" Eliora asked him. "Shouldn't

you have retainers and servants? These are no conditions for one of Alyssa's birth."

"Have you thought that perhaps I'm hiding here?" Yoren asked. "I can survive on my own. Only one hunter has spotted my fire, and I paid him well enough to leave us alone."

"Then he will only be the richer when he sells your secret for twice the amount," Eliora replied. "Don't be a fool. You must move elsewhere."

Again Alyssa expected an angry reaction, and again she was surprised by how docilely her lover reacted.

"If you think it wise," he said. His arms wrapped tighter around her, and sighing contentedly, she let him tuck her head underneath his chin. Her breath blew across his neck.

"It may not be too late," Nava suggested. "If we kill Lord Gemcroft before he can appoint a new successor, by law Alyssa inherits his wealth and business transactions."

"No," Alyssa said as she pulled away from Yoren's arms. "I don't want him killed. Whatever he's done to me doesn't deserve that. I worry for my family, my father included. These thief guilds will destroy everything my family has worked for. I can't allow that. That's why I must take over."

"She is the last," Eliora said. "Maynard might not remove her from his will, for if he does, the Gemcroft line dies with the stroke of his pen."

"Stop it," Alyssa said. "All of you. I will not let you kill him. He will not banish me, not forever. I know my father. Given time, he will accept me back."

"Time you may not have," Eliora said darkly.

"Ladies, I believe my lovely needs a rest," Yoren said. "If you might give us some privacy? Perhaps tomorrow morning we'll have a reasonable plan prepared. For now, I think we're all a bit upset over how things fell apart."

The faceless women slipped through the trees, with only Eliora glancing back. She said nothing, though Alyssa felt her eyes peering at her through the thin white cloth.

"I'm sorry," Alyssa said, shifting closer to the fire. She wasn't sure what for, but guilt weighed heavily on her shoulders. Whether by her own actions or not, she felt she had failed so many people. Yoren put his hand on her shoulder, and she was thankful for his kindness.

"Everyone makes mistakes," Yoren said. He paced behind her, and the silence she hoped he'd end stretched out longer and longer.

"I couldn't bear to see him dead," she said. Yoren's pacing made her nervous. What was troubling him so badly?

"Sometimes good men must die to further the cause of something greater," Yoren said.

"Yes, but I—"

Yoren grabbed her arms, yanking her to her feet and spinning her about. When she looked into his eyes, she saw that same fire that had always aroused her lust and called her to his bed. This time anger was mixed with the lust, along with a dash of contempt. She felt she looked into the eyes of a stranger.

"Listen to me," Yoren said. He was trying to remain calm, and succeeding only barely. "We have gambled everything on your ascension. Do you understand that? You are an outcast and a bloody fool if you think your father hasn't already written you out of his will. You are dead to him. He might as well be dead to you."

He paused as if waiting for her to answer. She nodded her head, unsure of what to believe. Would Maynard cast her out so? Would he believe she'd been behind the attack by the faceless? Yoren loomed over her, and for the first time she felt vulnerable in his presence.

"We have done everything to put you into power," the man continued. "And will *continue* to do everything. Do not let your emotions get in the way of this, Alyssa. Everything is before us; all we need is to shed a little more blood. One day, our children will inherit the Gemcroft fortune, and our grandchildren will dance in the mines your father chokes with axes and slaves."

They are liars, girl, echoed her father's voice in her ear. *Liars and thieves and conniving men...*

"The Gemcroft name is doomed," Yoren said. "You knew that when we came here. Your father is weak. A strong leader must arise." He brushed her hair. "A leader like me."

And that was it, then. Alyssa looked upon the man not as her lover, not as a dashing man with a hint of danger in his smile. She saw the poised viper, saw in his smile a crawling beast that would take all her power and leave her shriveled and dead. They would not be equals, not once the wedding bells rang.

And right now her life was in his hands.

His face brushed her neck, and his arms held her closer against him. For once, it did not excite her. Instead she fought down her revulsion, pretended to be aroused as his tongue flicked across her skin. As his hands fumbled across her breasts, she swallowed her anger and shame and let it burn away her self-delusions. To the ground by the fire they went, and she spread her legs for him as he pulled down his trousers. She let him think he'd convinced her, let him believe himself still in control. She was a Gemcroft, and could endure the man's touch for a little while longer. But she swore that should she somehow assume control of the estate that was rightly hers, she would not let a dog like Yoren have a single taste of its power.

Father was right, she thought as Yoren grunted louder. *I am such a stupid girl. But that girl dies tonight.*

Yoren would be the next to die, and unlike her, he would not be reborn wiser, stronger. He'd just stay dead.

CHAPTER

8

Given the mansion's numerous closets, secret pathways, and gardens, Aaron couldn't have been happier with his new home. He'd spent the past few days lurking more aimlessly than normal. Since the attempt on Aaron's life, his father had not appointed a new teacher in weaponry, stealth, or politics. With little else to do, Aaron had begun picking random workers and stalking them. He'd watched fat Olivia slaving away at the ovens for nearly four hours before she noticed his presence. Deciding a busy, unskilled person like that was no fun, he moved up in difficulty. Senke had caught him in less than four minutes; Will in less than two.

But Senke and Will were gone, as was Kayla, whom he hadn't worked up the courage to stalk yet. He'd discussed her with Senke plenty, blurting out how beautiful and skilled she was. Senke, the wily woman-lover that he was, had been more than sympathetic. But then he'd gone on and said the worst three words in the world to Aaron: "You're too young."

With the king sending soldiers to kill him, Aaron didn't think growing older that much of a guarantee. He'd spent the last two hours hiding atop an old wardrobe. Floor planks opened up nearby to one of the many tunnels leading in and out of the mansion. Aaron had watched people come and go, observing their reactions as they stepped into the light. For a few, he'd even scratched the wood with his fingers or let out a quick cough. None had noticed. Aaron found himself missing Senke even more.

Aaron thought perhaps he should be in bed, but the Spider Guild was far more active at night than during the day. More active meant more interesting. He wandered the hallway, listening for something to watch. On a good day he'd catch several members of the guild gambling with dice, and he'd watch the twitches of their faces and the nervous movements of their hands. Aaron had gotten quite skilled at guessing who would win by the severity of their tells.

As he wandered, he found his spirits dropping. He bypassed only a couple of men, all alone and looking almost annoyed at his presence. When he passed by the front door, Aaron crossed his arms and leaned against it. "So bored," he sighed.

Then he felt the door behind him shudder, as if someone was grabbing the iron handles on the other side but not yet pulling. Voices drifted inward. Aaron wasted no time. Before the door could creak open, he was already hidden in a shadowy corner.

Senke entered first, and Aaron's initial joy at seeing him was tempered by the deep scowl across his face. Kayla followed. There was blood on their clothes, and numerous cuts across their bodies. Aaron sank farther into the darkness, watching with a mixture of curiosity and fear.

Will entered, an old man held in his arms. It took a moment before Aaron realized who it was: Robert Haern, the kindly teacher who had risked his life to help him escape the soldiers. His face was bruised, his hair dirty, but enough of the man remained to clearly identify him. Aaron felt an initial inclination to reveal his presence, but he fought it down. They had entered through the front door. No one was permitted to use the front door.

"He still with us?" Kayla asked, gingerly touching a gash on her forehead with her fingertips.

"He lives," Will said. "But his sleep is deep."

"We'll let Thren wake him up," Senke said as he ducked his head outside, looked about, and then shut the door. "Perhaps during his questioning he'll forget the fact that we walked through the front gate and door with the whole world watching."

"The whole world is sleeping," Kayla said, her voice sounding very tired.

"No it's not," Will said. "Not the part that matters to us. But the old man would not make it through the tunnel. Which order do you want to disobey: the ban on the door, or the command to bring Robert here by morning?"

Their voices grew softer as they hurried deeper into the mansion. When they were far enough away, Aaron darted after.

He stopped for just a moment at his father's study, peering around the corner of a hall. Sneaking in through the door would be tough. He desperately wanted to know what was going on, but whatever the matter, he would probably hear the dreaded "You're not old enough" speech and then be sent to his room.

Decision made, Aaron waited until the door closed before he bolted to its side, pressed his ear against a crack by the hinges, and listened.

* * *

In his dream he was lively and youthful. Darla was at his side, her thin arms wrapped about his body. He nuzzled his face against her neck, inhaling deeply. Instead of her normal perfume of roses, he smelled blood. Something hard struck his face, and then he opened his eyes.

Darla vanished, the arms around him gone too. He was on his knees, stained with blood and filth. Before him, his face an unreadable mask of stone, stood Thren Felhorn.

"Welcome to my home," Thren said, his icy voice robbing any meaning from the greeting. "I trust you'll find it more comfortable than your last abode."

"I take whatever comforts are afforded to me," Robert said, dismally wishing he could be back in his dream. He wanted Darla, his beloved wife Darla, not a heartless interrogation. If he only closed his eyes, perhaps she'd be waiting for him, her face shining with light as it had in the prison...

Another blow to his face jolted him awake. The giant man towered over him, blood on his knuckles. Robert chuckled. Compared to the pain in his shoulders, the punch was little more than an annoyance.

"I know you must be tired," Thren said, walking out from behind the table. A hand on one knee, he knelt before Robert. "Tired, and in pain. I do not wish to add to either, old man, but I will. Tell me, what was your part in all of this?"

"My part?" Robert asked. "My part was to hang from chains. What is it you speak of?"

Thren narrowed his eyes, but he stayed his hand.

"The king dared cross a line he should never cross," he said, his voice quieting. "My son... did you have a hand in my son's capture?"

"Capture? So he didn't escape?" Robert let out a sigh. "I'm sorry, Thren, I tried, but he was just a boy, trained perhaps but... do you know if he is alive or dead?"

Thren only shook his head. "You were fond of this saying yourself, Robert. Do not ask questions you already know the answer to."

The old man rubbed his chin, letting his tired, sluggish mind slowly work through the cobwebs.

"He died," he said. "If he lived, you would not waste time rescuing me, nor would you wonder what role I played. When the soldiers came, I helped him escape through a window, but they must have surrounded my home too well. Listen to me, Thren. I was no party to his death, but I know of your reputation. If your son is dead, my life is forfeit. I ask you make it quick. I am an old man, and have waited long enough for the mystery of the hereafter."

Thren stood, drawing one of his short swords. The sound it made as it cleared its sheath made Robert shiver. The three who had rescued him stepped aside, leaving the matter solely to their guildmaster.

"Swear it," Thren said as he pressed the tip of his sword against Robert's neck. "Swear you had no involvement with the king. Speak truth, old man, and go into the afterlife without the weight of lies about your neck."

Robert slowly stood to his full height.

"Truth or lie, I die the same," he said. "And I do not fear the fate your sword promises."

Anger flashed across Thren's eyes. His mouth curled downward as his frown deepened. The whole room quieted, the very air thickening with the certainty of impending death. Then the door slammed open, Aaron's angry cry breaking the silence.

"He did nothing wrong!" Aaron screamed. "Nothing. Don't you kill him, don't you..."

The big man grabbed him by the neck and yanked him away from Robert. Thren watched his son, his visage not changing in the slightest. The tip of his sword still pressed against Robert's neck, but despite it Robert smiled.

"I see the boy lives," he said. The movement rubbed the tip against his flesh, drawing a tiny drop of blood. "I wonder if it is you with the weight of lies around his neck, Thren?"

"Do not mock me, old man," Thren said. His voice seemed torn out from a deep cavern, reluctant and heavy. "Kayla told me of Gerand's exit. You spoke with him before the attempt on my son. I want the truth, all of it. Any more lies and I will force the heavens to wait for your arrival while you rot in a cell."

Robert glanced at Aaron, who stood with the big man's arms wrapped around his chest. His lip quivered, but he showed no tears, and Robert felt a strange sense of pride. That was a boy worth training, he realized. One who would defy the will of his own father, and reveal his own inappropriate spying, all to spare a life he deemed innocent.

"Very well," Robert said. "I speak not to save my own life, but for the sake of the boy's trust. When you first asked me to train Aaron, I meant to say no, but Gerand's spies discovered the proposition and went to the king. They decided I should use the opportunity to learn more about you. All we hear are half-whispers, rumors, and exaggerated tales of your amazing excellence. The chance to learn even a shred of truth about the war being waged outside the castle walls proved too alluring. I had my orders, and that was to train the boy while keeping my eyes and ears open.

"Gerand, however, seemed to have his own plans. Troops surrounded my home after you left. When I discovered his plan, I struck him with my cane and then released Aaron. After that, I was beaten and taken to the prison, where you later found me. That is my tale. I am an old advisor doing the will of his king, and though you may call me a betrayer to your name, I was betrayed all the same. Do to me what you will."

Robert and Thren stared eye to eye, neither flinching. At this point Robert was too tired to care anymore what happened to him. When his role as the king's advisor had ended, he'd thought himself free of the games, the constant backstabbing and rumormongering. He just wanted to teach. Was that so horrible?

"While in my services, you betrayed information about me and my son," Thren said. "I have killed men for less."

The words hung in the air. Robert narrowed his eyes. Something about the way Thren stood, without any anger or fury, hinted at something more. No, the guildmaster looked far too pleased with himself.

"However," Thren continued, "you also saved the life of my son despite knowing the punishment you would receive. So now I face a dilemma, for anyone who saves the life of my heir I reward greatly. How do I reward a man whose life is forfeit?"

Robert sensed the opening being given and took it.

"Let me swear what little remains of my life to you," he said. "I shall be your slave and do whatever tasks you set before me, however difficult or demeaning."

"A worthy suggestion," Thren said. "For the sake of my son, I grant your request. You will have food and lodging here in my estate, and you shall train my son when you are not aiding with various duties that Senke will set up for you."

Robert bowed low.

"Thank you," he said.

"Follow me please," Senke said. "I've got a room near Aaron's that should do nicely. Clothing might be a bit rough, but the former occupants left a few extra outfits they couldn't cram into their wagons, so we'll make do. Oh, and we'll get someone to check you over. You took a beating in that prison..."

"Wait," Thren said. He turned and crossed his arms, facing his son. Aaron lowered his head, then quickly raised it, as if fighting off his initial fear.

"Yes, Father?" he asked, his voice just above a whisper.

"You spied on our proceedings."

"It is what you train me for."

"You misdirect me with your answer," Thren said, his eyes narrowing. "Trained or not, that does not explain your actions. Why did you listen in? Is it because of Robert? You were with him only a day. He cannot mean enough to risk my wrath."

Robert watched, curious that Thren would conduct something so private with others watching. Was he testing Aaron? Or perhaps making a show of the fact that no one was immune to punishment, not even his own son?

"I want to know," Aaron blurted, his voice no longer a whisper. He pressed on, speaking faster and faster as if to outrun his own doubt. "What we do, what we are. I train and train, but I am still treated as a child. I know so little of the city, and if it weren't for Kayla, I'd be in a dungeon. Or dead."

"That still does not give you permission to spy on my activities!"

Aaron expected the boy to cower. Thren's fury was like a monster all its own, and against that raised voice even Robert had felt a momentary flinch of panic. But instead Aaron only tilted his head, and then spoke so softly.

"But spying on you is how I saved your life."

The battle-hardened guildmaster was struck by the simple pronouncement. He looked at the young man before him, and he looked lost in a past Robert knew nothing of. The old man looked away, for some reason worried that if Thren should realize he watched, he'd react violently against him.

"You're right," Thren said, his fury subsiding. "Just a child you were, yet you killed without hesitation." Thren looked to Robert. "Killed his own brother, even. That is the level of his loyalty, that he would remove that brash, unworthy fool so he might become my proper heir. I do not want him coddled, not anymore. When you teach him, teach him the truth, no matter how painful."

Thren put a hand on his son's shoulder.

"Though you disappoint me with your trespass, part of the blame is mine. From now on, you will be at my side at all times. My life is not safe, Aaron, as you will soon discover. But know that regardless of the risk, I will bring you with me."

"I'm not scared," Aaron said.

"Even I am sometimes afraid, as will you often be."

The boy shook his head.

"Scared or not," he said, "I'll never show it."

A foolish boast, one Robert had heard a thousand times. But looking at that child, seeing his resolve and courage, Robert knew without a doubt that he believed him.

CHAPTER 9

The message had come yet again, and this time James Beren was tempted to shout out his Ash Guild's response at the top of his lungs. At least that would get Thren off his ass. Either that, or a dagger stabbed into it, but by this point he might have preferred the brutal attempt of force over the sickeningly sweet diplomacy Thren seemed prone to lately.

"Shall we give our usual answer?" asked Veliana, his right-hand man…although since she was a woman, he figured he should change her title, but crude amusement kept him from doing so. She was a pretty thing with cream-colored skin, red hair tied in a long ponytail, and dazzling violet eyes. Several daggers were clipped to her belt, her skill with them almost legendary, especially for one her age, and she was rumored to have a bit of magic in her as well. A few had murmured about how the little girl of eighteen had slept her way to James's side, but that was all hogwash. Her mind was as sharp as her dagger, frightening in its deadliness.

"His plan is suicide," James said, pacing within the warmly lit study. They were holed up in a safe house deep within the slums of Veldaren. Hundreds of families provided ample cover for their coming and going, and a bit of well-placed coin and occasional bread did wonders to ensure those families' discretion. A few hanging bodies had helped as well.

"Perhaps such a risk must be taken to end this," Veliana said. "He writes that we are the last holdout; all the other guildmasters have signed on."

"That's because he's killed everyone who disagreed," James said, a bitter edge creeping into his voice. "And the rest he cowed with a few subtle threats dripping with poison. He's grown desperate and delusional. Surely you can agree with me on that?"

Veliana smiled at him, a practiced smile that hid any of her true emotions from James. He felt her watching him as he paced. He also felt every bit of his forty years graying his hair and wrinkling his face. The Ash Guild was the smallest of all the thieves' guilds, but it was certainly not the weakest. With small size came added secrecy and stealth. They did not need to pad their numbers with riffraff and lowborn drunkards who couldn't steal a diaper from a suckling babe. But despite that core strength, they could not challenge the Spider Guild. Not yet.

"I'm not sure I can agree," she said, not revealing whether she meant with Thren or with James. "But we've entered the fifth year. We've tried hurting their wealth, and the gods know we have, but it's like bailing water out of a river. It all just runs back. We steal from the Trifect, and then our men spend it on wine, food, clothes, and petty trinkets, and who do you think supplies every one of those?"

"But all of us?" James asked. "This plan, this assault during the Trifect's Kensgold, will certainly result in bloodshed, but I fear the bulk of it will be ours, not our enemy's. Does Thren really think with all the thief guilds combining together that someone won't leak word to the Trifect? His plan requires an almost impossible level of secrecy. One errant word and we're all hanging from nooses... if we're lucky."

"If he's only contacted the guildmasters," Veliana said, "it is possible to keep silence, at least as long as necessary."

"And those guildmasters will tell advisors or close friends, just as I have told you. And then they will tell their close friends, and then one of them will leak word to a turncoat for Connington or Keenan, and then we're all fucked."

Veliana laughed.

"Then tell him no," she said. "Stop asking for delays."

"Do that and I become just another body at Thren's feet," James said. He sounded tired. "I didn't live this long, clawing and climbing my way past friends and enemies, just to watch it all vanish in smoke and ash."

"Ash is what we are," Veliana said, tossing the note from Thren Felhorn into the fireplace and watching it be consumed. "And ash is what Veldaren will be soon. Do what you think is best, regardless of whether I agree or not, but at least make sure you do *something*. Waiting for Thren or the Trifect to act will get us killed."

"You're right," James said after a length. "Either we aid him, or stop him. He is either friend or enemy. The question is, can we afford Thren as anything other than a friend?"

"That," Veliana said, "is a very dangerous question, and worse is the answer. Thren doesn't have friends, James. He only has men he hasn't yet sacrificed."

Her guildmaster let out a sigh.

"Then we stand firm, regardless of the wrath Thren brings

down on us," he said. "Hopefully his plan erupts in his face, freeing all of Veldaren from the bastard's presence. But what do we do until the Kensgold?"

Veliana smiled at him.

"What we've always done," she said. "Whatever is necessary to survive."

Gerand wound his way through the halls of the castle with an expertise acquired over fifteen years of serving the Vaelor family. Servants scuffled past him, and he listed off their names silently. Every new scullery maid and errand boy had to be vetted by Gerand personally. If something seemed the least bit off, he sent them away. Ever since the thief war had begun, King Edwin Vaelor had feared poison, a death that could come from even the youngest of hands. Personally, Gerand found the whole ordeal exhausting. Edwin jumped at shadows, and it was Gerand's duty to hunt them down. It never mattered that he always revealed dust gremlins and empty corners. The monsters would come back, acid dripping down their chins and dried blood on their dagger-like claws.

The bruise on Gerand's forehead pulsed with every beat of his heart. He touched it gingerly, wishing Edwin had listened to his advice and outright killed Robert Haern instead of imprisoning him. The Felhorn whelp had escaped because of the meddlesome old man. But Edwin's spine seemed more akin to fat than bone, and he had been unable to execute his former teacher, no matter how estranged they might have become. Still, Gerand would find ways to punish Robert for the blow his cane had struck him. He'd never say so, but Gerand felt the castle was his, not Edwin's, and he would command its workers and soldiers right underneath the king's nose if he must.

Up the circling stairs of the southwest tower he climbed, ignoring the creaking of his knees. The night was dark, and although the lower portions of the castle were alive with men cutting meat and women tossing flour and rolling dough, the upper portions were blessedly deserted. At the very top of the stairs Gerand paused to catch his breath. He leaned before a thick wooden door bolted from the outside. Tired, he lifted the latch and flung it open. Inside had once been a spytower, but the strange contraption of mirrors and glass was long broken and had been removed. The room had briefly been a prison cell, but over the past ten years it had fallen into disuse.

Waiting inside was a wiry little man wrapped in a brown cloak.

"You're late," the man said, speaking with inhalations of air instead of exhalations, which gave him an ill, out-of-breath sound.

Gerand shook his head, baffled as to how his contact always made it up the tall tower without being spotted. Unless he had the hands of a spider, he surely could not climb the outer wall. No matter how, every fourth day at an hour before dawn, Gileas the Worm waited for Gerand in the cramped room, always smiling, always unarmed.

"Matters have gotten worse," Gerand said, rubbing the bruise on his forehead without realizing it. "Ever since our involvement with Aaron Felhorn, King Vaelor has grown even more fearful of his food and drink. He has suggested rotating his cooks and keeping them under watch at all times. I've told him a food taster would be a much simpler answer, but for a cowardly son of a bitch, he can be so stubborn . . ."

The advisor realized just how out of place his speech was and halted. He glared at Gileas, his warning clear, but the Worm only laughed. Even his laugh sounded sickly and false.

"As amusing as informing the king of your candid talk

would be, I'd only earn myself a noose for the trouble," Gileas said.

"I'm sure you'd hang just as well as any other man," Gerand said. "Worms pop in half when squeezed tight enough. I wonder if you'd do the same."

"Let us pray we never find out," Gileas said. "And after what I come to tell you, you may discover my presence easier to bear."

Gerand doubted that. The Worm was aptly named, for his face had a conical look to it, with his nose and eyes scrunched inward toward his mouth. His hair was the color of dirt, another detail that helped enforce the adopted name. Gerand didn't know if Gileas had come up with the title, or if some other man had years prior. It didn't matter much to Gerand. All he wanted was information worth the coin and the trek up the stairs. Most often it was not, but every now and then...

The gleam in Gileas's eyes showed that perhaps this was one of those times.

"Tell me what you know, and quickly, otherwise Edwin will soon believe me to be one of his lurking phantoms."

The Worm tapped his fingers together, and Gerand did his best to suppress a shudder. For whatever vile reason, the man had no fingernails.

"My ears are often full of mud," the ugly man began, "but sometimes I hear so clearly, I might believe myself an elf."

"No elf could be so ugly," Gerand said.

Gileas laughed, but there was danger in it, and the advisor knew he should choose his words more carefully. In those cramped quarters, and lacking any weapons or guards, the Worm had more than enough skill to end his life.

"True, no elf so ugly, but at least I am not as ugly as an orc, yes? Always a light of hope, if you know where to look, and I pride myself in looking. Always looking. And I listen too, and what I hear is that Thren Felhorn has a plan in motion to end his war with the Trifect."

"I'm sure it's not his first, either. Why should I care about his scheming?"

"Because this plan has been sent to the other guildmasters, and all but one have agreed."

Gerand raised an eyebrow. To have so many guilds agree meant this was not some farfetched fantasy of Thren's, but something significant.

"Tell me the plan," he ordered. The Worm blinked and waved his finger.

"Coin first."

The advisor tossed him a bag from his pocket.

"There, now speak."

"You command me like I am a dog," Gileas said. "But I am a worm, not a dog, remember? I will not speak. I will tell."

And tell he did. When he was finished, Gerand felt his chest tighten. His mind raced. The plan was deceptively simple, and a bit more brutish than Thren most likely preferred, but the potential was there . . . potential for both sides to exploit.

Only if the Worm speaks truth, he realized. *But if he does, come the Kensgold, we might finally end all of this . . .*

"If what you speak of comes to pass," he said, "then I will reward you a hundredfold. Tell no one else."

"My ears and mouth are yours alone," Gileas said. Gerand didn't believe it for a second. He left the room and shut the door behind him, for Gileas demanded secrecy for his departure, just as he did for his arrival. His head leaning against the splintered wood of the door, Gerand allowed himself to smile.

"You finally erred," he said, his smile growing. "About bloody time, Thren. Your war is done. Done."

He hurried down the steps, a plan already forming in his mind.

* * *

Veliana waited in the corner of the tavern, a small place frequented more by soldiers than by rogues of the undercity. Her beauty was enough to keep her welcome, and her coin smoothed things over with those who still persisted in questioning. If she ever wanted something done without the denizens of the night knowing, she arranged for it in that tavern.

The door opened, and in walked Gileas the Worm. He saw her at her regular seat and smiled his ugly smile.

"You are as beautiful as you are intelligent," he said as he took a seat.

"Then you must think me a horrible sight," she replied.

Gileas scoffed.

"Forget it," she said. "Tell me, did he believe you?"

The Worm grinned, revealing his black, rotting teeth.

"Every word," he said.

CHAPTER 10

The temple to Karak was a most impressive structure cut from black marble and lined with pillars. A roaring lion skull hung above the doorway. The priests within were quiet, subdued men wearing black robes and with their long hair pulled tight behind their heads. They wielded powerful cleric magic, and had done all in their power to further the cause of their dark god of order. They played no part in the policy of the king, not officially, but Maynard Gemcroft knew that the priests had informed the royal crown of the dangers involved in exposing their presence to the city. If war was ever waged between the priests of Ashhur and Karak, the streets would soon be cluttered with the dead.

Maynard Gemcroft, in disguise and escorted by two of his most trusted guards, arrived at a building that looked nothing like the temple. Instead it looked like a large though plain mansion, with hardly a light lit within.

"I see you for the truth you are," Maynard said, putting his hand upon the gate, and then the image changed, the vision broken to reveal the temple in all its ominous glory. When he lifted his hand, the gate opened, and inside they went.

"Pelarak will see you shortly, Maynard," one of the younger priests said to them as he opened the double doors leading into the temple. Maynard did not respond. A bit of annoyance at not being called *Lord* in such a formal setting rumbled in his chest, but Pelarak had explained long ago that the priests would refer to no one as *Lord* other than Karak.

The hour was late, but inside the temple, routines went on as if it were midday. Younger men, boys really, traveled from corner to corner, lighting candles with thin, long punks. Purple curtains were draped across hidden windows. Following their guide, Maynard and his guards stepped into the great congregation room. Maynard had never considered himself a religious man, but the statue of Karak always made a deeply buried part of his mind wonder if he was in error.

Chiseled in ancient stone, the statue towered over those bowed before it. Its image was of a beautiful man with long hair, battle-scarred armor, and blood-soaked greaves. The idol held a serrated sword in one hand, the other clenched into a fist that shook toward the heavens. Twin altars churned violet flame at his feet, yet they produced no smoke.

Many men knelt at the foot of the purple flames, crying out heartfelt prayers for forgiveness. At any other time Maynard would have found the noise annoying and somewhat embarrassing to the wailer, but before that statue it seemed perfectly natural. In awe as he was, he was glad when Pelarak approached from the middle aisle and shook his hand. With his attention diverted, the statue seemed to lose a bit of its power.

"Welcome, friend," Pelarak said, smiling.

"After last night, it is good to hear you call me friend," Maynard said. He didn't know what to make of Pelarak's puzzled expression. Perhaps it was an act, but he didn't think so. If he was right, then everything he'd hoped for was true. The actions of the faceless women were unknown to Pelarak.

Surprise is on my side, Maynard thought. *I had best use it wisely.*

"I'm not sure what else you would be," Pelarak said as he led them off to the side of the aisles, where his own private room was attached. "If anyone should be worried about our loss of friendship, I should think it us. A man's heart and his gold sleep in the same bed, and the Gemcroft estate has been very . . . heartless in recent years."

The rebuke stung, but Maynard kept his tongue in check. Let Pelarak think he was in control. When the truth of his minions came to light, those stings would be forgotten.

"Times are harsh," he said. "Trust me, when the rogues are defeated, your coffers will be filled with the gold no longer needed to fill the pockets of mercenaries and sellswords."

Pelarak shut the door. Maynard's two guards remained outside. The room was small and sparsely furnished. Maynard sat in a small, unpadded chair while Pelarak crossed his arms and stood beside his bed.

"You speak truth, Maynard, but you did not come here wearing that amusing wig and beard to talk to me about tithes. What is the matter, and why do you worry about Karak's friendship?"

That was it, no dancing around the matter, no more stalling. Maynard let the truth be known while he carefully watched the high priest's reaction.

"Last night, three of your faceless women assaulted my mansion and kidnapped my daughter."

Maynard was in no way prepared for the cold anger that flooded Pelarak's eyes.

"I would ask if you were certain, but of course you are," the priest said. "You would not be here if you were not. Women of darkness and shadow, their bodies wrapped in purple and black? Who else could they be?"

Maynard felt a bit of fear bubble up in his throat seeing how tightly the priest clenched his fists. So much for thinking he was in control, the one with all the surprises. In truth, he knew very little about the faceless women other than that they existed, and that they were deadly. He had never actually sought their aid, and knew of no one else who had.

"Did you know of their involvement?" Maynard asked.

"Know? Of course not," Pelarak said. His normally smooth voice was sharp and abrupt. "They are whores and adulteresses, slaves to their sex and disobedient to Karak's commands. They live their lives outside the temple to atone for their sins. I had thought my command to remain neutral in your troublesome war sufficient, but perhaps I should have tattooed it into their flesh instead of merely asking."

"I lost several guards," Maynard said. "And my daughter, Pelarak, *my daughter*!"

Pelarak sat down atop his bed and rubbed his chin. His eyes seemed to clear, as if the clouds had parted in his mind.

"You know who did this," the priest said.

"I believe I do."

"Then who?"

"The Kulls," Maynard said. "I have reason to believe it was the Kulls."

"Forgive me, but I am not familiar with the name," Pelarak said. "Are they a lesser family of Veldaren?"

"They don't live in the city," Maynard explained. "And lesser doesn't describe what they are. Theo Kull is the head tax collector at Riverrun. He does all but steal from the boats traveling down the Queln River to the Lost Coast. I control much of the lands there, and it's been a point of contention between us who I pay taxes to. By paying here in Veldaren, I avoid the triple amount he takes in Riverrun. He knows the courts are no friend of his, at least not the ones that matter."

"How does your daughter come into play?" Pelarak asked.

"A few months back, Theo sent in some of his mercenaries to claim all my assets in Riverrun to pay my supposed debt. I have my own mercenaries, however, and they are of far greater skill and number. The Kulls wanted my large stretches of bountiful land around the city, plus my stores of valuables. They can't get to them, not with my guards, but if those guards were suddenly sworn to my daughter Alyssa instead of myself..."

The priest made the connection.

"They hope to use her to supplant you, and when that happens, through debt or loyalty, obtain what they desire in Riverrun."

"Those are my thoughts," Maynard said. "And not just Riverrun. What if they want everything I've built, every scrap of coin I've earned over my lifetime? I've thwarted them twice now, though with the faceless aiding them, I don't know how much longer I may last."

Pelarak resumed his pacing. His fingers tapped against his thin lips.

"I do not know why the faceless women might have chosen to aid Theo Kull in this matter, though I suspect the land near Riverrun may be the reason. Regardless, I will punish them accordingly. Fear not; the hand of Karak has not turned against you and the Trifect."

"Not good enough," Maynard said, standing to his full

height. He was a good foot taller than the priest, and he frowned down at him with an outward strength he struggled to match in his heart. "You have stayed neutral for far too long. Not once have I heard a valid explanation for doing so. These thieves are a danger to this city, and they represent the total opposite of the order Karak claims to love."

"You speak of Karak as if you were intimate with his desires," Pelarak said. "You demand our allegiance to your war. What do we stand to gain, Maynard? Will you offer us tithes, making us no better than the mercenary dogs you employ?"

"If you will not see reason," said Maynard, "then perhaps self-preservation will suffice."

He pulled a letter from his pocket and handed it over. Maynard felt his heart pounding in his ears, but he would not let such a cowardly sign show. This was it. He had crossed a bridge, and that letter was the torch to set it aflame.

"That letter is to be read aloud seven times a day to the people of Veldaren upon my death," Maynard said. "And it matters not how I die, by poison, blade, Kull, or Karak."

"You would announce our existence to the people," Pelarak said as his eyes finished skimming over the words. "You would blame their troubles on us? To force our obedience, you threaten to tell lies and half-truths to the city? We fear no mob."

"You should," Maynard said. "My people will be among them, and I assure you, they are excellent at inciting violence. Once people die, the king will be forced to send his soldiers. Tell me, how does one win over a city after slaughtering its people and its guards? Even better, how does one preach to a city after one's death?"

Pelarak stopped his pacing and focused his eyes on Maynard's face with a frightening intensity. His old voice was deep and firm as a buried stone.

"Every action has its cost," the priest said. "Are you prepared to pay?"

"When his patience ends, every man is willing to pay a little bit more," Maynard said as he opened the door to leave. "My patience ended years ago. This war must end. Karak will help us end it. I'll await your answer a week from now. I pray you make the right decision."

"Perhaps you're right," Maynard heard the priest say just before he closed the door. "Perhaps we have remained neutral for far too long."

And then the door closed, and without another word being spoken to him, Maynard was led out of the temple, out of its grounds, and back to his home, left with nothing but guesses as to what the cunning priest planned.

CHAPTER 11

Two of the men jumped as Veliana kicked open the door to the small room, abandoning their dice and reaching for their blades, but Kadish Vel slapped an open palm atop the table to stop them.

"No bloodshed," the man said. "Put your swords away. Veliana did not come here to slit our throats."

He saw the rage burning in her eyes and thought perhaps he was wrong, but he would not admit so openly. His thugs sat down, their hands lingering on their hilts. Veliana remained standing, though she at least had the decency to close the door behind her before she continued talking. Behind her were the people drinking and eating in the tavern, and far too many were staring.

"What game do you play, Hawk?" she asked him.

Kadish Vel, master of the Hawk Guild, smiled at the question. It was no secret he liked games; he would let the puppet of the Ash Guild explain further lest he reveal more than she already knew. When he smiled, his teeth flashed red in the dim light. His underlings claimed it was from the blood of women he dined upon in the waning hours, a rumor he himself had started. In truth, it was because of his love of chewing crimleaf, an expensive habit few could indulge as much as he did.

"I play many games," Kadish said, winking. Veliana slammed a fist atop his table, scattering dice to the floor. He ignored the outburst. "You seem distraught. Did you lose this mysterious game you are referring to? I don't remember playing with you, and I must say that sounds like something I would remember."

Veliana glared, making Kadish only smile all the wider. He adjusted the eye patch he wore over his right eye. In truth he could see just fine, but he liked the way it made him look. Let the other guildmasters try to be stealthy and secretive. Kadish preferred to be well-known, and liked. It helped with the survival rate.

"Enough," Veliana shouted. "Why are your men pushing into our territory? You know damn well everything south of Iron Road is ours, yet for the past week I keep finding your bird's eye scrawled over our territory markings."

"You know the manner of guilds," Kadish said, waving a dismissive hand. "The strong take from the weak. If you are so worried about lost homes and bazaars, then do your job. Defend them. Not here," he added when he saw her reach for her daggers.

"But you're not stronger," Veliana said. "If war breaks out between us, we will bury you in days. Pull back, now, or you'll suffer our wrath, you spineless little shit."

If Veliana expected the insult to rankle him, she was wrong. Kadish let out a laugh, feeling amused all the way down to his leather boots.

"Do you really think me so blind?" he asked. "Yes, open warfare between our guilds would devastate us. James is so good at recruiting, after all. I mean, he got you, didn't he? Perhaps even into his bed. But it's time you, and all of your pathetic Ash Guild, realized what world we live in. Instead of you making threats and demands, how about I ask some questions, and you give me some answers? Just a yes or no will do. The Serpents, have they also taken some of your territory? And everything along the eastern wall, does the symbol of the Wolf begin to cover your Ash?"

"It's all just a farce," Veliana said, her voice calming. A deadly seriousness had replaced her anger. "Take our territory, all of you, it doesn't matter. Soon all symbols will be the Spider. You know that, don't you?"

"You know nothing," Kadish said, scratching the skin below his eye patch. "And you can't see the future. I, however, am smart enough to view the present. As long as you hold out on Thren and his Spider Guild, you are lost. We've accepted his plan, and will move the moment the Kensgold arrives."

Veliana could have screamed. The Kensgold was a gathering held every two to four years by the Trifect, a massive collection of merchants, servants, family members, and every lowborn fool with a scrap of coin wanting to partake in the egotistical showing of power and influence. There was food, ale, and enough mercenaries to overthrow a kingdom.

"We can't attack during their Kensgold!" Veliana insisted. "How can all of you not see that? We're not an army, no matter how much Thren wants to pretend otherwise."

"And you're not in a position to lecture anyone," Kadish said. "If you're not with us, well, then you're just a corpse waiting to be picked clean. We'll take your members, your streets, and if we must, your lives. We all want this war to end. Tell James we will not suffer him and his guild to keep us from that finality. Tell him if he wants to have a guild at the end of the month, pledge his men to Thren Felhorn."

"You know," said one of the men beside Kadish, an ugly brute with scarred lips and a missing ear, "perhaps James might be more willing if we had his pretty lady here for ransom."

This time Veliana did draw her daggers, but Kadish stood and glared at his men.

"This meeting is done," he said to them. "We will not debase ourselves with such talk. The Ash Guild will see wisdom, I am sure of it. Good day, Veliana."

The woman spun and left, slamming the door behind her. When she was gone, Kadish rubbed his chin as his underlings snickered and made lewd comments. His mind raced through possibilities. If Veliana was so worked up that she'd storm into one of his own taverns to make empty threats, then panic was spreading through the upper ranks of the Ash Guild, if not to James himself.

"They're vulnerable," he said. "Rasta, take a few of your boys and have them scour the Ash Guild's streets. Find out just how badly they've been pressed, and which guilds are taking what."

"Planning something big?" the earless man asked.

"Keep your mouths shut for now," Kadish said. "But if James has lost more than we anticipated, perhaps it would be better to remove them entirely instead of waiting for them to finally bend the knee to Thren. Keep your numbers small, and move quickly. Even beaten and outnumbered, James is a dangerous foe. If we're to gamble with our lives, I prefer the odds stacked firmly in our favor."

Rasta stood and left while the earless brute recovered the dice from the floor, shook them in his hands, and rolled.

* * *

Aaron leaned against the wall to the open training room, holding back a wince of pain. His shoulder throbbed where Senke had struck him. Ever since the meeting the week before, and Thren's promise to include him in all things, his father had made him spend hours training each day. Senke was his trainer, the wiry rogue second only to Thren in skill with a blade.

"If you'd stop making mistakes, you wouldn't hurt so much," Senke said, pacing before him. "To your feet. It's time to dance."

Aaron pushed himself off the wall, knowing Senke would continue whether he was ready or not. For hours they'd danced, blunted practice swords whirling and clanging as they parried, riposted, and blocked. Of all his teachers of combat, Senke was by far the best, as well as the most enjoyable to be with. He laughed, he joked, he said things about women that made Aaron blush. When it came to swordplay, though, he took the dance seriously. The joy would fade from his eyes like a fire buried in dirt. After an error, he'd explain to Aaron what he'd done wrong. Should he react too slowly, or too foolishly, that'd be corrected as well. Sometimes he explained in great detail what to do, and when. Most often, though, he smacked Aaron with his sword and let the pain do the teaching.

This practice was particularly brutal. Senke wanted to hone Aaron's dodging ability. Denying him the ability to use his sword in defense, or to strike back, Senke swung and stabbed with incredible speed. The problem was that Aaron's initial reaction was always to block or parry, not dodge. Other teachers might have taken away his sword, but Senke would have none of it.

"You'll learn to control your instincts, otherwise they'll control you," the man said. Again and again the sword cracked against his shoulders, his head, and his hands. Whenever he tried to raise his sword, Senke's other blade would shoot out, parry it away, and then slap him across the face.

At last, when both were exhausted and dripping with sweat, Senke called the training done.

"You're getting better," the man said. "I know it's tempting to show off how good you are at positioning your blades, but sometimes, especially with stronger opponents, it is best to just get out of the way. Once you're reacting quicker, we'll work on integrating those dodges into your normal defensive patterns."

And with that, Aaron was dismissed. His teacher gone, he rubbed his shoulder, part of him wanting to ask a servant to massage it for him. But massages meant pain, and pain meant failure, at least when it came to training with Senke. After all, if he would just dodge like he was supposed to, he'd not have a bruise on him. So he put it out of his mind as best he could, wiped more sweat from his face onto his sleeve, and hurried down the hall of the mansion. He did not skulk, and he did not try to hide. This time he had a specific place he wanted to go, and without bothering to knock upon arriving he stepped into Robert Haern's room.

The furnishings were few but expensive. The chairs were padded and comfortable, the walls painted a soft red, and the carpet a luxurious green. Robert sat on the bed, piles of books on either side of him. Aaron wondered how he could possibly sleep on it, then wondered if the old man even slept in the first place.

"You're here," Robert said, smiling when he looked up. "I had begun to worry that Senke would knock all reason and wisdom out of you."

"My ears are clogged," Aaron said. "The wisdom stays in."

The old man chuckled.

"Good for you, then. Sit. We have old matters to attend to."

Aaron sat down, wondering what he could mean. Over the past week Robert had gone to great lengths describing the various guilds and their guildmasters. He'd gone beyond recent times and into the past, beating into Aaron's head why their colors were what they were, why each symbol had been chosen, what the symbols looked like, how they were drawn, and every other possible fact that seemed totally irrelevant. No matter how obscure it was, Robert would frown deeply and reprimand whenever Aaron missed an answer.

"In the darkness I might have taken away a light," Robert had said that very first day they resumed tutoring sessions. "But here I have nothing to take from you, so instead I do this: for every error you make, I will treat you like a child. I will tell you tales instead of truth. I will dismiss your questions like foolish inquiry, instead discussing matters that only a *boy* would be interested in."

The threat had worked.

"What old matters?" Aaron asked as he sat cross-legged on the carpet.

"Do you remember that first day? I was to have an answer from you, but forgot after my...brief stay in the dungeons. I asked you why the Trifect would declare war on your father after he had built up an alliance of guilds over the course of three years. Do you have an answer?"

Aaron had not given the matter much thought. He went with his initial guess, hoping it would be right. Robert always insisted that Aaron would know the answer to all questions he asked, and no other answer seemed to pop out at him.

"Thren became too powerful," Aaron said. "He was stealing

too much gold, so the Trifect forced this war with him and the guilds."

Robert chuckled.

"A child's answer," he said. "Coupled with a child's trust in his father. You couldn't be more wrong, boy. Perhaps we should read the story about Parson and the Lion instead of discussing such adult matters."

"Wait," Aaron said, his voice rising above a whisper. Robert seemed to notice, and he looked pleased.

"Do you have a better answer?" he asked. "Since your first one was so embarrassingly wrong?"

Aaron's mind raced. He had to figure it out. Anything was better than the fairy tales.

"Thren didn't grow too strong," he ventured, each sentence coming out as if stepping on ice to test its strength. "If he had, then the Trifect wouldn't have openly opposed him. The Trifect weighs all options, and this war has cost them greatly. Thren would not have stolen as much in twenty years as they have spent in the past five."

"Now you're making sense," Robert said. "The Trifect does not take on strong foes. They weaken them, poison their insides and rot their hearts. Once their target is desperate and fearful, then they strike."

"But the Trifect forced this war," Aaron said. He rubbed his thumbs together, as if trying to coax the truth out from an invisible coin. "And my father is not weak. Not then, and not now. The Trifect acted outside their normal behavior."

"Did they really? You say Thren was not weak. How do you know?"

Aaron paused, and his head leaned back a little as if he had smelled a bad smell.

"How could he be weak?" Aaron asked. "We've survived

against the Trifect. We've killed many of them, and thwarted every attempt to defeat us."

"Not every attempt," Robert said. "Must I get out the children's rhymes? Your father has suffered many casualties, and his coffers are near empty. This war taxes both sides. Never think you are invincible and your opponent a whipping boy. Rarely do matters work out that simply."

"Still, my father was not weak."

"You are wrong," Robert insisted. "Even a weak Thren Felhorn can withstand for many years. That is irrelevant. Have you ever heard that sometimes the *appearance* of weakness is just as dangerous as true weakness?"

Aaron nodded. He had heard such a sentiment before.

"Then consider this...five years ago, your father was consolidating power, but then other guilds broke away from him. Too many wanted control, and Thren's reputation was not yet established, though he built much of it during that time, brick by brick with the blood of his would-be assassins."

He paused, and Aaron sensed the unasked question. With the information given, he should be able to piece together the rest. He thought, his fingers pressed against his lips. He puzzled it over, and Robert did not hurry him.

"The Trifect realized how dangerous he was," Aaron said at last. "They knew he would eventually succeed in uniting the guilds against them. So when they saw the infighting, they tried to kill him."

"Exactly," Robert said. A bit of a smile touched his face. "They saw Thren's power as brittle and tried to smash it with a hammer. They did as they always did, Aaron, by striking when their opponent was weakest. But they erred, for your father erred, one of the few times in his life, but also the greatest. Just before the war between the Trifect and the underworld began, a weak guild, the Mantis Guild, tried breaking away. Instead of crushing that rebellion, your father let it last for several months."

"Why would he do that?" Aaron asked.

"I should ask you," Robert said. "You should know."

Again Aaron puzzled it over. He thought of Senke and of all the times he had let Aaron nearly score a blow or let a slash slip through his defenses, only for it to fall just short.

"Father wanted to teach the guild a lesson," he ventured.

"A wise guess," Robert said, "but still wrong. Try again, and remember my words."

He replayed the conversation again and again, and then the words struck.

Sometimes the appearance of weakness is just as dangerous as true weakness.

"He was plotting against the Trifect," Aaron said. His whole face flushed with pride at discovering the reason. "The Trifect would not suspect my father of doing anything drastic until the rebellion was finished."

"Quite right," Robert said.

"That was when the Trifect struck," Aaron continued. "They thought him weak, his alliance breaking, and so they sent in their mercenaries."

"Your father wanted to solidify power in secret," Robert said. "He used that rebellion to hide his strength, to make him seem weak, all so he might surprise the Trifect when he unleashed his collected power upon them. Every time someone rebelled before, Thren crushed them with brutal efficiency, but not the Mantises. That semblance of weakness unraveled all of his plans. If the Trifect had correctly gauged his strength, they would have bartered for peace and waited until Thren reached an age where he was too old to keep the rest in line. Instead they sent their mercenaries into the streets, killing thieves in their guildhouses. When your father tried for peace, it was too late. The Trifect had tasted blood and victory, and they set up a trap instead. Leon Connington nearly stabbed your father to death when Thren visited him in his mansion, and Maynard Gemcroft had his archers fire from their windows upon another of the Spider Guild's men sent to broker peace. That betrayal left your father in a hopeless position. Either he dies, or the three leaders of the Trifect die."

Robert pointed at a few books outside his reach, and Aaron fetched them. The old man opened them, his eyes not scanning the pages. It was as if the act gave him comfort.

"The city needs this fighting to end. The few who have remained neutral, like the king and the priests of Karak and Ashhur, will one day take a side to end the bloodshed. Your father is too strong, Aaron. He should have lost years ago. The guilds would have fractured, some great men would have died, and then the petty theft and trade of vice and flesh would have resumed as always. But not now. Each side has lost too much. They're like two stags staring eye to eye. The first one to blink loses..."

"Is this your advice to my son?" Thren asked from the doorway. Neither had heard his approach, nor his opening of the door. His arms were crossed and his face a mask. "My strength is a weakness; my war a mistake?"

Aaron fought an impulse to back away as if caught doing something wrong. Instead he bowed his head respectfully to both his father and his teacher.

"Robert speaks the truth as he knows it," Aaron said. "I need his honesty, not stories lying about the Trifect's power and twisting blame to where it does not belong."

Thren nodded, clearly pleased.

"Teach truthfully," he told Robert. "Never lie to my son. He is old enough for every truth, no matter how harsh. And he was right, Aaron. I was a fool. I let the Mantis Guild survive. I let an enemy live when I should have ended their existence. Sometimes even the most clever man can outsmart himself. You don't build an elaborate maze to kill a roach. You crush it with your heel. Now prepare your things. I go to a man who has lied to me, and want you at my side. There are lessons that one does not learn from books and study."

Aaron did not ask where they were going, though he very much wanted to. The boy knew his father would tell him when he was ready, no sooner and no later. They both wore the gray cloaks of their guild. Much of Aaron's outfit was new, from the soft black leather of his boots to the faded trousers and the thick gray tunic. He was most proud of the sword that swung from his hip, a thin rapier shortened to match his height.

"Say nothing, not even if you are directly addressed," Thren said as he led them through the dark streets. Morning was fast approaching, but until then the city would be still empty and quiet. The few men about them had their own business to attend to, and hide, so the father and son were left alone to wander.

"What if you demand I speak?" Aaron asked. Thren glanced back at him, looking bewildered.

"Why would I?" he asked.

Aaron nodded, his face flushed red.

They continued down the streets, which Thren named off as they passed, as well as what guild lay claim to them.

"Our territory is never something to give up lightly," Thren told him. "Every home, every run-down business, brings us profit. The businesses pay us protection money so we will not rob their stores. The street women give us coin for the privilege of using our streets. The people buy our drugs, supply us with recruits, and provide simple prey for our younger members in training. Every thief guild in Veldaren is trying to build an empire, and the one thing an empire needs more than anything else is land."

"You talk as if we're at war with the other guilds. I thought the Trifect was our enemy?"

Thren crossed his arms, his look hardening.

"In time we'll crush the leaders of the Trifect. We'll scatter their wealth to the four winds, and a dozen other lords and ladies will scramble like dogs to pick up the pieces. In that chaos there will be so much for us to take, so much profit to be made. Aaron, who do you think will be competing with us for that wealth?"

Aaron looked away, embarrassed.

"The other guilds."

"That's right, my son. They are not our friends. No thief guild, not the Hawks, the Ash, the Serpents, the Wolves... not a one is to be trusted. They are allies now, united only by a common foe. When that foe dies, every truce is broken. A new war will be upon us, and it will be one we must win, no different from the one we face now. Never stop looking to the future, nor forget the past. The other guilds were our enemies. They will be our enemies again."

They continued as the moon faded, the morning sun fast approaching. Before a large building marked with a sign painted entirely red, Thren paused and put a hand on Aaron's shoulder.

"We approach a brothel. Do you know what is done there?"

When he nodded, a small frown tugged at the corner of Thren's mouth.

"I'll assume Senke is to blame. Remember, women are a weakness to you. I want you pure, Aaron. I want you perfect. No strong drink will touch your lips. No womanly flesh will your hands caress. No priest will sway your heart. Power is all that matters, power and the skill to keep it. You have so much to learn, but once you are older, you will learn directly from me. Men fear my name, Aaron, but they will fear yours a hundred times more."

With morning close, the brothel was mostly empty. The women had slipped into more comfortable clothing. No men lingered drinking or chatting with the women before heading up to the more comfortable private rooms. The few who did remain were fast asleep. When the sun rose over the walls of the city, the ladies would prod them awake and usher them home to their wives, children, or professions.

"Welcome, Thren," said a middle-aged woman with flaming red hair and matching lipstick. "You have not graced us with your presence in far too long."

When she noticed Aaron, she smiled.

"Is this the young Felhorn? He looks so much like his father, he does. You brought him to the right place, Thren. I have some younger girls, and they know how to be gentle so that..."

"Enough."

His word struck her like a slap. Her lips closed, and the joy left her eyes, replaced with a cool, calculated gaze.

"Very well. Why are you here?"

Thren pointedly ignored her. He glanced at his son to ensure he had his attention and then began lecturing.

"This is Red. She is in charge of the women here. It helps to have a woman deal with the younger girls, plus her experience makes sure that they know how to do their jobs properly. Every brothel has someone like her. They are never fools, and they are always dangerous. They hear more than anyone else in this city. Men are stupid when in bed."

"Sometimes out of bed too," Red said.

Thren flashed her a dangerous smile.

"Where is Billy Price?" he asked. Red gestured toward a flight of stairs leading to an enclosed balcony.

"Leave your swords here," she said. "You don't need them if you're on business."

That dangerous smile on Thren's face never changed.

"You are not one to give orders to me," he said. "And death by the sword is *always* my business."

Aaron was surprised by how calm Red remained before such a glare. He decided she must be threatened often to be so calm. Either that, or she held very little regard for her life.

"Upstairs then," she said. "You may keep your blades if you insist. I only repeat what Billy tells me. You should know that."

Thren dismissed Red as if she were a servant or a slave, then went up the stairs. Aaron followed.

Billy was a fat man, astonishingly so for how short he was. When the Felhorns entered, the man stood, his gut swishing like it was made of curdled milk. His hair was cut short at the ears and dyed a pale brown. When he smiled, his two missing teeth made him look like a gaping schoolchild. Aaron wondered how such a fat, ugly man like that could run a brothel. If his father had not forbidden speaking, he would have asked.

"Welcome, welcome," Billy said, clapping his hands as if excited. He had been seated in a chair woefully small for his body. Behind him was a thick ornate railing, and beyond that a spectacular view of the city. "So good of you to join me in my humble establishment. The Bloodshot rarely gets company of your esteem, my great and powerful master of guilds."

The compliments flowed like honey from his tongue and

sounded as natural as running water. Aaron felt like part of his question had been answered.

"We come on business," Thren said, his hands resting on the hilts of his swords. He leaned forward just enough that the sides of his cloak hid the movements of his hands.

"Yes, of course, why else would such a noble man bother yourself with scum such as I? Why else would you dirty your hands with the doorknob of my wretched abode? Sit, please, I will not have you stand. Your son as well."

Thren remained standing, but he nodded at Aaron, who obediently sat down.

"I have looked over your books," Thren said. His face was a cold mask. "Something is odd about them, Billy. Perhaps you know what?"

"Odd?" Billy said. His smile was grand, and he wasn't even sweating, impressive for a man his size. Aaron watched him for all the signs of guilt he had been taught to look for. So far he saw none.

"Of course things should be a little odd," the fat man continued. "I run an odd place where men ask for odd things, gross things I wouldn't dare discuss in front of your boy. But my payments are in full. I dare not cheat, not when dealing with a man as frightening as you."

"It is your coin that intrigues me," Thren said. "And how much you have paid."

"What could possibly be the matter?" Billy asked. "At the risk of sounding proud, I pay more than any other brothel in this city! I know, for I hear the other owners whining, but I smile and think that I spend my money well for Thren's protection."

"That is exactly the matter," Thren said.

Aaron saw a tiny twitch at the right corner of Billy's mouth. His father had finally struck a chord.

"How is that the matter?" Billy asked.

"I've compared your coin to that of the other brothels under my protection, as well as spoken with those whining owners who pay the Hawks or the Ash. So tell me, Billy...how does a pathetic little brothel like the Bloodshot manage to outperform much grander places like the Silk or the Dandycushion? Your women are no prettier, your beds certainly not cleaner. Tell me, do you have an answer?"

A drop of sweat. Aaron grinned. Billy had no answer to the question. Before he could begin a wave of groveling and worship, Thren held up a hand and continued talking.

"For the past week I have had your building under watch. Most brothels have their men come to them, but you send out your girls to other places, drab places owned by men of no worth. But the men who own those places, or have loaned money to them..."

Aaron tried to make the connection. He had an idea what his father was getting at, but something was missing, some piece. Billy, however, clearly knew what the matter was. Aaron saw him grab at a dagger strapped to his belt, then stop. He must have decided, wisely, not to fight if things turned ill. He did not look like a man who could last long in a fight.

"I strictly forbid selling whores to the Trifect," said Thren, an icy edge to his voice. "All the other guilds have agreed, and you were no different. While the others suffer, you somehow thrive..."

"I charged any member of the Trifect triple," Billy said. All false affection and worship were gone. He was pleading now. "I'm practically stealing from them. All that money I send to you, to help you. Gold spent on my girls is gold not spent on swords!"

Not even Aaron saw the next movement coming. Thren's

hand caught Billy by his fat throat and flung him back. He slammed into the railing, which groaned in protest. A kick knocked him to one knee. Before he could cry out, the blade of a sword pressed against his breast.

"When I give an order, I expect it obeyed," Thren said. "You broke your word to me. You succumbed to easy coin."

"I gave it all to you!" shouted Billy. "Please, the girls needed work, and the Trifect was desperate! All of it I've given to you, I'd never cross you, I'd never..."

Thren grabbed Billy's hand, pressed it against the railing, and then slammed his sword down. The sound the flesh made as it tore reminded Aaron of a butcher shop. As Billy screamed, Thren tossed the hand off the balcony.

"I checked your books," Thren said. "And I compared that to what my men saw coming and going. You did give nearly everything to me, the rest to the girls. That is why you live, Billy. Now you listen closely. Are you listening?"

Billy nodded. He sat on his enormous rump, his stump pressed tight against the folds of his fat to stem the bleeding.

"I want the Trifect starved. I want them without drink, without drug, and without whores. They have made my life miserable, and I will do the same to them. Coin gains me nothing. Their suffering is all I want. Will you remember that the next time they send for your girls?"

"Yes, my lord," Billy said. His jowls jostled as he nodded. "I'll tell Red. I'll remember."

"Good." Thren cleaned his blade on Billy's shoulder and then turned to go.

"Thank you," Billy called out as Aaron stepped in line behind his father. "Thank you!"

They left the stairs, Aaron glancing back only once.

"Remember this," Thren said as they descended. "I cut off

his hand, yet he thanks me for not doing worse. That is the power you must one day command. Let them think every breath of theirs is a gift, not from the gods, but from you. Do this, and you will become a god among them."

Because of his father's order, Aaron could not reply. If he could, he would have mentioned that brief flash of anger he saw in Billy's eyes when his father turned to go. He would have spoken of the dogged determination lining the fat man's pained face, and the potential enemy Thren had just made. But Aaron could not, so he let the matter go.

Power was hurting a man without fear of retribution. That was the lesson Aaron learned.

Exiting the brothel, Aaron was surprised to see an ugly man waiting by the door. His clothes were ratty, his face strangely scrunched. By the way he reacted, it seemed he had been waiting for them.

"Master Thren," the man said, dipping his head and rubbing together his fingers, which had no fingernails, just fleshy red bruises where they should have been. "If you would only lend me your ear, there are things I could tell you. A great many things, if only you would pay the price..."

CHAPTER 12

The road was quiet. On one side was a small bakery. On the other was a smithy known for its owner's teaching abilities rather than his actual work. Six men approached from the east. They showed no weapons, but their rust-colored cloaks hid much of their bodies. They split, three on one side, three on the other, and then hurried down the road. Each of the groups had a member carrying a small pail of paint.

On the sides of both buildings, hidden so as to be glimpsed only in passing, was a smeared circle of ash. The men with the pail wiped it with their cloaks, then dipped their brushes into the dark red mixture. It looked like blood when they began drawing their symbol. They painted an unfilled outline of a hawk's talons, followed by three drops dripping from the foremost claw. The others stood about, watching for guards of both the royal and seedy kind.

They did not see any, for they did not look up. Crouched on the roof of the bakery waited Veliana and two of her men.

"This deep down Warden Street?" Veliana muttered as she watched them paint. "Have they truly grown so bold?"

"They've gone unchecked," said Walt, crouched beside her. His face was tanned and lean, his smile missing many teeth. By no means was she friends with him, but he was skilled in battle and reliable when it came to matters of stealth. For those reasons she kept him close. Crouched shoulder to shoulder with him atop the roof, she wished the man would at least take better care of his teeth. Someday his breath would give them away, she just knew it.

"Unchecked?" Veliana said, her voice deeply bitter. "I'm surprised they haven't encountered the rest of the guilds slicing through our territory. They're like wolves fighting over a dead deer."

"Tonight that changes," said Walt. "Tonight the deer shows it's not so dead after all."

"They move," said Vick, the other man atop the roof with them. He was young, with short blond hair and a scraggly mustache that failed to thicken no matter how long he went without shaving.

Veliana watched as the six men bolted around the buildings. She unsheathed her daggers as beside her Walt readied a crossbow.

"Six on three," he said. "I'll get two before they turn. That leaves four for you and Vick when you're on the ground. Think you can handle that?"

"Don't insult me," Veliana said as she leaped off the roof. Her silent landing went unnoticed. High above her a crossbow bolt whistled through the air. It struck one of the Hawk thugs square in the back. He lurched gracelessly to the ground. The remaining five spun. A second died, a bolt piercing his throat. The others charged, weaving from side to side in an attempt to thwart the crossbowman.

Vick should have been rushing alongside her, and Walt should have been firing more bolts from the roof. When neither happened, Veliana risked a look behind, just in time to see Walt's body hit the ground. Her heart sank at the disgusting sound it made. She had only a moment to glance up and see Vick sneering down at her before daggers cut at her slender frame. She batted them away, but with four to her one, she was sorely pressed.

The Hawks spread out farther, trapping her in the center of a diamond. Desperate, she lunged at one of the men, thinking that if she could kill him quickly she might escape. Her skill was great, and the man would have died under her assault, but then she felt a great weight slam into her. Stunned, she looked down at the bloody bolt protruding from her shoulder. Blood poured across her clothes.

Her daggers faltered, her meager blocks batted aside like children's defenses. Something hard struck the back of her head. She had just enough time to curse Vick's name before blacking out.

When Veliana awoke, she was blindfolded and shackled to a wall. She felt uncomfortably warm, which made even less sense when she realized she was naked. As the rest of her senses came into focus, she heard the popping and crackling of a fire. That explained the sweat that covered her body. But where was she?

"Wake her up," she heard a voice say. Hoping to hear anything she could use, she kept her body still and pretended to be asleep. To her left she heard rustling, and then something sharp, like a needle, stabbed the tip of her forefinger. She cried out. The sound was just barely coming out of her mouth before a fist struck her. Blood dribbled down her lips. Her tongue ached where she'd bit it.

Someone yanked the blindfold off her face. With blurred vision she looked at her captor. She saw the gray of his cloak and the short swords swinging from his hips. The way he stood before her, as if she were a peasant in the presence of a man who owned the world, told her who it was before she ever saw his face.

"I put word out I wanted you brought before me," Thren Felhorn said. "Consider yourself a gift from Kadish Vel and his Hawks."

"I hope you're pleased with your present," she said. She tried to turn her head to spit, but the shackles around her head and neck prevented it. Feeling horribly sick, she spat the blood from her mouth. Her stomach curled as it dribbled down her neck and between her breasts.

"That'll depend on your answers," Thren said. A giant muscular man stood beside him. They were outside the city, somewhere on the northern side judging by the trees that grew within touching distance of the wall . . . the wall she was helplessly strapped to by buckles and shackles.

"Will, clean her off," Thren said to the giant man. Will obliged, cleaning the blood from her chest and neck with a clean rag. She expected him to fondle her breasts or let his fingers linger on her neck, but the man did no such thing.

"Thank you," she said. She felt her head clear a little. Two torches were stuck in the ground on either side of her, and their light disrupted her eyes' attempt to adjust to the dark. She thought she saw another form standing beside Thren. It made no sense, though. She thought she saw a young man, someone twelve, maybe thirteen.

"I've been patient," Thren said. He crossed his arms and stood directly before her. "I've given James Beren plenty of chances to come to my side. Your Ash Guild is strong, and I hold more respect for it than for any other guild. Yet you and James did something stupid, girl. You plotted against me."

"No," she said.

Thren's fist smashed her face. Will's rag was there immediately, soaking in the blood she spat. The rage coupled with kindness only confused her more.

"Don't lie to me," Thren said. "The Worm came to me last morning and told me everything you'd arranged for him to do...for a price, of course."

Gileas, Veliana thought as she felt her stomach sink. *You bastard.*

"Is that why I'm here?" she asked. "Figure a little torture will help make your point to the rest of the guilds?"

"What I want," Thren said, leaning closer, "is you."

She opened her mouth, closed it.

"I don't understand," she said at last.

"I need the Ash Guild's men," Thren said, pacing before her. "All of the guilds must be united in this plan if we are to crush the Trifect come the Kensgold. For this to happen, the other guildmasters must trust me, and if they are to trust me, they must all join the plan willingly. The second I force loyalty, the other guilds will break away for fear of absorption and disbandment. Now, your dear James has proven stubborn. As satisfying as it would be to kill him, I cannot. Too many whisper of me doing such things as it is. I cannot dignify those mad ramblings with a kernel of truth."

"You want *me* to kill him," she said, guessing where his thoughts were leading. "I take over, bend knee to you, and suddenly the Ash Guild is just a toy in your pocket, to be used whenever necessary."

"You're smart, strong, and beautiful," Thren said, not denying her accusation. "It wouldn't be difficult for you to consolidate power should James die by your hands. You already have your reason for it. James had you contact Gileas, hoping to use him to sell information about our plan to the king. Doing so puts all of us at risk. Put an end to him. With but a word, I can declare the Ash Guild a friend, and the rest of the vermin will stop pressing your territory, stealing it away from you street by street. You can rule, Veliana. Do you have the strength to do so?"

Veliana thought of betraying her guildmaster, and the very idea made her sick. He was a good man. A better man, worlds better, than Thren could ever be. And all for what? So Thren could rely on the Ash Guild's aid when he launched his suicidal plan?

"This is folly, Thren," Veliana insisted. "We're thieves, thugs, brutes. We're not an army, yet you would have us launch a combined attack against all three leaders of the Trifect during their Kensgold, the one night when they're at their most powerful? We'll be slaughtered and broken."

Thren ran a hand through her long red hair.

"Do not let loyalty cost you everything," he whispered to her. "Either accept my proposal or suffer the consequences. What is your choice?"

Any other street rat would have turned on their leader. Veliana was unlike any other member.

"James has saved me a hundred times," she said. "Kill me or let me go. I will not turn traitor and knife him in the dark."

Thren sighed.

"A shame. I will not kill you, Veliana. That was not part of the deal. Gileas required you as his price for telling me of your conspiring with Gerand. I had no intention of paying it, but then again, I never thought you'd refuse the position I offered you."

A shiver of disgust ran up and down her spine. Now she understood why they'd stripped her naked. They'd even healed the wound on her shoulder where the arrow had pierced clean through. She closed her eyes, trying not to think of the ugly man's black teeth, twisted face, and stubby fingers. She almost changed her mind. Thren paused, as if waiting for her to break. When she didn't, he put his back to her.

"Remember, Aaron," she heard him say. "Things will never go as you plan. Prepare for anything, and be willing to sacrifice everything, even beauty."

Veliana saw the boy standing next to Thren, staring at her with his blue eyes. She could not decipher his look, his face remarkably controlled. And then he spoke the words that sealed his fate to her.

"Yes, Father," she heard the boy say.

If Gileas didn't take her life, Veliana swore revenge. Not on Thren, not directly. She'd only fail against someone so skilled. But the boy, the groomed heir, him she could kill. Him she could make suffer. Maybe, just maybe, Thren might feel as helpless then as she felt now.

Aaron took one torch, Will the other. They walked away from the forest, toward the western gate. The torches faded away and then died. In the starlight, she watched them pass a hobbled form approaching the other way. Her way. She didn't want to imagine what they might do to James. She was their only real hope for easy manipulation of the Ash Guild. What might they do now? Crush it completely, perhaps. Or perhaps nothing. The rest of the guilds were doing a fine job of rending the Ash Guild to pieces.

Veliana struggled against her chains. Their original purpose had been for the execution of criminals outside the city, who were left for wolves and coyotes to come and eat. While the punishment was gruesome, the spectacle was rarely witnessed and too random in its length. Fifty years ago the Vaelor line had instead instituted beheadings held before the castle steps. Quicker, bloodier, and a much better spectacle. Given how old the chains were, Veliana pleaded for one of them to break.

They didn't. From the corner of her eye she could see the manacle on one of her wrists. Black steel, clean and polished. Thren had brought his own chains. Of course he had. He wouldn't make such a stupid mistake as letting her escape because of some rusted manacles.

Gileas was getting closer. He was a fat shadow sliding across the wall, worse than any monster in her childhood stories.

"Please gods," she whispered. "Any god. Get me out. I'll do anything, but get me out of here."

She pulled so hard on her bindings that her wrists bled. Don't cry, she told herself. Don't cry. Don't cry.

"Hello, girl," Gileas breathed into her ear.

Tears trickled down her cheeks.

"Ooh, no, no, no," he whispered. "Don't cry."

"Fuck you," she whispered back.

He laughed, not at all bothered. She was shackled and helpless. He had all night.

"Nothing personal," Gileas said as he pressed the tip of his dagger against her right eyebrow. "I'll milk Gerand and the crown for all the gold I can, then take just as much from Thren and his ilk. I'll turn the rats on each other, and grow so very wealthy from it."

He pressed the dagger into her flesh. Blood trickled around her eye. She blinked against its sting.

"All night," he said as he slowly dragged the dagger downward. "I have all night."

He cut her eyebrow, her eyelid, and then her eye. She screamed.

Gileas rammed his mouth over hers, drinking in her scream like it was a fine wine. His smell hit her, followed by his tongue. It was slimy, wet, warm. She vomited into his mouth. He drank that too.

He pulled back, smiled at her, and then flew to the side from a brutal kick to the head. He rolled along the hard ground, stopping only when he struck the wall.

A woman wrapped in black and purple stood before Veliana, a serrated dagger in hand. She put her free hand against the vicious wound on Veliana's face, her fingers gently touching the flesh. Blood pooled across the cloth around her fingers, yet strangely was not absorbed into it. Veliana looked into the white cloth over her rescuer's face, seeing only the faintest hint of green eyes.

"You made an offer," the woman said to her. "Will you honor it? Swear to Karak your life, and I will take his."

Veliana could barely see Gileas out of the corner of her good eye. He was retching on the ground, one arm leaning against the wall to prop himself up. Blood continued pouring down her face, her neck, and her slender body. The eye was useless, completely useless. What did it matter if she swore her life to a nonexistent god? She wanted vengeance. She wanted to live.

"I swear it," she said.

"Good," the faceless woman said. Her hands were a blur about Veliana's body. One by one the locks clicked open. Veliana collapsed into the woman's arms, unable to stand.

"Your name?" she asked as she clutched the woman's shoulders, one eye crying tears, the other blood.

"Zusa," she replied.

Gently she put Veliana to her knees on the ground and then turned toward Gileas. The Worm had stood and put his back to the wall. He still had his dagger. Clutching her sides gently, Veliana knelt and watched.

"Uncalled for," she heard the Worm say as the faceless woman approached. "She was given to me. Given..."

He spun, his dagger lunging for Zusa's chest. It never came close. Zusa slapped it away with an open palm, kicked him in the groin, and then slammed an elbow into his forehead. Gileas collapsed, grunting in pain. When Zusa grabbed his hair to yank his head back, he laughed.

"Can't stab a worm," he said. "We just keep wiggling."

She stabbed anyway. Her blade punctured only air. Gileas's clothes were an empty pile on the grass. Zusa kicked them away but saw nothing. She looked as startled as Veliana felt.

"A worm," Veliana said. "He can't possibly be..."

But there was nothing there. He was gone.

"Come," Zusa said, taking Veliana's hand. "Follow me to my camp. You must meet my sisters."

The fire in the center of the camp had dwindled down to nothing. Zusa tossed on some branches while Veliana huddled against a tree, cold and naked. Winter was approaching, and the night air bit her skin. Zusa drew out two small red bricks and clapped them together above the fire. Sparks rained down upon the wood, instantly restarting the fire.

Veliana knelt beside it, eager for its warmth. She kept her right eye closed, wishing she could slow the bloody tears she was constantly wiping from her face. She was stronger than this, knew she was, knew she had to be. But staring into the fire, she kept seeing Gileas's dagger, heard the sound of her flesh tearing as the blade descended, kept remembering the pain as it stole away the vision in her eye.

"Where are your sisters?" she asked as shivers ran through

her body. Her revulsion at Gileas's touch remained strong, though it felt like the fire was slowly purifying her body of it.

"They will return in the morning," Zusa said. "I remained here to keep an eye on another charge of ours. I expected his idiocy to get him and his woman killed, but instead I found you tied to the wall."

"I was as surprised as you were," Veliana said. She turned her back to the fire, her arms crossed over her breasts.

"I'm not sure I have clothes appropriate for you," the faceless woman said. "Perhaps I could go and retrieve the strange man's..."

"No," Veliana said, suppressing another shudder. "I'd rather be naked."

Zusa tilted her head to the side. Veliana swore she could see green eyes studying her through the white mask across her face. Suddenly Zusa lifted the cloth and untwisted the wrappings about her head.

Veliana startled at the woman revealed beneath the wrappings. She was gorgeous by anyone's standards. Full lips, smooth cheeks, and vibrant eyes. Their deep color reminded her of pine needles. The woman ran a hand through her short dark hair, pulling out tangles, no easy task given how tightly it had been restricted and how covered with sweat it was.

"You're..." Veliana started to say, then realized how ridiculous it sounded.

"I know," Zusa said. "Trust me... I know."

She handed the wrappings to Veliana.

"They're not much, but you should be able to hide your nakedness."

Veliana started wrapping the black and purple cloth across her chest, pulling it tight to get as much coverage as she could. As she did, Zusa removed more and more of her wrappings from her chest and waist. Beneath she wore a dark shift, the color so thick she needed little of the extra cloth to keep her modesty. Veliana accepted the extra wrappings and continued looping them about her body. If she walked through the streets in broad daylight she'd earn herself many scandalous looks, but at least she was no longer naked.

"Thank you," she said, sitting down once more by the fire.

Zusa did not respond. She moved about the camp, preparing a tent that had been left behind unassembled. From a pack nearby she pulled out some tough meat and handed it to Veliana. She wasn't hungry but ate anyway, preferring the salty taste to the lingering offense of bile and Gileas on her tongue.

"Why did you save me?" Veliana asked.

Zusa glanced up as if the question were stupid.

"Because I wanted to."

Veliana smirked. It felt like an answer she might have given.

"Be that as it may, I've sworn my life. I'd like to know what I'm sworn into."

The faceless woman punched the last spike of the tent into the dirt with the hilt of her dagger and then stood. Without the wraps, her body looked far more relaxed and feminine. Her breasts actually had room to breathe, and Veliana couldn't help but feel both jealousy and annoyance. To have that much beauty and hide it? What was the point in that?

The thought of beauty stung her deeply. She ran her fingers along the bloody wound from her eyebrow to her chin. No one would think her beautiful now. She was a scarred freak. The eye, what was left of it, ached with every breath she took.

Zusa watched her trace her finger over the cut, her lips curled into a frown.

"We are the faceless," she said, looking away into the forest. Her short black hair fell across her face, hiding her pained expression. "There are only three of us, all priestesses of Karak, and all expelled. We are considered slaves to our sex, so weak and vile that we must live outside the temple with the rest of the sinful world."

"What did you do?" Veliana asked. She forced her hand away from the wound on her face. It would do no good obsessing over it now.

"I bedded a priest in training," Zusa replied. "A young man named Daverik. We were young, foolish. When we were caught, he was given lashes and a ten-year penance. I was forced to become one of the faceless."

Veliana huddled closer to the warmth of the fire and let the words sink in. A beautiful woman caught in bed with a priest. Rather than deal with the issue, they forced her out, hid her beauty, and declared her vile. She felt anger stir within her stomach. How could she be sworn to become one of them? Why were the gods so cruel as to put her in such a situation? Again she promised vengeance upon Thren and his son.

"Your sisters," Veliana said. "They're beautiful too, aren't they?"

Zusa nodded. "We all are. Do you understand why I saved you? To see another woman hurt, humiliated, her beauty stolen by a man... I couldn't bear it. Better that you become one of us."

"One of the faceless."

"My faith in Karak has not wavered," Zusa said. She sat at Veliana's side. Gently her fingers traced the dagger wound across her eye. "I will see what Pelarak can do about that. He is our greatest priest and strongest healer. I must also have his permission to fully induct you into our order."

It was all insane. Thren might think her dead, or he might hear of Gileas's failure. She couldn't possibly leave James alone and vulnerable, could she? The guild needed her. James needed her. Karak was nothing. The Ash Guild was family.

"I can't," Veliana said. "Please. I belong to a guild, the Ash Guild. If I don't hurry back, Thren might destroy everyone I know and love."

Zusa tapped at her lips, her gaze momentarily distant.

"No," she said at last. "Not yet. You must meet the high priest. I must hear his words. But afterward, I promise you, I will give you a chance to save your friends. Can you accept this, Veliana?"

The idea burned her stomach, but Veliana nodded in understanding.

"So be it," she said. "To the temple we go."

CHAPTER 13

Potts hated this part of his job. He could deal with Leon's general slobbery, his impatience with setbacks, and even his temperamental, dangerous mood swings. What the old man could not stand, however, was informing Leon of current events while the man bathed in his wooden tub. Even though his rolls of fat effectively censored him, that only seemed to make it worse. Two pretty maids worked him over with brushes, scrubbing ferociously against his skin in between splashes of hot water. Through it all, Leon giggled as if being tickled.

Master of the Connington fortune, one of three lords of the Trifect, thought the advisor, *and yet nothing more than a fat child in a bath. If there are gods in this world, they have cruel tastes for amusement.*

"I've been given word from the Green Castle," Potts said after clearing his throat twice to get his master's attention. "They've sent yet another wagon of wine from their stores, though they insisted we pay extra since we've already cleared out half of their vintage."

"Tell them I'll pay them that extra when I actually get the blasted bottles," Leon said, his giggles replaced by an annoying whine. "Those rogue bastards think to starve me of drink and food. It used to be just the city, but now the entire countryside is overrun with thieves and brigands. Perhaps we should send a whole army of mercenaries along the west highway. I'll get my damn wine then."

"Speaking of, uh, wine," Potts said, "Our own stores have gotten uncomfortably low. Nearly every seller in Veldaren refuses to deal with us, or part with a single bottle. Not for any price, no matter how outrageous."

"I told you they meant to starve me!" Leon howled. His fat shifted in the bath, splashing the two maids. They winced but held their tongues. Potts held his as well, not daring to say that he felt Leon could use a solid week of starvation.

"It appears Thren has begun a new tactic," Potts said instead. "Instead of trying to bankrupt us, he's doing what he can to make our lives miserable. He's disrupted the Gemcrofts' caravans as well."

"Make us miserable?" Leon fumed. "They live in guttershite and eat out of assholes yet they try to make *me* miserable? Well, he's succeeding! Remember my wagon of peaches that Thren ambushed on the Kingstrip? He had his men piss all over them before feeding them to herds of swine. I'd love to piss all over that bastard's head. I'm telling you, Potts, we must strike back. This nonsense has gone on far too long."

"Perhaps, if you have a plan, you can bring it up at the Kensgold?" Potts suggested.

"Ugh," Leon said, sinking deeper into the bath. More water splashed out the sides. The two maids were thoroughly soaked by now, but if they were disturbed by their contact with Leon and his dirty water, they hid it well. "I grow so tired of these Kensgolds. Didn't they used to be every four years instead of two?"

"They did," Potts said. "But when the Trifect declared war on the guilds, it was decided that meeting more often would be best for coordinating our efforts at destroying them." The advisor coughed. "It was your idea, master."

"Bah. Then I was an idiot."

You still are, thought Potts.

"One last thing," Potts said, determined to finish soon. If not, he'd be forced to endure the thoroughly grotesque sight of Leon getting out of the tub, the water dripping down from his fat in a wide circle around the floor. The maids could never get the towels around him fast enough to suppress the horrible spectacle.

"What's that?" Leon asked.

"It appears that the rest of the thief guilds have turned against the Ash Guild. They've taken nearly all of their territory except for a few streets."

"Really?" Leon asked. "Did their guildmaster die?"

"No, James Beren still lives. Truly, there doesn't appear to be any good reason for the cannibalism, not that I have heard."

"Hrm." Leon scratched his chin as he thought. "To have so many guilds attack them implies a severe weakness. Thren must have turned on them. It's the only thing that makes sense. Try to capture one of the Ash Guild's members before they're all dead. We might be able to snag ourselves an ally."

"As you wish," Potts said with a bow. He saw Leon grab the sides of the bath, preparing to stand, so he beat a hasty retreat.

Kayla sat alone in her room, feeling restless. For whatever reason, Thren had not taken her and Senke with him, only Will and his son. Senke had told her it had something to do with the Ash Guild, but would not elaborate. He had run off to do a spot of wenching, which left her alone, bored, and restless. Ever since she'd rescued Robert Haern from prison, her duties had dwindled to nothing. She figured in a day or two she'd beg for something as simple as leading a caravan robbery, just so she could have something to do.

She practiced with her daggers to pass the time. She had mentored under an elderly man many years ago, and from him learned many stances and techniques. She ran through them one by one. If she was to serve Thren, she'd need to be at her finest. Her daggerwork was far from the best. If Thren's life ever depended upon her, mediocre would not do the job.

How many hours she practiced, she didn't know, but when she finished her body was coated with sweat and her arms throbbed. She collapsed on the bed and gasped in air. When someone knocked on her door, she was too exhausted to bother getting up.

"Come in," she said. "It's not locked."

The door crept open. Kayla had expected Senke or Will, maybe even Thren, but instead Aaron crept inside and quietly shut the door behind him.

"This is a surprise," she said, sitting up on her bed. She caught his eyes wandering, then realized her shirt was unbuttoned at the top. Fighting away a blush, she fastened a few of the buttons, feeling silly all the while. She'd shown far more to men to get her way. Still, Aaron was young, and she was well aware of his crush on her.

"I have something for you," he said.

"Oh, do you now? Let me see."

Kayla outstretched her hand. He stared at her fingers, and she caught his lips trembling as if he were struck with indecision. Remembering how much she'd hated being his age, and how uncomfortable everything had always seemed to be when she was thirteen, she tried to prod him onward.

"Don't make me wait," she gently teased. "You've said you bring gifts, so give them to me. I may steal and spy, but I like presents just like any other girl."

His neck flushed a bit, just around the collar, but then he outstretched his right hand and dropped a set of earrings onto her open palm. They sparkled with sapphires and white gold. Kayla gasped. She had expected cheap jewelry, a flower, or some poorly written poetry. The gift in her hand seemed more appropriate for a woman of royalty.

"Where did you get this?" she asked.

"Father has begun paying me for my aid," he said. "He says I need to be treated like any other of his men if I am to earn their respect."

"He must pay you well," Kayla said, holding the earrings close so she could admire their sparkle. Clearly they had been polished and well cared for. A part of her felt too cheap and dirty to wear them.

"You're beautiful," Aaron said. His voice, his eyes, his demeanor: everything about him, normally so quiet and secretive, made no attempt to hide the plain truth he spoke. He thought she was beautiful, and that simple belief was enough to have her put the earrings in her ears, pressing them through scarred-over holes from earrings she had worn as a girl. A bit of blood ran across her fingers, but she made sure none dripped across the gold.

"Thank you," she said. She kissed his forehead, amused at how red his ears turned.

"Senke says I'll owe him for the next five years," Aaron said, babbling. He clearly didn't know how to react to the kiss. "But I'll keep paying him, and it shouldn't be a problem, unless I die, but then I don't need to worry about paying him back, do I? Not unless he can find my ghost and..."

"Shush, Aaron," Kayla said. At the invoking of his name, his whole body seemed to shrivel inward and slip behind a protective mask.

"Haern," he said. "Aaron isn't allowed to be friends with a woman. Call me Haern."

"Sorry," Kayla said. "This kiss is for Haern, then."

She kissed him just above his right eye.

"You're a cute boy," she said. "Now run along and do something appropriate for your age."

He nodded, the blush from his ears and his neck having connected at his cheeks. His apparent love, so juvenile and simple, was enough to brighten Kayla's night. She ushered him out the door, then plopped back down on her bed. As she spread her arms through the fabric of her covers, she let her mind wander. Aaron was cute and, more important, Thren's son. Once he got older, maybe sixteen or so, perhaps she could arrange for a marriage. Her place in the guild would be solidified so completely she'd rule once Thren died.

Assuming Thren ever died. The tough bastard looked ready to live another forty years. When he did pass away, she wondered if the Spider Guild would even survive.

What am I thinking? she thought. *Of course it will last. Thren won't spend his whole life building a castle of cards. He wants a legacy.*

Of course, any plot to use Aaron as a means of solidifying rank wouldn't work if what he had said was true. His father was denying him the friendship of any woman? Why was that? The cynical side of her wondered if it was to prevent the very idea she'd just had. But Thren's focus, his determination, his desire for a legacy...

Just what did he want Aaron to become?

Deciding her life far more likely to endure if she gave up pondering, or even worse, getting involved in such things, she closed her eyes and tried to relax. After a while she dozed off, her light sleep broken by a firm knock on her door. A tingle in her temples told her to open it herself. Her warning was correct: Thren stood waiting, his arms crossed, his swords hanging from his belt.

"You should be more alert when I am gone," he said as he stepped past her into her room. "Alert, instead of slumbering. If something should happen to me, an attack on our guild would immediately follow."

"A silly worry," Kayla said as she shut the door. "Since when can something happen to you?"

He looked at her as if deciding whether to smile or scowl. So instead he shrugged.

"Even the impossible tends to find its way into our everyday lives. I have a task for you, Kayla, one suited to your talents. A troublesome man named Delius has been actively encouraging the lowborn folk to turn against us, and such a . . ."

He stopped. She felt a moment of self-conscious worry spike through her. Was her shirt open again? Her hair messed up in some strange way? She followed his eyes, then realized he was staring at her earrings. Of course he'd noticed them. Besides being new, they sparkled like stars, almost screaming for attention.

"Your son gave them to me," she said, not daring to lie.

She was not prepared for the rage that roared to life in his eyes, his hands, and his snarl. Thren slammed her against the wall, her wrists pinned. Before she even knew she was in danger, she was helpless.

"Listen carefully," he said to her. Somehow his rage never reached his voice. "Aaron must remain pure. He has the chance to become something incredible. I will have my heir, and I will not risk its ruin to the caress of a woman, the stupor of drink, or the delusions of gods and goddesses. Do you understand me?"

"I'll give them back," Kayla said. She almost nodded, then realized that would dangle her earrings, and she feared that might set him off.

"Not just that," Thren said. "I want his heart broken. Give it a scar that will never heal. When you are done, meet me and Senke in my room. I still have that job for you."

"As you wish," she said.

He let go of her hands, glanced about the room, and then left.

Kayla felt her knees tremble, and when the door was shut she let her fear out in a single sob. The fear didn't last long. Anger raged upward in her breast. Aaron's adoration of her was so simple, so embarrassingly pure. And Thren would have her crush it, have her make his son's heart bleed, all so he could have his damn legacy?

She took off her earrings, put them in her pocket, and then left for Aaron's room. Despite what Aaron had said about his father treating him like the other men, his room was separate from the rest, isolated and private. She knocked on the door.

The look of mixed excitement and fear on Aaron's face did little to settle the knot in her stomach.

"May I come in?" she asked, wondering how many of his young fantasies started with her saying exactly those words. He didn't answer, only nodded.

She stepped inside. The room was spacious, with a tall ceiling and several windows, but the decorations were sparse. He had a bed, a trunk for his clothes, and the rest was weapons, training equipment, and books. From her quick glance, it appeared all of it received equal attention.

"Your earrings," Aaron said, immediately noticing their absence.

"Here," she said, taking his hand and plopping them atop his palm. "Take them back."

She saw something breaking in his blue eyes.

"Why?" he asked.

Kayla opened her mouth, a lie on her tongue. She knew she could lie well enough for him to believe her, and more important, she knew for her own safety she should. Doing the right thing was not often something she worried about, but deep down she knew she was the first woman Aaron had ever reached out to. If she cut him now, if she broke his spirit at such a fragile time in his life...

But then again, this was Aaron Felhorn, son of Thren Felhorn. She knew the stories the rest of the Spider Guild told about him. The stories they told about Randith Felhorn.

"Answer me this question first," she said. "Did you really kill your brother at the age of eight?"

He sucked in his lips and bit. He was staring at her ears, mainly where the earrings no longer were. She brushed them once, realizing they still bled.

"Yes," he said.

She felt her heart wince a little, but that wasn't what mattered. The second question was what mattered.

"Why?" she asked.

Aaron answered without the slightest hesitation.

"Because my father wanted me to."

Of course. What else mattered in Aaron's life? He was being steadily created, a work of art only Thren Felhorn could find beautiful. To see such parental devotion twisted and turned to murder and fratricide...

"Listen to me," Kayla said, lowering her voice. "I can't love you, Aaron. I can't even treat you with kindness, and my reason is the same as why you killed your brother. Take the earrings. Don't hide your hurt. Don't be ashamed of your tears."

She took his chin in her fingers and tilted his head upward.

"But you were right," she said. "I can love Haern. I'm not sure what Aaron might become. He may scare me, may even hurt me at his own father's request. So you must keep Haern hidden and safe. Keep him alive. Can you do that for me?"

His tears rolled down his cheeks, but he nodded. She saw that strength and felt beyond proud.

"Aaron must never love me," she said as she turned to the door. "Not while under the shadow of his father."

She opened the door, paused halfway through it.

"But Haern can."

"I'll remember," Aaron said as she left. Down the hall she went, all the way to Thren's room, where he waited. She knelt before his table.

"My task?" she asked.

"Were you successful?" Thren asked her first. Knowing her life was on the line, Kayla kept her smile hidden deep inside her breast.

"Beyond expectations," she answered.

As Kayla left, Aaron grabbed one of his many swords and slammed the side of a training dummy. He had learned another lesson about what it meant to have power. It meant crushing the will of another to meet your own. To learn that lesson, to know that it had been brought down upon him by his own father...

For the first time Aaron felt rebellion growing in his heart at the very notion of wielding that same power. He choked it down. Those thoughts didn't belong to Aaron. They weren't who he was, and he could never think them. Not when his father might see.

He cut one of his blankets in half, poked in a few eyeholes, and then wrapped it about his face. Lost in his training, he swung his sword about the room, shifting from stance to stance. Feeling somehow freed, somehow unchained, he let his anger rage and his rebellion grow, for he was Haern now, and those thoughts belonged to him.

CHAPTER

14

Wearing the same disguise as before, Maynard returned to the priests' temple a week later as promised. He dismissed his guards when he reached the gate, confident his threats were more than enough to keep him safe. It was the ruffians and cutthroats who wandered the streets that worried him. He didn't want to imagine the celebration that might erupt in the underworld if he was found and killed in the open.

Not surprisingly, his reception was far less warm than on his first visit. He was immediately led to Pelarak's room and then made to wait. The high priest arrived shortly after.

"You have put us in an uncomfortable position," Pelarak said as he shut the door behind him.

"Welcome to the rest of Veldaren," Maynard said. "No one is comfortable, not while vermin pretend to be kings."

"When men pretend to be gods, things are just as dire," Pelarak said. Maynard ignored the thinly veiled insult.

"I've come for my answer. Will you aid us in destroying the thief guilds, or will you cling to your worthless neutrality?"

Pelarak walked around him and then sat at his desk. He tapped his fingertips together, then put his forefingers to his lips.

"You must understand that I do what Karak desires of me," Pelarak said. "This decision is not mine, but his."

Under normal circumstances, Maynard would have paid lip service to Pelarak's faith. With his daughter missing and his estate lacking a true heir, he had no time or patience. He rolled his eyes.

"Don't feed me that nonsense. You are in charge here, high priest, not some voice in your head."

"You doubt Karak's power?"

"Doubt it?" Maynard said. "Would I be so insistent you help me if I doubted it? I just don't want to hear any nonsense about prayers or obscure promises and prophecies. I want an answer. The correct one."

Pelarak smiled a wolfish smile.

"You won't get it. Not the one you want."

"I will carry out my promise," Maynard said.

"And we believe you," Pelarak insisted. "Listen to what I have to say."

He gestured to the chair opposite him. Annoyed, Maynard sat down. Part of him knew he should calm himself. He was being hotheaded and rash, something he always dismissed in others. The priests had vexed him for years, however. If diplomacy and bribes did nothing for them, it was time to try threats and brute force.

"Look for a moment from my perspective," Pelarak said. "Let's assume I agree with you: the rogues need to be put in line, and this nonsensical war ended. But if I join now after you hold a sword over our heads, what prevents us from being puppets of the Trifect instead of servants to our god? We have killed kings for making the same threats you made."

Maynard felt a bit of his hotheadedness leave him. Something very dangerous was about to happen. Pelarak did not make threats lightly, and Maynard's assumption of safety seemed to be arrogance in hindsight. The priests could kill him with a wave of their hands. All his power and gold meant nothing if they felt Karak wanted his head.

"Rudely put, perhaps," Maynard said, falling deeper into his political persona, "but you do speak a bit of truth. We need your aid, Pelarak. For if you are not with us, then I fear the actions of your female assassins place you against us."

"I will deal with them in time," Pelarak said. "I told you, they do not represent us. Karak is our lord, and I am his closest servant. He wishes this war over. How, though, is where you and I will disagree."

"Presumptuous," Maynard said. "How will we disagree?"

Pelarak stood, smoothing out his black robe as he did. One hand rubbed his balding head. Maynard did not like this at all. The high priest was very rarely hesitant. This was bad. Very bad.

"We will aid you, but only under the condition that you give us someone into our safekeeping, someone to join our order. Someone you will remember the next time you wave a sword over our necks."

Maynard felt his heart sink.

"Who do you want?" he asked, already knowing the answer.

Pelarak might have smiled or gloated, but that was not the man he was.

"Two of the faceless sisters came to me last night to inform me of their actions. I did not reprimand them, not yet. They have your daughter, Alyssa. She must join our order."

Maynard felt his world tear and twist in chaotic ways inside his mind. Alyssa, a priestess of Karak? She would be safe from the Kulls, perhaps, and certainly no threat to his estate. But would he ever see her again? And when he did, would she still be the same free-spirited girl he loved? Could that spirit survive cloistered within the walls, battered daily with Karak's rhetoric of order and obedience?

Then he saw the danger right before him. If the faceless women had Alyssa, then they could do to her whatever they wished. If he refused their offer...

"I must accept," he said.

"Good," Pelarak said, a smile spreading across his face. "I am glad we could reach an agreement. We aid one another, as friends, not master and servant."

"Of course. You speak most wisely," Maynard said, the lie bitter on his lips.

When he turned to leave, Pelarak stopped him with a word.

"Maynard," the high priest said. "Make sure she is still heir to your estate. If you render her worthless, we will do the same."

A shard of ice grew inside Maynard's heart.

"I wouldn't think of it," he said.

"Good," said Pelarak. "Go with Karak's blessing."

He did, though if he could have, he'd have tossed any blessing of Karak's into the foulest open sewer and leave it to rot. If he could have, he'd have had Pelarak suffer the same fate.

"Forgive me, Alyssa," he said as he left the temple, giving one last look to the priests and priestesses bowed before the giant statue of Karak, their heartfelt wails reaching to the ceiling. He thought of Alyssa on her knees beside them, and the image twisted the ice in his heart.

Alyssa was already dressed and sitting beside the fire when Yoren awoke. It blazed healthily as she tossed on a few extra branches so she could watch them burn.

"Good morning, love," Yoren said.

"Morning," Alyssa replied, her voice dull. She might have been talking to a rock.

Seeming not to notice, Yoren hopped up, stepped behind a tree, and began urinating. When he finished, he stepped back around and only then caught the stare Alyssa was giving him.

"Something the matter?" he asked.

"Nothing," she said, turning her gaze back to the fire. "Only nothing."

He grunted but let her cryptic comment pass.

"Stay here, and keep that fire roaring," he told her. He retrieved his small bow and bundle of arrows from his tent and slung them across his back. "I'll see if I can nab us a rabbit or squirrel for breakfast. Don't do anything stupid while I'm gone. And if the faceless return, tell them to wait for me as well."

Then he was off, trudging deeper into the king's forest. Alyssa knew he wouldn't be gone long. During her time at Felwood Castle, when Yoren had often visited, he'd shown himself a competent hunter. To pass the time she tossed more wood onto the fire, watching it burn and finding comfort in that somehow. When he returned, he carried a dead gray rabbit by its back legs. He dropped it on the dirt beside the fire. Alyssa took it without question.

"I'll need a knife to skin it," she said.

Yoren paused, then shrugged and tossed her a slender dagger from his belt. She caught its hilt in the air, doing her best not to show irritation at the idiot for tossing it so carelessly toward her.

Any other time she might have felt squeamish about the blood and guts. She played the tomboy well enough with her foster families, or when she wanted to irritate her father, but it was mostly an act. Though they might never admit it, she'd long ago learned young men treated her better, more respectfully, when they believed she could wield a knife and not squeal at the sight of something dead. But pretending to handle blood and actually handling it were two different matters.

She pretended the rabbit was Yoren's head. It did wonders for her stomach.

When the rabbit finished cooking, Yoren gave her the bulk of the meat. He was once more playing the dashing suitor, as if the angry condescending brute from the night before had only been an illusion. She flashed her prettiest smile at his jokes. The lies came more easily to her than she preferred.

"Come," he said when their meal was done. "It looks like we'll have to trust the faceless bitches to find us. Clean yourself up a little; you've got grease on your face."

"Where are we going?" she asked as she wiped her chin and lips with the inside hem of her dress.

"To meet with my father."

He looked her up and down, scowling. She was wearing the same clothes as when her father had thrown her into the cells, and they were torn and faded from the recent abuse. Although she'd brushed her hair as best she could with her fingers, it had done little to remove the dirt and damage. She looked more like a haggard maid than an heiress to a mining empire.

"This will never do," Yoren said. "You must look like my queen, not my servant. Where are those blasted women? Surely they know a thing or two about primping."

"Yes, because their beauty is seen so often," Alyssa said. Her sarcasm was stronger than she'd expected, the cut of her comment deep enough to narrow Yoren's eyes and make him doubt her docility.

"By now Maynard has every cutthroat he owns in the city searching for you," he said. "Otherwise I'd take you to a bath-house and make you look respectable. But it looks like I'll have to bring you as you are to my father."

He scattered the fire and took her hand.

"Oh, and dear," he said, smiling at her. "Hold your tongue in my father's presence. I'd hate for you to make a fool of yourself."

Her mouth twitched but her eyes remained dead.

"Yes, milord," she said.

He completely forgot about the dagger that should have been safely tucked inside his belt, the one that had disemboweled the rabbit.

The one Alyssa hid underneath her skirt.

They walked south for over an hour before Theo Kull's encampment came into view.

"A warm fire, thick blankets, and, thank the gods, horses," said Yoren.

"Such charming accommodations," Alyssa said as he held her hand. Safely out of sight of the city's walls and the prying eyes within, Theo's camp stretched out for several hundred yards. Wagons formed its outer perimeter, some covered, some not. Several fires blazed within the circle. On one side were twenty smaller tents, shelters for the mercenaries. On the other was a single large pavilion of a faded green color.

She felt his grip tighten, and she wasn't at all surprised when it slid up to latch onto her wrist.

"Your barbed tongue makes it seem like you don't appreciate all we've done for you," he said.

"Forgive me," Alyssa said. "It is only the stress and exhaustion. I will feel better after bathing, I promise."

Yoren kissed her cheek, then looked her up and down.

"I hope so," he said. "You need it."

At their approach a couple of mercenaries drew their swords and beckoned them closer.

"Your name?" one of them asked.

"Yoren Kull," he answered. "Take me to my father."

The mercenary spat.

"Follow me."

He led them through the camp. Alyssa took in what she could. From the way the men lazed about, it didn't appear that they'd be marching anywhere soon. Most of the armed men were busy eating, telling stories, or gambling with wooden dice. A couple sneered at her, and given the state of her clothing and hair, she didn't blame them. She hated them for it, but she didn't blame them.

Theo sat in an ornate chair in the center of the pavilion. He didn't stand when they entered through the flap. Alyssa had met him only once, what felt like a lifetime ago. He was a big man, with big hands and an even bigger beard. He had a hungry smile, and beady brown eyes that seemed to covet everything he saw. He gestured to two chairs at the table before him. A snap of his fingers, and two servants hurried over with cups, plates, and dinnerware. A third servant filled the cups with wine while a fourth plopped servings of meat and bread atop the plates.

"Welcome back, my son," Theo said. "And I see you've brought your lover back from the Abyss. She looks it too!"

He guffawed. Yoren laughed along. Alyssa only stared.

"Come now, I only jest in good nature," Theo said. "I would never be amused at seeing a woman in such a state. Would you like some of my girls to bathe and dress you before joining us? Nothing would trouble me more than an uncomfortable look crossing your face."

"She's only uncomfortable with me in the bedchambers,"

Yoren said as he took his seat at the right hand of his father. "Though I fear I inherited that wonderful fault from you."

Theo burst once more into laughter. Alyssa felt her heart cool. He might have a silver tongue, but Theo was a piggish brute. If Yoren flung her to the ground right then and there with the aim of raping her, he wouldn't bat an eye. If anything, he might try to join in.

Alyssa shuddered, and it did not go unnoticed.

"Forgive my son," Theo said. "He offends when he means only humor. Let's see, Mary? Mary! There you are, girl. Clean her up, will you? I remember her a lovely one, so let's make her match my memory."

Mary was an older woman with gray hair tied behind her head in a bun. She had been the one directing the other servants who had laid out the food and dinnerware.

"Come with me," Mary said, grabbing Alyssa's hand. Her voice was firm but comforting. The look in her eye was one of guarded sympathy.

Next to the pavilion was a smaller tent for the servants. They slept on blankets on the ground, fifty of them crammed together in a tent meant for twenty. Beside the servants' tent was a giant wooden tub. After a word from Mary, several younger girls rushed off carrying buckets to fetch hot water from the fires.

"It'll be cold for a bit," Mary said as she began stripping off Alyssa's clothes. "Once we get some heat, maybe a few hot coals, you'll be better."

Alyssa glanced inside the tub. The water was hazy, but she'd bathed in worse when staying with her foster families. She let Mary strip her naked, glad that the two tents offered protection from the mercenaries who wandered about the rest of the camp.

"We'll get these washed while you bathe," Mary said. "Though heaven knows you deserve better. I'll see what we have stashed in the..."

She stopped as Yoren's dagger tumbled out of the clothes bundled in her hands. Alyssa's entire body froze. She'd forgotten it amid the frenzy of servants preparing the bath and tugging at her dress. Mouth locked open, she met Mary's eyes. In them she saw a hard, worldly understanding.

"A dangerous toy for the bedchambers," Mary said.

"Not when you want the bedchambers quiet," Alyssa replied.

Mary guided the naked Alyssa into the bath. True to her word, it was cold. When the first of the servants arrived with a bucket of boiling water, Mary took the bucket from her and poured it in herself. As the steam rose, the older woman leaned closer so that none might hear her.

"You kill him, the monsters here will ravage you," Mary said. "Keep it hidden. Keep it safe. Wait until you're truly alone."

Then she was gone in search of finer clothing. More buckets of hot water were poured into the tub, banishing the rest of its chill. Allowing herself a moment of luxury, Alyssa washed her hair and let the servant girls scrub her skin red.

Mary shortly returned, holding a blue dress of fine material.

"It belonged to Theo's younger sister," Mary explained. "I've already asked him, so don't worry."

They pulled her out of the bath, toweled her off, and then flung the dress over her head. The laces across the back seemed old-fashioned and overly elaborate, but Mary navigated them with ease.

"Suck your breath in more," Mary ordered. Alyssa obeyed. The laces slid tighter. Alyssa's chest heaved upward, looking twice its original size. When she looked down at her own body, the cleavage seemed obscene.

"Bear through," Mary said, recognizing the look. "A man thinks with his nether regions. The sight of you will stir him, and as long as a man's stirred, he's stupid."

"What if he's stupid before?"

Mary put her calloused fingers on Alyssa's chin and pulled her face close.

"Watch your tongue, girl," said the elder. "Men may be stupid, but women talk, and all around you are ears."

The girls dabbed her with perfume, combed her hair, and draped a multitude of necklaces across her neck and chest. When they were finished, she glanced into an offered looking glass, hardly recognizing the woman in the reflection. She knew that the Gemcroft name allowed her the luxuries she wore, but never once had she felt compelled to decorate herself so outlandishly.

Mary dismissed the rest of the servant girls.

"For your sake, remain patient," she told Alyssa. "You'll gain yourself nothing but bruises if you resist ineffectually. Deep down the Kulls are animals, dangerous animals. Do whatever you must to keep them calm."

Alyssa shook her head, wondering how her future had turned so grim. That night Yoren would come for her, as he would the next, and the next. More and more she wanted to turn him away, to deny his touch, but Mary's meaning was clear. Resisting meant beatings, or worse. Cruel as it sounded, she felt she deserved her predicament. From the moment she'd started listening to the lies Yoren had whispered in her ear as they cuddled in her bed, she'd earned this. She had believed his silver tongue and turned against her father. For that she was thrown out, and now she was chained to Yoren's true nature.

The skirt she wore had several layers. Mary separated them, making sure that Alyssa watched. The innermost was thin, white, and silky. Along the inner thigh was a single pocket. Mary slid the dagger inside.

"Never let him find it," Mary said.

Alyssa nodded.

"Thank you," she said.

"Come," said Mary, extending her hand. "You have a meal to attend."

This time Theo did rise at her entrance. A stupid grin spread across Yoren's face. Alyssa knew that at one time she had thought it charming, and that only enhanced her conviction that she had been an idiotic girl. Blind. Stupid. Careless. She was starting to run out of ways to insult the girl she'd been only days earlier.

"You look stunning," Theo said. "Isn't that right, Son?"

"Breathtaking," said Yoren.

Without being asked, Alyssa took a seat beside Yoren. She could tell he was pleased by the obedient-wife act. That was good; it'd keep him unsuspecting, but more important she hoped it would keep her from being dismissed from their planning. Despite their setbacks, she knew they still eyed the wealth of her family. The more she knew, the better her chance of minimizing the damage.

"We were actually just discussing returning you to your rightful position among the Gemcroft family," Theo said, sipping wine from a gaudy gold cup. "It seems we were foolish to trust those Karak bitches to do anything right."

"It was not their fault," Alyssa said, hoping it might incite a bit of anger, and therefore information. "My father was ready."

"He usually is," Theo said, his words dripping with bitterness. "I remember sending my men to grab what was rightfully mine, but even all those miles away from Riverrun he was still prepared. It wasn't just the gold, Alyssa, it was deeds, titles, and information. Everything east of the Queln River should be mine. Those lands deserve a true lord! Lord Gandrem has no rightful claim. Let him have the plains. He belongs with the grazing cattle."

If she'd meant to incite anger, she'd done exceedingly well. Though she knew of Theo's feud with Lord Gandrem, the current ruler of much of the lands north of Veldaren, she'd never heard of the Kulls' attempt on her father's safe houses in Riverrun. If she had, she'd have seen Yoren's courting in a whole new light.

"My lord, a visitor requests an audience," said a guard as he poked his head in through the flap.

"What's his name?" asked Theo.

"Her," the guard said, looking a little flustered. "And she says she has no name."

Theo let out a humorless chuckle.

"Send her in."

Alyssa felt a bit of hope as one of the faceless women entered. She was fully clad in her black and purple wrappings, her face a mask of white cloth. By her build, Alyssa recognized her as Eliora.

"I have come to listen," the woman said.

"Listen?" asked Theo. "To what?"

"She means she needs orders," Yoren said. All three watched as shadows seemed to curl off her firm body and fade away like smoke.

"Yes, well, we'd have those ready for you if we weren't always being interrupted by bothersome women," Theo said. "First Alyssa, now you. Well, since we're all here, let us get down to business. Maynard's got to go. Before he does, we need to find a way to reinstate Alyssa as the lawful heir to the Gemcroft estate."

"Wills covered with blood are rarely followed," Eliora said.

"I know that," Theo said. "I'm a Kull, not an idiot."

Alyssa thought they were one and the same and had to feign coughing to hide her laughter.

"There is another way," Yoren said. "The rest of the Trifect won't dare let one of its members appear weak for very long. If we kill Maynard and then march on their mansion, the others will make sure the matter is settled quickly and quietly. Who'll give a fuck if he wrote her out of his will? She's his own daughter, the last of his flesh and blood. There's a thousand ways we can discredit his death wishes."

"A good plan, though almost insulting in its simplicity," said Theo. "I have only a hundred swords here in my name. When could we possibly storm the estate successfully? We number only one-fifth of his house guards. I can't even guess how many more mercenaries he also has on retainer."

"When the head is gone, the body can only thrash for so long," said Eliora.

"We have a philosopher," Yoren said dryly.

"Is that an offer?" Theo asked. Eliora shrugged.

"We promised to do so once. We can do so again."

"You also failed once," said Theo. "Can you do *that* again?"

The shadows flared around her body. Alyssa wished she could back away from the two men. The faceless were dangerous, and to insult their professional pride and ability seemed beyond rash.

"We will not fail," Eliora said. "Tell me when you will strike and I will tell my sisters."

Theo scratched his chin.

"There's only one time I can think of that we can catch the old goat unaware."

"When?" asked Alyssa, unable to stop herself.

Theo's grin belonged on a bear more than a human.

"The Kensgold," he said.

CHAPTER 15

The king was waiting for him when Gerand arrived.

"What plans for today, Crold?" Edwin Vaelor asked as he made his fifth attempt at tying his elaborate sash correctly. Gerand frowned at his fumbling attempts, and when it was clear the king would do no better on his sixth, the advisor reached out and set the sash correctly.

"A few squabbles among farmers and some petty lords from the Northern Plains," said Gerand. "The troubles from Angelport will be a bit more difficult."

"Angelport? What's bothering Lord Murband now? He has no rivals in the entire Ramere, not a single bloody count or noble to bicker over his territory."

"But he has the elves," Gerand said. "And you know how much he likes to talk up their threat."

The king sighed as he slipped a gaudy necklace of gold and rubies over his neck. The Ramere was isolated in the far southeast of Dezrel, tucked in between the Erze Forest, the Quellan Forest, and the Crestwall Mountains. Lord Ingram Murband owned everything there from the Thulon Ocean to the Kingstrip, yet he complained more than any of the other lords. And it was always about the blasted elves.

"Don't they insist they're our allies? Granted, I have no trust in their claims. No one lies like an elf, right?"

"Too true," Gerand said dryly. "However, Ingram claims that the Quellan elves have begun shooting arrows at his loggers."

"He go too far into the forest again?" the king asked with a chuckle. Gerand was not amused.

"He's asking for permission to declare war."

King Vaelor scoffed.

"You're telling me he's to be the rough part of my day? Bring in the old goat. I'll laugh in his face and tell him if he wants to cut down the whole Quellan Forest he's more than welcome to, but he'll use his *own* soldiers as arrow bait, not mine."

"Any provocation in the south may cause the Dezren elves to retaliate in kind," Gerand warned. "We have many farming villages stretching north from the Erze Forest. Thousands of acres of crops might burn."

Edwin pulled on his thick crimson robe hemmed with white dove feathers.

"It won't happen," he said. "If Ingram sends in any troops, they'll be dead in hours, and then all *his* precious farmland will be vulnerable. He won't dare risk conflict if he knows I won't protect his idiotic ass."

"Your wisdom is unquestionable," Gerand said. He clucked his tongue, immediately angry at himself afterward for doing something that announced his nervousness. So far the conversation had gone as expected. This next part, however, was what really mattered. Murband and his elves could go dive into the Bone Ditch for all he cared.

"One last item," Gerand said. "I've received word that Thren Felhorn is expected to kill the Trifect at their Kensgold."

"What's a bloody Kensgold?"

Gerand mentally swore. The last time the Trifect had held a Kensgold was two years ago. The king had only been fourteen at the time.

"A Kensgold is a meeting of all three houses of the Trifect," the advisor explained. "They meet at one of their estates. They brag about their riches, compare trade agreements, discuss the downfall of any competitors, and overall spend a frightening amount of gold. It's a show of wealth, power, and solidarity."

"So which member of the Trifect are they to kill, exactly?" Edwin asked as he stared at himself in a mirror, turning this way and that to see if anything seemed out of place.

"All of them, Your Majesty," the advisor said. "The heads of all three families, to die within minutes of one another. Supposedly he's to gather the members of every single guild together into an army and assault the Kensgold when the celebration is at its highest."

The king whistled appreciatively.

"The wretch hasn't lost his balls, but perhaps his brains. Clearly we can't let him go through with it. Send word to one of them, Leon Connington maybe, about their plan. Let them find some devious way to scheme it to their benefit."

"I'm not sure that is the best course of action," Gerand said, broaching the subject carefully. He was well aware of the king's paranoia, and he planned to use that to his full advantage.

"Why is that?" Edwin asked. He grabbed his gold sword from a chair beside him. Gerand turned and coughed, using the excuse to roll his eyes. The king had commissioned the sword in one of his first orders of rule when he ascended the throne at age twelve, officially coming of age. The long sword wasn't tinted gold or covered with gold at the hilt. The whole bloody thing was made of solid gold: heavy, cumbersome, and thoroughly impractical. It shone beautifully in the light, though, and that was all Edwin cared about.

"Mercenaries from all over Dezrel will come pouring in for a taste of the coin the Trifect will be spending during the Kensgold. Hundreds upon hundreds, some from as far west as Ker and Mordan. At their last Kensgold, our best estimates put them at having over ten thousand men on their retainer, not counting their house soldiers."

King Vaelor looked at Gerand as if he were insane.

"That's thousands of men sworn to one banner inside my walls."

"Within a short walk from your castle doors, yes," Gerand added, unable to resist.

"Fuck. How long does this blasted Kensgold last?"

"Just a single night," said Gerand.

He could already see the fear spreading in Edwin's eyes. One night was enough to assassinate a king. One night was enough to supplant the hierarchy with the rule of coin and trade.

"We must stop them," Edwin said. He clutched his gold sword tight, as if he were going to draw it and strike some unseen enemy.

"There's no way we can," Gerand said, feigning defeat.

"There is. Ban the mercenaries from our city. Get rid of them. They can't pass through our walls if we don't let them."

Gerand nearly choked. He had been hoping Edwin would call for a sharp curtailing of the Trifect's power. A massive increase in taxes, plus a crackdown on some of their more illegal activities, would have done wonders to subdue the Trifect's smug flaunting of power. Banning all mercenaries, however, was about as far from what he wanted as the Abyss was from the Golden Eternity.

"Your Majesty, you can't," Gerand said. At the king's frown, the advisor corrected himself. "You shouldn't, I mean, not unless you want the thief guilds to thoroughly destroy the Trifect. Without their mercenaries they are vulnerable. Their house guards do well to protect their estates, but everything else, from their warehouses to their trade caravans, is protected by men bought by their coin."

"Why should I give a rat's ass about their coin?" Edwin shouted. He turned and struck the mirror with his sword, pleased at how it shattered. "I could tax every shred of wealth from their hide if I wanted to. If they're so frightened of our city's vermin, then let them flee to one of their hundred different holds strewn throughout Dezrel."

There was only one card left to play, a trump card with a dangerous cost attached to it.

"If you do that, my king, then you will be signing your own death warrant," Gerand said.

The king grew shockingly quiet. He sheathed his sword and stared at his advisor with crossed arms.

"How so?" he asked, his voice just above a whisper.

"Because Thren Felhorn thinks you attempted to kill his son. He will neither forgive, nor forget. Once the Trifect is dealt with, he will turn his focus on you."

"He won't dare strike at a king," Edwin said.

"He will," Gerand said. "He has before."

The king's eyes widened with understanding.

"My father..."

"There is a reason you became king so young, Your Majesty. Thren needed instability in the castle to set up his war against the Trifect. You were so young, you'd not wield full power for many years. Thren took the heads of your parents, Edwin. Took them in their sleep."

Edwin's hands trembled.

"Why was I never told this?" he asked.

"I made certain of it, and for good reason. I didn't want you to do something that might cost you your life. Your Majesty."

The king pointed a shaking finger at Gerand, the tip waving in front of his nose.

"You damn manipulative fool," he nearly shouted. "You told me Robert would just teach the boy, informing us of whatever he might overhear. How the Abyss did that turn into an attempt on the boy's life?"

Gerand remained silent. An errant word now might cost him his life. No doubt the guards stationed on the other side of the bedchamber doors were already drawing their blades.

"You will answer me," Edwin ordered.

"Yes, Your Majesty," Gerand said, knowing his fate was sealed. "I ordered his son, Aaron, to be captured. We failed. I thought with him as a hostage, we might force an end to the squabbles between the Trifect and the guilds."

The king struck him with the back of his hand. Gerand fell to one knee, his head throbbing where the king's many rings had left deep imprints on his skin. The scar on his face ached, and when he touched it, he felt warm blood on his fingers.

"This needs to be handled, immediately," King Vaelor said. "I can bear the Trifect, their wealth and their arrogance. Castle walls and guards protect me from their mercenaries. But I will not have some sewer vermin kill me over your mistake, especially that heartless bastard Felhorn. We know their plans for the Kensgold. Turn that against them."

"Yes, Your Majesty," Gerand said.

"Oh, and if you should fail..."

Gerand stopped and turned around, his hand still against the door.

"If I fail, I will willingly go to Thren, kneel at his feet, and announce my guilt in the attempt against his son."

The king beamed as if he couldn't be more pleased.

"See, that's why you're such a great advisor," he said, and he meant it.

Idiot, thought Gerand as he exited the bedchamber.

Aaron was getting good at choking down his curiosity. Any time he went somewhere with his father, he was never told where they were going or for what purpose, at least not until they were almost there. This particular task he followed his father on was already different from the others, further inciting his curiosity. They moved in daylight instead of at night.

"What if we're recognized?" Aaron asked as they neared the more populous parts of the city. More and more merchants were lined up on the sides of the street.

"We're just two of many," Thren said. "Don't give anyone reason to suspect otherwise."

Thren wore the plain gray cloak of the Spider Guild. Because of Aaron's age, it would seem odd for him to be ranked as anything above a cutpurse, so instead of a cloak he had a thin band of gray cloth tied around his left arm. Thren had cut Aaron's hair short just in case some of the guards might remember what he looked like. The bounty on his son had lasted only a single night, and not at all according to the castle records. Still, being reckless was not something Thren was known for. He kept his hood low, and had charcoal smeared across his face.

Thren had hammered into Aaron the importance of not

acting scared or in a hurry. They merely went on their way, not rushing, not dawdling. They were on a job, and very few would be stupid enough to interfere.

"I've never met our target," Thren said, talking casually as if about the weather. "Watch for a tall man with red hair and beard and white robes. He'll be attracting a crowd, most likely."

Aaron watched, not convinced he'd be much use considering he was shorter than his father, his view blocked by the rest of the midday traffic. He had to try, though. Even if it was hopeless, he had to throw his entire concentration behind the task.

Then he saw Kayla staring at him from afar. She blew him a kiss. He looked away and hoped his blush would go unnoticed. Kayla was trailing after them, though he didn't know why. Was it just for protection? Usually his father kept Senke and Will with him if he was worried about his safety. What then?

"There," Thren said, nodding ever so slightly to the east. Aaron followed his eyes. A crowd had gathered near a gap in the various merchant stalls. A few were jeering from the outer limits, but most were listening with rapt attention. Those closest to the center clapped and cheered.

In the center of the crowd was their target, a middle-aged man with deep red hair and a beard of the same color. His robes were white, and clean despite the color. He seemed handsome enough. Whatever speech he was giving appeared intense, yet he smiled while giving it.

"What's his name?" Aaron asked when he realized his father had stopped to listen.

"Delius Eschaton," Thren said. "Now be silent."

Aaron listened to Delius as he preached, at first from simple curiosity, then more and more because of the speaker's sheer oratory skill.

"Night and day we bemoan the fate dealt to us," Delius

shouted. "How many of you fear walking the streets at night? How many of you bite your tongues for fear of earning poison in your wine or death inside your bread?"

Delius pointed to a small girl behind him. She appeared no older than eleven, and she blushed at the sudden attention.

"I fear for my daughter. I fear she might not have the life she deserves. How many of you have daughters and sons that have entangled themselves in the thief guilds' lies? How many trade decency and conscience for a dab of food and a glut of blood? Do you mourn for them, mothers? Do you pray for them, fathers? Do you know what those prayers accomplish?"

Someone had placed a small pail before him, and all throughout his preaching men and women tossed in small copper coins in appreciation. Delius abruptly kicked the pail, scattering the coins throughout the crowd. Only a handful stooped for them. The rest stood enraptured. They all expected an explosion of sound and rage, but instead Delius's voice fell to a stage whisper.

"Nothing, for we do nothing. We are afraid."

A murmur slipped through the crowd. Delius let it spread as he turned and accepted a drink from his daughter. He handed it back, wiped his lips, and then turned to the crowd. His boisterousness suddenly returned.

"Afraid? Of course we're afraid. Who wants to die? You might think me mad, but I *like* this meager existence we call living. But the only reason the guilds and the Trifect bathe our streets in blood is because *we let them*. We turn blind eyes to underhanded dealings. We keep still tongues about guards we know take bribes. We fill our own pockets with sinful gold and bloodied silver, but hard coin is an ill pillow. Can you sleep at night? Do you hear Ashhur's voice whispering for something better, something more?

"We deny righteousness in fear of our own safety, and in doing so forfeit the future of our children. We let them live in a dead tomorrow because we fear bleeding for it today. Ashhur has called you! He longs to forgive you! Will you accept it? Will you help remove the darkness from our city and let in the blessed light?"

As men and women surged forward, crying out for healing and prayers, Thren shook his head.

"He is too dangerous to live," he said, glancing down at his son. "This city needs to be warned what this high-minded drivel will earn them. Faith has its place, and that place is far from us. I've waited too long as it is to kill him, so this message must be a strong one. Consider this your first real test, Aaron. No games. No training. We're spilling real blood."

He tilted his head and scratched at the side of his nose. Kayla saw from afar and closed the distance between them. Instead of talking, though, she moved right past without saying a word. She bullied through the gathered throng to the front. Thren knelt down so Aaron could hear him over the rising volume of prayers and shouts.

"Kayla will handle Delius," he said. "Kill his girl. Return to the safe house when you escape."

Thren slipped deeper into the crowd, nearing the front while staying on the opposite side of Kayla. Delius was kneeling near the center, his hands on the sides of an elderly woman. Both were crying. The scene felt strange and alien to Aaron. He had never been to any religious ceremony before, let alone a spontaneous one broken out in the streets. The fervor of the people's prayers was shocking.

He saw the girl standing behind her father. A hard knot grew in his stomach. Fingering the dagger Thren had given him, he eased his way around the back. The crowd was thinnest there, arranged single file with their backs to a wall. Aaron crossed his arms and watched the proceedings. He could see Kayla slowly working her way toward where Delius prayed with the others. Thren remained where he was, one row back on the opposite side.

Not sure what signal he should wait for, Aaron decided to be patient. The professional part of his mind knew the easiest time to kill Delius's daughter would be in the chaos after Thren and Kayla struck. The Haern part of him only looked at the young girl in horror. She was so pretty, with red hair as fiery as her father's. Whenever she smiled, huge dimples grew on her cheeks.

Aaron remembered Kayla returning to his room, the earrings in her hand. Rejected, and why? Because his father wanted him kept pure of women. Staring at the girl, he had an inkling as to why.

"Father," he heard Kayla shout. "Father, please, pray with me!"

She was directly next to Delius. The man smiled at her and took her hands. He knelt beside her, and Kayla bent her head as if in prayer. They were huddled together, seeming somehow intimate and private although a massive crowd was gathered around them. Delius's body shuddered. His head snapped back. Kayla was already running through the crowd before anyone realized what had happened. Delius collapsed on his side, the hilt of a dagger sticking out of his chest.

Shocked screams of two nearby women alerted the rest. The whole crowd fumed. Men turned this way and that, shouting for the guilty party, asking who had seen what. It was chaos, and if a few souls had seen what Kayla had done, they were not heard above the rest of the din.

Thren chose that moment to leap to the front, standing

on a small stool that Delius had sat upon at times when he preached. He was already a tall man, and the stool made sure that the guildmaster towered over the rest. He put his fingers to his mouth and whistled sharply. More gasps filtered through the crowd as people realized who he was.

Aaron did not watch him. He was still staring at the girl and the horrified expression on her face. Twin paths of tears ran down her cheeks. When her lower lip quivered, he felt the cold stone in his gut turn into a blade. Though he had done nothing, only watched, Aaron felt guilt creeping around his shoulders, wrapping tightly about his neck.

"This fate," Thren shouted, gesturing to the dead body, "belongs to any who dare turn against the rightful rulers of this city. Keep your righteousness out of our shadows. It has no place there."

And then he turned and jumped. His hands caught the top of the wall and flipped him over, deeper into the trade districts of Veldaren.

The crowd exploded. Furious shouts coupled with heartbroken wails. Some gave chase. Aaron stood shocked, his hand clutching his dagger so hard his knuckles ached. Then the girl turned and ran. He almost didn't notice. When he did, he shouted to her.

"Wait!"

He couldn't believe how stupid it was to shout that. Trying to push his emotions down, he chased after. He didn't know where she was headed, or for what purpose. Perhaps she knew she was in danger. Perhaps she only wanted to get away from the massive crowd of strangers and back to what might remain of her family.

She turned down a small alley in between two bakeries. The air smelled of yeast and flour. The girl ducked behind a large refuse container and didn't reappear. Aaron realized she didn't know she was being chased. She just wanted to be alone.

His dagger still sheathed, Aaron stepped around the corner of the bin and saw Delius's daughter.

She sat with her back to the wall, her head buried in her knees, arms wrapped around her legs. Tears wet her dress and face. Her eyes were closed. Aaron couldn't believe what he saw and heard. She was praying.

"Please, Ashhur," he heard her say. "Please, please, oh god, please..."

He drew the dagger, never making a sound. His hand trembled as he held it. She would by no means be his first kill. All his victims flashed before his eyes, from assassins to guards to his own brother. All had been armed. All had lived a violent life. There was something about donning a thief's cloak or soldier's helmet that made death forever possible. But what had this girl done? Why would she die? For nothing.

No, not nothing. She'd die because his father desired it. Aaron was becoming little more than the extended will of his father. He looked to the girl, so close to his age, so wounded, so alone. Gods damn it all, how could he kill her while she was praying? Praying!

Her eyes had still not opened. He had a chance. He had a choice. Kayla's words flashed through his head.

You must keep Haern hidden and safe. Keep him alive. Can you do that for me?

If he killed the girl, he'd be killing the part of him that was still free. The part that could love Kayla. The part that wasn't wholly enmeshed with his father. Killing her meant killing Haern.

Aaron sheathed the dagger and stepped back out of sight. He leaned against the wall on the opposite side of the refuse bin.

A soft sigh escaped his lips, unheard through her sobs. His eyes lifted to the sky, and there he saw Kayla watching him from the rooftops.

His heart leaped in his chest. His legs turned to water. How long had she watched? Had she even known his task in the bloody affair?

As if in answer, she looked to the girl, looked to him, and then smiled. Moments later she was gone, vaulting along the rooftops.

"Please, Ashhur, please give him back," Aaron heard the girl beg. "Ashhur, please, I can't, I can't..."

He ran, unable to listen to any more.

CHAPTER 16

Veliana wondered what James would think if he saw her like this. Her eyes were blindfolded by one of Zusa's wraps. She detected the faintest hint of sweat on it. She kept her hands at her sides, and was thankful they weren't tied. Zusa didn't seem worried that she'd run off but had insisted quite strongly that she not. Veliana had sworn her life to the faceless. If she tried to leave, her life would be forfeit, for it was no longer hers. It was Karak's.

It seemed appropriate enough, so she thanked Karak that the streets were so empty. At least they sounded empty. Zusa rushed her along at dizzying speed. If the other faceless women were nearby, she wasn't aware of them.

Veliana's knowledge of the streets was superb. With every turn she tracked where they were. A few times she had to guess, and the speed at which they hurried was no help, but no matter the twists and loops they made, she was certain they had traveled into the northeastern district.

They stopped. A gate rattled. Zusa yanked the cloth from Veliana's eyes to let her see. Before her towered the temple to Karak, impressive with its black marble and rows of pillars. Through a trick of her eyes, she swore she saw the lion skull hanging above the door turn and rattle its teeth.

"Welcome home," Zusa said.

The doors opened. They were ushered in by a young man with a pockmarked face. Once they were inside the main foyer, the priest left them between the rows of pews arranged before the giant statue of Karak. Veliana looked around as subtly as she could, doing her best to appear unimpressed. In truth the praying men unnerved her, their ululations stretching too loud and too long. The very air seemed thick with energy. It felt like magic.

"Who have we come to speak with?" Veliana asked.

"For matters of such importance, we must speak with the high priest. His name is Pelarak, and the name he carries is a great honor, given by Karak himself when he ascended to his position." Zusa gestured about the room. "Every man here would throw himself upon a sword to protect Pelarak's life. Do not fight him, and do not argue, even if he kills me."

"*Kills* you?"

"Hush," said Zusa. "He approaches."

An elderly man approached from the front of the temple, having just prayed with a young, overweight acolyte. He wiped away a few tears from his eyes and then smiled at Zusa. From the chains he wore, and the way every other priest turned his head and nodded in reverence as he passed, Veliana knew he could only be Pelarak.

"Welcome," he said.

"Thank you for accepting us, my glorious high priest," Zusa said, offering a quick bow.

"It is good to hear your voice, Zusa," Pelarak said.

Veliana found the comment unintentionally biting.

"We must talk in private," Zusa insisted. "Our time is short, and our matters urgent."

"I can imagine," Pelarak said, his kindness fading away as if it were a mirage. "Who have you brought with you?"

"That is part of what I wish to discuss."

Pelarak gave Veliana a look that froze her blood. He was dissecting her with his eyes.

"So be it. Follow me."

He led them to his meager chambers, holding open the door for them like a gentleman. Once they were inside he closed the door and crossed his arms.

"You have done much without my approval," Pelarak said. "What madness has come over you lately?"

"How so?" Zusa asked. She ushered Veliana toward a seat, but no one sat.

"Attacking the Gemcroft home? What part of my orders to remain neutral and apart from the shadow war did you not understand?"

Zusa shrugged her shoulders.

"The Kulls offered land for a temple in Riverrun. They have connection to neither the guilds nor the Trifect."

"Do you think Maynard cares?" Pelarak shook his head. "Karak made it clear as night that we were to remain indifferent. You have put our entire temple in danger because of your recklessness."

Veliana would have given anything to see behind the white cloth over Zusa's face.

"What did you tell him?" Zusa asked.

"With him threatening to send the starving masses after us?

I offered to aid him, but only if we admitted his daughter as a priestess to ensure he made no such threats again."

"Alyssa Gemcroft is under our protection," Zusa said, her voice steel.

"You answer to me, faceless," Pelarak said, his voice rising to match her intensity. "I don't care what you've done with her. I don't care who you've promised her to, and I don't care what you have to do. Bring her here."

"As you wish," Zusa said. She seemed to be staring down the high priest, even though he couldn't see her eyes.

Pelarak broke his gaze from her and finally moved behind his desk to sit. Veliana sat down opposite him and crossed her arms. She hoped that the conversation didn't last much longer. The sooner she left the temple the better. She felt oddly comfortable among Zusa and her faceless sisters. Inside the temple, however, she felt like an intruder waiting to be caught.

"I come to ask that Veliana may be admitted into our order," Zusa said. Pelarak raised an eyebrow.

"Women are not 'admitted' to the faceless, Zusa. It is a punishment and a dishonor. What has this woman done to deserve such treatment?"

"She has sworn her life to me, and to Karak."

"Then let her join the temple, if her vow is to Karak. You hold no position to accept a life into your hands."

Zusa took a step forward.

"My priest, with her talents, I feel her place would be best . . ."

"I will decide what is best," Pelarak said, his voice nearly shaking with a cold intensity. "Your kind has functioned far too long without supervision. If you cross my orders again I will disband the faceless and send you into exile. Your place is one of penance, not command, Zusa. If you value your faith in Karak, you will learn this quickly."

For a long while Zusa remained silent. When she moved, it was suddenly.

"Come," she said, grabbing Veliana's arm and yanking her to her feet.

"Where are we going?" asked Veliana.

"I said come."

If Pelarak was upset at her leaving instead of staying to be a priestess, he didn't show it. He remained in his seat as they left, not bothering to see them out. Veliana wasn't sure if it was a conscious choice or not, but Zusa didn't blindfold her when they exited the temple. As they marched south, Veliana interrupted the silence between them.

"Is it really so terrible to do what he says?" she asked.

The shadows seemed to curl off Zusa's body like mist off a pond. It was as if anger fueled them.

"If we do as he says, the Kulls will be furious," Zusa said. Her voice trembled with rage. "How dare he deny me an apprentice. How dare he!"

As they neared the wall, Veliana glanced over, an idea blossoming in her mind.

"Who do you serve?" she asked.

"Karak," Zusa replied.

"Help me out here, Zusa. In this matter, is it Alyssa or is it the Kulls?"

"The Kulls have offered land for a temple in Riverrun, a prosperous town that has long denied us permission to establish a presence."

"Land owned by the Gemcrofts, correct?"

Zusa halted and looked at Veliana. At least, Veliana assumed she did from the way her head tilted. It was hard to know with that damned cloth over her face.

"What are you saying?" Zusa asked.

Veliana shrugged.

"Seems if you're doing all this for the land, then the Kulls are irrelevant. We just need a promise from Alyssa."

Zusa crossed her arms.

"What do you get out of it?" she asked.

"Give me two days," Veliana said, winking her good eye. "I need to find out what happened to my guild. Can you keep Alyssa safe and out of Pelarak's hands until then?"

The faceless woman thought for a long time. The shadows swirling about her slowly cooled.

"Very well," Zusa said. "Return to me afterward. I am not releasing you from your oath."

Veliana drew her two daggers and laughed.

"I wouldn't dare risk you lovely ladies coming after me when I sleep," she said. "But let me seek my revenge on Thren, and I'll behave... enough."

Zusa watched her go back into the heart of the city. She crossed her arms. Their plan was already fragile. Cutting out the Kull family would make matters even more precarious. Everything seemed to hinge upon the Kensgold.

A Kensgold that would be starting in only a few days.

"Forgive me if I go against your wishes, Karak," Zusa whispered as she turned and dashed into the dark alleys. "But Pelarak is only a man. He is not you. We will do your will as we know best."

The bar was empty but for an unconscious man slumped over a table, a lone serving wench cleaning around him with a cloth, and two lovers feeling each other up in the corner. Gileas would have preferred them all gone, but he couldn't afford to be choosy. With Veliana still alive, his days were numbered.

After what he'd done to her, there was no way she wouldn't come for vengeance. He sat in the corner opposite the lovers, leering at them, enjoying the sight of the woman's thigh. When she finally glanced over and saw him, she flipped a finger at him and then returned her attention to her lover.

Gileas pretended not to notice the man from the Spider Guild entering the tavern. He kept his head down, staring at the table as if stuck in a drunken stupor.

"Strange place for a worm," said the man as he sat down across from him.

"Soil beneath the wood floor," Gileas grunted. "And you're late, Senke. I'm pushing my luck as it is."

Senke chuckled as he glanced about the room. The serving wench seemed determined not to acknowledge his existence, so he decided against a drink.

"Second time now you come calling with supposed valuable information," Senke said, sounding vaguely amused by the idea. "I'm not sure if I believe you have it or not, but apparently my master is willing to listen."

Gileas handed over a yellow piece of paper. Senke flipped it open, read it, and then raised an eyebrow.

"This is her location?" he asked. "You're sure?"

"Would I lie to the great and mighty Spider Guild?" Gileas asked. "Spiders kill worms, or at least, they would if they fought."

"Yeah, but worms eat the spiders after they're dead."

Gileas laughed as if this were the funniest thing he'd ever heard. Senke shifted in his seat, clearly uncomfortable.

"A good laugh is priceless, but my information is not," said Gileas. "Where is my pay?"

Senke reached into a pocket of his long gray cloak and pulled out a small bag of coin. He tossed it onto the table.

"You'll get the second half when the information pans out," Senke said. Gileas snorted.

"Keep the other half for yourself, or donate it to some orphans. What I have is all I need to leave for a more, hrm, friendly environment? Once a few certain people are dead, I'm sure I'll come back to sell you the rest of my little secrets."

Senke shrugged.

"Your loss. I'll find some orphanage suitably run-down to match your charming personality."

Gileas laughed.

"To think I'll miss your wit," he said.

"And to think I'll miss your lies."

Senke tugged at his hood in a mock salute, then left the tavern. Gileas nibbled on the ends of his fingers, waiting a minute or two to make sure Senke wouldn't see him leave. He heard the door creak. He looked up. No one was there.

"Hrmph," he said.

A dagger plunged into his back. He shrieked. The lovers in the corner dashed out the door, the guy struggling to pull up his pants and looking damn foolish doing so. The wench shouted something about no blades, but Gileas didn't hear it. He twisted to one side, hoping to keep the blade from pushing in farther, but then a hand grabbed his head and slammed it against the table. Stars swam before his eyes.

Someone yanked the dagger out. Gileas clutched his arms against his chest, rocking back and forth as pain shot through his body. Warm blood ran down his spine.

"Hello, Vel," he said as Veliana sat down opposite him. Twirling in her left hand was a bloody dagger, flecks splattering across the table. The tavern owner neared and started to speak, but a single glare from Veliana shut him up.

"This is guild business," she said. That was all the tavern keeper needed to hear.

"I just saw a Spider Guild officer leaving the bar," she said when the man was gone. "What did you sell him, Worm?"

"Nothing," he said. "Only lies and promises and empty air."

She grabbed his hand and thrust the dagger through his palm. To his credit, he didn't scream.

"Try again," she said.

"You're a fool," he said. "I wouldn't have killed you. I never would have. So angry..."

"Look at me!" she shouted. She jammed a finger toward her scarred eye. "Look!"

The pupil was milky white, the outer edges bloody. From her forehead to her cheek, the inflamed scar overwhelmed whatever beauty she might have had.

"You think I give a rat's ass if you meant to kill me or not?" she asked.

Gileas coughed. He felt like his back was on fire. With how wet his cough sounded, he knew she'd pierced his lung. It wasn't fatal, not yet...

"I can pay you, enough for a healer. There's a chance they can heal your eye. Not enough to see, I doubt, but at least it won't be so ugly."

Veliana yanked the dagger out and then rammed it back downward, this time penetrating his wrist. He screamed.

"What'd you sell him?" she asked. "You already sold me out to Thren. Who else did you ruin? What remains of my Ash Guild?"

Gileas laughed in spite of the pain it caused him.

"They're hiding, Vel. Hiding. But worms crawl everywhere. Thren knows where they are now. He knows, and you'll all die.

He'll have his plan, his stupid, doomed plan. Oh, how I cannot wait to see the Kensgold as it unfolds, and the chaos it will unleash."

Realization hit Veliana like a cold fist in her gut.

"You told Gerand the truth," she said. "Not that all the guildleaders would be massing at Thren's hideout tomorrow. You told the king's advisor the goddamn truth."

Gileas's black-toothed grin was all the answer she needed.

"You son of a bitch," she said, her voice seething with rage. "The king's soldiers were going to save us all from that overconfident bastard and his war!"

"Who knows who Gerand's told?" Gileas said. He coughed, and blood spilled across his lips. "Who knows what plans they've spun? The Kensgold will be a fun night. So much fun..."

"You'll watch nothing," Veliana said. "You're going to do Dezrel a favor and fucking die."

She yanked her dagger out and thrust for his chest. The dagger punched through his clothes but pierced no flesh. They were empty, and already falling as if dropped from the ceiling. The clothes piled on the chair, looking like some strange joke. Veliana stared at them, her mouth open in shock. She'd thought the first time that she was delusional from her pain and trauma. This time she knew magic was at work.

She picked up his shirt and shook it. Nothing. She used her dagger to shift his trousers from side to side. Still nothing. Curses on her lips, she turned to leave when something caught her eye.

Crawling on the floor toward a small crack was an eight-inch black worm. As it flexed, she saw a thin cut along its side.

"Not possible," she said. No wonder he had been nicknamed the Worm. He'd probably given the name to himself to mock every single person he dealt with. Every joke about living in mud, digging through walls, listening with ears clogged with dirt... it was all true.

It was almost to the crack. Veliana hurled her dagger, wanting to get nowhere near the strange creature. The dagger pierced the worm just above its midsection. It twisted and squirmed, its body cut in half. Still it crawled toward the crack, leaving its lower half behind.

Veliana crushed it with her heel. Innards spurted across the floor. She held in a wave of vomit. It reminded her of when he had kissed her. She pulled the dagger free, wiped it clean on her pant leg, and then sheathed it. It took a couple kicks to get the worm body through the crack. The carcass was shockingly heavy for being only a worm.

When done, she turned and saw the tavern keeper looking at her with wide eyes.

"Burn the clothes," Veliana said as she tossed him Gileas's bag of coins. "Consider that ample payment for keeping your mouth shut."

With no time to waste, she hurried out the door. Everything was a mess. If the king knew of Thren's plans for the Kensgold, then most likely the Trifect did too. That changed everything.

Before she could worry about that, she had to deal with her most pressing danger: Thren knew where the Ash Guild had holed up to hide. Preparations for an assault would have already begun. Thren had long learned never to let an enemy last a second longer than necessary. She ran a list of safe houses through her mind, trying to decide which one James would flee to first.

Faster and faster she ran, praying no guild member caught sight of her. Her guild was dying, and the scent of blood would bring every last cutpurse down on their heads.

CHAPTER

17

When Aaron arrived in his father's room, Kayla was already there, waiting.

"As I was telling Kayla, this was a perfect hit," Thren said to his son. "Delius is dead, in the middle of a crowd in daylight, no less. No one saw the killer. We've heard confused reports already claiming it was a man instead of a woman. The entire city knows I am responsible, but no court will ever judge me, no soldier will ever find me. That is how you send a message, my son. That is how you frighten a population, by showing that even with common knowledge of our guilt, their justice will never reach us."

"Yes, Father," Aaron said. His voice was barely above a whisper. Thren noticed his subdued nature and then rubbed his chin. He stared into Aaron's eyes, trying to decipher the reason.

"The girl," he asked. "Did you kill her?"

Aaron shook his head. He almost lied. He wanted to claim she'd died, and that the trauma of killing a young girl in cold blood had left him ill. But he couldn't. His entire insides chilled at the very thought of his father finding out he spoke a lie.

"No," he said, stealing a glance at Kayla. "She ran away while the crowd was still gathered. I failed."

Thren caught the glance and turned his attention to Kayla. She only shrugged as if she didn't understand.

"No matter," Thren said. "Kayla, go fetch me one of our cutpurses. I don't care who."

Aaron waited with his eyes downcast. His father never said a word.

"You called for me?" asked a clean-shaven man with thick circles underneath his eyes. His black hair was cropped and pulled back into a ponytail.

"I did. Aaron, this is Dustin. Have you met him before?"

Aaron shook his head.

"I don't believe so."

"Look upon him," Thren said to his son. "And listen carefully. Instead of spending time thieving, assaulting caravans, or working the streets, he will instead track your failed target. He will spend our money bribing men and women to find out the girl's name and location. He'll risk his life in these endeavors, to both rival thief guilds as well as the Trifect's men. Coin, time, and manpower, all wasted because you couldn't do one simple job."

Aaron kept his eyes down, accepting his father's rebuke.

"I understand," he said.

"Good." Thren turned to Dustin. "Her last name is Eschaton, daughter of a priest who died earlier today. Find and kill her."

"Am I allowed to have any fun with her beforehand?" asked Dustin.

"I want my message hammered home," Thren said. "Do as you please. Make sure she dies afterward."

Dustin's grin was ear-to-ear.

"Be a pleasure. I'll leave her bits on Ashhur's temple door."

Aaron felt his neck flush. He desperately hoped his father wouldn't notice. But of course he did.

"You have plenty of growing up to do," Thren said to him. "You wanted to be at my side, and now you are. Start living up to your expectations."

"Yes, Father," said Aaron.

"Begone," Thren said, waving a dismissive hand.

Aaron didn't go to his room. Instead he went to Robert Haern's.

"Come in," the old man said after Aaron knocked. The boy crept the door open, slipped inside, and then shut it. When he turned around, Robert was staring at him.

"What troubles you?" Robert asked.

Aaron bit his lower lip. He so badly wanted to ask a question, but he knew the potential danger. What he wanted to know, his father would disagree with. But he had to know. It would just eat at him for months if he didn't find out.

"I saw a priest today," he said. "He wore a symbol, like this, around his neck."

Aaron drew a single line in the air with his finger. It looked like an *M* with one side much higher and sharper than the other. Robert picked up his cane and walked over to his desk.

"Did it look something like... this?"

Robert opened a drawer and pulled out a gold medallion hanging from a silver chain. It also had the strange line. Aaron nodded.

"That line is the Golden Mountain," Robert explained. "It has two peaks. The lower one represents Dezrel, and the height we can ascend to in our lives. The higher one represents the Golden Eternity. As you can see, nothing in this world can ever make one rise as high as in the afterlife."

"Who is Ashhur? And why do people pray to him?"

Robert raised an eyebrow.

"Where have you heard people praying to Ashhur?" he asked.

A brief memory flashed before Aaron's eyes, that of the red-haired girl sobbing in front of him as she called out to Ashhur.

"Nowhere," he said.

"Hrmph. Ashhur is brother to Karak, who I'm sure you know a little bit more about, considering who your friends and associates are. Ashhur represents justice, mercy, grace . . . things that most would consider the finer parts of mankind. That is why someone would pray to him. They seek comfort, or forgiveness, or protection."

Robert went to put the amulet back into the drawer, then paused. He saw how Aaron was looking at it, and the old man bit his lip.

"What is going on, boy?" he asked. "Why do you come in here asking about gods?"

Aaron didn't want to answer, but Robert was his teacher. If he refused, then the next time he came in asking questions, he might get only silence.

"Kayla killed a priest of Ashhur today. I was ordered to kill his daughter, but I failed."

"Failed?" asked Robert. It was as if he could see right through him. "Or refused?"

Aaron felt his cheeks flush. If his father had read him as clearly, then their conversation might have taken a very different turn when Thren was scolding him for his failure.

"She was crying," he whispered. "She didn't even know I was

there. Her father, killed right in front of her. I've killed before, I've, but she's not like us, not like, not..."

Tears swelled in his eyes. Aaron couldn't believe it. He wiped them away, the blush in his cheeks fierce. He felt so stupid, so young.

"I'm an embarrassment," he said.

"No," Robert said, putting his hands on Aaron's shoulders. His beard wasn't tied behind his head like normal, and it reached down to his waist. It made him look older, less controlled and more grandfatherly. His whole face seemed to sag a little, as if he had dropped a layer of armor from his flesh.

"Listen to me, Aaron," he said. "Your father is raising you to be something terrible. He'll deny you everything, even his love, to make you into what he wants. Do you know what that is, boy?"

Aaron almost denied it, but he remembered what Robert had always said: any question he asked, Aaron should already know the answer to. And Aaron did know the answer. It terrified him more than anything.

"A killer," Aaron said, his voice once more a whisper.

"The perfect killer," Robert gently corrected. "He'll starve you of love, affection, friends, faith... everything but the blade and the shadows."

Aaron sniffed and rubbed his nose against his sleeve.

"What should I do?"

Robert handed him the amulet. The boy took it as if it might burn him. His eyes were wide as he traced a finger over the gold.

"Pray, Aaron. Pray for anything and everything. We live in a harsh world. One day your father will place you at the edge of a cliff. I've heard the stories about you. I know you killed your brother when you were but a child. You can jump down that ravine, or you can stand tall and refuse him."

"I know what happens to people who refuse my father," Aaron said. "They die."

Robert smiled.

"We all die, son. The question is, who are we when we do?"

Aaron lifted the amulet before his eyes.

"Everything good about mankind?" he asked.

"Everything we wish we were and most often fail to be, Aaron," said Robert.

But he wasn't Aaron anymore, not then.

He put the amulet in his pocket, where his father wouldn't see it. When he turned to leave, he paused, then glanced back at his teacher.

"Do you pray to Ashhur?" he asked.

Robert sighed.

"I know I should not answer," he said. "But what I have said is already enough for your father to kill me. Yes, I pray to him, Aaron, though not as much as I should. And nothing like I did when I was younger. The world is harsh, Aaron. Sometimes it seems like Ashhur isn't even listening."

He thought of the girl, pleading to Ashhur to give back her father. The hurt in Robert's eyes was so plain, Aaron wondered whom he had prayed for Ashhur to send back.

How cruel a world, thought the boy as he left Robert's room, a plan forming in his mind. *But I won't be its cruelty.*

Not anymore.

He searched the entire compound. Dustin was nowhere to be found. Holding in a curse, Aaron went looking for Kayla. He found her in the mess hall, eating with several men. His mind raced, trying to think of a way to talk to her without letting it be obvious. If anyone might help him in protecting the girl, it'd be her.

Summoning his courage, he walked straight up to her. If there was no subtle way, then being brazen about it would be less likely to draw attention than some half-assed secret communication.

"Kayla," he said, feeling the eyes of the others on him. No matter where he went, he was Thren's son, and the thieves acted like a word from him might be their deaths. It might have been true, but it still made him feel uncomfortable. Of course, any attention made him feel uncomfortable. He preferred the corners and the shadows, not front and center.

"Yes, Aaron?" she asked.

He felt even more awkward with Kayla looking at him. He kept thinking how pretty she was. It didn't help that with her leaning toward him, he had a nice view down her shirt.

"I need to find someone," he said. Kayla shrugged and stood from the table, having already finished eating. A couple of others mocked her for leaving a glass full of beer, but another cheerfully volunteered to finish it for her. When they were far enough away, Aaron blurted everything out at once.

"I need to find Dustin," he said. "The one you fetched for my father."

"Dare I ask why?"

"I'm going to kill him."

Kayla held her surprise well.

"Again . . . dare I ask why?"

They were at the door to the mess hall. Aaron waited until she pushed open the door, then used its creak to help hide his voice.

"Because he'll kill her," he said.

Kayla opened her mouth to ask a question, then closed it, having figured out the answer.

"Shit," she said. "You're out of your mind. He's a pro, Aaron."

She led him down the hall. In the quiet their voices seemed more ominous, their whispers carrying far. Kayla led them to her room as quickly as possible.

"You can't," she said once she shut the door. "You don't even know her name. You're throwing your life away, don't you understand?"

Aaron clenched his fingers around the medallion through the fabric of his pants.

Everything good about mankind, Aaron thought. *Everything good about me.*

"I have to try," he said. "Please, tell me where he went."

Kayla bit her lip and stared at him.

"Fuck it," she said. "I joined this guild for a fearsome reputation and a bloated amount of coin. So far I've rescued an old man from prison and murdered a helpless priest. It's not like I can do any worse. I risk my own life telling you, you do know that, right?"

Aaron blushed, realizing how stupid he was not to have thought everything through.

"I can't," he said, turning to leave. "I can't risk your life, not for me, not for her."

"Aaron," she said, grabbing his shoulder and turning him around. She smiled at him, even as her lips trembled with fear. "I researched the Eschatons before the job in what little time I had. Delius was a noble who turned to the priesthood only a few years back. He has a mansion in the western district. It's sparsely furnished and poorly staffed. He gave away much of his wealth to the temple. The girl might be there, or she might be in the temple. If she's in the temple, you haven't a prayer of getting to her. Either way, that mansion is the first place Dustin will look."

"Thank you," Aaron said.

Kayla gave him directions to the mansion, as well as a brief description of what it looked like from the outside.

"Dustin's started ahead of you," Kayla said. "But he'll need to ask around first to find out where they live. You might be able to beat him there. Hurry out, and try to be back before sunrise."

Aaron hurried to the door, and he heard Kayla's voice call out after him.

"And for the love of all that's holy, don't let anyone see you!"

CHAPTER 18

Aaron felt oddly exhilarated. He'd never been out at night on his own. Thren had always insisted someone accompany him on his rare excursions out of the complex. Usually the reasons involved safety, the Trifect, and rival guilds wanting to settle a million old grudges. More and more, though, Aaron decided his father wanted to keep him from having a taste of freedom.

He ran along the rooftops. With so many nearby logging towns, especially those on the northern edges of the King's Forest, the houses were built sturdy, tall, and with mostly flat roofs. The wood and plaster easily held him. He landed as softly as he could, but he also ran fast. Bits of gray cloth trailed in the air behind him, the ties to the mask that covered his entire face. Only his blue eyes were visible.

As he neared the western district, the going got rougher. The west was far from the wealthiest of districts, but every part of the city had its betters, and they always clumped themselves together. As the buildings grew fancier, the roofs grew more slanted, with multiple floors, odd decorations and stone creatures, as well as the sharp triangular rooftops that had been fashionable at some point. Instead of racing along, he leaped and climbed. Sweat poured across his skin, the air was devilishly cold, but through it all Aaron smiled.

I'm Haern now, he thought. *I'm free. Haern is powerful. Haern can rebel.*

It was strange thinking like that, but it made sense somehow. Let Aaron be shy. Let Aaron cower before his father and steal as ordered. Haern would hide, and he would survive. And tonight Haern would kill, but unlike Aaron he'd do it for good. He knew just enough about sex to know that whatever Dustin planned to do, it'd be horrific torture before he actually killed the girl. He couldn't let her go through that, especially knowing it'd be his fault. His cowardice, his inability to lie to his father to protect her.

At last he found the mansion. He was atop an even larger home on the opposite side of the street, his arms wrapped around a stone statue of what looked like a deer crossed with a man. His fingers drummed against the antlers. Despite the darkness, he could see far. The moon was bright, the clouds only wispy ghost fingers stretching across the sky.

There was no sign of anything amiss. No windows were broken, the door was shut tight, and he saw no shadows skulking around the sides. Of course, based on what Kayla had said, he had to assume that Dustin would be a bit more subtle than to just walk up to the front door and kick it in.

If the girl was there, she most likely wasn't alone. Or she could be in the temple of Ashhur. Sitting there across the street, there were a million things Aaron didn't know, and he'd find out none of them from his current perch. Tapping his dagger to give himself courage, he climbed down and approached the mansion.

The place lacked the security of higher wealth. No worn paths circled the building from a patrol of guards. No fence surrounded it, and no dogs prowled about. Many times Senke had led him to various estates, pointed out weaknesses, and made him sneak in when the night was young. He never had to steal anything valuable, just something to prove he had gone deep inside the home. From what he saw of the Eschaton mansion, Aaron thought Senke never would have given him a place so easy except as a warm-up.

Aaron slipped around back, checking each of the windows. He found one unlocked near the very back. His heart stopped as he realized that Dustin may have been the one to unlock it. Stepping back, he scanned the area, seeing no footprints. There was undisturbed dirt on the windowsill. Carelessness then, Aaron decided. Thank Ashhur for that.

He slid it open, doing so quicker than he might have normally. He didn't have time to be patient. If Dustin spotted him, he'd want to know what was going on. Aaron might be able to get the jump on him if he hurried. With the window halfway open, Aaron slipped inside and onto the hardwood floor within. His landing made far more noise than he'd have liked. If any of his former teachers had been there, he'd have been given a solid, but quiet, smack to the head.

It took him another moment to decide what to do about the window. Part of him wanted to leave it open for a quick getaway. Then he realized that if he was trying to make a quick getaway, he had already failed terribly. Better to make sure Dustin got no wind of his being there. He shut it and readjusted the curtains.

Aaron could only guess as to the layout of the mansion.

Thick curtains covered the windows, making the rooms far darker than it was outside. He waited a minute for his eyes to adjust, then worked his way toward the back. When his feet touched carpet, he smiled. Off of the hard surface, he'd make much better time.

He had entered a long hallway with three windows facing out. The direction he'd guessed led him to a small kitchen, small by rich men's standards, anyway, though it appeared well stocked. Aaron slipped on through, drawing his dagger as he exited into a short hallway ending at a door. He pried it open, cringing at the noise the hinges made. An alert guard might have heard, but inside he saw only a large bed. An elderly lady slept on the side closest to him, her mouth open, drooling. Her hair was completely gray. Lying beside her was Delius's daughter.

Aaron couldn't believe it. Her father murdered that morning, by the Spider Guild, no less, and no one had thought to give her a guard? Not even a man of the house? Instead she was with an aunt or a grandmother. Helpless.

That's what I'm for, Aaron thought as he scanned the area. The room only had one door. If Dustin was to get to them, he had to go through the kitchen, followed by the short hallway. Knowing his time was running out, Aaron planned through the upcoming encounter. When Dustin arrived, he was determined to have surprise on his side.

"You're sure that's where she is?" Dustin asked, dancing a copper piece along his knuckles.

"Yeah," said the drunken man opposite him. "Delysia's not old enough to be by herself, not with her brother off being trained to be some kind of mage or whatnot. Her granny's with her. Stupid old bag, I'd have slapped her a dozen times if she wasn't so quick and eager to call her son to save her."

"I don't care about her," Dustin said. "Why wouldn't they take Delysia elsewhere?"

The other man shrugged. He looked ready to pass out. When Dustin had begun asking around the bars about the Eschatons, he'd been given blank looks until, at the fifth, a man had pointed to the corner.

"Ask for Barney," he'd been told. "Guy worked for him, guard or something."

Barney had actually been a gardener, though he had often implied that he'd been an actual guard when asked what he did. Dustin had been worried about loyalties to his employer, worries that quickly died when he found out Barney had been fired earlier in the day.

"Windbag thinks they can't afford me," Barney grumbled. "I'll show her. Bet that Delius bastard had a ton stored away. No one just gives their shit to the poor. They'll say they do, but they never do."

Dustin had already bought the man three drinks. He tossed him the copper, not caring that it rolled off the table and to the floor. For a moment it didn't look like Barney even noticed.

"What you want them for anyway?" he asked after a lengthy belch.

"Unfinished business," said Dustin as he walked out of the bar.

The Eschaton estate wasn't very far. It appeared Barney liked to drink close to home. Dustin kept to the shadows as he approached, his hand casually resting on the hilt of his mace. With its solid round head, it was more of an iron club. A good blow could smash a man's skull like a pumpkin. Dustin always got a much bigger thrill breaking bones than spilling blood. People bled all the time. Cuts were on the outside. Bones were inside, and the way people howled when he mangled their fingers or obliterated their kneecaps...it gave him shivers just thinking about it.

There was also one extra benefit to having the mace instead of a sword. He slipped around to the back, found the first window on the eastern side facing away from the street, and then smashed it in with his mace. Barney had made it quite clear that it was just Delysia and her grandmother, and that they had no guards. Even if they did awake to the sound of breaking glass, what would they do? Fight back?

Dustin chuckled. He hoped so. He wasn't much for old ladies, but Delysia was supposed to be ten or so. Her pleading and struggling would be damn exciting.

Once inside, Dustin pushed his back against the wall beside the doorway. If someone came to investigate the noise, he'd have an easy blow to the back of their head. No one came. He shook his head. Whoever these Eschatons were, they were a stupid lot. He walked silently into a modest kitchen, careful not to disturb anything. He had been sloppy with the window, he knew that, but making too much ruckus searching for the girl would be pushing his luck. Besides, if they tried to flee, he wanted to make sure he heard them.

He was not prepared for what he saw when he reached the other side of the kitchen. A boy dressed in Spider Guild grays knelt next to a door at the end of a short hallway. Dustin stopped, unhidden in the middle of the doorway, and wondered if he had somehow entered the wrong house.

So far the boy's back was to him. Dustin glanced around, saw a crumb of hardened bread crust, and flung it. It smacked the boy in the ear. His tiny body jumped, and Dustin winced at the noises he made. They weren't loud, but he guessed a bedroom was on the other side of the door.

"What the bloody Abyss are you doing here?" Dustin whispered fiercely once the boy was with him in the kitchen. The boy looked back, only his eyes visible through the mask over his face. Dustin figured he was one of their younger thieves, but he didn't have a clue who. "And what's with the mask?"

"I'm correcting a mistake," the boy whispered back.

Dustin gestured to the door, then made a circular motion with his finger beside his head, showing what he thought of that plan.

"You're a kid, now go home," Dustin said. "I have work to do."

When he tried to push him aside, the boy grabbed his wrist and held firm.

"She was my kill first," he whispered far too loudly. The hairs on the back of Dustin's neck stood on end. Something was wrong here. Those eyes seemed so familiar...

"Aaron?" he asked, tugging his arm free.

"No," said the boy. "My name is Haern."

Pain spiked into Dustin's side. He spun on reflex, only dimly aware that the boy had stabbed him. His spin forced the dagger out, flinging blood across the lower drawers of the kitchen. He swung his mace, grunting as it broke the door frame. Haern rolled underneath the blow, kicked off the table, and then lunged with his dagger.

Dustin parried with the length of his mace, set his left foot closer, and then swung back, hoping Haern would trip when dodging. Instead the boy ducked underneath, looped his own leg around Dustin's foot, and stabbed his dagger into Dustin's calf.

Choking down a scream, Dustin swung his mace back down. One good hit and he'd splatter Haern's brains across the floor. Problem was, the boy was too fast. He darted from side to side, barely avoiding every swing. How the noise had not attracted attention, Dustin didn't have a clue. On his fourth swing, Haern parried the mace to the side, then cut back quickly enough to slice a thin gash along Dustin's hand.

The older thief abandoned all pretense at silence. Any underestimation of Haern's skill was gone. He stepped back, hoping to go on the defensive to see if Haern made a mistake. Instead Haern lunged, his sudden aggressiveness startling Dustin. More dagger cuts lined his legs, which already throbbed with pain.

"Have her," Dustin said, backing toward the window he'd entered. "You can have her, just fucking kill her afterward, all right?"

This only seemed to enrage Haern further. Dustin turned to run, knowing the boy would never let him leave. He took only two steps, and then spun. His knee slammed into Haern's stomach, knocking the wind out of him. Before the boy could dart away, he followed it up with a vicious elbow to the side of his face. He felt grim satisfaction at the sight of blood spurting across the carpet, blood that wasn't his.

"What is your problem?" Dustin asked as he knelt down. Haern was on his stomach, his dagger lying several inches out of reach in the kitchen. He grabbed Haern's leg and pulled him closer, determined to remove the mask. He had his suspicions about the boy being Aaron, but needed to know for sure. If it was Aaron, he'd leave and let Thren dole out whatever punishment he felt appropriate. If it wasn't, well...

He readied the mace in his other hand.

"Let's take a look, eh?" Dustin said as he spun the boy onto his back. When Haern rolled, his leg shot upward, kicking Dustin in the chin with his heel. Haern used the momentary confusion to continue his roll, breaking free of Dustin's grip. The mace missed and struck the carpet, breaking the wood floor underneath. The boy lunged for the dagger, scooped it up in his hands, and then whirled.

Dustin's jaw dropped as the dagger flew through the air and buried itself in his chest. Before he could react, Haern was already chasing it, his foot slamming into Dustin's throat. Dustin retched as he fell. His mace smacked the floor twice, never once hitting flesh. Haern straddled him, his knees pressing in against Dustin's elbows. Dustin felt the dagger yank free of his chest, then press against his throat.

"You can't kill her," Haern said.

"Your father will figure it out, Aaron," said Dustin, hoping his guess was right and the boy's real name would startle him.

Instead his whole face darkened, a frightening gleam in his eye.

"I'm not Aaron," he said. "Not when I have a choice."

The dagger stabbed downward, and then Dustin saw the gleam no more.

Haern sheathed his dagger and tightened his mask. He was bleeding from the nose, where Dustin had elbowed him, and, with nowhere else to go, the blood was seeping into the mask and running down his lips. His stomach felt like it had a terrible cramp from his being kneed there. Sniffling, he stood up and held in a shiver.

Now he'd actually killed Dustin, he had no clue what to do with the body. He thought about leaving it there for the old lady to clean up. Surely she knew some younger men to help deliver it to proper gravemen.

Haern frowned. That wouldn't do. If Thren found out one

of his men had died on the job, he'd send another to finish it. He never left things undone. He needed Dustin gone; that way he could claim the kill for himself and act as if Dustin had never shown. Thieves went missing all the time for a million reasons. Surely he could think of one that sounded convincing.

His stomach heaved again, and he fell to his knees. When he vomited he saw blood, hoped it wasn't something serious. His heart was pounding in his head, and once more he looked to the dead body, as if to confirm it was still there. Amid his pain, he heard the padded footsteps only a moment before something blunt struck the back of his head. His vision swam with dots, and his whole body lurched to one side. He spun as he fell, just in time to see something large and black come swinging in at his face. Right before he was knocked out cold, he wondered how many days until his father forgot he'd ever existed.

"Stay back, Delysia," said the old woman, holding a heavy iron pan. "These vermin are dangerous even at a young age."

"Don't be silly, Gran," said Delysia. "You hurt him bad."

Gran stood over both bodies, wielding the pan with both hands as if it were an ancient weapon of legend. She gently prodded the young man's body with her bare foot before stepping back into the kitchen.

"He dead?" Delysia asked.

"Don't look like it," said Gran. "Maybe if I were twenty years younger I'd have sent his brains flying out his ear, but looks like I just rung his bell a little."

"What do we do?" asked Delysia. "Tie him up?"

"Don't have the rope for that. Here, help me drag him into the pantry. We'll just lock him up in there for now."

She stepped around and grabbed the boy's feet.

"Ugh," she said. "Blood all over the carpet."

"Gran!"

The old lady looked up at her granddaughter.

"What?" she asked.

Delysia's face was pale, and with a limp hand she pointed to Dustin's lifeless body. Gran, whose real name she hadn't gone by for at least fifteen years, turned around and looked.

"Keep forgetting how sheltered you've been," Gran said. "Delius did a good job of that, at least. If he had let you go to market on your own once in a while you'd have seen plenty sights worse than this lying in the gutters."

Delysia's eyes teared up at her father's name. Gran saw this and quietly muttered a curse to herself.

"I'm sorry, girl. It's been a rough day, and this ugly business is so much more than you deserve. Your father was a good man, and I'm sure he was doing what he thought was best for you."

Delysia nodded and wiped away some of her tears. Trying to be brave, she grabbed the boy's hands and helped lift him off the floor. They dragged him to the pantry door, then dropped him so Gran could remove the dagger from his belt.

"Most likely we'll let the guards have him," Gran said as she put the dagger on one of the tables.

The pantry was large enough for three people standing side by side, so one unconscious young man easily fit. Gran dropped her end unceremoniously on the floor. Delysia lowered hers a bit more gently, not wanting to hurt his head. They shut the door, leaving him sprawled across the floor.

"Bring the candle closer so I can see," Gran said. Delysia promptly obeyed. They had two candles lit, one for each of them from when they had sneaked out of their bedroom to see what was going on. Delysia put one on the counter next to the pantry and left the other one on the table beside the dagger.

"Need a lock," Gran said as she examined the pantry door. "Give me that chair. No, darling, the other one, the one that didn't cost your father ten farms' worth of dairy milk."

The pantry had a slot for a lock in case the servants' fingers got too sticky when they were cooking and cleaning. It was up high, far beyond reach of Gran's stooped shoulders.

"Hold it steady for me," said Gran after returning to the table and grabbing the dagger.

"Yes, Gran," said Delysia.

Gran climbed up, putting both feet on the cushion.

"You want me to split my head open like a watermelon?" Gran snapped. "Hold that blasted thing still!"

Delysia clutched the chair tighter, doing her best to keep it from rocking. She wondered what might happen if the thief inside woke up and tried to open the door. Gran would go sprawling, perhaps even taking Delysia down with her. She prayed he stayed unconscious.

"Hope this'll fit," Gran said as she pushed the dagger into the hole intended for a lock's latch. It slid in about a third of the way before catching. Gran grunted and pushed harder, but the dagger wasn't budging.

"We'll have to hope it holds," Gran said. "I'm coming back down now."

She stepped off, looking very relieved when her feet touched solid floor. Her wrinkled hands clutched the back of the chair as she regained her breath.

"Was a time I could go leaping tree to tree without a care," Gran grumbled. "What I'd give to be *that* crazy gal again."

"Do you want me to fetch the guards?" Delysia asked.

"You?" asked Gran. She looked at the young girl as if she'd asked to drink hard liquor and then run naked through

Merchant Way. "Don't be daft. Two men snuck in with aims to rob and kill you. I'm not letting you run about on your own."

"We have to get someone," Delysia insisted. "What if more come? I want the guards, Gran. Can't you go get the guards?"

Gran's whole face turned sour.

"Of course I want the guards. Something needs to be done about this, a dead body and a locked-up young man. But by Ashhur's beard, I'm not letting you out at night. Gods damn it, I should have had one of the servants stay overnight. Thought you could use some quiet time to grieve, but what do I know?"

Delysia shifted uncomfortably as her grandmother muttered and looked around the kitchen.

"All right," Gran said. "I don't like this one bit, but here's what we'll do. I'll hurry out and find a guard. You stay right where you are. If that boy starts kicking and shoving at the door, you watch the latch at the top. That dagger starts moving, or the wood starts to break, you run your skinny ass out to the streets and the nearest guard station. Am I understood?"

Delysia tucked her hands behind her back and lowered her head. That always seemed to please Gran best when she was lecturing.

"Yes, Gran," the girl said.

Gran was still frowning when she hurried back to her bedroom. She was only in her shift, and dead body or no dead body, she wasn't going out indecent. Once she had on a dull beige dress and a red scarf, she returned to the kitchen and kissed her granddaughter on the forehead.

"Be safe, and may Ashhur watch over you," she said.

"I'll be careful," Delysia said. Gran's eyes darted over to the pantry as if a monster lurked within.

"You better. Remember, second it looks weak, you run like the wind."

When she was gone, Delysia sat down on the expensive chair. She picked at the fine cloth on the cushion, not seeing how it was really any different from the other chair. She'd left it in front of the pantry door, thinking maybe if the door burst open it might cause the boy to stumble. With his mask on, she hadn't had a chance to see much of his face, only his blond hair peeking out from the top.

The candles slowly flickered and burned. The longer Gran was gone, the more slowly the seconds seemed to crawl. Delysia hadn't realized just how quiet the mansion had gotten. For as long as she could remember, cats had lived underneath the floor of their home, sneaking in and out of holes her family could never find. She heard them crawling now, thumping against boards and beams. Every time she heard one, her skin crawled. They'd never bothered her before, but now she imagined men with daggers instead of cats with kittens.

In that quiet, she heard a muffled noise within the pantry.

Delysia tensed. Even her breathing halted. She listened for something, anything. Another noise, this time like a foot dragging along the floor. The young man was getting up. She thought about shoving the back of the chair against the pantry door, but knew it would do no good. There was nothing for it to hook under. She'd have to trust the dagger.

Suddenly the door rocked outward. She heard objects rattling within, and the wood creaked as the dagger caught inside the latch. Despite herself, Delysia let out a shrill scream.

That seemed to puzzle whoever was inside. She heard him speak, his voice muffled but still understandable.

"You're alive?"

Delysia wasn't sure how to respond.

"Of course I am," she said. "Why wouldn't I be?"

She heard a loud thump within. It sounded like he'd sat down with his back against the door.

"Then I didn't fail," she heard him say, though whether to her or himself, she didn't know.

"My granny is getting the guard," Delysia said, thinking if she could keep him talking he wouldn't start beating on the door. Of course, with that being her plan, she realized how dumb it was to admit guards were coming. She smacked her forehead and hoped she hadn't screwed up too badly.

"Guards?" the boy said. "Good, you'll be safe."

Delysia stared at the door, certain she had misheard.

"What was that?" she asked.

"I said good, you'll be safe."

She blinked. Why would someone who had broken into her home care if she was safe, unless...

"What are you doing here?" she asked.

"Protecting you," said the boy.

"From who?"

"The men who killed your father."

That sent an icy chill down her spine. She'd tried to forget the body in the hallway, tried to forget the horrible moment when her father had collapsed amid his followers. Why did people want her dead? Why did they want her father dead?

"We never hurt anyone," she said, tears forming in her eyes. "Why did they do this, my father was good! He was good, real good, more than I'll ever be... why did... why..."

Delysia cried. The young man inside remained silent the whole while. For some reason she found that rather kind of him.

"My name is Haern," said the pantry once her crying died down to just sniffles.

"Hello, Haern," she replied. "I'm Delysia Eschaton."

"Delysia..."

To her it sounded like he was feeling over the word with his tongue, applying it to some unknown memory or picture. Perhaps he was trying to imagine what she looked like...?

"You stay put, all right?" she said. "I'll tell the guards you behaved when they come."

"It won't matter, Delysia," said Haern.

"Why not?" she asked.

"Because they'll kill me."

Delysia shivered, wishing she had worn something warmer. The blankets of her bed were not far away, but she didn't want to leave sight of the pantry for a second. So far Haern hadn't tried to get out, but he might be biding his time.

"They won't do that," she said.

"They will. You're not safe. You have to get out of the city, Delysia. When my...when Thren realizes Dustin failed, he'll send another after you. He won't stop until you're dead."

She wanted to believe he was lying. If he was, he was really good at it.

"Who is Thren?" she asked.

A soft chuckle echoed from within the pantry.

"You really don't know? Thren Felhorn, leader of the Spider Guild. He's dangerous. He's the one who killed your father. You should have died when he did, but the other killer..."

His voice trailed off. Delysia's hands trembled like little birds. In every corner she imagined the man from the hallway. He held a metal club in his hand, his pale face lit with a grin.

"I don't know where to go. Dad's will gave all his farms to the workers. We have money, but Gran won't listen. She never listens to me. Can't we just hire some guards?"

Another soft laugh within.

"Guards? You really don't know anything, do you?"

Her anger flared.

"Well, at least I'm not the one stuck in a pantry!"

He didn't seem to have a comeback for that. A minute passed in brooding silence. Haern cracked first, and that alone made Delysia feel a little better.

"I'm sorry," he said. "How old are you, Delysia?"

She puffed out her chest, even though he couldn't see it.

"I'm ten, almost eleven."

"I'm only thirteen," said Haern. "I don't think either of us know anything, do we?"

She almost took it as an insult, then let it drop. Sitting there, scared and alone and wishing her Gran were back, she found it a little hard to argue.

"You really think someone else will come for me and Gran?" Delysia asked.

"Yes, I do."

Delysia sighed. She felt like crying some more, so she did. Again Haern waited patiently for her to finish. She wondered how much time had passed. Surely Gran should be back with guards by now?

"Why are you here?" she asked after wiping her face with the hem of her shift.

"I said already, to protect you."

"But that's stupid," she said. "You're barely older than me!"

"The man in the hallway is dead, isn't he?"

The way he said it gave her another chill. Delysia curled her knees up to her chest and hugged them. She stared at the pantry, oddly curious as to what Haern's face looked like underneath his mask.

"The guards won't really kill you when they get here, right?" she asked. "You're just saying that so I let you out."

"They know who I am. That alone will earn me death."

Again she thought of his mask.

"You know who is after us," Delysia said. "That means you can help us. Can you? I know you're young, but you stopped that man before. Can you do it again?"

"I don't know," she heard Haern say. "Maybe you should leave me for the guards."

That seemed to stoke a bit of fire in her.

"If you can help me then say so! I won't have you dying in there because of who you are. Daddy says . . . Daddy always said to judge someone by what they do, not by their name or what they say."

"Some names are so bloody they must be judged," Haern said quietly.

Delysia shook her head. Her father had hammered home certain things in his lectures, and that was one.

"Grace is stronger than blood," she said.

On the far side of the house, the door opened. Delysia's heart jumped, but then she heard Gran shouting at the top of her lungs.

"Del? I'm here, sweetie! It's Gran, and I've got the guard!"

She looked to the hallway, then to the pantry. She couldn't do it. She couldn't leave him to die.

Even though she was still young, she was as tall as Gran was. It wasn't because she was extraordinarily tall, more that Gran had never been tall to begin with, and her back had bent with age. Delysia climbed atop the chair and stretched for the dagger lodged in the lock. On the second tug it broke free, showering a few splinters atop her head.

"Say something, hon, you're scaring me!" Gran shouted.

"I'm in here," Delysia shouted back as she pulled the chair away and then flung the door open. Haern stood waiting for her, his mask pulled tight around his face. Blood had soaked it throughout. For a brief moment she expected him to attack her. He didn't. He only stared at her with the strangest of expressions.

"Don't stand there," she whispered. "Hide!"

When Gran arrived, accompanied by two gruff-looking men in the brown armor of the city guard, Delysia was sitting in the chair facing the pantry. She looked up and smiled at Gran, but her eyes were wild with fear.

"Are you all right?" Gran asked as she scooped her granddaughter into her arms. The guards had stopped to examine the body in the hallway. When Delysia didn't respond, Gran glanced at the pantry door and saw it slightly ajar.

"Did he hurt you?" she asked, her eyes suddenly widening with fear.

"I'm fine," she said. "He got away is all. He wasn't dangerous."

"Wasn't dangerous? Wasn't... did you even see what he did to that man? He cut his damn throat, you stupid girl!"

At this point one of the guards entered, looking around with a distant, tired expression.

"Where'd you say the boy was?"

"Um, er, he's..." stammered Gran.

"He got away," Delysia said. "He kicked open the door and ran."

"Hrm," muttered the guard. "You see what he looked like?"

"He had a mask," Gran said, finally composing herself. "I didn't think to remove it."

"Can't do much about that, then. What do you reckon happened to the thief back there? Those cuts don't look like a boy made them."

"I've told you what I know," said Gran.

The guard shrugged and left the kitchen. They examined

the body a few minutes longer, then gave the estate a lazy search, finding nothing. When a third guard showed up with a wagon for the body, they picked it up and carried it outside.

"I'd reckon you should get yourselves some mercenaries," one said to them. "Place like this, it looks like you should be able to afford a sellsword or two."

Delysia stayed in her seat the whole while, not once getting up to leave the kitchen. Gran wandered about before dismissing the guards. When she returned to the kitchen, her face was a lively red.

"Well that was embarrassing enough," she said. "I tell them stories of a dangerous young man locked in my pantry, and all I can show them is dust bunnies and some rotted cabbage!"

Gran caught Delysia's eyes drifting over her shoulder and turned to look. Sitting on top of the counter, a cabinet door open below him, was Haern. Delysia winced as Gran screamed bloody murder.

CHAPTER 19

The third safe house was the correct one. Veliana glanced around to make sure no one watched, then pushed aside a false brick in the giant wall surrounding the city. When she did, a lever snapped within the wall, unseen gears turned, and the dirt below her shifted as a circular sheet of metal lifted upward. Replacing the brick, Veliana climbed down a small ladder, and then replaced the lid. It would be visible under close inspection for a day or two until the dust settled over it and a few walked across it.

Not that it mattered. If Gileas really had told Thren its location, they had less than an hour to get out.

In the darkness that overcame her when she replaced the lid, Veliana had to feel around to get her bearings. There was only one direction to go, back toward the city in a cramped tunnel. She squirmed on her belly, elbows tucked tight against her sides. About twenty feet in, the tunnel started sloping upward.

Another twenty feet and she bopped her head against a solid piece of wood.

"Shit," she said as she touched her throbbing forehead. Normally, close to the false bottoms of buildings, there'd be light sneaking through the cracks. Here there was nothing. Feeling around blindly, she found a small lever and pulled it. Grating noises from both sides filled her ears, and then a whoosh of air above her signified the board's removal. She climbed out.

It didn't take long to figure out why there was no light warning her of the false bottom. She was in the basement of a rather large mansion. She'd known of the entrance to the safe house but never been there before.

James must have fled here, she thought. *This place looks to be enormous.*

The basement itself was not lit, but to her right she saw light spilling down a staircase and she worked her way toward it. She kicked a crate once, biting down on her tongue to hold in another curse. She walked more carefully after that. At the bottom of the stairs she looked up. A man was leaning against the door frame at the top, his back to her.

"Make him roll again," the man shouted. "I saw Jek shaking them bones a bit too crazy. He's probably got a rigged pair in his pockets."

As he finished talking, Veliana pressed the tip of her dagger against his neck, having climbed all the way up without alerting him to her presence.

"A lousy guard is a dead guard," she told him as he jerked his head around, his whole body stiffening.

"Hey, Vel," he said, smiling nervously at her. "Glad to see you're back and cheery as ever."

Veliana recognized him as Jorey, a low recruit, promoted most likely because of the attrition caused by the other guilds.

"Out of my way," she said, giving him a shove. Several other men in the light grays of the Ash Guild jumped from their seats around a table. Two of them grabbed daggers, while the rest just gawked.

"You're supposed to be dead," said the man holding the dice. She presumed he was Jek.

"Hate to disappoint," she said. "Now where is James?"

"What the fuck happened to your face?" asked one of the thieves. She ignored him and continued glaring.

"Upstairs," said Jek.

"All right. I want torches lit and stuck in the basement. Get two men watching it, and I mean *watching* it, not sitting at the top of the stairs waiting for a crossbow bolt. What about the front doors to the building? Who's watching them?"

"Just Gary," said another. "It's been quiet here. The guilds have started leaving us alone since James agreed to Thren's plan."

This stopped Veliana in her tracks.

"He agreed?" she asked. "When?"

"Earlier this morning," said Jorey. "Where have you been, Vel?"

Veliana shook her head, trying to match things up in her mind.

"No time," she said. "I've got to talk to James. The rest of you, get to the doors, with at least one man patrolling the windows."

"Why the attitude?" asked a fat man from the corner.

"Because Thren knows we're here," she said. "He won't leave us be, not now, not ever."

"But we agreed to what he wanted," said Jek. "Surely he won't..."

"The next person that argues with me gets a knife in the throat," Veliana shouted.

That shut them up, she thought as she stormed through the house, searching for a way upstairs. When she came upon a spiral staircase she grabbed the railing and used it to climb up the steps two at a time. Once on the second floor, she looked about, seeing a hallway leading in either direction. She chose one, her head on a swivel. She stopped when a voice called her name.

"Veliana?"

She spun, stepped two doors down, and found James sitting on the edge of his bed, naked. Refusing to blush or even avert her eyes, she crossed her arms behind the small of her back. A young blonde lay sprawled out on the bed beside him, her slender form barely hidden by the thin blankets wrapped around her.

"Apologies for the bad timing," she said. "I hope I arrived at the end, and not the beginning."

James chuckled.

"We Berens like to think there are no endings or beginnings," he said. "Just brief interludes in between."

He stood and pulled on his trousers. His movements stirred the woman beside him. She pulled the blankets closer and then rolled the other way.

"Who is that?" Veliana asked as James stepped out of the room and shut the door behind him.

"One of Leon Connington's maids. Why?"

Her jaw dropped open.

"Are you mad? She could tell him where our safe house is!"

James laughed.

"You know how he treats them. He'll be lucky if he even *gets* his maid back, let alone any information."

James's joy drained away as he truly saw her face for the first time.

"By Ashhur, what happened to you?" he asked, gently touching it with his fingertips. "Is it still tender?"

"Hurts like a bitch," she said. "It won't heal, either. What is this I hear about you making a deal with Thren?"

James sighed. He walked into the room opposite his own. There were no furnishings or portraits, just a single yellow curtain he pulled back so he could stare out at the city through the diamond-shaped window.

"Thren's plan may be suicide, but there's still a chance of it succeeding. If we opposed him any longer, we'd never last another night. They burned us out of our last two safe houses. Did you see?"

She nodded. James shook his head, his hand curling as if he wished he had a drink to hold.

"We've lost so many. Our territory is almost nonexistent. Even after this, we'll still lose most of our members to other guilds unless we get lucky and hit a large haul somewhere. What would you have me do, Vel? Stand and fight him, fight the combined might of all the thief guilds?"

"Other guilds must be getting nervous," Veliana said. "Thren tried to recruit me to take your place. He feared others would abandon him if he tried to force anyone to his side."

James laughed.

"He didn't do any of this. He planted whispers, ideas, and let the rest of the guilds eat us alive. Those who were closest to the Spider Guild got the best territory... *our* best territory. He wanted you because it was easier. A quick coup, a few dead bodies, and then he's got another puppet running another guild. Instead he had to spill a bit more blood. It wasn't hard. You know Kadish Vel? His Hawks have wanted everything north of Iron Road for months. Now he's got it. Five years we've fought that bastard's war, five fucking years, and now because we don't play along, we get thrown to the dogs."

"And the Shadows, Hawks, and Serpents," Veliana said. "We have no friends. We never have."

James gestured once more to her face.

"Who gave you that? Is that why you barged in here looking for me?"

Veliana turned away, suddenly self-conscious of the wound.

"That, no, Gileas did it, but he's dead, I killed... James, Gileas sold information to one of Thren's men less than two hours ago. He gloated over letting Felhorn know where we were hiding."

"It means nothing," insisted James.

"But he was so certain," Veliana said. "He also claimed to have told the king's men about Thren's plans for the Kensgold."

At this, James's face darkened.

"Thren won't believe you," he said. "We tell him a dead man leaked his plan to the king, then demand he call it off? He'll only assume we're seeking a new way to sabotage his plan without outwardly opposing him. Worse, he'll think we told the king ourselves. Damn that little worm."

Veliana knew she should have found that funny, but didn't.

"We can't go through with this," she said. "We can't throw our lives away with him."

James wrapped his arm around her and pulled her close.

"Tell me everything," he said. "All that's happened."

Veliana told her tale, of being captured and left for Gileas, and her encounter with the faceless women. She hid nothing, not even her trip to Karak's temple. When she finished, his face was the calm, angry stone she most often saw when he was contemplating death.

"So Vick betrayed you to the Spider Guild?" he said. "I knew he was gone, though I assumed he died in the ambush that had killed Walt, and presumably you. He must be laying low. We'll find him in time and teach him the revenge of the Ash Guild."

"What do we do?" Veliana asked. "Gileas was supposed to tell them where Thren's guildhouse is located, and convince him all the guildleaders would be there, working out a plot to kill the king. An entire army should have descended upon that Felhorn bastard's base, but instead Gileas fucked that up and told him the truth. Now we're sworn to a promise that means death, yet can't back off from it else we find death in a whole new way."

James squeezed her shoulder.

"We'll play along," he said. "I plan to survive, and settle our score with Vick and Kadish. But come the Kensgold, we will not be the ones dying that night."

"What do you mean?" Veliana asked. "Surely you don't..."

"I do," said James. "What night will Thren be more vulnerable? What night will his entire reputation hinge upon? The Kensgold is the key, Vel. We wreck him, and everything he's built fractures. We'll negotiate our own peace with the Trifect. Let the others fight the mercenaries. We'll make ten times their coin from our whores alone."

"I'll trust you," Veliana said, pulling out from his grip. "I'll even help you after I return to the faceless women. But first you have to promise me something."

"What's that?" he asked.

"Leave his son, Aaron, to me."

Gerand Crold sat in his chair, feeling particularly vulnerable even though the thick stone of the castle's walls surrounded him. He went over that morning's conversation repeatedly in his head.

"Thren would have a word with you," one of the kitchen boys had told him, someone Gerand failed to recognize.

"And why would I agree to that?" Gerand had asked in return, not bothering to ask why such a child would know. The Spiders seemed to spin their webs everywhere when they needed to.

"It's important. It's about the Kensgold. Be in your room, and be alone, or people die."

And then the child had vanished as Gerand stood frozen still in the hallway before the throne room. The Kensgold? Did Thren know that Gerand had been tipped off about his plans for the Kensgold by the Worm?

Gerand had gone through the day trying to remain calm, but it'd been a farce. The idea of someone sneaking into his bedroom should have been ludicrous. His quarters in the castle were small but luxurious and, more important, extremely safe. He was surrounded by guards and protected by sheer walls of stone and roving patrols of soldiers. Never before had he worried for his life when his door was locked and his window barred.

Yet for years he had listened to the wild tales of Thren Felhorn's exploits. The man had killed an entire royal family, two if the rumors were true. He had stolen the family jewels from Connington's very head without the man noticing. He had killed Ser Morak, the greatest swordsman from the nation of Ker (though whether fairly or not was under constant debate). To a man like that, what were a few walls or a door?

Gerand put down his glass and started pacing the room. He wished his wife were there, but he had sent her away, and not to their small estate. Deep in the southern district he owned a modest jewelry shop, and he had instructed her to hide there for the next two days. Now he wondered if that would be safe. Sure, they had some guards, enough to deter any regular thieves and cutpurses... but Thren?

"Damn it," said Gerand, striking the top of his dresser. "He's a man, not a ghost. Walls and doors mean the same to him as any other man."

Strong, angry words, but they did little to calm him. Therefore he walked over to his bed and pulled his rapier off its wall-stand. Holding the cold hilt in his hand, he felt a little better. Perhaps he wasn't as good as Ser Morak, but he was a fine bladesman in his own right. At least he might die fighting instead of gagging on poisoned food.

The hours crawled by, the night slowly deepening. Gerand read when he could calm himself enough to focus, his rapier across his legs as he turned the pages. Other times he looped the weapon through a few stances, trying to remember the last time he'd sparred. It had been a year or two, he decided, and that was a year or two too many. He'd have to find a partner, and a good one. Perhaps Antonil Copernus, the guard captain, would suffice...

A knock on his door sent Gerand spinning, his blade cutting air. When he realized the door was still closed, and no specter had come for him, he felt incredibly foolish. He slid his rapier into his belt and put his hand on the handle.

"Who is there?" he asked.

The door blasted inward, wrenching his hand. The solid oak slammed his forehead. As he fell he tried to draw his blade, but then his back smacked atop the small chest at the foot of his bed. The rapier clattered uselessly along the stone floor. He reached for it only to have a heavy boot slam atop his fingers.

"Get up," said a voice. Rough hands grabbed the back of his clothes, yanking him to his feet and then flinging him into his chair. Clutching his wounded hand to his chest, Gerand got his first good look at his attackers. One was a woman with raven hair tied back. The other was most certainly Thren Felhorn. Gerand had never met the man before, but he'd both heard and read many descriptions.

The woman drew one of many throwing daggers from her belt and twirled it in her fingers while Thren shut the door to the crowded room. When Gerand's eyes flitted over to the rapier, the woman threw her dagger, piercing the chair so close to his skin it cut the cloth of his robe. She shook her head at him but said nothing.

Thren gently pushed the woman out of the way and then stood before Gerand with his arms crossed. He frowned down at Gerand. Death was in his eyes.

"Do you know who I am?" Thren asked.

"I do," Gerand said, doing his best to sound brave. How many times had he belittled Thren to the other nobles, even the king? He took every word back. Gods damn it all, where were his guards?

"Do you know why I'm here?" Thren asked.

Again Gerand nodded.

"I believe I do," he said.

"Kayla, could you hand me his rapier, please?"

The woman retrieved the sword and handed it hilt-first to Thren.

"Thank you," Thren said as he quickly inspected the blade. "Solid craftsmanship, if a bit on the self-indulgent side. A man could live for a month on what this single ruby in the hilt would fetch him. I've known of you for some time, Crold. Your family line has been as decadent and pointless as the hilt of your rapier. Always aspiring to be bootlickers and ass kissers, never to be leaders."

Thren drew one of his short swords and held it in front of Gerand's face.

"You see this?" he asked. "Plain, but well made. Nothing

beyond the necessary. You have forgotten you are a tool, Gerand Crold, and nothing more. To pretend to be something else can lead to... dangerous circumstances. Tell me, my dear advisor to the king, which would you rather be pierced by: my short sword, or your rapier?"

Gerand glanced between the two blades.

"My rapier," he said.

"A good choice," said Thren before stabbing Gerand in the chest with it. He made sure to hit nothing vital, just the meat near the shoulder. Gerand choked down his pain as blood spilled across the violet of his robes.

"People will always fear me over you," said Thren. "That is why I am more powerful than you, more powerful than the Trifect, more powerful than even the king. I will not have you interfering in my affairs. You play games, I deal in blood, and my son is not one of your pieces!"

Son! thought Gerand. *He's here because of his son? Not his plan for the Kensgold?*

The blood drained from Gerand's face. Suddenly there were multiple reasons for Thren to kill him. He hoped the torture would not last long.

"He looks like he's going to pass out," Kayla said.

Thren twisted the rapier, flaring pain in all directions throughout Gerand's body.

"I should kill you," Thren said. "But I won't. You are too useful to me where you are. I want the Trifect humiliated. You are in a position to do that for me, Gerand. Your word is the king's word in all stately matters. Do you understand what I'm telling you?"

Gerand nodded.

"I understand," he said. "I hold no allegiance to the Trifect. I can do as you ask."

Thren chuckled.

"You can, but will you? Once I'm gone, how do I know you'll keep your word?"

"Hostages work wonders," said Kayla, right on cue.

They both paused so Gerand could understand the meaning of their words. The advisor looked back and forth between them, the whole while his heart sinking.

"You have Martha," he said.

"So he can think after all," said Kayla.

"I have not taken her yet," Thren said as he pulled the rapier out of Gerand's chest. He acted as if he were about to sheath it, then instead pushed its bloodied tip against Gerand's throat. "But I know where you hid her. I'll have eyes on her every day until the Kensgold ends. You try anything, to sneak her out, or bring extra guards, and I'll make you suffer. You do as I say, or I'll make sure every member of my guild has a turn with her. Doesn't matter how hard you try to hide her, or protect her. In time she will be ours. Have I made myself clear?"

"Perfectly clear," Gerand said in a voice suddenly grown raspy and weak.

"Your orders are simple," Kayla said as Thren backed off and tossed the rapier atop the bed. "The flood of mercenaries for the Kensgold should be arriving any day now, if they haven't already. Among them will be massive caravans of wine, food, and dancers. Tax them all. Heavily."

"But the Trifect will be..."

Gerand stopped, realizing how stupid his complaint was. Kayla caught it and laughed.

"That's the point," she said. "Everyone they hire will demand more to compensate for the tax. Next, you will pass a law forbidding more than fifty mercenaries to be gathered together in any one area, event, or function."

"Call it an attempt to secure peace," Thren chipped in.

"Make it clear you'll fine the mercenaries themselves," Kayla said. "Keep them worried about their pockets."

"I will do what I can," Gerand insisted. "Though it won't be easy."

"Third," said Kayla, "and most importantly, the Trifect has hundreds of merchants in their employ that have not paid their taxes. That money is instead going to the mercenaries, and for years you have turned a blind eye. That stops."

"I'll collect from them what I can," Gerand said.

Thren shook his head.

"I don't want them taxed. I want them arrested."

"Arrested? What for?" When Thren reached for the rapier again, Gerand paled. "Very well. Tax evasion is a serious crime. Most will plead out and pay their fines within a day or two. Will that suffice?"

"That'll do," said Kayla. "When the Kensgold ends, we'll leave her be."

"I'll even give my word to never again threaten harm to her," Thren said. "But only if you cooperate. Is that clear?"

It was.

Kayla slid open his door and looked out. When she saw no guards, she pulled her gray hood over her head and beckoned for Thren. Just before the guildmaster left, he knelt close and whispered into Gerand's ear.

"I won't kill you. I'll chain you to the wall in a cell, your wife's body in front of you. Once I cut off your eyelids, you'll watch her rot until she's nothing but bones. Pass the laws, and make sure you *enforce* them."

Kayla dashed out the door, and Thren followed.

CHAPTER

20

Once Gran calmed down she finally offered to listen to what the young thief had to say. Of course, that was only after her attempt to beat him with a pan had failed, and he'd knocked her into a chair.

"Please listen," he said once she quit shouting for help. Delysia stood at her side, stroking her hand and doing her best to reassure her.

"You stole into my house, killed a man, hid from the guards, and then expect me to sit still and listen?" Gran asked. "Even for a young pup, you're a fool."

"Gran," whined Delysia.

"Oh all right. What is it, boy?"

"His name is Haern," Delysia said.

"Fine. *Haern.*" Gran spat the word out as if it were a curse. "What do you have to say?"

"Delysia is not safe in the city," Haern said. He leaned

against the pantry door. Pieces of dry leaves stuck to his outfit from when he had brushed a hanging tomato plant in the dark. He held one of the two candles Delysia had lit; Gran held the other.

"No one's safe in the city anymore. Why is Delysia any different?"

"Thren Felhorn of the Spider Guild ordered her father dead," Haern said. He kept his eyes on Gran, as if ashamed to look at the girl but too proud to stare at the floor. "I was there when it happened."

"You mean you were to take part," Gran said. "I'm not daft. Look at the colors you're wearing: thief guild colors. What were you, a spotter? Were you to watch for the guards, or just loot her poor father's corpse after everyone was gone?"

Haern slammed a fist against the pantry door. The motion knocked one of the leaves free from his sleeve, and Delysia watched it fall to the floor.

"It doesn't matter," Haern said. "The man I killed was sent to finish the job. With him dead, Thren will send another, and another, until the job is finished. He doesn't leave things undone. Delysia needs to get out, as fast and secretly as possible."

"I think he's right, Gran," said Delysia.

"Of course you do," Gran said dismissively. "You're a young girl ready to believe any story a boy tells you. What if he's wrong, and Thren had nothing to do with your father's death?"

"You know damn well the Spider Guild is responsible," Haern said.

"You watch your tongue with me, boy, or I'll wash it out with lye!" snapped Gran.

To both their surprise, Haern shifted from foot to foot and lowered his head.

"Sorry," he said.

"Well, at least you have some manners," said Gran. "Though I'm worried that you're right. That horrible murder in the street was bad enough; having a thief break in is just as bad. I may be old, but I've kept enough wits to know that wasn't a coincidence."

"Where can we go?" asked Delysia. She looked close to tears. Given how horrible her day had been, Gran couldn't blame her.

"There's no *we* in this, child," the old woman said. "As much as it pains me to say it, we have to put you where not even the sneakiest of thieves can get you. Your father was well respected by the priests of Ashhur. I'm sure if I asked, they would accept you into their care. Once inside their white walls, you'll be dead to the world for as long as you're there."

Delysia sniffed.

"But what about Tarlak? Will I ever see him again?"

Gran pulled her close and kissed her cheek. "I'm sure you will. Your brother's off safe with that wizard teacher of his. Now we need to make sure you stay safe, otherwise he might find me and turn me into a mudskipper for letting something happen to his dear little sister."

"I don't want to leave you," she said. Gran gently shook her head.

"I don't want to leave you either, but I've already lost my son. I couldn't bear to see Dezrel lose you as well. I'm old, and you've got no mother to watch after you. The priests and priestesses will give you a good home. I promise."

Delysia returned the kiss, then turned. There was no one there, just a half-closed pantry door. Haern was gone.

"An odd boy," Gran said. "I hope he keeps his mouth shut about where you're going."

"I trust him," Delysia insisted.

"Trust him? Hah." Gran laughed until she coughed. "You probably love him too. Dashing, mysterious boy in a mask. Every damsel wants one of them to come sneaking in through their bedchamber window."

Delysia scrunched her face and poked Gran in the side. When Gran poked back, they both broke into laughs.

"It's good to see you smile," Gran said. "I'll have that one last laugh to keep with me for the end of my days. Now go pack up your things. Not much, now, just what you can carry. I dare not wait a minute longer before bringing you to the temple."

Gran watched her hurry back into their bedroom. Gran's face became a sorrowful mask, her lip quivering and her eyes wet. When Delysia returned, her arms full of dresses, Gran smiled away her tears, hid them with a laugh, and then led her granddaughter out the door and away.

Pelarak was furious. For two days he had waited for Zusa and her faceless to return with Alyssa, and for two days he had not heard a word. He hurried through his morning sermon. He never lost his place or misquoted a scripture, but his mind was elsewhere and his faithful knew it. Anger crept into his words, and his call for penance and the destruction of chaos was particularly moving. Afterward he knelt before the great statue of Karak, letting the purple light bathe him.

"Something troubles you," said a man as he joined him on his knees.

"The world is a troublesome place," said Pelarak. He opened his eyes, and then smiled when he realized who was with him.

"Ethric, so good to see you!" Pelarak stood and hugged the man. "Your arrival here is so well-timed Karak himself must have had a hand in it."

Ethric smiled. He was a tall man, and the only reason Pelarak could throw his arms around his shoulders was that Ethric had remained on his knees. He still wore his dark black plate mail, having arrived so recently he'd had no time to remove it. A two-handed blade hung from a sheath on his back. He was completely shaven. Across his bald head and face were a myriad of tattoos dyed in a dark purple ink. They looped and curled in an ill pattern.

"Your priests make their way to Ker less and less," said Ethric. His voice was rich and pleasant to the ear. "Carden hurried me off to see how things were going. The troubles between the Trifect and the guilds have lasted so long we've heard of it all the way across the rivers."

"Come," Pelarak said. "Are you hungry? Join me in a meal."

Deep in the recesses of the temple was a rectangular room bare of decorations. A long table stretched along the center with wooden stools for seats. A mere look from Pelarak sent the staff running, young priests still in training in their devotion to Karak.

"It is hard remembering you were such as these boys," Pelarak said. "I've seen so many grow up and take their armor or their robes. Many aspire to greatness, but so few reach it."

"I wonder which I will be," said Ethric as he sat opposite him at the table.

"A dark paladin every pup of Ashhur learns to fear, if Karak is kind," Pelarak said.

Children surrounded them, carrying bowls, spoons, and a large pot of soup. Once they were served, both bowed their heads and prayed silently for near a minute. Ethric dug in afterward with a healthy appetite, while Pelarak only sipped occasionally.

"I must confess, I come here with reasons beyond your warm

words and food," Ethric said when his bowl was half finished. "Though Karak knows I needed both. Haven't had a solid meal since the Stronghold, and that feels like a thousand miles away after so many months of travel."

"Did you encounter any trouble on the road?"

"A foolish brat thought he could slay me to earn admittance to the Citadel." Ethric chuckled. "I'd hardly call that trouble, though. More of a nuisance. I was almost to Kinamn, where the pathway winds through all those rocky hills. Imbecile was hiding among the rocks shooting arrows whenever he thought I wasn't looking. I'm sure he planned a more heroic tale for when he brought my head to the Citadel doors."

"At least he had more fight in him than Ashhur's paladins have had as of late," Pelarak said, dropping his spoon. "Though I fear we have too much of that fight in our own ranks here in Veldaren."

"Which is why I am here," insisted Ethric. "You told Carden you were troubled. Tell me what it is so I may scorch it with fire and cut it with blade."

"Do you know of the faceless?" asked Pelarak.

Ethric furrowed his brow as he thought.

"No," he said. "I've not heard of them."

"Come," Pelarak said as he stood. "Let me show you."

He led him into the deep recesses of the temple, down a flight of stairs, and into a large but cramped storage room. Crates were piled this way and that, huddled against the walls or the many pillars that supported the ceiling. Pelarak lifted his hand. Purple fire surrounded his fingers, giving them light.

"About two hundred years ago the priests of Ashhur succeeded in a massive conversion of our brethren. It was then that our presence in Veldaren weakened, and our kind were banished from the city. We fought them bitterly, as you can imagine, and with heavy hearts. A score of priests repented, sneaking away from Ashhur's temple and throwing themselves at our temple doors in Kinamn."

The whole time he talked, Pelarak led them through the maze of old armor, racks of swords, crates of cloth, and jars upon jars of food. He stopped, scratched his chin as he thought, then turned toward a stack of paintings propped against each other. Each of them was rectangular, the length of a man lying on his side.

"We tested their faith," Pelarak said as he looked through the paintings. Even though his hand swirled with purple fire, it did not burn the material. "Those that lived were admitted into the priesthood, but not entirely. The high priest at the time was a brilliant man named Theron Gemcroft."

"I know of him," Ethric said, watching the elaborately framed paintings flip forward one after another. He saw mostly portraits of former high priests, though among them were scenes of warfare, battles between angels of Karak and Ashhur, and even serene depictions of nature. "Forfeited his fortune to devote his life to Karak? Carden was particularly fond of his sayings, and used them often in his sermons."

"How is that old goat?" Pelarak asked.

"Hard as nails and brutal as a mailed fist," Ethric said with a small smile. "What are we looking for, my priest?"

"This," Pelarak said as he lifted up one of the paintings. Ethric grabbed a corner to help. Together they held the picture and stared. It showed seven men and women, their bodies wrapped in black cloth. Only their eyes were visible through cuts in the wrapping. They held daggers, staves, and swords in hands hidden by waves of shadow that rolled off their bodies like smoke from a fire. At their feet lay over twenty dead paladins of Ashhur.

"Well painted, if a bit overdramatic," Ethric said.

"They are the faceless," Pelarak said, his eyes going distant. "Theron knew that to welcome the traitors back without penalty could weaken us. He also knew that their devotion could be of great use, but only if the traitor-priests were forever reminded of their failure. So he wrapped them in cloth and ordered them to never reveal their skin until the end of their days. They slept separate from the rest, dined away from the rest, and eventually attended their own sermons."

"This is fascinating, Pelarak, but I'd swear you had a point. I'd love to be patient, but it is too damn cold down here, and the warmth of your soup is wearing thin."

Pelarak laughed, but his voice lacked any mirth.

"My point is that we do not actively recruit faceless. They are a punishment, not an honor. We have only three now, women who let their sex control their actions. Their faith in Karak, however, remained strong. So we put them separate from us, let them live and operate outside the temple. For years they remained obedient, performing tasks to further the cause of Karak. But now..."

"They've done something," Ethric said, figuring where the story was going. He looked at the seven in the painting, their bodies bathed in blood and darkness. "They've gone feral, haven't they?"

"Putting our entire temple in danger," Pelarak said as he clutched the painting with his burning hand. "This spat between the Trifect and the thieves benefits no one, certainly not us. We gain nothing siding with either, and only risk revealing ourselves to the public at large. This cannot happen. Yet they have acted out on their own, struck against a lord of the Trifect, all while telling me lies and half-truths. Now one comes to me, seeking to increase their number, as if it were a privilege to be a faceless. Too many times I have given them orders, only to watch them be disregarded entirely."

"You want them killed," Ethric said. It was not a question.

"I do," Pelarak said. The fire on his hand changed from purple to red. The painting began to burn. "I want their bodies sacrificed before the statue of Karak. Their very order is one of shame and disobedience, and now they have gone too far to be useful any longer. What good is a servant that will not obey? These three faceless sisters have a captive by the name of Alyssa Gemcroft. She was supposed to be brought here, to be placed under our watch, but instead Zusa and her sisters have kept her hidden. Find the faceless women and kill them. Alyssa *must* remain alive. All our plans mean nothing otherwise."

Ethric watched as the fire spread across the painting, not at all bothered by the smoke that washed over his face. When the flame reached his bare hand, he flexed his arm. Black fire swarmed over his fingers. The frame broke, crumbling into ash in his fingers. In one giant whoosh, the painting and its frame were consumed. As the ash rained down to the floor, Ethric drew his sword and made his vow.

"Until my death, I will hunt them," he whispered. "No child of Karak is greater than his master."

CHAPTER 21

Privacy was something Alyssa found she could rarely obtain, but despite all their food and supplies, Yoren still liked to hunt. It was then she could be alone, and she cherished those opportunities. That morning, like most others, he went off with his bow to prove his abilities and come back with yet another animal he could boast of slaying. That morning Alyssa fled to the far edge of the camp, racing around the bottom of a nearby hill so that she could not be seen even by their guards.

A small stream flowed near the bottom, barely more than ankle-deep as it ran toward the nearby Kinel River. Into its water Alyssa stared, glad she could not see her reflection due to the mud. No doubt she would have seen the circles around her eyes, angry red veins filling the whites.

"Do you miss me?" she whispered, thinking of Maynard in his giant, empty mansion. "Do you miss me, Daddy?"

Yoren had convinced her that he didn't. That she'd been sent to John Gandrem's to be out of the way, to wait like a good girl while the men did their business. And she'd believed it. She splashed the water with her hands, disrupting whatever reflection she could see. The cold clung to her fingers, and she held them against her dress to dry them off. That hand brushed the dagger she still kept with her, and for the first time she thought to use it not on Yoren, but on herself instead.

"It's not safe to hide beyond sight of Theo's guards," a voice said behind her. Alyssa flinched, fingers tightening around her dagger, and then she relaxed.

"Why is that, Zusa?" she asked. She'd finally learned to identify all the faceless women by their voices. It was either that, or constantly look like a fool asking the name of whomever she was speaking to.

Alyssa glanced back and saw the woman standing with her arms crossed, covered face staring at her. At least, Alyssa thought she was staring at her. The daylight reflected off the thin white cloth, making it impossible to peer through it. How Zusa could see at all baffled her.

"Something might happen to you," Zusa said. She hesitated a moment, then took a seat beside Alyssa before the stream. "Something unfortunate."

"I'd see any bandits coming for miles," Alyssa said, gesturing to the grasslands beyond.

"You act as if I speak of threats beyond the Kulls' own camp. It is Yoren who might do something unfortunate should he fear you attempting to flee."

Alyssa swallowed, and she stared into the water in hopes of keeping the strange woman from reading her reaction.

"Why would he think I'd be fleeing? He is my love, after all."

At this Zusa let out a laugh. It was so rough, so sudden, that Alyssa jumped.

"Yes, yes. Of course. Your true love. That is why you flinch just before he touches you at night. That is why you smile when he looks at you, yet never before, and never after his eyes leave your face. Yoren may be a fool, Alyssa, but do not treat me as such, nor my sisters."

Alyssa felt her neck turning red. Was she really so terrible at hiding how she felt? Or was the other woman just that good at reading people? Seeing that masked face, that aura of danger that settled around Zusa as comfortably as the gray cloak she wore, Alyssa dared hope it was the latter. She tried to decide how to continue their conversation, if at all. Yoren and Theo were the faceless women's employers. Yet she seemed to speak only with contempt of Yoren . . .

"Forgive me, then," Alyssa said. "Sometimes we must share a bed for reasons other than love."

"Such as?"

"Power. Safety. Respect."

"If you think Yoren gives you any of that, then you are as big a fool as he. Come back to the camp, Alyssa. I'd hate to see you punished needlessly."

Zusa reached out, grabbing her arm. Alyssa refused, instead pulling away and glaring.

"I am no fool either!" she said. "What else am I to do? My father will have banished me, blaming me for the attempt on his life you damn women made. I was once heiress to one of the most powerful families in all of Dezrel. Yet what am I now? Nothing but a warm place for the cock of a fat, disgusting tax collector's son. I know he would use me, but one day he'll learn just how wrong he was to ever dare to do so."

Zusa stood there, arm still holding her. Alyssa met her unseen stare, not caring anymore, not willing to keep up the act. She was alone, damn it, this was supposed to be her tiny sliver of solitude.

Slowly the wrapped fingers released her.

"Alyssa..." Zusa started to say, then paused. "What if... what if I were not in the Kulls' employ?"

Alyssa swallowed, remained silent.

"What if," Zusa continued, sitting down cross-legged before her. "What if the only reason we serve is to bring land into Karak's possession, land currently owned by the Gemcroft family?"

"Land promised to you after my father was dead," Alyssa said, easily piecing it together. "Land promised to you after I was wed to Yoren."

"Land you could promise to us as well."

Alyssa shook her head.

"I can make no promises, Zusa. You have to know that. Even if I could somehow convince my father to take me back and accept me, I cannot guarantee he would give up any land to Karak's temple. You tried to kill him, and Maynard is not so forgiving."

"What if your father were no longer alive?"

Alyssa dug her fingers into the dirt beside her.

"No," she said. "No. Then you are no better than Yoren and his shit-eating snake of a father. Go back to camp if that is all you can offer me. I want to be alone."

Zusa stood, her cloak rustling as it folded around her, hiding her slender form.

"I know you keep a dagger in your dress," she said, just before leaving. "You will have only one chance to use it. Just one. But know there are two types of mercenaries. There are those who work only for coin, and those who think for themselves."

"And which are you?"

"We are the best of the best, Alyssa."

She waited until Zusa crested the hill, then ran. Her feet

were bare, and they sloshed through the mud of the stream easily enough. She held her skirt up high as she could, but still the muddy waters splashed across it. No turning back, she thought as she rushed along the other side. Everyone wanted her father dead, wanted her to pledge power she didn't deserve to people who had not earned it. Enough was enough. She would rather risk the wild, rather go to her father and throw herself at his feet and beg for mercy, muddy dress and all.

Alyssa looked back once, saw Zusa watching her from atop the hill, and swore.

Whatever distance she'd made suddenly seemed irrelevant. Her legs pumped as she flew across the grasslands, but she'd already tried fleeing them once. The faceless were bizarre creatures, impossibly fast. Her only hope would be to lose her, but how? All around were grass and gently sloped hills. There were no trees, no buildings, no real way to hide. Her teeth clenched, she choked down her scream. Why did she have to remain? Why did the woman have to lurk and watch and ruin whatever hope she had of escape?

Barely visible in the distance she saw the Kinel River, and she wondered if she might be able to use its current to float away. Its waters would be ice, though, and she wondered if she could endure it for any length of time. Her feet, caked with mud, already were turning numb. Her breath burned in her lungs, and she ran and ran, but it did not matter. Hands touched her shoulders, a foot slipped beneath hers, and then she tumbled. She rolled along the grass, which was wet and loose from proximity to the river. Zusa followed, collapsing atop her as she sank into the cold ground.

"Why?" she nearly screamed at Zusa. "Why couldn't you just let me go?"

Zusa grabbed her shoulders and twisted, forcing Alyssa to

look at her as she pinned her to the ground. As Alyssa watched, she tore off the thin white cloth to reveal her piercing green eyes.

"Because I would have you *face* this," Zusa said. "You will not run. Running gets you a knife in the back. But a lord's daughter stands tall, dagger in hand."

"And dies stabbed in the chest," Alyssa said, feeling tears slide down the sides of her face.

"Never. No matter what happens, no matter whose bed you sleep in or what your family name becomes, I will not allow it."

Alyssa felt a lump in her throat, and she tried to swallow it down.

"Why?" she asked. "Why would you do that for me?"

Zusa stood, then offered her a hand.

"Men have twisted you, treated you as a piece in a game or a toy for a bed. I understand this far more than you can understand, Alyssa. But it will not repeat itself, not this time. Not when I have the strength to prevent it."

It took all her strength, but Alyssa reached out and accepted that hand. Pulled back to her feet, she looked about, feeling lost and dazed. What did this mean? What did it change?

"Come," Zusa said, still holding her hand. "Back to the camp, before they notice your absence."

Alyssa remained silent, daring in her heart to trust the strange woman. Upon their reaching the camp, one of the guards noticed the mud on her dress but said nothing. He might normally have asked questions, but Zusa's presence stilled his tongue. Toward Yoren's tent they went, Zusa with no apparent desire to leave Alyssa. Alyssa hoped to change clothes before Yoren returned, but instead they found him already there, sitting before a bonfire in the center of the camp. Before him was a large rabbit, its fur already peeled back.

"My dear?" Yoren said, looking up and noticing the mud and the tearing of her clothes. Alyssa thought for an answer, but was not given time.

"She slipped near the stream," Zusa said. "But do not worry, she is strong as ever." Eyes still uncovered, she looked Alyssa's way. "Isn't she?"

"Yes," Alyssa said, praying it was true, yet not willing to believe it.

Her fingers touched the dagger in her dress as Yoren resumed skinning the rabbit.

Not yet.

CHAPTER 22

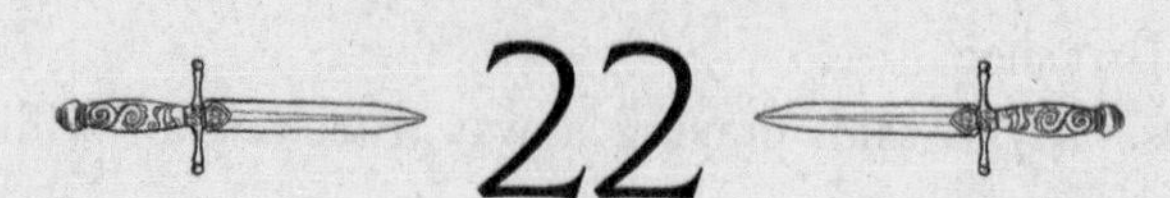

Thren hadn't felt this good in ages. So far two riots had broken out in southern Veldaren. The king's advisor had done his work well. With soldiers arresting dozens of prominent merchants, goods had been left unprotected as taxes were collected. Those who were released found their stalls and warehouses ransacked. Thren had personally burned down several. The price of the remaining goods and, most important, food, doubled and then tripled. Mercenaries flooding into the city in anticipation of the Kensgold found their employers unable to pay them. Some went away, while others...

Thren laughed. Others had eagerly joined his own guild to ensure their work with a blade received adequate pay. Those who hadn't taken up with the guild, well, they died easily enough. Given the hunger, the frustration, the gouging of customers, the poor southern section of Veldaren was all too eager to let its anger loose. It wouldn't be long before the hungry and destitute made their way north into the rest of the city. If Thren's spies outside the walls were correct, Laurie Keenan and his family would be making their grand return to the city sometime that afternoon. Hunger riots, jobless sellswords, and overeager castle soldiers demanding taxes were one fantastic greeting.

Laurie would get the message immediately: Thren controlled the city, not he. If everything went according to plan, the slaughter during the Kensgold would send an even stronger message.

"Sir," shouted Kayla, hurrying after him. He was on his way to his son's room, wanting the boy to accompany him on a routine collection of protection money from the merchants still active amid the riots. Given the circumstances, he was certain they'd be eager for all the protection they could get.

"I am no sir," Thren said as he turned. "I am no knight, and no noble."

"Sorry," Kayla said as she slowed to a walk. "I'm not sure what to say that would be seen as respectful."

Thren gave her a look of honest confusion.

"What could be more respectful than my own name?" he asked.

"Right," Kayla said. "Anyway, we still have no word from Will."

"He's been gone far too long," Thren said as he resumed his walk down the hall. "Taking Gerand's wife shouldn't have been difficult, not for someone as skilled as him. I doubt any mercenaries could capture him, not alive anyway. If Will is in hiding, he has a reason, and I'm sure he'll..."

He opened the door to his son's room and took a step inside. Aaron was on his knees, his hands clasped together underneath his chin. His elbows rested on the side of his bed. His eyes were closed, though they snapped open at Thren's sudden entrance.

Thren's jaw dropped. Hanging from a silver chain looped around Aaron's fingers was a golden pendant of Ashhur.

Before anyone could react, Thren slammed the door shut, spun, and struck Kayla with his fist. As she slumped to the ground, he shouted for his men. The mansion was large, but even so, gray cloaks rushed toward him in seconds.

"Where's Senke?" he shouted as the men stared with a mixture of confusion and curiosity at Kayla slumped on the floor, holding her cheek with a stony expression upon her face.

"Here," Senke said, pushing his way to the front of the men.

"Find Cregon," Thren said. "I'll need his spells. And you two," he said, pointing, "find Robert Haern and bring him to my room. Kayla too. I want them bound tight."

Thren reopened the door to Aaron's room. Aaron sat on the bed. The amulet lay beside him, as if he knew hiding it would be a pointless gesture. Thren stepped inside, grabbed the amulet, and then beckoned to his son to follow.

Aaron walked down the halls a step behind his father, feeling his heart race. His stomach roiled as he tried to think of what punishment awaited him. Robert had given him the pendant. Kayla had encouraged him to rebel. There was also the matter of Delysia and Dustin. While he had run off to protect Delysia, Thren had sent for him. So far he had not demanded an explanation for his absence. Now it looked like the matter would soon explode in his face.

"Keep your mouth shut until I ask you a question," Thren said as they walked.

If there was anything Aaron was good at, it was keeping silent. He nodded.

They took a long, looping path toward Thren's room. Aaron

realized his father was buying time, most likely wanting whatever he had ordered prepared ready by the time they entered. The thought was hardly comforting. He felt like throwing up. He'd made a mistake, a stupid one at that. Only twice before had he prayed to Ashhur, and both times he'd felt a combination of silliness and embarrassment. Afterward he'd remembered the way Delysia had prayed when he stood unseen before her. Whatever he was doing was not the same, he felt it in his gut.

So he'd tried again, this time because he'd heard no word either way on whether or not she'd lived. And now he might have endangered her life. If Thren tortured him, he'd talk. He held no delusions about that. Once Thren knew where she was, she would die. Gods damn it all, how could he have messed up so badly?

"Remember, I do this for your own good," Thren said when they finally arrived at his room. Two men stood guard before it, bowing respectfully as they passed through.

Inside the room Senke had cleared away the chairs of the table. Robert Haern knelt at one end. Kayla knelt on the other, a large bruise spreading across her cheek. Senke stood between them, his hands on the hilts of his swords. A heavyset man leaned against the bedpost of the extravagant bed, his arms crossed. He was sweating, often wiping his face with his hands. Aaron had seen him rarely, but the fat man was hard to forget. He was Cregon, a mage who had long been in the employ of his father.

"Stand here," Thren ordered, pointing beside Senke. When the guildmaster walked over to Cregon and began talking, Senke whispered down to Aaron.

"What the fuck did you do?" he asked.

"I prayed," Aaron whispered back.

"Shit," Senke said, then clammed up. Thren was returning with the mage.

"Stay still," Cregon said, his voice thin and reedy. "All of you. If my concentration breaks, I won't be able to try again until tomorrow."

Aaron entertained shouting out a bizarre stream of cuss-words to disrupt the mage, but decided otherwise. Instead he watched Cregon cast his spell. The man was a poor mage, in both money and abilities, hence his easy recruitment into the Spider Guild many years ago. He spent most of his days sequestered apart from the rest of the men, reading books and pretending to advance his skills while in reality doing his best to drink the days away.

Arcane words of power passed through Cregon's lips, sounding clunky and odd. Aaron had little experience with spellcasters, but he thought their casting should sound more fluent and natural than what he heard.

Cregon abruptly stopped and wiped his sweating brow. Aaron felt a slight tingle shoot up his back, as if someone were rubbing him with flower petals.

"There. The spell is in place," said Cregon.

"Excellent," Thren said. "Leave us to our business."

The mage looked happy to oblige. Once he left, it was just the five of them. Thren paced before them all, the icy fury of his face gradually growing.

"Kayla, Robert, I brought you both here because of certain actions by my son. I know the rest of my men well, but you two are new to my home. Too long I have turned a blind eye. No longer. Senke, draw your sword."

Senke did as he was told.

"There is a spell over all of you," Thren continued. "When

you talk, the spell will silence any lies. I will hear only truth on these matters."

"Even me?" asked Senke, a wry grin on his face.

"Test for yourself," said Thren. Senke shrugged. He said something. Aaron read a few of the words on his lips, *virgin* being one of them, but heard not a sound.

"I'll take that as a yes," Senke said.

Thren paced before his two prisoners as everyone watched him.

"Who gave Aaron the amulet?" he asked. For a moment no one spoke. Then Robert glanced upward.

"I did," he said.

"I thought as much. You are a teacher, and as with many teachers, you took your desire to impart knowledge too far." Thren tossed the amulet he held aside. "If it had been just this, I would have only given you a warning. But instead there is the matter of Delius and his daughter."

At this, Aaron's heart sank. So the truth would come out. None of them could tell a lie. He'd risked everything, and for nothing. His own life might be forfeit for killing a fellow guild member. Thren glared at him, and Aaron averted his eyes.

"You should have killed her when Kayla killed Delius, but instead she somehow escaped. I now see hesitance where I once saw inexperience. I see mercy where I once saw misjudgment. One of you planted these horrible ideas in my son's head. I want to know who."

Neither Kayla nor Robert said a word.

"Keep silent, then," Thren said as he paced. "It is better than lies. I sent Dustin after Delysia, yet he and the girl vanish like ghosts in the barrows. Few knew where Dustin was going. You were one of them, Kayla. So what happened? Did my son come sniveling, crying to you for help?"

All three of the accused remained silent.

"Answer me!" shouted Thren. "Whoever killed Dustin dies tonight. Now I will hear a name from one of your lips!"

Aaron's eyes flicked between the two of them. He could spare them. If he admitted to requesting information about Dustin, demanding it really, perhaps he'd spare Kayla's life. The same went for his teacher. It was Aaron who'd come to them. Surely his father would understand that? He opened his mouth to speak, but Kayla spoke first.

"I know who must have killed him," she said. The fact that Aaron heard her meant she spoke the truth. He felt his heart drop into his gut. Kayla glanced over to Robert, and Aaron swore he saw a tiny nod of approval.

"Who?" asked Thren.

"It was Haern."

Silence filled the room. Aaron looked to his teacher, a cry of denial on his lips, but Robert's stern glare kept him quiet. He realized then what was going on. The old man would die to protect the young. Hot rage pulsed through his veins.

Thren turned to Robert, his eyes cold steel.

"Did you somehow arrange for Dustin's death?" he asked.

Robert remained silent.

"Did you teach my son about Ashhur?" he asked.

Robert remained silent.

"Did you make his heart weak with words of compassion and mercy?" he asked.

Silence.

"Aaron," Thren said, pushing Senke aside and taking his short sword. He held the hilt toward his son. With a shaking hand, Aaron accepted the offered blade. He felt strong hands take his shoulders and guide him before his teacher. Robert knelt, his arms tied behind his back. Tears were in his eyes.

"I don't want to," Aaron said. All there heard.

"I will suffer none to betray me," Thren said. "Kill him. Let his blood cover your hands so you know the price of weakness. Dabble in betrayal, dabble in death. Now do as you're told."

He looked once more to his teacher. Impossible as it seemed, the old man was smiling.

"I forgive you," Robert said. "Now do it."

No lie. Aaron couldn't believe it. Forgiveness before the sin was even committed, unasked, undeserved. As he held the short sword, he felt Aaron dying. To kill his teacher for a truthful lie spoken by Kayla, all to save his own life...

He swung the blade. Warm blood splashed across his arms. Robert gagged twice, his windpipe cut, then slumped over and died.

"Well done, Aaron," Thren said.

"Haern," the boy whispered back. Thren did not understand the importance of hearing that single word spoken aloud, but Kayla did.

"I'll clean up the body," Senke offered.

"No," said Thren as he took the sword from Aaron's hand. "My son made the mess. Let him clean it up."

Senke untied Kayla's hands and helped her to her feet. She rubbed her raw wrists while watching the guildmaster from the corner of her eye. Thren reached out and touched her face with his fingers.

"Forgive me for the blow," he said to her. "I struck in anger and false assumption. Robert's time alone with him was clearly ill spent."

Kayla was wise enough to keep her mouth shut.

"Come," Thren said, walking beside Kayla as if nothing were the matter. "I want to make sure Laurie's entrance to Veldaren is as memorable as possible."

They left Senke alone with Aaron, who remained standing before the body. He felt dumb struck, and was on the verge of tears.

"I have nothing to clean up the blood with," he said, his voice oddly distant. Senke tried to laugh, but it came out more as a choked cough.

"There's a closet in the corner with a bunch of spare sheets. You can use one of them."

Aaron obeyed, moving in a stiff, methodical manner. Senke watched him, all the while rubbing his fingers across the front of his chest.

"I've had sex with a horse," he said as Aaron walked back. Aaron paused, but Senke laughed again, his face flushing a pale shade of red.

"Just testing the spell," Senke said. "Clearly it's worn off."

"Clearly."

Aaron knelt and began mopping up the blood. He kept his eyes straight down, afraid of seeing the body. The sight of it seemed so . . . wrong.

"Listen," Senke said as he knelt down. "That was a special man, and an old one too. He was ready to go, and I don't think he was too upset with you about it, all right? I know how much pressure Thren's putting on you. He wants you to replace him one day, and to be a name the whole world fears."

"I don't want the world to fear me," Aaron whispered. "I want them to love Haern."

"Haern?" asked Senke. "I'm not sure I . . ."

Aaron glanced up at him, his stare hard and full of killing. Senke's mouth dropped open.

"It's strange an old man could kill someone like Dustin," he said carefully. "It'd have to be someone younger. Someone who could slip out without being noticed . . ."

Aaron swallowed, returned to wiping away the mess.

"I could get killed for this," Senke said as he stood. He glanced around, as if looking for spies listening in on their conversation. "Fuck me like a Kerran whore. You're Haern. You took a new name."

At Aaron's icy look, Senke broke out into nervous laughter.

"Up, down, and sideways, as our dear Kayla likes to say. I know grown men who would have crumbled and confessed sooner than you did, boy. How old are you again?"

Aaron ignored the question, focusing instead on mopping up the rest of the blood. Senke saw the sheet he held was completely soaked so he retrieved another. He tossed it over Robert's body, shaking his head as his grin faded.

"We've all got secrets, Aaron," Senke said as he rubbed his chest again. "Some we tell, and some we keep hidden. Yours must stay hidden. Do you understand that? If anyone finds out what you did, they'll go to Thren in a heartbeat. I don't want to imagine your father's fury. He'll kill everyone who knew about it, including me and Kayla. I don't know about you, but I'm quite happy with living, and would like to continue doing so for the next couple of decades."

"I don't see a way out," Aaron said as Senke tucked the sheets around the body. "And what was the point? I prayed, and people died. Hardly mercy. Ashhur's not even real. He's... he's just a fucking dream."

Senke *tsk*ed at him.

"Such language," he said as he knelt down. He looked to the door, as if expecting it to bang open at any moment. Just in case, he put his back to it and acted as if he were busy wrapping the body. While Aaron watched, he pulled out a small medallion of the Golden Mountain from underneath his leather armor.

"I'm not the most faithful," Senke said as Aaron's eyes widened in shock. "I treat it more like a good-luck charm than anything else. Doing what we do makes prayer hard sometimes, you know? But whatever you want to say, or want to learn, I'll do my best. I might be signing my death warrant, but if you need help with girls, love, or faith, you can rely on me. You're a good kid, Aaron. I'm not proud of all I do, but it's better than what I did before joining the Spider Guild."

Aaron stopped scrubbing, seeing that whatever blood was in the carpet wasn't going anywhere through his meager efforts. He tossed the wet crimson sheet on top of Robert's body, glad that his head was covered. He didn't want to see those sad eyes staring up at him.

"Everyone needs friends," Senke said. "Even people like you and me. Thren seems determined as the Abyss to keep you from having any. Don't tell anyone, but I've been making plans to get out for a while now. Until then, you can trust me, and talk to me about anything. Understand?"

Aaron nodded.

"What do we do about the body?" he asked.

"Leave it here," Senke said. "We've done enough. I'll get a few of our lower ranks to smuggle it out one of the tunnels. I think it's time you and me got something stiff to drink."

Aaron smiled.

"Senke... thank you. You don't know how much this means to me."

Senke winked.

"Keep it to yourself, *Haern*."

CHAPTER

23

For over a mile stretched the wagon train. Some wagons were covered with dried hides and white tarps, while others were open and piled high with pumpkins, squash, and winter corn. In one wagon was a whole troop of dancers, singing and laughing at the sight of Veldaren's walls. Another two were full of hard men, their faces and hands scarred from the sellsword life. All around the wagons walked servants, cooks, highborn maidens, and lowborn camp followers. At the far end trailed a small herd of cattle and sheep, ready for butchering. When the Kensgold started, they would have fresh blood and meat for their festival.

Ahead of it all rode Laurie Keenan.

"We're bringing twice what we brought last year," said Torgar, riding next to him. "I hope you know what you're doing."

"I know more than most," Laurie said, his voice oddly soft and gentle. "Like how I know you should watch your tongue, Torgar, lest I cut it out and feed it to the ravens."

The sellsword captain laughed at his employer. Laurie was a smart man, but he was often full of idle threats and ambiguous comments. His eyes were dark, his complexion more so. Riding next to the sellsword, he seemed skinny and weak. He wore his hair long and braided, in the popular fashion of Angelport where the caravan had originated, following the highway out from the Ramere and north through the Kingstrip.

"I don't understand why we bother to return," Torgar said, ignoring the warning to watch his tongue. "This must cost you a fortune every time we make this trip. Why not make Leon and Maynard come to you? It's far safer in Angelport than Veldaren, anyway."

"Because if all three of us left Veldaren, there might not be a city to return to," Laurie said. His face was clean-shaven except for a thin strip of hair growing from the center of his chin that hung halfway down his neck. Laurie twirled it with his fingers as his caravan wound around a small hill on its way to the city's western entrance. The southern gate was closer and would have saved them a good twenty minutes of traveling, but the king had forbidden merchants from entering there. That, and being among the poor was not one of Laurie's favorite pastimes; the south was just crawling with the empty-pocketed cretins.

"A shame you can't just hire that Thren guy to work for you," Torgar said after glancing back at the caravan to make sure nothing looked amiss. "Imagine what a man like that might have done as your right-hand man."

"Trust me, I've tried," said Laurie, sounding tired of the topic. "He's a hard man to get ahold of. Most of my messengers wind up dead, at least the ones offering him the position. I think he views it as an insult."

Torgar laughed heartily.

"Only a fool would turn down working for you, milord.

Food's good, the women are fine and clean, and there's always a steady stream of idiots to kill with a sword."

"Speaking of idiots with swords," Laurie said, pointing to the western entrance. The gates were open wide, but there was a lengthy line of peasants, merchants, and mercenaries winding out from it. A thick grouping of guards was the cause.

"Did they check our things last time we came?" asked Torgar.

"That was only two years ago. Have you taken so many blows to the head that you can't remember even that far?"

Torgar kept his head shaved, and he rapped it with his knuckles and made a hollow knocking noise with his tongue.

"My ma scooped my brains out when I was four. Left just enough to swing a sword, ride a horse, and bed a woman."

Laurie chuckled.

"I think the third one occupies the most of your meager intelligence," he said. "Come. Let us find out what the fuss is about before we have a thousand people trampling each other to get through."

Torgar led, and Laurie followed. They rode around the outer edge of the line, ignoring the few angry calls from lowborn merchants and farmers. When they reached the gate, the crowd swelled in a semicircle, making their progress difficult.

"Look for a spare guard," Torgar said. "I'll see if I can pull him aside. They're bound to shit their drawers when they see our caravans coming."

Torgar looked but saw none. Sighing, he dismounted and started pushing his way through. When a man cursed him and moved to strike, Torgar grabbed the hilt of his long sword and drew it enough to reveal naked steel.

"I draw, it ain't going back in without blood on it," Torgar growled. The man, a haggard farmer with a cartload of pumpkins drawn by a donkey, paled and mumbled an apology. One of the guards, hearing the threat, pushed aside an angry woman and called out to them.

"Draw no blades, or you can sleep outside the walls tonight," the guard shouted. Torgar stood to his full height so that the guard's eyes only came up to his neck.

"Hope you brought friends," Torgar said, but his grin was playful.

"Enough, Torgar," said Laurie, following in his wake. He glanced about nervously, disliking being at such close quarters with the unwashed rabble. "Are you in charge of the gates here?"

"Just helping," the guard said. "Listen, if you're in a hurry, you'll still have to wait just like everyone else."

"I'm not like anyone else, nor will I wait like anyone else," Laurie said. He turned and pointed at the massive caravan of horses, wagons, and carts in the distance, billowing dust to the sky. "Those are mine."

"Damn, never can catch a break," the guard said. "Which ones are yours?"

"All of them."

The guard paled, and he seemed to look at Laurie with newly opened eyes. For a moment he chewed his lip, and then the connection hit him.

"Lord Keenan?" he asked. "Oh shit on me, I'm sorry, milord. I've a half-dozen merchants all pretending to own Dezrel, and I figured you just another..."

"That's fine," Laurie said, interrupting him. "What is your name, soldier?"

"Jess. Jess Brown, milord."

"Well, Jess, before I bring my convoy through the gate, I'd like to know what is going on. I take it there is some sort of tax or toll?"

"There is," Jess said, glancing once at Torgar. "Though you might not like it. King Vaelor, Ashhur bless his name, passed the laws not two days ago. There's some fines involving mercenaries, which you'll learn about soon enough. The short of it is taxes, though, on all goods and services traveling into the city."

"On *all* goods?" asked Laurie. He grabbed his long green cloak and wrapped it tighter around his shoulders, as if a bit of his heat had escaped him. "What nonsense. Tell me the taxes."

Jess did. As he ran through a memorized list, Laurie's face turned darker and darker. Torgar could see him mentally counting with the mention of each item of food and clothing, each servant and animal. By the time Jess was done, Laurie's neck had turned a deep crimson. Even Torgar could tell that such taxes would amount to a small fortune.

"All this just to enter?" Laurie asked, his quiet voice poorly hiding his anger.

"Forgive me, milord," said Jess. "Gerand Crold has been most insistent about enforcement. He's ordered any man caught turning a blind eye or accepting a bribe to be strung up from the wall by his thumbs and left to the ravens."

"I can't blame you for your orders, nor for enforcing them with such threats hanging over your head," Laurie said. He took out a single silver coin and handed it to Torgar, who then passed it on to the soldier.

"Thank you, milord. You are most generous."

"And thank you for your time," Laurie said. With a quick nod to Torgar, the two pushed their way out of the crowd and back to their horses.

"The thieves must have gotten to the king," Laurie said as he mounted his horse. "Either that or his advisor, Crold."

"More likely the advisor," Torgar said. "He's been around awhile, if my meager memory serves me well. How many kings has he seen die? Probably views himself as one. Might not be the thieves involved either, just greedy hearts knowing you was coming."

As they rode back toward their caravan, Torgar raised an eyebrow at his master.

"So...how much did it all come to, anyway?"

"Twenty times the normal fare," Laurie said with a sigh. "I know you're not the best with big numbers, so let me keep it simple. I'd be paying an entire month's worth of income just to walk through their bloody gate."

"Huh," Torgar said, guiding his horse around a giant rut in the road. "Almost makes you think twice about entering, eh?"

Laurie stopped his horse. Torgar slowed his own and then looped around, his hand on his sword.

"Something amiss?" he asked.

"Nothing," Laurie said. "But what you said, it might make a bit of sense. Look there, at the two hills we just rode beside. Couldn't we set up camp on their peaks?"

Torgar scratched the stubble on his jaw, thinking.

"Could put yours and Madelyn's things on the big hill, surround the lower parts with the wagons so it'll be easier to guard. Wouldn't be too tough to put our men in the gaps. That smaller hill could be for your servants and soldiers, ring the lower parts with tents and then build fires at the top."

"Could you guard it as well as you could our estate?" Laurie asked.

"As well?" Torgar asked. "Course not. Your mansion's got spiked fences and more traps than even I know about. Out here we'll have men and wagons. Wagons can be climbed, burned, and cut through. Men can be bought, confused, and killed. But if you're asking if you think anything could happen out here, I say no. With as many men as we'll have ringing the camp, you'll be safer than the king."

"Come then," Laurie said. "Let us tell my wife and son."

With its master gone to the gates, the rest of the caravan slowed its approach, which Madelyn Keenan was greatly thankful for. She sat in the back of the largest of the covered wagons, which was pulled by six gray oxen. Far too quickly, though, her husband returned, his vulgar sellsword captain at his side. The two followed after her wagon so they might talk.

"How did things fare at the gate?" Madelyn Keenan asked from her cushioned seat. She wore what she considered an outfit designed for travel: a tightly fitting dress with a plunging neckline. The outfit exposed her slender legs, which she had stretched out from underneath the tarp in hopes of getting what little sun she could before winter arrived in full, along with its dim light and numerous clouds. She'd tied her brown hair into a ponytail so long that it wrapped twice about her waist before clipping into her silver-leaved belt.

"The king, may Karak curse his name, imposed an outrageously high tax on all goods entering the city," Laurie said as he accepted her outstretched hand and kissed her fingers. "So it appears we must camp outside the walls."

"Must we?" asked Madelyn. "You'll deny us a roof over our heads all for a silly tax? Bribe the guards and get us through. I've heard quite enough of the serving girls bitching about the bumpy trip. I don't want to imagine how they'll whine about this."

"Guards won't take bribes," Torgar said. "King's riding them hard on this one. And if it is a roof you want, milady, we have more than enough tents for that. We'll erect you a fine pavilion to call your own."

Madelyn rolled her eyes and turned her attention back to her husband. She'd never liked the smelly sellsword, especially the way he looked at her. When it came to dress, attitude, and words, she knew how to drive men wild, and in doing so control them. When it came to Torgar, though, she never felt that control. Instead she felt like he was the one ready to dominate her, status and repercussions be damned.

"What about Maynard and that fat Connington fellow?" she asked. "Will they bring their wealth out of the walls and join us here in the wild?"

"We're within spitting distance of the walls," Torgar said. "This ain't the wild, woman."

"Remember what I said about your tongue and the ravens?" asked Laurie. "Think on that for a while, and leave me be with my wife. Oh, and find Taras. He's probably getting friendly with the camp followers."

"As you wish," Torgar said with an exaggerated bow.

"Must you make him so involved in your decisions?" Madelyn complained after the sellsword was gone.

"His usefulness makes up for any of his faults," Laurie said. The wagon jostled and slowed, so Laurie pulled back a bit. He looked around as he did, then swore.

"Forgive me, I must go. The wagon leaders are unaware of our change of destination."

Madelyn watched him ride around the wagon and out of sight. She tucked her legs underneath her knees, realizing she would see more of the fading sun than she'd prefer over the next couple of days. The journey north from Angelport had been far from pleasant, even with the cushions and the company of her servant girls in the giant wagon. They were so excited by arriving at the city that she'd forced them away so she could have a moment of peace.

The lady gazed around at the multitude of gently sloping hills covered with grass that grew up to the thigh. Hopefully that thick a bed of grass would soften the rocks that seemed to lurk everywhere just below the soil. She and Laurie had made love once on the grass during their journey north, and her back had ached for days because of it. She'd rather be bedded on a plank of nails. At least that way the pain would be uniform across her body.

She felt unease growing in her stomach. Seeing the many hills, void of walls, lampposts, and guards, seemed to have awoken an old fear within her. It was one thing to trust her guards; it was another to lock her door and bar it with a thick plank of wood. Here she would have... what had Torgar called it? "A fine pavilion to call her own"? She couldn't lock a pavilion. By the Abyss, they didn't even have doors to shut, just thick flaps.

"They've been told," Laurie said as he came back, startling her. "Something amiss?" he asked when he saw her jump.

"No, only thinking. Are you sure this is wise? With the thief guilds still trying so hard to survive, wouldn't it be safer in our estate?"

Laurie settled his horse into a gentle trot that matched the wagon's speed.

"Truth be told, I think we'll need to be diligent no matter where we hold the Kensgold. But do you know what I see when I look at those hills? I see no rooftops for assassins to hang from. I see no shadows in which to hide. I see no crawl spaces, basements, hidden ways, or forgotten doors. Whatever traps Thren and his pets have planned for me, I know damn well they weren't made with wide open fields in mind."

"I'd much rather have my room, *our* room, in our mansion, safely tucked in city walls," Madelyn insisted.

"Do you desire tight spaces so strongly?" he asked, frowning.

Madelyn sighed.

"I don't know. Perhaps when your camp is made I'll change my mind. Just promise me, if I desire to return to the city, you will let me go? I can take some of the sellswords, and I doubt I will be hard-pressed to find a legion of servants and working girls wishing to come with me."

Before her husband could make such a promise, they were interrupted by the damned barbarian.

"I've found the boy," Torgar shouted as he rode up from the south.

"A boy no longer," Laurie said, turning to greet them. Taras Keenan rode beside Torgar, looking more the son of the sellsword than of the thin noble. He was on the cusp of his seventeenth birthday, and had spent every day of their slow trek to Veldaren practicing with the mercenaries. More annoying to Madelyn, he had grown rather fond of Torgar and chosen him as his favored teacher and sparring partner.

"Until I fight a man in honest combat, I'll still be a boy," said Taras.

"That sounds like Torgar talking," Madelyn said, her tone disapproving.

"It is only a gentle reminder to you that I'll still be your precious child for a little while longer," Taras said, smiling.

"Good to know you have your mother's tongue instead of Torgar's, at least," Laurie said. "But now I have something a bit more important for you, Torgar. Go to both the Connington and Gemcroft estates and invite them to our lovely hills. Do your best to convince them. Remind them it is my year to host, and they cannot refuse a place given once I have tables down and food to eat."

"Mention food and we'll get Leon down here, even if it's in the middle of a pigsty," Torgar said with a deep laugh. "Heard he's having a hard time getting his delicacies with all the guilds running amok. Shall I bring the boy with me on my duties, milord?"

Madelyn's glare was a clear no, and that was enough to make up Laurie's mind.

"Aye, you should," he said. "Remember, Taras, I have given Torgar charge in these matters, not you, so do not contradict him unless absolutely necessary."

Taras could hardly contain his excitement. He hadn't been to Karak's city of stone since he was nine, and had asked questions of the place without ceasing on their ride.

"Come," he shouted to Torgar. "The city's waiting for us!"

He galloped off, the sellsword dashing after. Madelyn scowled and looked away. When Laurie saw this, he frowned again, and this time did not try to curb his temper.

"He must learn responsibility in these matters," he said. "Dealing with the other members of the Trifect will do him good."

"It'll do him dead," Madelyn said. "You send your own son into Veldaren with a single mercenary to guard his back? We'll find them rotting in the sewers, all because you'd rather camp under stars and save yourself an orc-scrap of coin."

"Mind your tongue," Laurie said.

For a minute they rode in silence, Laurie's horse trotting slowly behind the wagon as Madelyn sat with crossed arms atop her cushions. When the wagon halted suddenly, Laurie veered to one side. They'd come to the first of the hills, and slowly the lead riders were heading off into the high grass, moving carefully with men on foot scouting ahead to make sure no holes or sudden dips threatened their wagon wheels.

"We're here," Laurie said. "We'll have a comfortable camp set up for you in no time."

"No you won't," Madelyn said. "I'm going home. Our real home."

When Laurie glared, she glared back. The man swished his tongue from side to side as if swallowing something distasteful.

"I will miss you dearly," he said. "But go to the city if you must. I'll get you an escort. Two armed men traveling together may not appeal much to the mob, but a gaggle of servant girls and a noble lady in her litter will prove a different matter entirely."

He rode away, in a far fouler mood than when he'd returned from the gate.

Thren led the way, the rest of his guild following, minus Aaron and Senke who were still busy cleaning blood off the floor. They weaved through Merchant Way, their hands for once staying out of foreign pockets. The riots would soon be there. Thren had personally started two fires, and his men had started three more. They did not burn homes. They torched the storehouses, rendering food all the more precious. Butcher after butcher retreated into his shop, persuaded through either coin or dagger. Bakers fared no better. They either shut their ovens down for a day, or shut them down forever.

"The tradesmen will point their fingers at you once this day is done," Kayla said as she traveled beside him. Thren only laughed.

"After this day is done, I don't care. Today we need hunger and riots."

With quick hand gestures, Thren positioned his men up and down the road. In every corner, in every stall, the Spider Guild occupied Merchant Way. Thren stood at the intersection with Castle Road, the main throughway that led north to south from the wall to the castle. A few of his most trusted men had discarded their cloaks and joined the hungry, complaining masses in the south. If they did their jobs, the riots would surge north at a frightening pace.

For twenty minutes they waited. Thren kept his hood pulled low, and he smiled at those who noticed him. He felt unafraid. Only a full troop of mercenaries would give him concern. Beside him was a modest jeweler selling baubles in preparation for the Kensgold. Accompanying Laurie Keenan to Veldaren would be a host of camp followers, not to mention the many servant girls, dancers, and singers. Every one of the jeweler's trinkets was sold with the promise of irresistible allure to those women.

"My things are safe?" the bald jeweler asked him at one point. Thren nodded.

"You've been good to me, Mafee," the guildmaster said. "When I draw my sword, take your merchandise and go."

More minutes crawled by. The only tense moment was when a squad of mercenaries marched through. They didn't give the gray cloaks a second look, instead hurrying on toward the castle. Thren scratched at his chin, his signal to leave them be.

A chorus of shouts rose from the south. Thren looked down Castle Road and was pleased at the sight. Over four hundred made up the first wave. He recognized one of their shouts as an anthem Senke had devised. "Bread or blood," they shouted. One or the other, they'd have it, and Thren knew which one he preferred. He drew his sword and placed the tip by his right foot. All down Merchant Way, gray cloaks did the same. Mafee saw it, shoved his cheap jewelry into a burlap sack, and bolted into his home, directly behind his stall.

"Bread or blood!" Thren shouted as the mob reached him.

"Bread or blood!" the mob shouted in return, led by spies of the Spider Guild. The mob had meant to travel north to the castle, but through skillful prodding turned down Merchant Way instead. Stalls for bakers and meat carvers were empty and unguarded, and as the mobs passed, gray cloaks kicked and tore them apart. Given a taste of carnage, the mob wanted more.

More of Thren's men appeared, holding lit torches and shouting angrily. More stalls were tipped over. Wagons burned. Donkeys bled out, their mournful screeches haunting the chaos. The crowd swelled in number, joined by looters, bullies, and the coldhearted who felt power in the mob. A human swarm, they tore Merchant Way to pieces. Fires spread along the houses, yet no men came rushing with buckets.

Thren personally set fire to Mafee's house. Those pathetic trinkets were a disgrace, and even worse, he'd paid a pittance for protection compared to the money he drained from the desperate and the clueless.

"Stay safe," Thren said, the demonic grin on his face flickering in the light of the fire.

He whistled long and loud. Their work was done. Guards had begun pouring in from the north, chasing away the looters and rioters with shield and blade. At first some resisted, but the men of the Spider Guild shouted false cries of fear and fled. When blood spilled across the streets, the rest followed. It would take several hours to put out the fires. Merchant Way looked like an army had invaded. Laurie Keenan would have his greeting, and if Thren was lucky, they'd thrash his wagons, harass his mercenaries, and steal ungodly amounts of his food.

One of his men came rushing in from the west. Thren recognized him as Tweed, a simple yet skillful man he'd appointed to watch for the Keenans' approach.

"Problems, we gots plenty now," Tweed said, talking with a lisp. "Keenan's not coming inside. The rest are going out to him."

Thren pulled him off the main road, certain he had misheard due to the horrid commotion.

"Tell me again," Thren said. "Make it clear."

"I've seen them, the Keenans, putting up big, big tents and circling their wagons," said Tweed. "Looks like the new taxes set them off. They ain't going to see the riots, only hear about them."

Thren's jaw clenched tight. He sheathed his sword and grabbed Tweed by the shoulder.

"Answer me carefully," he said. "Did you see anyone from the caravans come inside? Anyone at all?"

"I saw some before I leaped off the wall," Tweed said, looking a little nervous. "Not many, a soldier here, a boy there. Only large group was some women surrounded by a few guards. I thought they was just some mercs taking their whores in to look for beds and drinks."

"You did good, Tweed," Thren said, releasing his shoulder. "Hurry back to the gate and watch for any other large groups. Report to me immediately if you see any."

Thren looked about, calling over members of the Spider Guild with his hand. He wished Senke were with him, and he felt foolish for leaving such a sharp-witted man behind to baby-sit his son while important matters were afoot. There was a chance the group of women and soldiers was nothing, but his gut told him otherwise. Once he had about five men beside him, he gave his orders, trusting them to relay the message throughout the guild.

"Only alive?" one asked when Thren was done.

"Death causes anger and sadness," Thren told them. "Capture inspires horror and desperation. Cut a single strand of her hair, and I'll scalp you. I want Madelyn Keenan as a hostage, not a corpse."

CHAPTER 24

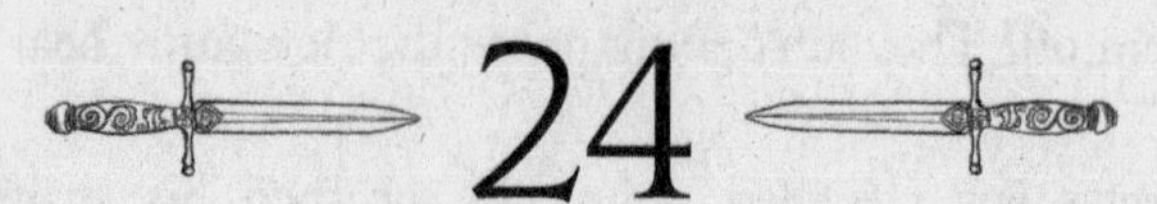

They'd been inside the city for less than a minute when they saw the first sign of riots.

"Look there," said Susan as she pointed above the houses to their right. "Is that smoke?"

"Looks like someone better be grabbing some buckets," said Nigel, an older mercenary missing half his teeth. He'd been put in charge of seeing Madelyn safely to her estate.

"What say you, Susie? Shouldn't you get to running?" he asked, smiling a gapped smile.

"Let their houses burn, long as they aren't ours," Susan said with a huff.

"Never let a fire burn, for the next home that catches could be your own," Madelyn said, feeling light-headed. The walk from their wagons to the city had been lengthy and steep. After so long riding in wagons and on horses, the exercise was unwelcome. The sweat on her fine clothing made it stick to her body, cold and uncomfortable. She'd almost taken a litter, but Laurie had insisted the added attention would be ill-advised with so many thieves and ruffians running loose in the city.

Still, her litter had curtains and walls, something she sorely missed amid her servingwomen and house guards. Holding a hand to her face, she looked at the smoke curling into the air.

"Several fires," she said. "Either it spread, or they were started on purpose..."

"Leave it to Thren to give you such a welcome," said Nigel.

"That's not our place, is it?" one of the other girls asked, suddenly worried. Madelyn rolled her eyes.

"Wrong part of the city. Your mind moves as slow as tree sap. Did you think you'd be the first to realize our home was ablaze?"

The girl blushed and stepped away from Madelyn, toward the outer ring of servants that surrounded her.

"Sorry, milady," she murmured.

"Lay off the brat," Nigel said. "I was thinking the same thing myself. Not everyone has been to the estate. It's been, what, two years since we've returned?"

"Four," Madelyn said, her voice tired. "At least for me. I let Laurie attend the last Kensgold alone. I tired of cloaks and daggers long ago."

The twelve mercenaries encircled the women as they marched. When they reached the start of Merchant Way, they drew their weapons.

"What in Karak's name happened here?" one of them asked.

It seemed the wind had shifted, so the smoke now blew in their faces. Stalls lay smashed, their signs broken and their boards cracked as if by hammers. The windows of every store were shattered. Fires had consumed a block of five stores on the north side, with three more along the south. Castle guards stood around the smoking wreckage, killing the flames while men and women arrived carrying buckets of water pumped from Veldaren's wells.

"Not good," Nigel said. "We're in the middle of Veldaren with no clue what's going on. We should have waited, damn it! Should have sent someone to make sure things were calm."

"Too late for second-guessing," Madelyn said, feeling his nervousness catching. "The estate's not far, and soldiers are about. But just in case, keep your swords drawn, and take no nonsense from anyone. I don't mind arriving at home with blood on my clothes, so long as the blood is not mine!"

They continued traveling down Merchant Way, approaching the wealthy eastern district. The closer they came to the center of the city, the more eyes watched their passing. Madelyn wondered how many belonged to spies of the thief guilds. Half? None? All? She thought *all* the most likely.

"We're not far now," she said aloud, trying to calm the girls around her. Most of them were younger than she, and they felt vulnerable despite the soldiers. They were not used to having so many eyes leering angrily at them. Madelyn clutched her hands tightly against her waist. Let the peons seethe with jealousy. She had earned her wealth, on her back as much as her feet. Laurie had fought tooth and nail to keep the wealth he had, as had the entire Keenan family line. She would not feel pity or guilt for the standing that was rightfully hers.

"It's in the eastern district," Madelyn continued. "Merchant Way ends in a fork at Iron and Cross. Not far up Cross Street is our estate. We'll be safe there."

The girls seemed to calm a little, although Madelyn's mind raced. She had seen several men following them, all wearing cloaks of gray.

"Gray is the Spider Guild?" she whispered to Nigel.

"Believe so," Nigel said, his eyes darting about as frantically as Madelyn's. "Could also be the Ash. Your dress might just get that blood you wanted, milady."

"Not wanted," she said. "But I'll endure if I must. Watch the rooftops as well. Spiders cling to rafters just as well as they hide under rocks."

A few of the gathered men and women shouted insults.

"Whores!"

"Hoarding bastards!"

"Cowards!"

The mercenaries raised their swords and cursed back. The first few skittered away, but more and more gathered to follow them. Madelyn felt the hairs rising on the back of her neck. There was something deliberate about the way the small crowd seemed to stalk them. More curses were hurled their way, but the mercenaries let them be. Soon they started having to push their way through. Nothing serious, nothing overtly deliberate, just a man standing in the center moving away too slowly, or a woman with her wash who refused to budge.

Two men rolled dice in the center of the street. Each wore a gray cloak. They looked up from their game, pulled their cloaks back to reveal their daggers, and then let them fall.

"Push through 'em?" asked Nigel. Madelyn looked about. She felt as if she walked through a forest of dry tinder, and every person traveling with her carried a blazing torch. A single false move meant fire.

"We're starving!" shouted a young man in dirty clothes.

"Bread or blood!" was the answer from someone unseen within the crowd.

"Move around them," Madelyn said, her decision made. "Do it quickly. I can almost see our gate."

"I see the Reaper's eyes," said one of the men as Madelyn's

group passed. She glanced down at the dice. Each showed a one.

They reached the fork at Iron and Cross. The south path on Iron Road seemed bare and quiet, but Cross bustled with a waiting gang of twenty. It seemed a merchant with a load of bread had been assaulted, his cart toppled. He lay unconscious, his face covered with bruises. With shouts of "Food," more and more came their way, jostling the mercenaries and smothering them with noise.

As the people rushed past, one slid a knife through the side of a mercenary. He crumpled, his pained cry the only alert they had. Two more dropped, blood spurting from cut throats.

"Stay back!" Nigel shouted, cutting down a woman who had dared step too close. Her blood coated his armor. "All of you, stay back!"

The rest of the mercenaries took his cue, swinging wildly at any who came too close. Their progress slowed to a crawl, and with one of their own fallen, the mob turned their attention from the bread to the blood.

"Murderers!" another unseen man cried.

"Butchers!" shouted another, this a woman with raven hair cut short. She wore the gray of the Spider Guild. When she saw Madelyn looking over at her, she shot her a wink and a smile.

None of the mercenaries carried shields, so when rocks pelted them, they could only duck. Susan collapsed, a heavy stone cutting across her temple. Two more servant girls fell screaming, bleeding from their mouths and noses. Once they were outside the protective circle of the mercenaries, the crowd assaulted them. They tore off their clothes, cut their hair, and smeared them with mud.

"Don't look back," Madelyn told the others. "Hurry for the gate, and for the love of Ashhur, don't look back!"

The screams of the other girls spurred them on. They fled north on Cross Street, past the toppled cart, and deep into the wealthy eastern district. Madelyn's eyes lingered on a dead merchant's body lying beside what must have once been his wares.

Cross Street appeared empty but for a single man standing in the center. He lowered his hood as he approached, his body wrapped in the thick fabric of his gray cloak.

"Madelyn Keenan," the man said, a pleased smile on his face. "It is so good to meet you."

The shouts of the mob seemed to have dimmed behind them. The mercenaries stepped closer together, and their pace slowed once more.

"What business have you with me?" she asked, her glare at Nigel urging him onward.

"I am Thren Felhorn. Everything and everyone inside Veldaren is my business."

The mercenaries stopped completely.

"What is it you want?" she asked him, struggling to keep her composure. "Ransom? Or perhaps words of truce or surrender?"

Thren laughed.

"I want your husband tearing at his tunic and dusting his head with ashes. I want your family praying desperately for your return. Do you know who they'll pray to when they do? I'll be the one who determines your death or release. They'll be praying to *me*."

Men in gray cloaks stepped out from houses and alleys, and even fell from the rooftops.

"Surrounded," Nigel whispered as he counted. "And at least twenty. Make an offer, milady. We won't win this fight."

"I have nothing to offer other than myself," Madelyn said. "You have armor and a blade. Do your job."

"Whatever she is paying you cannot be worth your life," Thren said. A few of his men stepped closer, while others drew loaded crossbows and aimed them at the mercenaries. Their strings were thick and the bolts thicker. Nigel was certain they would pierce right through his chain mail.

"Forget this," said one of the mercenaries. He threw down his sword. Before he could take a step, Nigel stabbed him in the back and kicked his body to the dirt. He pointed the bloody blade at Thren, then saluted. Thren nodded, and the rest of the Spider Guild took heed of the message: the mercenary captain was for their guildmaster to kill.

At the twang of the first crossbow, Nigel lunged. Thren drew his short swords, swinging them in a dance that was beautiful to behold. Two more mercenaries fell, their vitals punctured by crossbow bolts. The servingwomen screamed. Madelyn drew a dagger from her sash, determined to bloody the first man who touched her. The remaining house guards defended as best they could, their thick armor deflecting the stabs of the daggers, but they were horribly outnumbered and doomed to fall, and both sides knew it.

Nigel wielded his bastard sword with both hands, needing the grip to hang on when Thren smacked it aside with his blades. Madelyn knew the mercenary captain was an experienced fighter of many battles, and had even participated in the winter war between Ker and Mordan. But compared to armored men in thick lines, Thren was like a ghost. Every swing Nigel made seemed to cut air.

Blood splattered across his armor. His wrist had been cut, yet Madelyn had no clue how. Nigel stepped back and thrust. Thren parried with his left hand, then stepped forward and slashed with his right. Desperate, Nigel twisted so the blow would strike the thin pauldron atop his shoulder. It did, and the pain was brutal, but the deep bruise was far better than the gash it would have given his neck.

Behind him a few of the serving girls dashed away. Crossbow bolts tore into their backs. Another fell, a rogue slicing her ankle with his dagger before unbuckling his belt. He was on top of her in moments, not caring that several of the mercenaries remained alive.

No longer caring for her safety, Madelyn leaped from the group. Her dagger stabbed the man's neck. Blood gushed across his armor, and swearing softly, he rolled over and died.

"Oh gods," the young girl sobbed. Madelyn took her face in her hands and pressed their foreheads together. Blood covered them both, and its sickly-sweet aroma was all she could smell.

"Hush now," Madelyn told the girl. "Hush. We'll be fine. We'll all be fine."

Meanwhile Nigel unleashed a storm of curses at Thren, hoping to distract him. He'd retreated several steps, his shoulder ached, and he'd avoided death twice by the sheer thickness of his chain mail. Breathing was difficult. Thren, however, was still smiling. He had not a drop of blood on him.

"Are you ready?" Thren asked, suddenly hopping backward and letting his cloak fall forward to hide his weapons.

"For what?" Nigel asked.

"On the count of three, I'll kill you," Thren said.

"Overconfident ass."

Madelyn watched, desperately hoping the mercenary would pull off a stunning victory. Thren swayed left to right, as if waiting. Nigel lunged with the greater reach of his sword, hoping to catch him off guard. Instead Thren smoothly parried to the side.

"One," he said, stepping forward with his left foot.

Nigel looped his sword around above his head and struck for

Thren's neck. The rogue stepped forward again, blocking with his short sword.

"Two."

His foot curled around Nigel's. Their weight connected. Thren lunged forward, slamming his elbow into Nigel's face. The mercenary captain went down. A short sword stabbed through the crease of his chain mail underneath his armpit and into his chest.

"Three."

"Not dead yet," Nigel said, his voice sounding wet.

Thren laughed.

"A worthy attitude," he said as he kicked the blade from Nigel's hand. "Would you care to work for me, or die like the rest of your men?"

Nigel chuckled even as blood dripped down his lips.

"Cut my damn head off already," he said. "I ain't going to eternity as a traitor."

Thren shrugged as if it didn't matter to him either way. He pulled his sword out, raised its tip, and prepared to thrust it into Nigel's throat.

Before she could witness the execution, Madelyn saw a great burst of white, so powerful her eyes ached. She turned away, unable to watch. All around she heard voices shouting, many of them panicked. And then she heard singing. As her vision returned, she saw Thren was gone. Nearby, the rest of the serving girls sobbed, as did the petrified girl still in her arms.

A man stepped over to her and looked into her eyes. His bald head was smooth and rounded, as were his large ears. His mouth was pulled into a tight frown.

"Are you two all right?" he asked.

"Yes," Madelyn said, her voice quivering. All around she saw men in similar garb, white robes with gold chains. "Yes, we are."

"Good."

And then he left her, instead going to Nigel's side.

"Hold still," the man said to him. He put his hands through the armor and against the wound on his chest. Nigel coughed.

"Madelyn?"

"The noblewoman?" the stranger asked.

Nigel nodded weakly.

"I'm here," Madelyn said, still cradling the serving girl. "I'm well."

"Brave too, considering what she had to do. Be quiet. I must say my prayers without interruption."

The man closed his eyes and whispered words that Madelyn could not understand. White light glowed, as if his skin were luminescent. The bleeding in Nigel's chest stopped. When he coughed again, the cough was dry and healthy.

"Who are you?" Madelyn asked as Nigel slumped into a sudden, peaceful sleep.

"Calan, high priest of Ashhur," he said, turning to offer her a hand. "And as of now, consider yourself and your charges under my protection."

CHAPTER 25

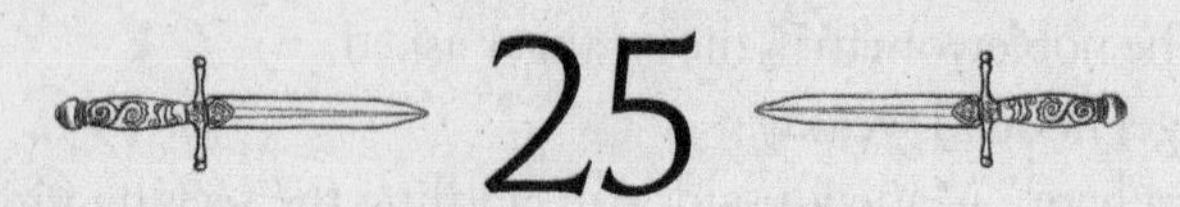

Ethric had been involved in many riots, but he'd never seen one created so spontaneously out of so little. Someone's hands were certainly behind it, and the manipulation involved left him impressed. He walked down the middle of the open street, almost euphoric at the chaos. Karak, being a god of order before his banishment by Celestia, should have frowned upon such activities, but Ethric felt them lift his heart. The only thing worse than chaos was false order, the kind established by faithless kings and the worshippers of Ashhur. Let chaos burn down the falsehood like fire upon a crumbling home. From the ashes, he and his kind would build anew.

At the western gate he came across a filthy beggar sitting beside the road. He was blind, and before him was a clay pot. Ethric watched as a chubby merchant wearing red and purple silks atop his tunic tossed in a handful of coins. Before the merchant could escape, the dark paladin was there, grabbing his arm while stabbing his sword into the pot.

"Let go of me," the merchant shouted as he tried to wrench his arm away. Ethric's grip did not loosen. When he pulled the sword out of the pot, the sharp tip had pierced through the center of one of the coins.

"What charity is this?" Ethric asked as black fire surrounded the blade.

"Help for those less fortunate," said the chubby man as he looked around for someone to aid him. There were none. Everyone recognized Ethric's black armor, the dark flame of his blade, and the white lion skull painted on his breastplate. Just like the priests of Karak, the paladins were forbidden from entering Veldaren, but when inside they were never seen. Better to safely ignore the darkness than call it out and risk death.

"Shall you buy your way into eternity?" asked Ethric. The coin slowly melted, the copper dripping down the length of the blade, bubbling and popping. "If copper to a blind man saves your soul, imagine your rewards if you threw gold to the feet of a truly holy man."

"You're evil," the merchant said. Ethric felt impressed by his courage.

"Evil?" he asked. He ripped the silks from the man's tunic and held them aloft. "You parade before a blind man in wealth that could feed him for years while tossing him a pittance you will never miss. That is not piety. That is disgusting."

He turned and rammed the silk into the blind man's pot. The merchant stood with his hands shaking, his eyes torn between the dark paladin and the silk.

"No fighting, have mercy. A kindness is a kindness, no matter the size," the blind man said, trying to defuse the situation.

Ethric only smiled and gestured to the pot. His sword still burned with fire.

"What is more important to you?" he asked the rich man. "Your wealth, or your supposed bribes to the fates?"

When the merchant reached down for the silk, Ethric cut him down. With two vicious hacks he separated the head and dumped it atop the pot. The blood poured freely, ruining the silk and drenching the few coins within.

"Gifts are always repaid in blood," Ethric said to the blind man. "Altruism is a delusion. Grace is weakness masked in lies."

By now a crowd had surrounded him, shouting and pointing angrily. The dark paladin smiled, and when he stretched out his sword, the people made him a path. With so many swarming the streets, it took a good while for the city guard to arrive. He heard the distant commotion behind him, but felt no fear that they might come searching. They would hear his description, and know him for what he was. That alone would prevent any real search. No city guard was dumb enough to challenge a paladin of Karak, not without an army at its back.

Despite the delay, Ethric's mood remained good. He had very little to work with in his search for the faceless women, but Pelarak had given him one tangible lead. On the inside of the wall, about half a mile north of the western gate, Pelarak had told him of a crack. It was wide, running lengthwise along the stones of the wall like a lone bolt of lightning. If Pelarak ever needed to contact the faceless women in urgency, he had an apprentice leave a note in the crack while the stars were bright. By morning it'd be gone.

Ethric found the crack, looking exactly as it'd been described to him. The street was quiet, modest homes with immodest fences on either side. They appeared new, most likely built after Thren's little war had started. He removed his glove and put his hand against the deepest part of the crack.

A smile lit up his face. His lengthy training had attuned his body to all things magical, both clerical and wizardly in nature. Deep inside the crack was a simple alert spell, one that would send warning to the caster whenever the ward was tripped. The faceless women would never need to check, yet would always know when they had a message and could retrieve it before the dawn. Seeing beauty in the spell's simplicity, Ethric reminded himself to treat his foes with greater respect.

Deciding to treat simplicity with simplicity, he found a large rock and shoved it into the crack, tripping the ward. Now the only question that remained was how long it'd take one of the women to arrive. Since he'd placed the "message" in the middle of the day, they'd certainly know something was amiss.

"Patience serves the wise," Ethric said, finding himself a seat beside a fence. He leaned his back against the bars. He was out of sight of any travelers on the road, and he doubted the owner of the home would be stupid enough to call him out from his position. All he had to do was watch and wait.

At some point he must have fallen asleep. Ethric remembered no dreams, but when his eyes snapped open he felt a distinct disorientation at the loss of daylight. The sun was barely visible through a pale scattering of clouds as it hovered above the western wall of the city.

Ethric knew he had awakened because of his finely honed instincts. At first he saw no intruders and heard no footsteps. But he was hunting skillful prey, and lack of sight and sound meant nothing. He looked to the wall. The rock wedged inside the crack was gone.

"I thought you'd wait until dark," Ethric said as he stood. His hand reached for the hilt of his sword. A dagger slid through a crease of his armor by his shoulder blades and pressed against unprotected flesh before he could.

"It seems the priests have grown desperate," he heard a voice behind him say. "A dark paladin alone in Veldaren in broad daylight? Will they soon announce their existence to the land, or are they just hoping a mob will kill you?"

"It would take far more than a mob," Ethric said. "Pull back your blade, woman. I know what you are."

She hesitated for a moment, and then the dagger withdrew. Ethric turned, his arms crossed over his chest.

"With whom do I speak?" he asked.

"I am Eliora," the faceless said. "What message do you bring from the temple?"

"Just that Alyssa must be returned, immediately," Ethric said. "Bring her to me at once."

Eliora clicked her two daggers together as she gently weaved back and forth.

"Matters are not as simple as Pelarak believes," she said. "Alyssa is surrounded by guards and protected by a wealthy tax collector."

"None of which should matter to a faceless."

Through the thin veil of white, Ethric could see hints of Eliora's face. He'd swear she winked at him.

"Only if we wanted her dead, Paladin. Escaping alive is another matter. I'm sure Pelarak told you she is worthless to us if harmed."

"Where is she held?" Ethric asked. "Tell me and you may go."

Eliora's swaying slowed, then came to a stop.

"Whom do the dark paladins serve, Karak or his priests?" she asked.

"They are the same," Ethric said. "His priests speak the word of Karak."

Eliora took a step back.

"Then I will not bring you to her. Karak has given us faith, and a mind to use it. We are not Pelarak's slaves, not anymore. We do the will of our god. *Our* god. Will you remain blind to Pelarak's manipulation and control?"

"You will bring me to her, or you will die."

Eliora cocked her head. She seemed to be staring into Ethric's heart.

"You would kill me anyway. Pelarak has made his move. So be it."

Ethric drew his sword and lashed out in a single smooth motion, the blade bathed in dark fire. The faceless woman fell backward, her spine arching and her knees bending. After the sword passed harmlessly above her, she snapped forward, lunging with her daggers. One scraped against his plate mail and caught in a crease while the other gouged the flesh underneath his chin.

Before she could finish the kill, Ethric rammed an open palm against her chest. The strength of Karak was with him, and she flew backward, a shock wave of sound and fire exploding from the contact. Eliora rolled, shadows splashing off her body and lying like deep puddles. Her feet touched ground, she spun, crossed her arms, and vanished in a puff of smoke.

A long shadow stretched from the western wall from the sunset, and out of that shadow leaped Eliora. Her feet slammed into the small of Ethric's back. He cried out in pain as he stumbled forward, his sword slashing behind him blindly. Its fire singed some of her wrappings, but cut no flesh. A dagger struck Ethric, cutting a thin but bloody wound across the back of his head.

Ethric fell forward, avoiding the vicious thrust aimed between his collarbone and neck that would have surely finished him. The dagger struck his armor. The magic in both collided, strength against strength. Sparks showered to the ground. The dagger dulled. When Eliora spun, thrusting it forward, Ethric twisted so she stabbed directly into his thick breastplate. The dagger exploded into shards that bit her hand. Blood soaked her wrappings.

"Yield and I will be merciful," Ethric said as he went on the offensive, slashing back and forth with his blade. Eliora ducked, shifted, and leaped away like a dancer, each cut passing close enough to burn more of her wrappings. When his sword stabbed forward, it should have pierced her heart. Instead he cut smoke, for she was gone.

Anticipating the attack, he spun, cutting the air between him and the wall's shadow. Eliora was there, her foot outstretched for a kick, but again his sword passed through only smoke. He coughed and retched as it swarmed over him, burning his lungs and tasting foul on his tongue. Within the smoke he heard laughter. Within the laughter he heard rage.

Something sharp pierced his side just above his belt. Warm blood poured down his thigh. He felt it twist, and the pain doubled. Ethric swung, but he felt blind and dull. His sword cut air and smoke, nothing more.

"I will not be treated as a fool," Ethric shouted. He struck the ground with his blade, both hands gripping the handle to increase his strength. Power rolled from the blow, pushing away the smoke. Clean air filled Ethric's lungs. Before his head could clear he saw Eliora lunging at him, her dagger aimed for his eye.

His reactions were quicker. He dropped his sword. His left hand shot up, blocking the stab with his vambrace. His right hand reached forward, grabbing Eliora's neck and crushing her throat. Before she could turn to smoke in his hands, he shouted the name of his god and let his full power roll forth.

Eliora's whole body went rigid. The wrappings around her

face blasted off, revealing her beautiful face locked in a grimace of pain. Ash billowed from her nostrils and open mouth. Her entire weight hung from the fierce grip of his hand.

"Chaos... must... end!" screamed Ethric. He slammed her headfirst to the dirt. As she gagged, trying to force air through a charred throat, the dark paladin picked up his sword.

"Karak will abandon you," she said, her voice hoarse and weak.

"Don't you see?" Ethric said, showing her the blaze of dark flame on his blade. "My faith is strong, and his presence in me is stronger. You're the one abandoned, heretic."

With one vicious stroke he cut off her head. So hot was the flame on his sword that her body never bled, the flesh and veins cauterized by its heat.

"Two left," Ethric said, leaving the body to rot. "Take her soul, Karak. Punish her as you please."

Eliora had told him enough. Before he'd left, Pelarak had informed Ethric of the entire matter of Alyssa Gemcroft, the thief guilds, and Theo Kull. *Tax collector* Theo Kull. At first he'd thought Alyssa was secreted away somewhere with the other faceless. To be with Theo Kull meant servants, living quarters, and mercenaries. Pelarak had never mentioned their being inside the city, which meant only one thing... they lurked outside the walls, and a collection that large could not hide from him.

Ethric traveled south toward the gate, determined to see his business done before nightfall.

CHAPTER 26

Madelyn Keenan sat in a small room that made her wagon outside the city seem like a castle. She had a plain wooden chair with no padding, a bare desk, and a bed stuffed with straw, not feathers. She wore a clean white dress given to her after she'd bathed. She still smelled the blood that had covered her hands and face.

Young girls had come and gone the entire day, attending to her needs. No one had ordered her to stay, but the unspoken desire seemed obvious enough. Madelyn lay on the uncomfortable bed, accepting pillows, warm tea mixed with honey, and the occasional girl coming in to ask if there was anything else she could do.

Calan had promised to send word of her safety to her husband, but Madelyn had not seen the high priest since arriving at the temple. He'd said something about attending others, and something more about patrols, and then he'd left. She wished she'd gone with him.

The walls were bare wood. The floor was stained a dark brown. There was nothing to read, nothing to do. She felt more a prisoner than she'd ever felt in her life, and this was in a place she'd been brought to for protection.

At last, when she thought she could take no more, the door opened and Calan stepped inside.

"Forgive my intrusion," he said as he closed the door. "The hour is late and I had much to do. So much, truly, that should have been done long ago."

"And what is that?" Madelyn asked, not really caring but not ready to have the conversation turn to her. She wanted time to regain her composure.

"Protect the city," Calan said, as if it should have been obvious. "There is much you need to hear, Lady Keenan. Things are changing, starting now. Will you listen?"

"I don't have much choice," Madelyn said, crossing her legs and trying to appear ladylike in the plain dress.

"You are free to go whenever you like," Calan said. "Though I think you might have a difficult time convincing your remaining mercenaries. They quite like it here. Most appear to be sleeping well for the first time in many nights."

"It's the first night they won't have to stand at their posts," Madelyn said. "Of course they're eager to laze about while taking my coin."

Calan shrugged as if this were all irrelevant.

"I have been high priest for only a day, Lady Keenan, so forgive me if I say things you already know. My predecessor was a man named Calvin. Most brilliant when it came to the scriptures but most timid when it comes to your Trifect and the thieves' guilds. He was adamant we stay out of your war. We watched as each side killed hundreds of innocents, and then did our best to clean up the damage."

"We have done no wrong," Madelyn said, picking at the fabric above her knee. "The guilds are illegal, immoral, and a drain on this city."

"As I'm sure the Trifect has done nothing illegal or immoral over the past five years," Calan said, his round face darkening a little. "But I am not here to assign blame, Lady Keenan, only to talk."

Madelyn made a small gesture with a hand, urging the priest to continue.

"Forgive me, milady. The days have been rough on us all. We are not used to such strife within our temple, but I'm sure that is something that you would care little about. Still, listen a little longer, for all of this will make sense by the time I am done.

"A few days ago a priest of our order, a man named Delius Eschaton, was killed in cold blood in broad daylight. We have little doubt that Thren and his guild were responsible, yet they are beyond the justice of the king. We almost convinced Calvin to act then, but Delius was going against our orders in his tirades against the guilds. To all our shame, policy and rule won out over blood and loss. Then, that night, we received his daughter in secret, for the guild had sent an assassin to kill her. From what we heard, he nearly succeeded."

The old man paused for a moment. Madelyn rubbed her hands. The warm bath she'd taken had done wonders, but still she saw the faded red stain of blood deep in the cracks of her skin.

"I'm waiting for where this affects me," she said when it seemed Calan was in no hurry to continue. She guessed he was waiting for something from her. The name Eschaton sounded vaguely familiar, but she couldn't place it.

"Such callousness," Calan said. "Still, I should not have expected different. That little girl, sobbing in fear as she said good-bye to the only home she'd ever known, was the final catalyst. When Calvin refused to act, we forced a vote and removed him as high priest. I took his spot, and that is what you should be clearly aware of, Lady Keenan."

Madelyn tried to summon a bit of her noble contempt, regardless of her modest dress and loose, undecorated hair.

"The doings of old men in stone temples are none of my concern," she said as she stood and crossed her arms. "I congratulate you on taking control, but it is time I left. I want to return to my home, where I can rest in safety."

"Calvin's removal and my ascension are the only reason you are alive, Madelyn," Calan said. His voice had grown quieter, and though the words themselves were harsh, his tone was not. If anything, he sounded like he was talking to a foolish child. "Riots and looting have gone on long enough. We set out in an attempt to restore order, and that is how we found you surrounded by men of the Spider Guild. Tell me, do you think you'd prefer Thren's company to mine?"

"A prison is a prison," Madelyn said, but her voice was already faltering. The old man had saved her, and here she was bickering and trying to insult him. What was wrong with her?

"I am not holding you prisoner," Calan insisted. "I am preventing you from walking off the edge of a cliff. Already I have sent a runner to your husband to inform him of your whereabouts. Would you wait for him to send you a guard, or would you prefer to brave the night streets alone?"

"But the rest of my men..."

"They are only three," Calan said. "And how many women would you take with you? Don't be foolish."

The high priest rubbed his hand against the side of her face, and for a reason she could not understand, she did not slap it away.

"As of tonight, we are ending the bloodshed," Calan said.

"We will wear holes into our sandals as we scour the streets. We will shine a light into every dark corner. We will sing a song of joy to drown out the ugly shouts of hatred. Our eyes are open, Lady Keenan. Sleep well on your bed, and know that you are safe here. Think on what I have said, and then when you return to your husband, tell him what you have heard. Do I truly ask so much of you?"

"I've long heard whispers that the thieves had bought off the priests of Ashhur," Madelyn said. "You should have helped us against the thief guilds, yet spent years doing nothing. Now you tell me to feel safe in your house? I will not sleep, old man. I still have my dagger, and with my back to the wall and my eyes to the door, I will wait for my husband."

Calan smiled a sad smile.

"Such spirit," he said. "A shame it is born not of love but mistrust and desperation."

He turned and left. True to her word Madelyn shut the door, sat on her bed, and stared at the doorway until it was only a barely perceived blur.

Safe or not, desperate or not, she would tell her husband what had transpired. Any veiled threat, no matter how gently given, would earn his wrath.

Daytime was surprisingly pleasant, but it was the nights that made Alyssa cringe with every wayward glance at the setting sun. In daylight she spent time with a charming Yoren and his favored mercenaries. She laughed as they sparred, told filthy jokes, and took turns trading verbal barbs at each other's prowess in blade, bow, and bed. Her meals with Theo Kull, of poorer quality than what she might have had at her father's, were still plentiful.

But every night Yoren came to share her bed. With teeth clenched she endured his grunting atop her, his careful movements slow and methodical. He was proud of himself, she knew. Every time she faked a moan or bucked beneath him, he acted as if he were the greatest lover the world of Dezrel had ever known. But she had to fake it. Had to play the part, as much as it sickened her. The worst was when he put his hands around her neck. Once it had only been a game, a thrill for someone as highborn as she to feel a man's threatening grasp amid the love play. Now those hands had an eagerness that frightened her, their actions too closely resembling what he'd do to her the moment the Gemcroft wealth was safely in his grasp.

"Something the matter?" Yoren asked, sitting beside her.

"Thinking of home," she said, hoping the comment innocent enough for the inquiry to end. The two sat before an enormous bonfire, their arms linked. The contact felt like a perverse lie to Alyssa. With her free hand she secretly fondled the dagger hidden in her skirts. She'd thought of using it several times. Once she had even reached for her discarded dress and the dagger hidden within, right when Yoren was climaxing and his hands seemed to clutch her throat with inhuman strength. As her fingers had touched the hilt, he'd finally relented, and so had she.

One of the mercenaries tossed another large log onto the bonfire, startling her from her thoughts with his shout.

"Where's the music we was promised? I've got a song to sing, yet no music to sing it with. I ain't singing without no song!"

Alyssa faked a smile. The cold of winter had come on strong with the approaching night, and the mercenaries had successfully begged permission to build a bonfire to ward off the cold. The bulk of the camp, minus some servants and patrolling men, were seated around that bonfire. Veldaren's walls were in the far distance, but Alyssa felt certain that anyone walking along their breadth could spot their fire with ease.

"Here's your music," one sellsword shouted, following it up with a loud burp.

"Give me some more of Gunter's cooking, and I'll give you some music of my own," another man shouted. Gunter, whose cooking was renowned, but whose priggish attitude was loathed, raised a forefinger and shook it at the mercenary. He got a finger right back, and it wasn't the forefinger. The men around him howled with laughter, and soon a chorus of bodily noises sang in Gunter's direction.

"I think the king should be treated to such skillful musicians," Alyssa said, laughing in spite of her dour mood. This earned her a chorus of cheerful agreements.

"A sign of a good leader," Theo said, sitting on the other side of Yoren. "You inspire love in men, Alyssa. Good things surely await your rule of the Gemcroft estate."

"A rule I may never have," Alyssa said, the naming of her father's house souring her smile. "But while the sun is setting and the moon rising, let us speak of more certain and happier things, such as the opening of another cask of cider!"

The mercenaries roared, and when Theo nodded in approval, they cheered.

"They wouldn't be so boisterous if they knew what I had planned for them on the morrow," Theo said, lowering his voice for just the three of them.

"They would," Yoren said, "but only after an extra round of drink or two. Keeping them in the dark is cheaper."

Theo laughed, and Alyssa laughed along, her mind racing. So far she knew little of what the two men planned. When one of their servant boys returned from the city with news that Laurie Keenan had moved the Kensgold to outside the walls, neither had been upset. In fact, they had seemed almost overjoyed.

A young servingwoman slipped through the men, doing her best to ignore the few comments she received and the occasional grab at her body.

"Milord," she said, bowing to Theo. "The two women are here."

Theo sighed.

"Send them on over."

The woman bowed and then hurried away. A minute later two of the faceless stepped into the light of the great bonfire. Neither bowed to Theo Kull upon arrival.

"Welcome back to my camp," Theo said. "Next time, please introduce yourself to my guards, not the servingwomen. Shadow-walkers or not, I'd prefer you to follow protocol like every normal human being."

"Your women argue less," said the one on the left. Alyssa recognized her sharp voice as Zusa's. "They also hold their tongues. Safer for all involved."

"That wasn't a suggestion," Theo said, his voice hardening. Neither faceless woman reacted.

"Why are you here?" Alyssa asked, hoping to move the conversation along. She liked having the women nearby. Even though they took payment from the Kulls, they didn't feel like a part of them. Perhaps she just enjoyed the company of someone not owned by Yoren and his father.

"We fear for Alyssa's safety," said Nava. "We must take her into hiding. Pelarak wants her imprisoned in the temple."

"We've paid you properly," Theo said. "Alyssa stays here with us, regardless of what your little priest says."

"It's not wise to tempt Pelarak," Zusa said. "You are a mouse dancing before a lion."

"Only the skull of a lion," Yoren corrected. "And I dance like a puppet for no one, faceless."

Zusa laughed.

"Pelarak will make you dance," she said. "Your bones are his toys. Your blood is his drink. Either flee or hide. Here is not safe. Give Alyssa to us."

Alyssa dared hope she could go with them. She'd forfeit her entire wealth for just one night away from Yoren and his hands. How she wished to sleep without fear of his rousing in the middle of the night, hungry for what only she could provide. With the faceless women, she would have respite.

"This is not a discussion," Theo interrupted. Alyssa felt her hopes dashed to pieces. "I will not hand over..."

A horn sounded from the north, followed by shouts. Armed intruders were at the edge of the camp. Alyssa looked toward the noise. When she turned back, the faceless women were gone.

Yoren stood, his hand falling to the hilt of his sword. Theo grabbed his son's wrist to stop him. All around them mercenaries put down their cups and drew their blades.

A moment later a man in leather armor came running from the north, sword in hand.

"Milord," the man shouted. "He refused to wait, or give us his name. He killed Geoffrey, and he wears the armor of..."

He stopped when he realized the man had already arrived. The other mercenaries formed a ring around the intruder. The great bonfire burned between him and Theo.

"Greetings, tax collector," the intruder said. Alyssa might have thought him handsome if not for the cold look in his eyes and the looping tattoos across his naked face and head. Just looking at them made her stomach queasy. He wore dark plate mail, the skull of a lion emblazoned in white across his chest piece. Fresh wounds marked his body, none of them remotely serious.

"Greetings," Theo said. "Though I'd prefer you call me by my name. Do the paladins of Karak know nothing of respect?"

"No less than the men of Riverrun," said the paladin. "I am Ethric, and you are Theo Kull. Consider our pleasantries exchanged." He pointed his giant sword at Alyssa. "I've come for Lady Gemcroft. Is this her?"

Yoren drew his sword and stepped in front of her. Before returning to Veldaren, Alyssa might have felt humbled by his chivalrous nature, but now she felt like a beautiful gem being squabbled over in the marketplace. Again she wished for the faceless women. Their offer of safety and concealment seemed all the more desirable.

"You will not touch her," Yoren said. "Alyssa is in our safekeeping. Karak has no claim on her."

"And you do?" Ethric asked. "Only a fool would believe himself above the desires of a god."

"She is my betrothed," Yoren said.

Ethric looked to his left, then to his right, pointedly dismissing the men who might come to Yoren's aid.

"Cover your steel, boy, or I'll put your blood on it," Ethric said.

"Begone from my camp," Theo said. "I dismiss you. You are not welcome here."

Ethric laughed.

"I am never welcome. This is your last chance. Hand her over."

"Fuck you and your lion god," Yoren said. "Kill him."

Alyssa let out a sharp cry at the sudden eruption of blood. The two nearest mercenaries fell back, deep gashes in their chests. Their armor did nothing to slow the blade. Ethric pivoted to the side and cut down another man, his finely crafted and god-blessed sword shattering the mercenary's cheap iron weapon. Two more died attempting an attack, their swords clanging uselessly off Ethric's plate mail or sailing wide from an impossibly fast parry.

"Cease this!" shouted a feminine voice, with such volume and authority that both sides obeyed. Nava walked into the light of the fire, her daggers drawn and dripping shadows.

"I wondered if you would show," Ethric said, taking a step closer and holding his sword before him. "Pelarak has ordered the disbandment of your order. You must return to the temple immediately."

"Alyssa is under our protection," Nava said. "Be gone, and tell Pelarak we no longer follow his command, only Karak's."

Hands grabbed Alyssa's wrist. Startled, she turned to shout, but a wrapped palm covered her mouth.

"Quiet," Zusa whispered. "Like a mouse, now follow."

Nava crossed her daggers before her chest as Ethric took a step closer.

"I hoped you would say no," he said. "I cherish the honor of killing another heretic. Eliora is dead, you whore. Your kind dies tonight."

If Nava was upset, she did not show it. Slowly she swayed from side to side. While Ethric watched, she cut just above her elbow and let the blood drip down onto her cloak. Like a drop of dye into clear water, the red swirled and spread across the dark cloth.

"Blood for blood," Nava said. "I'll bury you in my cloak."

She lunged across the fire, her cloak whipping around her

like a funnel, its length suddenly twice that of her body. When Ethric swung, his sword clanged off as if he'd struck stone.

Nava's foot snapped out, striking his head. He rolled with the blow, ending on his knees. He swung behind him, but Nava leaped over the blade and stabbed her daggers for his neck. Ethric turned just in time, one dagger striking his chest plate, the other slashing his cheek. He rammed his fist into Nava's gut, grinning in satisfaction at the gasping cry of pain she made.

The faceless woman somersaulted backward, her cloak twirling before him. He tried to push it aside, but he might as well have tried to push down a tree with his bare hands. Blood ran down his face, a trickle curling in at the corner of his mouth. He licked it and then spat.

"Fight me," he shouted as the cloak slowly drifted downward. He braced his sword, smoothly shifted between stances. Then she was there, ducking and spinning beyond his sword's edge. Normally he'd feel confident having such reach over his opponent's daggers. The length of his blade meant nothing, however, if she could weave around it as if in a dance.

She spun full circle about him, her cloak stretching longer and longer. Laughing, Nava jumped into the air, her cloak snapping behind her. Realizing he was surrounded, and soon to be crushed, Ethric poured every bit of his power into an overhand chop. A horrific screech sounded as his blade hit the cloak. The blood-red cloth shook, cracked, and then broke like shattered steel. All around him the red material crumpled to the dirt.

Sensing opportunity, one of Theo's mercenaries swung at Ethric's back. The paladin heard his approach and swung about. Fury raged in his eyes. He blocked the blow, then looped his sword underneath and upward. The mercenary crumpled to the ground, his intestines spilling from his belly like freed snakes.

Feet slammed into Ethric's back. The remnants of the cloak wrapped around his head. The blow jerked his body forward, but his head could not move. Pain flooded his mind as his neck wrenched awkwardly. Knowing her daggers would soon follow, Ethric fell limp, his sword swinging above his shoulder. The cloak vanished as Nava retreated.

Ethric spun on his knees, his weight resting on one hand as he gasped for air. His fight with Eliora had already drained him, and Nava was proving no easier.

"A shame," he said, hoping to buy some time. "You could do great things for Karak with such skill."

Nava began swaying from side to side, her tattered cloak only hanging down to her waist.

"But Karak wants us dead," Nava said. "Who is it we should pray to now?"

Ethric stood and gripped his sword. The black flame roared higher, his faith unshaken by the difficulty of the fight. He would kill the heretic. Of that he had no doubt.

"Ask Karak when you see him," Ethric said. He stepped toward the bonfire and suddenly punched his free hand into the flame. He was not burned. The fire turned from yellow to purple, its smoke from a deep gray to clear.

"Can you stand the heat of the Abyss?" he asked as he stepped back, his left arm completely wreathed with purple flame. Nava lunged, trusting her speed. Ethric parried her first two thrusts and countered a third. When she spun about trying to get closer, he opened the palm of his burning hand. Fire exploded as if from the mouth of a dragon. The fire swarmed over Nava's cloak, setting it aflame.

Nava wasted no time, jumping backward and slicing off her

cloak where it attached to the clasps atop her shoulders. But Ethric did not chase as she'd expected. Instead he stabbed his sword into the flame, turned it once, and then swung. A massive arc of fire lashed outward, catching her across the chest. All about, wagons burned and men died as the fire consumed them with frightening speed.

Faring little better, Nava dropped to a roll. The dirt did little to stop the burning. Ethric rushed after, and when she rolled underneath a wagon, he punched it with his fist. The fire left his arm and set the cover aflame. An upward swipe of his sword cut the rest of it in half. Nava was underneath, gasping for air and clutching her horribly burned chest. The wrappings were gone, revealing blistered skin blackened by the heat.

"Shouldn't . . . have burned me," she said with labored breaths.

"Karak has abandoned you for your heresy," he said, his sword held in both hands, the tip touching her breast.

Nava laughed even though the movement obviously pained her.

"Alyssa is gone, you fool," she said. "Zusa has her. You'll never see her again."

Ethric stabbed down and twisted. When he yanked the sword free, he spat on her corpse. He strapped his sword to his back and returned to the bonfire. All around, men were desperately tossing dirt with shovels to put out what fires they could. The rest of the mercenaries crowded before Theo and Yoren, who both stood with their swords drawn.

"Where is she?" Ethric asked as he approached. "Where is Alyssa Gemcroft?"

"Taken by the faceless," Yoren said. "What now, Paladin? Will you give chase?"

Ethric glared at them, then to the hills beyond. The last

faceless woman must have fled with Alyssa while he fought. He knew he could never track her, but the royal girl was a different matter. If he hurried, he might catch up to them...

"I go for the girl," he said. "If you want her back, then seek out Pelarak and the priests of Karak."

"We just need her alive," Theo said. "Will you harm her?"

Ethric laughed at their foolishness.

"We want her safe, you damn simpletons," he said. "She is our own protection against Maynard Gemcroft. We have a common enemy, yet you cower and feebly strike against me. Pray I never see you again."

He left their camp, circling around Theo's guards. The footprints were chaotic, but seeing a set leading directly south from the camp, Ethric gave chase. Two of the faceless women were dead, the third fleeing with his prey. His task was almost finished, and the night was young. Offering a prayer of thanks to Karak, Ethric ran on.

CHAPTER

27

Once he was certain everyone was asleep or occupied, Aaron donned a pale gray cloak and slipped out of his room. Something weighed heavily on his mind, and he knew of only one person who could answer him. Problem was, that person was currently hidden deep inside the temple of Ashhur. He doubted the priests would let him in to see Delysia, and equally doubted they would let her out.

Aaron had been shown how to hide, how to kill, and how to steal, but never once had he been shown how to break into a place with the goal of talking. The night had potential to be an interesting one.

The hallway was empty. He ran, tumbling into a nearby room. One of the floorboards was loose, and it came up easily when Aaron pulled on it. Below was a tunnel connecting to the others that spread underneath the estate like those of an anthill. Ensuring his dagger was tucked tightly into his belt, Aaron climbed down and replaced the board above his head.

The way was tight and dark. For a moment Aaron heard a noise, and he feared someone might be approaching from the other direction. He'd have no excuse or reason to explain his leaving. Thren would be furious. He heard another noise, sounding like the board he'd just replaced. Then silence. After five long minutes, Aaron resumed crawling, certain that no one was following him.

When he climbed out of the tunnel, he was underneath a giant, empty pile of crates that were never cleaned or removed from the alley in which they stood. Aaron pulled a thick strip of cloth from his pocket and tied it to his face, adjusting it so the eyeholes matched up perfectly.

He was Aaron no longer.

Haern dashed down the street, his pale cloak fluttering behind him. A moment later another figure emerged from beneath the crates and gave chase.

Madelyn felt sleep tugging at her eyes, but she refused its temptation. She wanted her eyes bloodshot and her actions slow and uneven when she met her husband. His anger would only grow at his seeing her thus.

Light spilled in from a crack in the doorway. Madelyn felt her heart halt and her fingers tighten on the dagger. So Calan had lied, just as she'd feared. They would kill her after all.

The door opened. Blinded by the sudden light, Madelyn winced and held a hand over her eyes. She saw a small figure, too small to be an assassin.

"Oh," she heard a girl say. "I didn't know…"

Madelyn lowered her hand as the girl thankfully closed the

door halfway. In the dimmer light, she could see. The girl stood with her hands behind her back. She wore a plain white dress that hung all the way down to her ankles. Her unadorned hair spilled down either side of her face, a beautiful red. Madelyn's best guess put her at no older than ten.

"I've been awake," Madelyn said. She realized she still clutched the dagger, and lowered it to the bed. That seemed to calm the girl a little.

"I was sent to get, um..."

She blushed and pointed at the chamber pot in the corner. Madelyn rolled her eyes.

"Just leave it," she said. "Come back for it in the morning."

The girl paused, clearly trying to decide which orders to follow. Madelyn stared at her face, seeing an odd familiarity. When the girl turned to leave, Madelyn spoke a name.

"Eschaton?"

The girl jolted as if shocked.

"How do you know my name?" she asked, turning back around.

"Just your last, girl. You've yet to give me your first."

The girl blushed.

"Delysia Eschaton. It is a pleasure to meet you, milady."

She gave a curtsy that was skillful as it was absurd in the plain long dress.

"I knew your father," Madelyn said. "Many years ago, when he was still a lord. You have his hair and eyes. We weren't close, but we talked on occasion. Then he let his faith override his senses and vanished into these cloistered halls."

Delysia didn't appear to know how to react.

"I hope what memories you have of my father are pleasant ones," she said at last. "Though it pains me to talk of them. I should go."

"Stay," Madelyn said, an idea growing in her head. "I've been locked alone in here for many hours, and it'd be good to have someone to talk with."

Delysia opened her mouth as if to protest, then decided otherwise. Madelyn patted the space beside her on the bed, and Delysia reluctantly took a seat there.

"Do they require you to have such plain hair?" Madelyn said as she brushed a hand through the fiery red.

"No. I haven't had time. I'm so new here."

Delysia tensed a little when Madelyn began braiding it, then slowly relaxed. Having spent a lifetime at courts, dinners, and extravagant parties, Madelyn had long ago learned how to read and manipulate others. Delysia was adrift, alone, and scared. Most important, she seemed to be craving a mother figure, judging from how quickly she'd relaxed after the braiding started.

Madelyn frantically racked her brain. Delius Eschaton... he'd been married, but what had happened to his wife?

"I'm so sorry about your mother," she said, deciding to keep it vague. No child as young as Delysia would be willing to discuss such a matter in depth. What was more important was the comfort Madelyn eased into her voice, the tender honesty and empathy.

"Daddy... he helped us through," Delysia said. Her whole body seemed to be shivering. "I miss him. I miss my brother. I miss my mom and my granny. I don't want to be here, I want to be home, I want to be..."

Her words ended in tears. Even with her manipulation, Madelyn was surprised by how quickly Delysia had broken down. The girl must have been on edge the whole day, just waiting for something to set her off. Knowing her timing must be perfect, Madelyn let Delysia cry just long enough before wrapping her shoulders in a hug.

"There now," she said. "Cry if you must. I know how you feel. I miss my husband. I worry for him too. For all he knows I'm hanging upside down from chains in one of Thren's hide-outs. If only I could feel him in my arms again."

"I heard others talking," Delysia said. "They said they'd send someone so he'd know."

"But are you sure?" she asked, letting her face harden just a little. After a moment Delysia shook her head.

"No," she said. "I guess I'm not."

Madelyn let the silence return. She'd finished two thin braids, so she began tying them together, high up near the top of Delysia's head. Lacking material, she tore a bit of her own dress and used it to tie the braids firm.

"Your brother is all you have left," she said, injecting a combination of curiosity and worry into her voice. "Do you know where he is now?"

"He's apprenticed to some wizard," Delysia said. "I could never pronounce his name right. Malderad? Maldrad? Something like that."

"Yes, wizards often have funny names," Madelyn said. "They think it gives them an air of mystery, but mostly it just makes them look like fools."

Delysia giggled softly.

Madelyn chose that moment to pull back her hands and set them on her lap. The sudden stop made Delysia turn to see what was the matter.

"I could take you to him," Madelyn said. "Surely you heard among the whispers who I am, Delysia. I am Lady Madelyn Keenan, and wealthier than the king. It seems cruel to keep you hidden here when your brother is out there alone and in danger. What if he returns to Veldaren? What if the thief guilds send for him too?"

Delysia twisted her fingers together, then grabbed her elbows and shivered as if she were cold. Madelyn paused a moment, then drove the final nail home.

"Delysia, does he even know your father is dead?"

Her eyes widened. She shook her head.

"Someone should tell him," Madelyn insisted. "I think it should be you. Come with me."

"I'll get in trouble," Delysia said, suddenly fearful. "Granny put me here, where it's safe. Who will I stay with, and what if Maldrad doesn't want me? I can't."

This was it. This was the moment to break her. Madelyn stood and crossed her arms, acting every bit the scolding parent. She was not going to stay in the temple the rest of the night. No matter how honest Calan seemed, Madelyn knew the way of the world. People wanted what she had, whether it be coin, power, or her body. Until she was safe with her husband she'd always be at risk, and no simple child would keep her from him.

"You can and you will, Delysia," she said. "I must return to my husband. You must return to your brother. Isn't that what you want? Forget what others expect of you. They don't decide your life. That isn't their right. I will ensure everything goes well for you, all for being a friend to me in my dark time. Help me, Delysia. Please. I'm asking you."

Delysia wilted under the barrage of words. She slowly nodded.

"You promise to take care of me?" she asked.

Madelyn smiled her sweetest smile.

"I promise," she said.

"Fine. Everyone else is asleep except me. Bertram was to help me with my nightly duties, but he's so fat he dozed off in his chair. I don't know if the door's locked."

"Only one way to know," Madelyn said, taking Delysia's hand. "Lead me there."

Haern scratched at his mask, wishing he had found something smoother to wear. When finished, he wrapped his cloak tighter about him. Other than his blond hair, he was a mess of gray lurking in the shadows. The temple was before him on the other side of the street. Haern hid beside a shop set up to take advantage of the temple's traffic, selling a multitude of sweet cakes and treats that got devoured after every service.

Looking at the temple, Haern wondered how the Abyss he was going to get inside. He saw no windows, just rows and rows of columns. The columns themselves were too smooth and wide for him to scale. The giant front doors were closed. They were unguarded but most likely locked and barred from the inside. The roof was sharply sloped, pointed in the middle but nearly flat at the edges, the shape created by a clever interlocking of additional tiles. A statue loomed on either side of the short white steps leading up into the temple. The left was of a noble-looking man in armor holding a set of scales. The right was of a young woman with her arms raised to the heavens as if singing in praise.

"Never abandon as hopeless something you've never tried," he whispered aloud. One of his earlier swordmasters had favored that saying. There was only one place left Haern could check, and that was the roof. So to the roof he went.

He'd taken nothing with him but his cloak and his knife, so he did what he could. At full speed, he curved to one side and leaped into the air. He kicked off the statue of the woman, vaulting himself atop the other statue. Not letting his momentum slow, he leaped again, his whole body reaching for the edge of the roof where it was flat.

His fingers brushed it, slipped, and then he was falling.

The front of the temple had large inset sections depicting mountains, fields of grain, and a rising sun. Below those carvings was a second edge jutting out just before the pillars began. Haern banged his elbow against the edge, twisting him midair before he could grab hold. A sharp intake of breath was the only cry he made.

He swung one foot up to the ledge, glad for once that he was still somewhat young and small. He had an inch and a half to stand on. More than enough with his feet turned sideways. He stood upon it, his back to the carvings, and looked down at the street. He saw no one. It seemed whatever activities might be normal for the night, they took place nowhere near the temple.

He was about to turn and jump for the roof when he heard a loud crack from the doors below.

"Hurry," said a woman's voice just above a whisper.

"I am," whispered back a girl. Haern's heart leaped. He recognized that voice. Then the two walked out from underneath him, hand in hand. Haern saw the red hair and knew for certain.

"Shit," he said, realizing where he still was. For all his efforts to get to the roof, Delysia had come out on her own, and now there was no easy way down...

Haern slipped back down to his fingers, took a deep breath, and then tried to fall forward instead of straight down. The higher up on the steps he landed, the better. Luck was with him, for he landed on the very top step, which gave him plenty of room to roll. His knees still ached, and there was no way for him to remain silent, but that was better than a painful tumble down the sharp edges of the steps.

Knowing time was short, he ran down the steps, chasing after the two who had hurried north from the temple. As if fleeing, they ducked between some stores. Haern felt his heart stutter. The way the older woman had led, it seemed like she'd been dragging Delysia. Something wasn't right at all. He sprinted faster, his dagger drawn.

"Why are we going this way?" Delysia asked once they hurried into the alley.

"I think I heard someone following us," Madelyn said, glancing back toward the street. "We have to be careful. Come closer."

Delysia realized the woman had taken out her dagger. Why had she taken out her dagger? And if she was afraid of someone following, why was she keeping her back to the road?

"I want to go back," she said, stepping farther into the alley. "I don't want to go anymore."

"I can't have anyone warned," Madelyn said. The compassion drained from her eyes. "Ashhur's priests have always been in the thief guilds' pockets, no matter how hard Calan insists otherwise. Your father was always a fool, Delysia. Kindness made him blind, and you're no different."

Delysia turned to run but the alley dead-ended at a thick wooden wall connecting the two stores. She spun back around and put her back to the wall. Madelyn stood in the center of the alley, dagger still in hand. There was no way past her; no way out.

"I won't tell anyone," she said, tears growing in her eyes.

"No," Madelyn said. "You won't."

Something knocked the dagger from her hand. Madelyn's mouth opened, and then a dirty boot struck the side of her face. Delysia let out a small cry as Madelyn went down, her hands outstretched to slow her fall. She rolled when she hit the ground, but Haern was already there, scooping up the dagger and kicking her in the stomach.

"How dare you try to hurt her," Haern whispered, his whole body trembling with rage. He held a dagger in each hand, and he looked more than ready to use them. Madelyn sat on her knees and glared.

"Don't," Delysia shouted. "Please, let her go."

Haern glanced at her, and Madelyn took the chance to run. Haern looked back, clearly debating.

"Please stay," Delysia insisted, and that was enough to keep him with her.

"What are you doing out here?" he asked, sliding both daggers into his belt.

"I was . . . I was doing something dumb. I'm sorry. I should get back."

"Wait," Haern said, reaching out and grabbing her wrist. Delysia tensed, but his touch was soft. He held her there, neither moving, only their eyes alive as they stared at one another.

"Please stay," he said.

"We'll be caught," Delysia said.

She heard the boy laugh.

"No, we won't," he said, sliding his grip down from her wrist to her hand. Then they were running, her heart hammering, and suddenly she was shimmying up the side of a house and onto the roof.

"We'll be safe here," Haern said once they were all the way up. They sat cross-legged before each other, the city stretched all around them, enclosed within the great wall. He gestured to his right, where the street was hidden from view.

"No one can see us passing by," he said.

Delysia nodded. She rubbed her arms with her hands, feeling both cold and afraid. The past few days had been a whirlwind of pain and confusion, and all she wanted was to curl up somewhere warm and sleep. Yet Haern kept looking at her with his blue eyes, so intense in their desperation. He wanted something of her, but what, she didn't know.

"Why did you come for me?" she asked, hoping to pry it out of him quickly so she could go back to the temple.

"Because I . . . it's about your father."

Delysia winced.

"What about him, Haern?"

Haern sighed and looked away. His mask helped hide his emotions, but it didn't erase them completely. He was reluctant and embarrassed. Delysia felt her fear hardening in her stomach. Whatever Haern had to say, she sensed she would not like hearing it.

"I helped kill your father," Haern said suddenly.

Delysia didn't move. Her thoughts returned to that day, but she remembered no boy. She only remembered tears, the surprised cries of the crowd, and then running far away so she could cry alone. Still, Haern's ache was too real to be a lie.

"Why?" she asked. "Why did you help?"

"Because my father asked it of me," Haern said. "That's not all, Delysia. I had a mission, one I failed. *You* were my target. I was to kill you."

Delysia suddenly felt paralyzed with fear. She thought back to her talk with him in the pantry. What if she had been a fool to let him out? He'd been stopped on his way to finish the job, and now here she was, helpless atop a roof with no way off other than a long fall.

"What do you want from me?" she asked, praying to Ashhur that the boy didn't draw his daggers.

"I followed you that day," Haern said. "You didn't see me, but I followed. I listened to you pray. It broke my heart. Do you understand? Listening to you cry, listening to you pleading so helplessly with your god, I couldn't..."

He stood and turned away.

"I couldn't let myself become such a monster. I've come close. I won't do it."

Delysia stood. The trouble inside him was so great, and her inner nature won out. She reached over and put a hand on his shoulder and turned him back to face her. Tears were in his eyes, wetting the cloth wrapped tight about his head.

"I want to know how to pray like you did," he said. "I want to have that kind of faith. Your father was dead, and you still believed. I've tried, but people died. I feel hollow and fake. What is it you know? What is it you do? Please, tell me, Delysia. I need this. I need something to cling to, otherwise I'll be lost forever. I'll become what my father wishes me to be."

Delysia blushed. She felt so young and foolish, and yet he was coming to her for help? She tried to think of all her father's lectures. The memory of his kind words and warm smile only hurt her more.

"Give me your hands," she said. There was one thing she remembered, one moment that nothing could ruin. It was the nightly prayers her father had said with her whenever she felt scared or lost. Tears in their eyes, she knelt, her fingers still interlocked with Haern's. The boy knelt with her.

"Bow your head," she told him.

"What now?" he asked.

"Close your eyes." He did, and then he waited.

"Think of everything you love," she said. "And pray it safe. Don't think about to whom you pray. Don't worry about whether it'll be heard or not. Just pray."

Haern opened his eyes and looked at her.

"What if I have nothing to love?" he asked.

The question pierced Delysia's heart. She'd once asked that same question of her father after they'd had a bad fight. She gave Haern the same answer he had given. Never in her life had she missed her father so much.

"Then you can love me," she said.

Her body lurched forward. Her mouth opened in shock, and it was only then she felt the pain. Blood seeped down the front of her dress as she fell, a small arrow shaft sticking out of her back.

CHAPTER

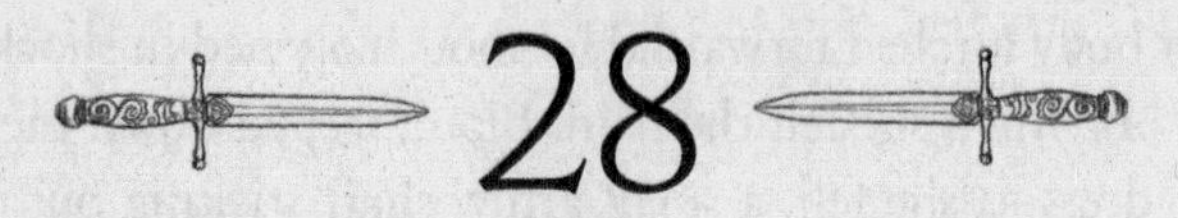

28

No!" Aaron screamed, catching Delysia in his arms. Kayla watched, her jaw clenched tight at the sight. All around him members of the Spider Guild leaped to the roof. Two houses over, Thren lowered his handheld crossbow and approached.

"Stay away from me!" Aaron shrieked, holding Delysia in one arm and drawing his dagger with the other. The men surrounded him, their weapons drawn. None approached, all waiting for their master. Kayla slowly closed the distance, and given how distracted the young man was, he did not sense her approach.

Thren leaped across the last gap and landed atop the house. He still held the crossbow.

"You have disobeyed me for the last time," Thren said. His voice was overwhelmed with rage. "Rooftop prayers? Hiding away with a priestess? What is the matter with you!"

"Stay back!" Aaron screamed again, tears streaming down

his covered face. Thren paid him no heed. He walked over and yanked the mask off Aaron's face, not at all worried by the dagger his son held.

"You disappoint me," Thren said.

That was it. She could see Aaron was ready to attack, and Kayla feared the repercussions. Taking a stone wrapped in thick leather by its short handle, she struck the back of his head. Letting out a garbled cry, he collapsed atop the dying girl's body.

"Carry him," Thren ordered his men. "Leave the girl."

Two of them hoisted the boy onto their shoulders and made their way toward the edge of the house. A group of three waited in the street below, catching Aaron when they lowered him down.

"Where are we taking him?" Kayla dared ask.

"These foolish notions need curing," Thren said as he put away the crossbow. "Ashhur is a disease infecting my son, and it seems I am incapable of removing it on my own."

Kayla followed the logic to its horrific end.

"You'll give him to the priests of Karak," she said.

Thren glanced at her.

"I do not like it either, but it must be done," he said. "They'll crush his faith in Ashhur, purifying him. I'm taking back my heir."

"Thren!" shouted one of the men, climbing back up to the roof. "We found her! We found Madelyn."

"Excellent," Thren said. "Get her bound. When I return, I'll set up a safe place for our dear noble hostage."

Kayla could hardly believe how easily Thren's frustration slid away upon hearing such a thing. His concern for Aaron, was it really that shallow? Kayla glanced back at the girl with the red hair as Thren leaped off the roof to join the rest of his men.

"Damn it, Aaron," she said. "I didn't know!"

Thren had ordered her to follow Aaron about. Once he'd stopped at the temple, she'd sent out a signal. And then when the girl had fled with Madelyn Keenan from the temple, Kayla could hardly believe the sight. She'd hoped Haern would stay away, would leave them alone, but he hadn't. By the time Thren arrived, Madelyn was running off through streets she knew nothing of, an easy catch. But Haern was still with the daughter of that idiot priest Kayla had killed, his very presence dooming her.

A presence his father had been alerted to by Kayla. The blood spilling across the roof was her fault.

She knelt down, touched the girl's neck, and was startled by the slow pulse she felt. The girl was alive.

"You owe me," Kayla whispered as she hoisted the girl onto her shoulder.

She was being stupid. She knew she was being stupid. Her survival instincts screamed to keep her hands clean and let the girl die. But she couldn't. If Aaron found out she was the one who had followed him, she couldn't imagine facing the sorrow and betrayal in his eyes. He'd trusted her, and this was how she'd repaid him?

"Stay with me," she whispered. "If your god is real, then hopefully he'll realize I'm down here needing all the help I can get."

Carefully she climbed down to the street, Delysia's body slung over her shoulders. The whole while she did her best to ignore whatever torture awaited Aaron within the temple of the dark god.

Thren was one of very few who knew the location of Karak's temple. Once they were near he took Aaron into his arms and ordered the rest to return home. The coming day and night would bring the most important series of events in the past five years. His men needed to be fresh, and he was already straining them enough. All because of his son. All because of Ashhur.

"I see through your illusions," said Thren when he stood before the thick iron gates surrounding what looked to be a luxurious but empty mansion. The image wavered. The fence opened on its own. Thren stepped through, walking along the smooth obsidian path leading up to an enormous pillared building of darkest black. The skull of a lion hung above the door, its teeth stained with blood.

The double doors swung open. A young man stepped out, his hair tied behind his head in a long ponytail.

"I ask that you remain outside," he said. "Pelarak knows of your arrival."

Not waiting for an answer, the man shut the door. Thren leaned Aaron's body against one of the pillars and waited. It had been many years since he'd come to someone for aid, and he wasn't entirely sure how to act. He had no intention of bowing before the priests, nor would he plead like a commoner. Perhaps a trade.

The doors opened. Thren snapped to attention, his hands falling to his blades out of instinct too engrained to deny.

"It is a strange night that grants me a visitor such as you," Pelarak said as he stepped outside and closed the doors behind him. The priest's eyes glanced at Aaron but he continued as if he saw nothing. "For you are Thren Felhorn, are you not? Master of the Spider Guild, puppet master of the thieves? To what do I owe this honor?"

"I need my son cured," Thren said.

"We are not as skilled at the healing arts as our rivals," Pelarak said. "Though I doubt they would aid you. I heard they ousted their former high priest after you killed one of their own."

Thren frowned. That was a damn shame. He had spent many months slowly working on Calvin, bribing him with every possible vice in search of the man's weakness. Once he'd discovered his love of crimleaf, the process had been considerably easier. Must everything fall apart so close to the Kensgold?

"You misunderstand the healing I desire," Thren said, forcing the subject back to the task at hand. "My son has taken foolish notions into his head that I want expunged."

Pelarak scratched his chin.

"He's fallen for the seductive grace of Ashhur?" he asked.

Thren nodded.

"This will require time," Pelarak said. "And more importantly, it will potentially ruin me. Maynard Gemcroft has threatened our very existence if I do not side with him against you, Thren. Tell me, what would you do in my place?"

"Destroy those who threaten me," Thren said. "Never let a man keep a sword readied above your neck."

"Words we cannot live by," Pelarak said. "Ashhur's presence here is too deeply embedded. Maynard could send mobs against us. Blood would fill the streets. Nothing of your little war with the Trifect would compare to the carnage we would unleash. But that would end our work here, which would sadden me greatly. So I have few choices."

Thren drew his short swords.

"I'd tread carefully," the guildmaster said.

Pelarak chuckled.

"Put those away. Even with your skill, you cannot match my power. I am Karak's most faithful servant, save for his prophet. If I wanted you dead I would not announce or explain myself."

Thren lowered his swords but did not sheathe them.

"What are your choices?" he asked.

"I can turn you away, making you a potential enemy. In doing so, I also remain a puppet of the Trifect. However, even that option has been denied to me. Maynard Gemcroft's daughter is missing. She was to be in my care, yet is not. For this alone Maynard will destroy us."

"There is another way," Thren said, realizing what Pelarak was leading to. "There is my way. Take my son. Cure him. Burn all remnants of Ashhur from his flesh so he may be pure."

"Can you kill Maynard Gemcroft?" Pelarak asked. "My time has already passed. By the end of the Kensgold he will carry out his threat."

Thren saluted with his sword.

"By tomorrow's eve Maynard will be dead," he vowed. "Can you save my son?"

"We will take him," Pelarak said. He banged twice on the doors. Two other priests came out. When Pelarak pointed to Aaron, they picked the boy up and carried him inside. As they did, Thren briefly described the events that had transpired, from Aaron's prayers and his amulet of the Golden Mountain to his secret meeting with the priest's daughter.

"How much time will it take?" Thren asked.

"A day or two at most, unless he resists our methods," the priest replied.

"Can he?" Thren asked, watching the double doors close with a groaning of wood and iron locks.

Pelarak laughed softly.

"Of course not. He's just a boy."

Thren bowed.

"May our endeavors aid us both," he said.

"Go with the true god's blessing," Pelarak said before returning inside.

Thren felt lighter as he vaulted over the iron fence and raced down the streets, taking a winding path back to his safe house. Matters were out of his hands now. The priests would convert his son. Any influence Ashhur had on him would be gone. Thren would save his killer, his perfect heir, the keeper of his legacy.

Assuming his plans for the Kensgold unfolded without error. But with Madelyn nearly gifting herself to him, he knew he'd taken a large step toward that goal. Now Thren could only hope his son would be saved in time to partake in the victory that would define the Felhorn legacy for centuries.

Aaron's awareness rose and fell, and as it rose he felt the pain. It stabbed into his wrists and forced him back down. Water splashed across his tongue. Dull chanting shook the rhythm of his dreams, flooding them with color that vibrated to the sound. He saw red and purple. The colors worked a sharp discomfort in his mind. More pain, this time in his ankles. Water dribbled up his lips. That didn't make any sense. Why up?

He opened his eyes. Expecting to be upside down, he was surprised to see a man standing before him. He was balding, with sharp eyes and a bitter frown. He wore dark robes. Hanging from his neck was a pendant shaped like the skull of a lion.

"Where am I?" Aaron asked.

"A room of faith," said the priest. "My name is Pelarak, and you are in a most holy place. Here Karak is master, not the goddess of the elves, not Ashhur, not the moon or the stars or the sun. Just Karak."

He held out his hand. In it was a waterskin. When he pressed against it, the water traveled up instead of down, splashing across the ceiling. The sight was so strange Aaron felt a sense of vertigo. He turned to the side, vomited, and then watched in horror as it smacked atop the ceiling, splattering a messy red.

"To be expected," the priest said. "Many things are strange here, and you will see only a blessed few. Karak is god everywhere, but we have consecrated this room with blood and prayers."

Aaron tried to move but could not. He looked to his wrists, where he felt cold iron chains. He saw nothing but air. The same for his ankles. As he struggled, he saw indents press against his skin, made by no visible source.

"Chains are a deceptive thing," Pelarak said. "Who makes them? What gives them their strength? It is shallow to call them iron and unbreakable, yet foolish to call them self-made. You have chains upon you. Break them."

Pelarak waved his hand as he gave the command. A sudden urge filled Aaron's heart. He could think of nothing but escape. Every flight response he had was triggered in his mind. Every muscle clenched and fought against the invisible chains. He felt his skin rub raw. His knees and shoulders throbbed in agony. Blood dripped upward in a perverse rain. Finally he flung his entire body forward, straining so hard against the chains his neck bulged and his forehead dripped sweat that drifted upward into his hair before pooling into thick drops that rose to the ceiling.

No matter how hard he tried, he could neither break the chains nor stop his trying.

"This is life," Pelarak said, watching emotionlessly. "We struggle against our bonds, unable to break them, but only because we are foolish. You have made those chains, Aaron. Break them."

He wanted to. Oh, how he wanted to. It felt like his heart would burst, each rapid beat like a hammer blow to his chest.

More blood floated upward from his wrists. His mind searched for the solution. Robert Haern had always insisted he'd know the answer to a question when asked, but did this priest ensure him the same fairness? What did he mean, chains of his own creation?

"I don't understand," he said, his voice cracking. His tongue felt made of cotton.

"Then try harder," Pelarak said. "Ignorance is not an excuse; it is a blindness fostered by this world. Your body will break, and you will die, all because of your ignorance."

The man was clearly a priest of Karak. Only one thing came to mind that might explain the chains, and why he would think them his own creation: Ashhur.

"I've prayed to Ashhur," Aaron shouted. He felt his maddening urge to struggle slowly subside. His breath shuddered as he hung limply from the invisible chains.

"Very good," Pelarak said. "You're making progress. Look to your hands and feet."

Aaron did. No longer were the chains invisible. Though they felt like iron, they appeared to be made of white marble. Golden Mountains decorated their keyholes. The room slowly darkened, though the chains remained bright, almost glowing.

"Symbols," Aaron said, his voice a whisper. "They lie as easily as men."

Pelarak's face seemed to darken at this.

"Keep your eyes open," he said. "I have something I want you to see."

He stepped back. The room turned completely dark, although both the chains and Pelarak remained perfectly visible. A fire sparked in the center of the room. Within its center Aaron saw the briefest image of an eye. The fire sparked again, then grew. It roared to the ceiling, enormous but without heat.

Its life was quick, and as it died a young girl stood before him, her fiery red hair tangled and unkempt.

"Aaron?" Delysia asked. Aaron felt his body tremble at the sound of her voice.

Just a lie, he thought. *Just another lie.*

But it was hard to believe that as she touched the side of his face. Her hand felt cold, but her touch was real. Tears flowed up his eyes and to the ceiling. Her dress was charred as if by fire.

"They do lie," the girl said. "The Abyss is cold. The fires give no heat. Ashhur didn't want me, so now I'm here. I gave no love to Karak, so he gives no love to me."

"You're not real," he said. It sounded like a plea. "You're with Ashhur. You went to a better place. You were good. You were *innocent*."

Pelarak laughed. Delysia cried. Her body faded upon an unfelt wind.

"No one's innocent," Delysia said through her sniffles. "But I worshipped something false. It didn't matter how I prayed. I prayed to deaf ears."

Aaron flung himself against his chains, desperate to touch her. She was fading away like a ghost. The darkness was claiming her, eating into her flesh so that it turned translucent. Pelarak waved a hand through her, scattering her image like smoke.

"You went to her," the priest said. "I spoke with your father. I know what you have done. Do you not see how foolish you are? A girl. A young, stupid girl, and yet you thought she had wisdom?"

Aaron slumped, and his eyes stared at a floor with no texture or shape.

"Her prayers were so real," he said. "She meant them. She felt them. That is what I wanted."

Pelarak grabbed Aaron's hair and jerked upward so they could stare eye to eye.

"Madmen gibber that demons live within them, and that their voices torment them daily. Do they not believe as deeply as that little girl did? Why not go to them for guidance?"

To this Aaron had no answer, but Pelarak did.

"Because she had a dream that you desired," the priest said, letting go of Aaron's hair. "You liked what she believed. It sounded sweet. But the only thing that matters is the truth. Would you willfully live a lie just because you like it? Should I tell you that your girl is fine, and that the world is a beautiful place, and that no one will ever hurt you? I'd love to live in that world, but that doesn't make it real. What is real, Aaron? What do you *know* is real?"

He thought of Robert Haern dead, killed by his student's hands. His hands.

"I know I've killed those I love," he said.

"Ah yes, and why?" Pelarak asked. "What is it that brought about their murders?"

A light flashed in Aaron's eyes. He knew. He saw his love and devotion, saw to whom he had given them. His guilt and shame coalesced into a hardened arrow, no longer aimed at himself. There was one person who deserved it all. The one who had strangled his soul and perverted his desires. The one who had used his love to inspire murder and destruction. His own father.

"I prayed to Ashhur," Aaron said. It was no lie. "Because of that, people died."

"Precisely," Pelarak said. "Is that Ashhur's power? Devotion leading to death? Karak is power, boy. He is the Lion. He is king of all, and all will tremble before his roar and bow to kiss his claws."

Suddenly Pelarak was gone. The chains cracked and broke.

Aaron crumpled to the ground, shivering in the darkness. He felt cold. His teeth chattered.

And then the Lion approached. It walked from afar, too far to be inside the small room. Its fur was fire, burning atop skin made of molten rock. Eyes swirling with smoke fixed upon his trembling form. When it opened its mouth, teeth the size of daggers glistened with fresh blood.

Behold the Lion, shouted a voice, impossibly deep and booming from every corner of the room. *Behold the power of his majesty.*

The Lion roared. Deep within its gullet Aaron saw a thousand weeping lives. They reached upward and wailed, their cries mixing with the mighty roar of a god. Aaron felt his soul quiver. He mashed his face to the cold dark stone. Tears flowed from his eyes. He couldn't think. He could only tremble in wonder.

Do you doubt my authority? the Lion asked. *Who are you to me, mortal? When your life ends, I am the Truth that awaits you. Where shall you stand in my eternity? Will you worship beside me, or will I consume you in fire and grind your bones in my teeth?*

Aaron sobbed shamelessly. He'd never felt such terror. He was naked before a god, pathetic and helpless. He pounded his fists against the floor. Sweat covered him like a cold sheet. The Lion roared again, and its breath was fire and steel. His clothes ripped and his flesh tore. Blood spilled outward in bizarre directions, as if the laws of the world had no bearing within Karak's sacred room.

Will you swear your life to me? the Lion asked.

A deep part of Aaron wanted to submit. He wanted the terror to end. The darkness would consume him, and it seemed wisest to surrender. Standing beside the Lion was better than the wailing he heard within. Infinitely better.

Aaron thought of what Robert had said. Ashhur was everything good in mankind. With tears in his eyes he looked up to the Lion, searching for that same goodness. He saw none of it within the fire. Death, consumption, anger, and condemnation looked upon him, smoldering in physical form. None of the love that had filled Delysia's prayers could live within that horrific creature. He felt his mind splitting, as if two paths were before him and half wanted to go down one and half the other.

Swear it! the Lion roared. *On your knees, swear your life to me. I will have it no other way. Death is your fate, child. I see it clearer than you see the sun and moon. You will die by the hand of a friend if you resist my mercy. Beside me, you will rule Neldar as a demigod, and your son as king.*

Two paths. Two beings. Two minds. His father desired that first path, the easy path, one of bloodshed and murder. But the desire Robert Haern had kindled, the one Kayla had protected and Delysia nurtured, led away into deadly light. Each filled him with fear. Deep down, he knew which was right. He knew the choice he should make. But he was afraid.

Choose! roared the Lion. *Now, or I will burn away everything that makes you who you are, and deliver unto the priests an empty shell.*

He couldn't choose. Terror overwhelmed him. Stars swirled in the darkness about the Lion, as if the very heavens circled the embodiment of Karak. Smoke billowed from its nostrils. Its eyes flared with impatience. The Lion opened its mouth and snarled. His time was up. The moment was gone.

Aaron felt the roar wash over him, stronger than ever before. It felt like the world would shatter beneath its strength. His ears would never hear again. His eyes burned with tears. The breath in his lungs halted, and his heart beat wildly. Within his mind a fire raged, consuming all. The choice. There was only one. Aaron knew it. The fire was an altar, and he laid down his sacrifice.

Everything that meant to be Aaron, to be the son of Thren Felhorn, to murder without guilt and devote everything to bloodshed and slaughter, he flung upon that altar. He openly welcomed the roar, now a cleansing fire. He let it destroy his fear. He let it obliterate his lack of remorse. It tore down his walls. In the midst of that roar, he laughed.

"Let Aaron die," he said. "Haern lives."

More phantom cuts lashed his arms and chest. The blood now flowed in the correct direction. Smoke poured into his lungs. His head swam, light and dizzy and free. His neck drooped. His eyes closed. A laugh still on his lips, he succumbed to unconsciousness as the Lion roared.

"Come," Pelarak said as he opened the door. Two more priests stepped inside, joining him in a small square room. The walls were bare and gray, the floor cool stone.

"Were you successful?" one of the other priests asked.

"He has seen the Lion," Pelarak said. "None but the most faithful have done so and lived. When he awakes, his heart will belong to Karak. Of that I am certain."

"Praise be," said the other.

They carried the young man out of the room. Pelarak watched them leave, a frown on his face. Something felt wrong, but he couldn't decide what. He hadn't heard the words of the Lion, nor seen its vision, but he had felt its awesome power as he watched Aaron sob and cry on his knees. There was something unsettling about how Aaron had laughed at the very end.

Determined to question Aaron when he awakened, Pelarak stepped out of the most holy of rooms. He'd devote an hour to prayer, then seek the sleep he most desperately needed. Perhaps things would seem better in the morning.

CHAPTER

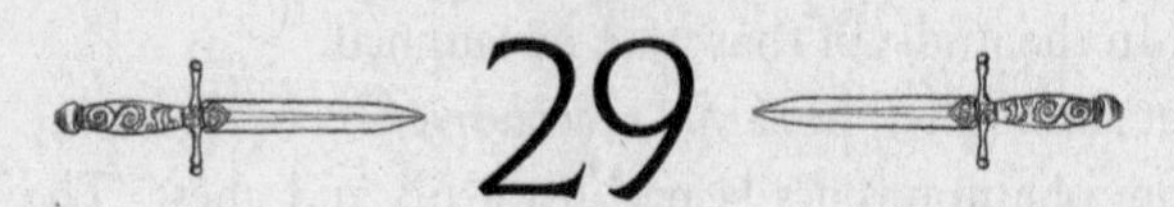

29

You mustn't stop," Zusa insisted as the two ran. "The paladin will follow. He will always follow."

Alyssa nodded. Her breathing had become ragged, and her left side ached as if a dagger was lodged within. They'd run west, away from the camp and away from Veldaren's walls. A few times they'd shifted direction, but only to avoid the hills that surrounded the area.

"Where," Alyssa said, feeling light-headed and unable to voice the rest of her question.

"The river is near," Zusa said. "We will use that as we must."

Alyssa did her best to keep up, but they had run for almost an hour after fleeing the Kulls' camp. She'd never felt herself out of shape, but the exertion was beyond even her capabilities. She started stumbling, dragged on only by Zusa's firm grip on her wrist.

"Not far," Zusa insisted. "Hurry. Not far at all."

The Kinel River ran south from the mountains, passing west of the King's Forest and looping a quarter mile from Veldaren before traveling south, marking the western edge of the Kingstrip. Despite her aching sides, weak legs, and ragged breath, Alyssa managed the final few minutes to its edge.

"We must get to the other side," Zusa insisted. "The river is wide, but not deep. The paladin will cross, but slowly. The plate mail will hinder him."

"Please," Alyssa said, falling to her knees. "Let me rest a moment."

"Rest on the other side," Zusa said. "He may be here at any moment. Life or death, girl. Choose."

She staggered to her feet and grabbed Zusa's shoulder.

"Life," she said.

The water came up to their necks, and it was shockingly cold. Alyssa's lips turned blue, and her teeth chattered. Zusa tugged her along, although Alyssa could no longer feel her hand clutching her wrist. She dreaded the coming feel of open air, but a dim part of her was certain it'd still be warmer than the water.

"Fire will bring him to us," Zusa said, even her gravelly voice chattering a bit. "But we have no choice. I can fight the paladin. I cannot fight the frost."

A minute later they emerged on the other side. Alyssa took a few steps before crumpling to her knees, doubling over with her arms crossed before her chest. She tried to speak, but her shivering was so severe she could not make the words.

Zusa knelt in front of Alyssa. Shadows curled off her body, moving sluggishly as if they too were affected by the cold. Zusa's hands touched the grass, her fingers digging into the earth.

"*Nuruta*," Zusa hissed. Purple fire erupted between them. It burned bright, then faded to the size of a man's head.

"Stay close to it," Zusa said. "The warmth is weak, but it will keep you alive."

Zusa looked back to the river. Alyssa followed her gaze. She saw nothing in the dim starlight, but evidently the faceless woman's eyes saw far better in the darkness.

"The paladin approaches," she said. "Half a mile away, perhaps farther. We have time for warmth."

The two huddled before the fire, feeling its heat fight away the wetness of their clothes.

"Karak has abandoned me," Zusa said as the fire popped. "My soul is already doomed to the Abyss. What does one more broken law matter?"

Alyssa watched as she peeled away the wet wrappings from her head. Her eyes were a sparkling green, her lips pale and supple. Her cheeks were smooth and round, as if Zusa had been carved from stone in the image of a goddess. Short black hair stuck to the sides of her face, but she pulled it back into a ponytail and tied it with one of her wrappings.

"If Karak would hide such beauty from the world, then he is a foolish, jealous god," Alyssa said. She looked to the river. "Can you kill his paladin?"

"We shall see," Zusa said. She glanced down at her wrappings, which were still soaked from the river. With a shrug she removed them and cast them beside the fire, along with her wet shift. Looking like a naked nymph of the forest, Zusa kissed her dagger and then approached the water's edge. Alyssa thought to do the same, then decided she would wait. If Zusa died, then her fate was sealed as well. She would not die naked.

"You are determined, servant of Karak," Zusa shouted across the river. With her back to the fire, Alyssa watched, her eyes adjusted enough to see the man standing on the other side. His armor was even darker than the night. He drew his sword, and black flame swelled about it.

"My name is Ethric, and my faith is fervent," the paladin shouted back. "But you have cast aside your wrappings, disobeying the order of our god. Will you fight me like a naked whore, or do you hope to distract me while you cut my flesh with your dagger?"

"When you are dead, I will cast your body to the river," Zusa shouted. "The fish will nibble on your eyes and worms will feed on your guts. Do you still desire to cross?"

Ethric laughed.

"Desire? My desires mean nothing. Karak has commanded your death and the return of Alyssa Gemcroft. I will cross, and I will burn your head and leave your body for the wolves."

He took a step into the water. Zusa crouched, her dagger held before her eyes. To Alyssa, she appeared some strange wildling, dangerous, calm, and insane. She shifted closer to the fire, feeling for the first time in her life an urge to pray. Whatever fate lay before her, she knew she wanted the dark paladin to have no part of it. But whom could she pray to in her desire for death other than Karak? Surely Karak would accept no prayers aimed at the destruction of his own champion.

"One more step," said Zusa. "Just one more, and I will kill you. The water is your death, Paladin."

Ethric waded into the river. At first it flowed to his waist, then rose until it was above his chest. He kept his sword held high, its dark fire absorbing the light of the stars so that it seemed a deep chasm floated above his head. Zusa remained still, her body crouched. Whispers floated off her tongue. The shadows grew about her, hiding her nakedness.

Protect her, Alyssa prayed, though she knew not to whom. *She may not deserve it, and neither do I, but protect her anyway.*

Once Ethric was in the center of the river, Zusa leaped. It

seemed the chains of the world had left her, for she vaulted high in the air. A cloak of shadow followed her even though she was naked. For a moment she soared as if on wings, and then curled her body downward, diving like a bird of prey. Ethric tilted his sword, but his movements were hampered by the deep water.

The collision was brutal. Alyssa gasped as shadows collided against shadows. Water erupted as if the ground had thrown up its contents and shifted the river. A single harsh clang of steel rang in her ears. When the river calmed and her eyes could see once again, she saw neither of the combatants. Her heart trembled. She thought to run. Freezing to death seemed far better than whatever fate the dark paladin planned for her.

The water rippled, and then Zusa stepped onto the shore, water dripping from her slender body.

"I warned him," she said, and then a smile broke out across her face. "He drowned. Make room by the fire."

Zusa sat beside her wrappings, crossed her legs, and leaned toward the purple flame. Hardly believing it, Alyssa stripped off her own wet clothing and huddled closer. Both of them naked, wet, and freezing, Alyssa laughed at what a sight they must be.

"I think many a man would love to stumble upon our camp this night," she said.

"One did," Zusa said, glancing to the river. "I pray he enjoyed what he saw."

They cuddled together for warmth beside the fire that never faltered.

Alyssa dreamed of Yoren approaching their camp, walking over the river as if he were a ghost. When he neared, he grabbed one of her nipples and squeezed it so tightly it hurt.

"I missed you," he said, smiling. His teeth, no longer gold, were crumbling ash. She screamed. He kissed her, ramming his tongue down her throat. Suddenly it was a snake, crawling down into her belly and coiling there. She thought she'd vomit, but when she did he shoved his hand over her mouth and forced her to swallow it back down.

When morning came, Alyssa groaned and reached for her clothing. The fire was gone, and her skin pale and covered with goose pimples. Zusa lay beside her, awake but still undressed.

"Your dreams were ill," Zusa said.

"They were," Alyssa said, pulling on her dress, which was blessedly dry but for a thin layer of dew. "I hope they're not a portent of things to come."

"I dreamed too," Zusa said. "Karak sent me warning of my path. I walked upon a road of flame, and every step burned the soles of my feet. Eventually I had to crawl, and when I could not crawl I collapsed. The fire wouldn't kill me, though. It only caused me pain. What is it you dreamed?"

Alyssa explained her dream. Zusa's eyes seemed so sad when she looked upon her.

"You are pregnant with Yoren's seed," she said. "The signs are obvious. He will take over your household through your child."

Alyssa opened her mouth, then closed it. A child? Part of her had hoped such a thing might happen when she'd lain with Yoren in their secretive nights. With a babe growing in her belly, her father never would have been able to deny the marriage she desired. But now? Now after seeing the monster Yoren truly was, now that she was destitute and alone? She didn't know what to think, what to do.

"The Kulls would make me a slave, or worse," Alyssa said. "I cannot bear it. We must flee."

"Even without you they will move," Zusa said. "They mean to kill Lord Gemcroft as an end to their problems. Besides, what did I tell you about running?"

"Then what am I to do?" she asked.

"There is a ferry a mile south," Zusa said as she started covering her body with her wrappings. When she reached her neck she stopped, and a playful smile came over her. She tossed the rest, leaving her face and hair exposed.

"We will talk along the way," Zusa said. "We tread a dangerous line, and you will find no help in either Kull or Gemcroft. You are trapped between vipers and a pit."

Her eyes twinkled.

"Still, even vipers may serve their purpose."

CHAPTER

30

Haern awoke on a simple bed stuffed with straw. A blanket covered him. Bandages wrapped the cuts across his body, every one of them stinging like a freshly opened wound. The room was dark and without windows, but light from the hallway crept in through the crack of the door, allowing him to see.

Tears filled his eyes as Haern fought down a wild laugh. He'd lived. He'd come face-to-face with the Lion and lived. His father would be furious... if he ever found out. Haern had no intention of letting him. His days as Thren's heir were done. He'd tear himself free or die trying. No matter what his fate, he'd make sure Delysia's death meant something.

"Please," he prayed. "I am in the den of lions. Keep me safe."

He slid off the bed. His gray clothes were shredded, but the cuts were thin and the cloth mostly intact. He wished he had his mask, though. Without it he still had the face of Aaron. His smile grew as he realized he wore the face of a dead man. How many would truly know that was the case?

His pillow had a covering, so he removed it and then quickly searched the room. His footsteps made no sound, and his fingers were like feather-strokes upon his surroundings. He found no weapon in the lone drawer, nor stashed under his bed or beside the door. Disappointed, he tied the covering across his mouth as if he were a lowborn bandit. It'd have to do for now.

Haern crept to the door and lay flat upon the floor. From what he could see through the crack, the hallway was empty. A lone torch flickered opposite, the source of his light. Now the real test. He stood and gently checked the door. It wasn't locked.

"Thank you," he whispered. "Now keep it up, all right?"

He heard no footsteps, no shuffling of a bored guard or soft breathing of a slumbering man. Taking in a deep breath, Haern pushed the door open a crack and slid out into the hallway.

It was empty. Haern gently shut the door behind him just in case. The carpet was thick and soft. He couldn't have asked for better. Small torches were lit every twenty feet, hanging from iron loops embedded in the walls. Bits of purple flickered in their centers. They released no smoke.

Faced with yet another choice, Haern glanced left, then right. The hallway ended in a sharp turn either way. He didn't have the slightest clue where he was within the temple complex. One way might lead out. The other might lead farther in. He decided to go right, and if it didn't look promising, to hurry the other way.

It turned out the way was correct, but still far from promising. Looming before him was the great open chamber of worship. The statue of Karak towered before him, still intimidating even in profile. The purple fires burned at his feet, the only light visible. Shadows danced across the pews. Two men knelt in prayer before their altar. A third slowly circled the room, softly singing something more akin to a funeral dirge than a worship hymn. His hands were lifted to the ceiling and his eyes half closed.

The two praying he might sneak past, but the circling priest was another matter. Haern leaned back into the hallway, knowing his time to escape was fleeting. He couldn't let three men stop him. He was the former son of Thren Felhorn. He wouldn't let three thousand men stop him.

"Keep circling," Haern whispered. When the priest was on the opposite side of the room, Haern ran as fast as he could, his upper body crouched down. The motion made his legs ache and his back twinge, but he recited a mental litany against pain taught him by one of his tutors. When he was halfway to the first row of pews, one of the praying men leaned back and shouted in a twisted cry of pain and triumph.

Haern's instinct was to freeze but he didn't obey it. That was something else he'd long ago been trained to ignore. He rolled behind the first row, then spun about to look. One priest stood before the statue, a knife in hand. Blood spilled from his other arm, his severed hand lying on the smooth obsidian altar. Haern's eyes locked upon the knife. It was a bit ornate, no doubt intended for sacrifice instead of battle, but it would have to do. He tried not to think on the horror of seeing a man mutilate himself in the name of his god.

The other praying priest stood and wrapped his arms around the bleeding man. The third continued his circling and singing as if nothing unusual were happening.

"Do not fight the pain," the unwounded one said. "In darkness we bleed to prevent the darkness spreading to others. We must give all to defy the chaos of this world. Your pain is nothing compared to the suffering of thousands."

Haern crawled along the right side of the pews. Time was running out. The hallway leading to the center aisle clearly looked like an exit, but if he didn't reach it before the circling priest came up behind him, he'd be spotted.

"Karak be praised!" shouted the mutilated priest. Haern felt his stomach tighten at another cry of pain. He didn't dare look, but it sounded like one of them was sobbing. The dire hymn continued in its low, maniacal consistency.

At last Haern was at the final row. He lowered himself to the ground, looking for the feet of the circling priest. Once he was on the opposite side yet again, Haern ran toward the center.

He immediately fled when he saw what awaited him down the long entryway hall: two priests leaning against the door, their heads bowed and their arms crossed. He couldn't see their eyes in the split second before he rolled to the pews on the other side. Their hoods were pulled low. They might be asleep…or they might have spotted his roll.

No shouts of warning came from the doors. He had gone unnoticed.

"Thanks, Ashhur," he whispered under his breath. There was no way he could sneak past the two of them, nor could he subdue them with his bare hands. Only one option remained. He made his way back toward the front. The bleeding priest had stopped crying, instead sucking loud, labored breaths in through clenched teeth. The other had begun reciting a series of scriptures that cooled Haern's blood.

"Only in death is life reborn. Only in blood is sin denied. Only in darkness is the world saved. Only in absolute emptiness is there order. Praise be to Karak."

"Praise be," the other priest stammered.

The circling priest switched hymns, his voice deepening and the words slowing. Haern couldn't understand the lyrics, but the song gave him the shivers. The two priests up front weren't helping either. Judging by the song, the man was near the door. Time was short.

Haern looked around the pew to the statue. The first priest had placed the dagger upon the altar, its hilt and blade covered with blood. Beside it was a severed hand. The other was clutching him, repeating scriptures while blood seeped into the bandages wrapped around the stump.

"Forgive me my theft," the wounded priest murmured, his skin pale and his eyes rolled back in his head. His words mingled with the scriptures, blending in perfect harmony. "Forgive me my theft, Lord. Wounded I enter, but enter I will."

"Only in blood is sin denied."

"Forgive me my theft, Lord. Whole I sinned, but wounded I enter."

"Only in darkness is this world saved."

"Forgive me my theft, Lord. I deny myself the chaos."

"Only in absolute emptiness is there order," the two repeated as one.

Haern chose that moment to strike. He kicked the unwounded priest behind the knee, the man's head smacking the altar on the way down. Planting his feet firm, Haern rammed his body against the other, elbowing the bloody stump. The priest cried out, staggering backward on weak legs.

Giving neither time to respond, Haern scooped up the dagger, spun, and slashed open the first priest's throat. As his body spasmed, Haern turned to the other and lunged. The dagger pierced the man's chest.

"Only in blood," the priest whispered with his dying breath.

A bolt of shadow struck Haern's side. He cried out, stunned by the immense agony. It felt like every nerve in the area was firing off sensations of pain. Rolling to avoid the next, Haern clutched the dagger with both hands. The hilt was slick with blood, and he might lose it if he wasn't careful.

"Killed amid worship!" the third priest shouted, his deep voice booming in the great room. "You will suffer for such blasphemy!"

Two more bolts of shadow flew from the priest's hands, splintering wood and cracking stone where they struck. Haern ran between the pews, using their wood for cover. The priest was halfway down the center aisle. Close enough. Haern stepped onto a pew and leaped with all his strength. His body stretched, the dagger lashing out. The priest, stunned by the sudden assault, tried to ward himself. The spell died on his lips as the dagger slashed his face.

Then their bodies collided. Haern screamed as his shoulder rammed the priest's chest, wrenching his whole body violently. He spun and landed awkwardly on a pew, his feet sticking into the air and his stomach pressed against the seat. The priest fared better, collapsing into a sitting position on the pew.

"Suffer!" the priest shouted. The word carried power with it. Haern rolled to the floor, his mind white with pain. His wounds from the Lion raged. Blood soaked his clothing, some his, some not. He felt the dagger slipping from his weakened hand.

"You cannot resist Karak's power," the priest said, reaching down to take away the dagger. "How such a simple boy could kill two of his..."

Haern put a leg underneath him and pushed, ramming himself into the priest's stomach before the man could close his fingers about the hilt. The man's hands clawed about him, flailing. Haern stabbed once, twice, then twisted the blade upon yanking it out. Blood shot across the front of his shirt.

"Karak is nothing to me," Haern said, feeling a sick joy at denying the man's dark god even as he died.

He had no time, though. The two other priests had come running down the long entryway and into the room beyond. Unlike the other three, they were not caught unaware. Dark magic crackled around their fingertips as they summoned the might of their god.

Haern ducked below the pew, cleaned the handle on the dead priest's robe, and then took a deep breath. With the sounds of battle, the rest of the priesthood would soon awaken and join them. He had one chance to escape, and that involved a head-on approach against two furious priests.

"Protect me, or make sure I die," Haern prayed, staring at the dagger. Either way, he had no intention of staying. Dagger clutched tight in his right hand, he made his charge.

Bolts of shadow struck the pews, exploding their wood into splinters. They hit to either side of him, for Haern had leaped over the first row, using the seat to catapult himself into the air. He flew heels-first, curling gracefully to land atop the very last row. More bolts chased him but he twirled into another jump, the dagger flashing with each spin as it caught the light of the altar's fire.

When he landed he did not engage but instead ran between them, his dagger lashing outward. The one on the right screamed as the tendons underneath his arm tore, blood rushing down his side. Haern went to cut the other, but the priest clapped his hands together. A wave of power rolled outward, knocking the boy aside as if he were an insect before a storm.

"Get back," the priest on the left told his wounded friend, who reluctantly obeyed. Haern took two steps toward the door as if to flee, then dropped flat on the ground. A blast of red lightning shot above his head, breaking the thick bar across the doors. Haern rolled to his knees and kicked. Instead of directly charging the priest he lunged to the side, ramming his shoulder against the wall. Another bolt of shadow struck the ground, missing by inches.

Both priests began their prayers for another spell, but Haern was too close. Their hands moved as if in a dream, their bodies surrounded by molasses. Haern kicked off the wall, spun once, and slashed his dagger into the nearest priest's chest. Without slowing he spun about the body, stabbed again, and then jumped toward the other. His foot crushed windpipe; his dagger pierced lung.

The priests fell. Haern tossed the sacrificial dagger.

"Karak can keep it," he told the bodies. With the bar broken, he pushed open the doors with ease. He avoided the obsidian steps, not liking the way they glowed in the waning moonlight. The soft grass felt wonderful to his feet, as did the sudden rush of fresh air. Only the fence blocked his way. Haern laughed. After five priests, a fence would be child's play.

He swung his weight from side to side as he shimmied up the bars, then somersaulted over the sharpened tops. The landing jarred his legs, adding more pain to his already impressive list, but he was out. He was free. Haern looked back to the temple, watching as it slowly turned into an earthly mansion, its columns fading into shadow and lies.

It seemed an appropriate place to entomb the sins of Aaron Felhorn forever. Free at last, Haern ran on, knowing he had much to do if he was to ruin his father's plans for the Kensgold.

Not long after the dawn, the first of many wagons exited the western gate of Veldaren. More followed. They were Connington's, loaded with barrels of wine and ale. Rows of mercenaries guarded them. Leon would have no repeat of the peach-pissing disaster. A few women went with them, trailing just behind. They were the first of what would soon be an army of camp followers.

The wagons circled the hills, held back from the peaks by Keenan's men. Tents occupied every open spot. Prostitutes drifted among the mercenaries, latching onto those who appeared handsome or wealthy. More wagons arrived, these carrying wood and utensils for building fires and cooking the enormous amounts of food soon to follow. Old tables snaked throughout the camp, mismatched in color and style.

By midafternoon the noise had grown so loud that those within Veldaren could hear the cacophony. Merchants not directly associated with the Trifect packed up their wares and shifted west, setting up shop beside the gates or along the winding path leading toward the camps. Coin was traded between a thousand hands. Lord Maynard Gemcroft's wagons arrived next, loaded with silks, chains, jewels, earrings, and a veritable army of mercenaries with swords drawn. The camp followers bedecked themselves in decorations far above their station, knowing the Kensgold would be their best night in years. Gold flowed at the Kensgold, as they always said.

The meat wagons arrived late from the southern farms, much to the ire of Leon Connington's cooks. Leon had appointed himself master of the meal, but that meal could not truly begin until the first cows arrived for the butchers. They dug a ditch in the dirt south of the hill and let the blood flow. Flies buzzed about it, stubbornly withstanding the chill of the newly arrived winter. As cooks cut and chopped the meat, small fires spread across the hill, surrounded by stones and covered with spits and cauldrons. Until the meat was ready, the men and women gorged on biscuits, honey, and rolls basted with spices.

Plenty of it was free, but far more was not. It never seemed to matter. The consumption grew. Atop the larger hill was a great pavilion, and within feasted the highest members of the Trifect. Leon had staggered up the hill, all fat and sweat and silk, and boisterously clasped Laurie's hand.

"I tell you, it's been many years since I feasted in the open air," he nearly shouted. "And the taxes? Preposterous! Thank the gods you thought of this place. You saved me a fortune on the cattle alone."

Leon's family was distant, since he was unmarried and was yet to declare an official heir. Various aunts, uncles, and cousins traveled with him, decadent in their clothes and obstinate in their attitudes. Laurie quickly ushered them all into the pavilion, promising warmth, food, and drink...much of it Connington's, but still he offered.

Maynard Gemcroft was the last of the three to arrive. He traveled in a caravan of over two hundred mercenaries, along with another hundred servants, tasters, singers, jugglers, and other performers. While Leon had declared himself master of the meal, Maynard had taken over the entertainment.

Slowly joining them in a steady stream were friends and families of the mercenaries, the cooks, the servants, the wealthy and the poor, along with many members of the thief guilds, their daggers poisoned and their eyes wide at the proliferation of gold and silver.

An hour before nightfall, the Kensgold officially began.

CHAPTER 31

While the Kensgold was gearing up, the leaders of the thief guilds met in a strange place for their kind: open air in broad daylight. They stood before the large fountain in the very center of Veldaren. Any gathering of so many leaders needed to be somewhere neutral, with many exits, otherwise no one would come. Given the absolute chaos of the Kensgold outside the city, traffic was almost nonexistent within. As if infected with a massive plague, the whole city had emptied outward, flooding the surrounding hills with torches, campfires, tents, and song.

Thren was the first to arrive. Any delay on his part might worry the others. Kadish Vel of the Hawk Guild was next, looking ugly as ever with his red teeth and loose eye patch. Then came Norris Vel, brother to Kadish and newly appointed master of the Serpent Guild after Thren had killed Galren, their old leader. The Shadow Guild had a new leader as well, a bulky man named Gart.

"Just Gart," the man said when introducing himself to Thren. His hands were meaty and his voice slow. "My last name's a bitch."

"What happened to Yorshank?" Thren asked.

"I'm slow," Gart said, flexing his hands. "He was slower."

James Beren of the Ash Guild was the last to arrive. All the leaders had been allowed to bring one trusted member, and Veliana was his. She glared at Kadish but wisely held her tongue.

"Where's the Wolf?" Kadish asked as they stood about the fountain, looking nothing more than a group of old friends gathering before joining the festivities. So far the only significant player in the underworld yet to arrive was Cynric, master of the Wolf Guild.

"He and his men are already scattered about the Kensgold," Thren explained. He kept his back to the fountain and the guildmasters to his front. "I will go to them with the real plan after discussing it with you all."

"Real plan?" Kadish asked. "What do you mean, real plan?"

Thren shrugged.

"Do you think I would propose a plan so simple, or trust you and your ilk to keep it from leaking to the Trifect?"

James stepped forward, unable to hide his anger. "You sicced your pets on me just so I would agree to a *false* plan, a suicidal assault on their camp amid the Kensgold that every one of us here knew would fail? Even you knew how stupid it was, yet we were made to suffer for refusing it?"

The other members grumbled, none of them happy with being taken for fools. Thren silenced them by putting his hand on the hilt of his sword.

"Enough," he said. "What is done is done. No matter how hard I might try, I knew the plan would reach the Trifect. That was the point. We will not launch an assault on the Kensgold, especially not with them outside the city. Without our walls, our shadows, our poison, we are nothing but an outnumbered army of children."

"Your Spiders may be children, but my Hawks spill blood like men," Kadish said.

"So what's the real plan?" asked Gart. "I still get to break necks?"

"Their mansions are empty," Thren said, a smile growing on his face. "They've taken the vast bulk of their mercenaries and helpers. Now is when we strike. We will split up, half assaulting the Conningtons' estate, the other half the Gemcrofts'. Kill everyone inside, and I mean *everyone*. Then we set our traps. When the Trifect return we assault them from the windows and rooftops of their own homes. We'll kill their family, their friends. When it is time to run, we burn their mansions to the ground. They will suffer tonight, and suffer greatly. If we are lucky, we might kill Leon or Maynard during the assault."

Thren looked to every single pair of eyes, judging their commitment. Despite their anger at being deceived, the simple but brutal plan seemed to excite their bloodlust. Five years was a long time. Suddenly an end seemed in sight.

"Who goes where?" Kadish finally asked.

"The Hawks and the Ash will take out the Gemcrofts. The Serpents and the Shadows will go for the Conningtons."

"And who will you go for?" James asked.

"My men will be split among each of you," Thren said. "That way I show no preference and therefore no risk of betrayal. As for who I go with . . . that is my own damn business."

"You can't make us go with the Hawks," Veliana insisted, her outburst earning her a glare from both James and Kadish.

"Come now, your lovely presence will make the proceedings all the more exciting," Kadish said.

"No arguing," Thren said. "No squabbles. No betrayals. We end this tonight. Understood?"

They all reluctantly agreed.

"I get to crush Connington blood," Gart said. He seemed tremendously happy.

"Wait until the sun has dipped below the walls," Thren ordered. "Move in concert, and keep it quiet. Once set up, things will take time. Kill any who might return early, and wait for the main force before you act. And no matter what, make sure the homes burn."

They all scattered in various directions. Just as they were the last to arrive, James and Veliana were the last to leave.

"His men are split and he hides his own destination," Veliana said to her guildmaster. "There is no way to betray him without betraying other guilds as well. Now we play along or make enemies of every living man and woman within Veldaren."

"Never said he was a fool," James said. "And you're right. The ambush we prepared was for him outside the city. We have nothing prepared, and cannot prepare with him hiding his location. It seems we were fooled, when we had no right to be. I knew that plan was too simple and stupid for someone like Thren."

"Then we put our faith in his new one," Veliana said, putting a hand on his shoulder. "Thren rules this day. Let us just hope that come the end of it, we're still alive."

Alyssa walked ahead of Zusa on their return to the Kulls' camp, knowing her lead would make things easier for the other woman. Most of the guards stared at Zusa's face as they passed, frightened by her skill yet drawn to her beauty.

"Alyssa!" shouted Yoren when he saw her. He stumbled over a pot, pushed aside another man, and then wrapped her in a ferocious hug. Kiss after kiss he planted on her face, and Alyssa found herself relaxing in his arms and returning the kisses. After a moment he leaned back and let her stand, and that was when he noticed Zusa's face.

"By Karak, girl, where's your wrappings?" he asked.

Zusa took a step back and crossed her arms as if embarrassed. "Gone," she said. "Why do you care?"

Yoren didn't seem to know how to respond, so eventually he shrugged and took Alyssa's hands in his.

"Come," he said. "Father will be thrilled to see you. And what of the dark paladin? Did you elude him in the night?"

"Zusa killed him," Alyssa said as they walked around the tents on their way to the large pavilion.

"Did she now?" He glanced back at Zusa. "At times I wondered about my decision to hire you. It seems you three were well worth the coin."

"Just one now," Zusa said. Alyssa heard the sadness in her voice, but Yoren prattled on without noticing.

"We didn't know what to do. Theo thought to send search parties to look for, well, your body. I meant to go to Veldaren and see if the priests of Karak had you. Better alive and imprisoned than dead in a field, I figured. But here you are! More than I could have hoped for."

Alyssa glanced back at Zusa, who nodded. That nod gave her courage to continue.

"Please, hurry me to your father," she said. "I have something he needs to hear."

"On what matter?" Yoren asked.

"For his ears alone," she said. "If I am to rule in my father's place, there are some details I would prefer to organize with Theo first. He is lord of Riverrun, at least in fact if not in name."

Yoren looked none too pleased about this request, but he did not argue. Hoping her nervousness did not show, Alyssa followed him into Theo's pavilion. The older man sat in a chair, the remnants of the morning meal splayed out before him on the table.

"By the gods, Alyssa Gemcroft, safe and sound!" Theo cried, shoving against his chair to aid himself in standing. "I thought my guards were just babbling nonsense; either that or some pretty whore from the Kensgold had wandered over and been mistaken for you."

"I'm flattered by the comparison," Alyssa said.

"You should be, girl, looking as you do. I've seen my dogs drag in less disheveled things than you. Twice now you've come to me in tatters. The Gemcroft line must be rolling in its graves."

Alyssa felt anger mix with her self-consciousness. Indeed, the wade through the river had dirtied her dress, and she'd torn the tight silk during her frantic run. Drying it by the fire had shrunk it considerably, and she'd torn it more putting it back on. Her hair was a frightening mess, and she'd have given just about anything for a hot soak. Still, she was Alyssa Gemcroft, heir to the northern mines, and she'd never willingly accept such insults.

"If you have any desire to remain in my good graces come my ascension, you should bite your tongue, or better yet, apologize for such remarks," Alyssa said. "You first compare me to a whore, then to shit your dogs drag in?"

Yoren flushed red at the sudden outburst, but Theo only laughed at the fire that suddenly burned bright in her voice.

"Quite right, and I do apologize, Lady Gemcroft. Come, let me fetch my servingwomen so they may bathe and dress you proper to your station."

"No," she said. "I have business to discuss, matters pertaining to my future holdings."

"Surely these can wait," Yoren began, but Alyssa cut him off.

"Now," she said, her eyes boring into Theo's. "Surely you would not insult a guest by denying them dealings? Or are the rumors I hear of the Kulls more truthful than I thought?"

The whole tent quieted. Theo's smile drooped, the joy drained from his eyes.

"So be it," he said. "Let us treat each other as partners of business. What is it you wish to discuss?"

"Not yet," she said, glaring at Yoren. "We talk alone."

Yoren scoffed but Theo was in no mood.

"Leave us," he said to his guards as well as his son. He pointed a finger at Zusa. "But she goes too."

Zusa bowed. The pavilion emptied until Theo sat alone, his fingers rubbing his silvery knife.

"You may sit if you desire," he offered. Alyssa refused.

"I have a question for you," she said. "My father has vexed you time and time again. Do you know why? Because you are a mere tax collector in a faraway city, scheming and fighting to take over a mere pittance of my father's property."

"Where is your question, girl?" Theo asked, his hand clutching the wide table knife dangerously tight.

"I can give you far more than some miserable land in Riverrun," Alyssa said. "Which is more important to you, your wealth, or your son?"

"What nonsense is this?" Theo roared. Alyssa reached into her skirt and drew the dagger hidden within its secret pocket. Two steps put her an arm's length from Theo's throat. The big man wisely paused, still clutching his knife as he tilted his head to one side.

"Forgive me," he said. "I am still waiting for a true question, as well as an offer of deals and trades. But you are a woman, and unaccustomed to such matters, so I will be patient and give you another chance."

"I will not marry Yoren," she told him. "You will not inherit the Gemcroft line. But if I am declared lady of the estate, then I will reward you handsomely. My father has several mines in the northeast, not far from your little town. Your taxes and harassment have made them near-unprofitable. I'll give them to you, as well as the properties you seek within Riverrun. You gain all this in return for disavowing any possible marriage between myself and your son."

Theo rubbed his chin.

"You seem to forget something," he said. "With your marriage, all of those would become mine in time, or at least my son's. Why would I give up so much just to gain what I would already have? And don't say because you threaten me, for I am not scared of your little toy."

Alyssa smiled. She was tired of being someone's plaything. It was good to finally be in charge. In the distance she heard a couple of scattered shouts from the guards.

"I knew you would say so," she said. "And even if you promised, I would never believe it. You speak in lies, all you Kulls do, and I was stupid to have believed them for so long. But give me my inheritance, Theo, and I promise to keep my word."

"Is that so?" Theo asked. "Just because you..."

And then he lunged at her, his arm swinging in a sideways arc to bat away her dagger. Alyssa parried it smoothly aside, stepped closer, and then smashed her elbow into his throat. Theo fell back into his seat, gasping for air. His knife thudded to the dirt.

"I've had enough training to deal with someone as slow as you," she said. "Are you listening, Theo? And are you watching? I hope you are."

More guards shouted, this time closer. The tent flap flung open, and in stepped Zusa. Blood covered her wrappings. In her hand, held out like a gift, was the head of Yoren Kull.

"Well done," Alyssa said with a smile. Guards gathered at the entrance to the tent. Alyssa pressed the tip of her dagger against Theo's throat and then turned to the men.

"Step inside, he dies," she told them. A quick nod from Theo ensured they obeyed. Despite her ragged appearance, her mussed hair, and her dirty face, Alyssa felt like herself once more, only stronger and wiser than when her father had cast her into the cold cells below their household.

"Tell us your orders, Lady Gemcroft," Zusa said.

Alyssa looked back to Theo, her smile growing wider.

"Mercenaries," she said. "They work only for coin."

And then she thrust the dagger. With their only hopes of payment dead, either stabbed or beheaded, the mercenaries switched allegiance with practiced ease as Zusa cried out the wealth of the Gemcroft family line.

"You have your army," Zusa said, sliding up next to her moments later.

"Because of you," Alyssa said, taking Zusa's hand and then kissing it in mid-curtsy.

Her beautiful face no longer hidden by veil and wrappings, Zusa smiled and curtsied in return.

CHAPTER 32

The outer limits of the Kensgold were filled with sellswords and the poor. The food and drink radiated outward from the many banquet tables and kegs. Thren had debated a more thorough disguise than his low hood, dirtied face, and slight limp, but decided against it. With near a thousand faces swarming about the area he'd need a fraction of his skill to go unnoticed. By Karak, he could have stripped naked and still struggled for attention considering the amount of sex going on everywhere. No doubt the whores would be sore for weeks, but even the ugliest of them clutched silver coins tightly between her fingers.

At the base of the two hills the parked wagons formed a perimeter, their gaps lined with mercenaries. Thren did not challenge their ring, instead joining the crowd that lingered nearby in the hope of catching the more private and privileged festivities. Beside him was a hastily constructed wooden platform kept empty by a couple of Leon's soldiers. Thren didn't know its purpose but assumed it was for some sort of loud singer or shameless erotic dancing troupe. He didn't care to find out, either. Where he stood was the southernmost portion of the larger hill, exactly where he'd told the Wolf Guild to meet him.

His patience was nearing its end when a man in a brown cloak and gray shirt approached.

"You stand well enough for one with a limp," the man said.

"The knee don't like bending," Thren replied, feigning an Omnish accent. "What right you got to be asking?"

"The right of a wolf," the man said, flashing him a toothy grin. His makeup was heavy, but Thren recognized those sharpened canine teeth.

"Your disguise trumps my own," Thren said.

"I was to be here longer than you," said Cynric, guildmaster of the Wolves. A pungent dye covered his gray hair with a layer of brown, the dirt on his face hiding his pale skin and ritual scars. For a moment each held his tongue, staring up the hill at the elite of the Trifect. Neither sensed watching eyes or attentive ears around them, so they continued.

"I've thirty men throughout the crowds," Cynric said. "They await my howl. I've counted the number of guards, ignoring those on the outer ring. Over four hundred protect the main hill, and another two hundred the smaller. Our claws are sharp, but they do little against steel armor. I hope you have a better plan."

Thren nodded, hearing nothing he hadn't expected.

"The plan is in motion, Wolf. We do not attack them here. Your men are a diversion, nothing more."

Cynric chuckled.

"I had thought as much. Gathering everyone here for a direct strike didn't quite...play to our strengths. So, would you care to share the real plan? I'd hate for my Wolves to miss out on the bloodshed."

"Once the Kensgold nears its end, you will join me in assaulting the Gemcroft household. Our kind will have already taken over their estate and set up traps throughout. We will seal their exit once they realize the trap is sprung and try to flee."

"They'll be like a wounded doe," Cynric said.

"You and your hunting analogies," Thren said, and he laughed in spite of himself.

Trumpets sounded atop the hill. A steady procession of sellswords moved directly toward them, Leon Connington in tow. From the west, mercenaries lifted a giant wooden cage on poles from atop a wagon and brought it toward the stage. The door was heavily chained and bolted. It had no gaps in its sides, hiding whatever might be within.

"What is going on?" Thren asked, bracing himself. Because of the trumpets, the crowd had surged in his direction, packed together so tightly he'd have a devil of a time pushing his way out. Given their position, he and Cynric had a front-row seat to whatever foolishness was about to begin.

"Leon's bragged about a special event planned to start the Kensgold," Cynric explained, not even bothering to whisper. The chaos around them would drown out anything they said. "As to what, I don't know. None of my men and women could find out through coin or flesh."

Thren nodded, feeling uneasy. He didn't like surprises, and even worse, he hated lacking a quick exit. Shoving aside a hundred bodies was no easy feat.

"Come, come," he heard Leon Connington shout as he hobbled after his guards. Maynard and Laurie traveled with him, and at the sight Thren felt his heart jump. All three leaders, there in the clear. If they were to die, the entire plan would be unnecessary. His war against the Trifect would be won.

"I don't suppose you have a crossbow on you?" he asked Cynric. Sadly the man shook his head.

"Damn."

The Trifect families stopped far up the hill, keeping a good distance between themselves and the crowd. Mercenaries surrounded them, looking serious and stiff in their patchwork armor. Grunting from the weight, the group of sellswords placed the covered cage down in the center of the stage. The crowd murmured, wondering what exotic creature might be trapped within.

An old man approached the stage and held up his hands for silence. Thren recognized him as Leon's advisor, Potts.

"This day, my Lord Connington brings a gift not to the Trifect but to you wonderful people of Veldaren!" the old man shouted. Those who hadn't quieted before did so now. The din lowered to a murmuring hush.

"Long they have stolen from you," Potts continued. "Long they have made you cower and hide in fear of poison and blade. We have fought them for you, bled for you, and died for you."

A few whistled, but not many. Given the sheer amount of free food and wine floating about, it would seem in bad taste to argue.

"What is going on here?" Thren hissed to Cynric.

"I told you, I don't know," the Wolf master replied.

Potts turned back toward the hill and pointed. A procession of five men walked down from the pavilion. They wore plain brown robes, their heads and faces clean-shaven. Thin tattoos circled their necks and wrists before traveling upward like veins toward their eyes. Both guildmasters knew who they were immediately. They were the gentle touchers, Leon's skilled masters of torture.

Thren felt his stomach drop as if full of lead. He suddenly knew who was within the cage.

"Damn them," he whispered. "Gods-fucking-damn them."

The five surrounded the cage and raised their hands. With a dramatic sweep of his arms, Potts ordered the cage opened. The gentle touchers yanked out the bolts from its sides. The cage collapsed, its walls coming apart like a broken child's toy. Standing perfectly still, his body tied to a thick pole, was Will. The gentle touchers rushed forward, taking the pole and jamming it into a hole in the stage, securing it tight. Will looked exhausted but unharmed otherwise. He had been stripped naked but for a plain loincloth. His thick muscles tensed against the ropes binding his hands and feet.

"Will the Bloody," Potts shouted. "The right hand of Thren Felhorn, the enforcer of the Spiders! We give him to you now, people of Veldaren. To you, and to the gentle touchers."

"Enjoy the show!" Leon shouted from the hill. "Give 'em blood!"

One of the gentle touchers put down a small table he had carried from the wagon. Another unrolled a canvas wrapping filled with instruments. They started with the small pins. Two focused on each hand, taking their pins and slowly pushing them underneath Will's fingernails. Two more did the same to his toes. The fifth constantly surveyed the ropes, tightening when necessary, grabbing hold of Will and keeping him still when he flexed his fingers or tried to bend his knees.

Once enough pins were in place, they split apart their duties. One took a small set of pliers and peeled back a fingernail. Another took a thin pin and jammed it into the exposed flesh underneath. A different gentle toucher used a hammer and a blunt piece of wood to smash down on the toenails with pins underneath. With each strike, Will's entire body thrashed against the ropes.

"Like art," Cynric said as he watched. "Like fucking art."

Thren's hands shook as he watched. He refused to look away. Somehow Will had been caught, and like a damn fool Thren hadn't gone looking for him. He might have spared his closest enforcer this terrible tragedy. Even better, he might have spared him the spectacle. Hundreds of people howled and cheered with every moan and scream he made. Two gentle touchers simultaneously grabbed Will's little toes with pliers and pulled them back until they were so out of joint they were perpendicular to the rest. Thren watched as Will the Bloody, the strongest, fiercest member of his guild, wept like a child.

And they hadn't even cut him yet. Only a little bit of blood trickled from his fingers to the wood stage. The gentle touchers ripped off Will's loincloth, taking their needles and pliers to his groin.

"Change of plans," Thren said. His face was an icy mask, his disguise barely hiding his rage. He pointed at Leon, not caring if any saw.

"He's mine," he said, his voice so cold that Cynric shivered. "I'll leave the Gemcroft ambush to you. If I can, I will join you, but I need to make sure that if Leon's taken, he's taken alive. No one else must kill him. That pleasure will be mine, and mine alone."

Cynric turned and shoved his way through the crowd, not desiring to watch anymore. Thren kept his hands clenched, refusing to be weak. No spectacle would defeat him. He stared at Will's eyes, hoping that for at least one moment they would meet his. He wanted Will to see Leon's death in his stare, to see the rage and know that no man, not even a member of the Trifect, could escape it.

After twenty minutes the gentle touchers brought out their knives. Ten minutes later Will died. The crowd cheered, thrilled with the spectacle. Their cheers rose when Will's head rolled off the platform. A few men kicked it about, laughing as if it were all a game. Another lifted it high above him, as if it were a trophy. Just before he left the throng, Thren stabbed him in the back and then vanished before anyone even noticed the drunken man was dead.

With so many processions of food and wagons moving westward, Haern had an easy time procuring himself something to eat. He kept his mask over his face, feeling comfortable only with it on. Afterward he found the main hideout for the Spider Guild and scouted for a hiding place. With the whole guild soon to move out, he only needed to follow one to find the rest. One of the nearby homes had a tunnel dug underneath, so Haern crawled in through the window of a finely furnished house opposite.

Thankfully the occupants were long gone, most likely enjoying the festivities. Haern grabbed some pillows from the bed and stretched out across the floor.

With his belly full and his body aching, sleep was welcome. He offered a single prayer before closing his eyes, and that was for no dreams. The prayer went unanswered. Haern dreamed of the Lion, snarling at him in fury. When he awoke, cold sweat poured off his body. The wounds from the Lion's roar had reopened and bled anew. Haern bandaged them using strips of the cheapest-looking shirt he could find, feeling a little guilty as he did. Whoever owned the home would certainly think him the oddest burglar ever.

When he glanced outside he saw the sun not far from setting.

Expecting the bulk of the activity to happen after dark, Haern straightened up, stretched his muscles, and then watched. An hour crawled by, quiet and boring. Just when he began thinking of switching locations, Haern spotted three men in the gray of the Spider Guild exit the front door. They hurried north, their cloaks flapping in the air behind them.

Haern didn't bother going downstairs. He propped the window halfway open, slid out, and then dashed along the rooftops. The buildings were close enough together that he could follow at a swift pace without any fear of being spotted. For a moment he wished he had the dagger he'd tossed back to the priests of Karak. Whenever it came time to act, he didn't like the idea of being weaponless. He'd have to find a way to arm himself, and quick.

The three men traveled through the alleys and back corners, avoiding the main roads whenever possible. Haern smiled. If he'd followed along the ground, it might have been troubling. Up on the rooftops, he took straight paths where they took winding ones. It didn't take much guesswork to follow them. They were traveling toward the Gemcroft mansion.

With how empty the streets were, Haern picked up occasional snippets of their conversation. Part of him was furious at how freely they talked. Sickness hit his stomach when he thought of how Thren would have punished them if he had known. To think he had loved a man like that. Haern shook his head. Still loved. He couldn't lie to himself. Thren was a monster, yet still his father. Turning blind eyes toward his feelings would only endanger himself.

"...of a fire," Haern heard one say.

"Can't wait myself," said another.

"What about James?"

"Wait until everything's crazy. Kadish will..."

And then they were too far gone. Haern scrambled about a chimney, leaped over a thin alley, then stopped at his new perch. The expansive Gemcroft mansion stretched out before him on the opposite side of the street. Below him the three men of the Spider Guild gathered and waited—for what, Haern was not sure.

They were talking again. Haern took step after careful step along the roof, testing each one to make sure it would hold silently. Once he was near, he lay flat on his stomach and put an ear to the edge. If the men had been whispering, he wouldn't have heard, but their discipline seemed to have vanished with their excitement.

"...Abyss are those blasted Hawks?" said the one on the left.

"We're still early," said the one on the right.

"Ash Guild ain't here either," said the middle, cleaning his fingernails with his dagger. "Wonder if those cowardly skirts will even come."

"Thren got to James," said left. "The Ash boys will show."

"Wouldn't bother me none if the Hawks stayed roosting overnight," said right. "All of them fuckers would sooner kill you than rob you. They turned a little turf war into some goddamn bloodbath. No decency among them, none at all."

"People get that from their leader," said middle. "Kadish is to blame. Guy likes to eat flesh, people flesh. Everyone knows it."

Haern scoffed. The three idiots below him certainly didn't take after *their* guildleader. A part of him hoped Thren would show up while they still were talking, just so Haern could hear their chastisement. A much larger part hoped he'd never see his father again.

"Look, that way," said right, pointing farther down the street. A group of eight men in the dress of the Hawk Guild marched openly in the center of the street. Curved daggers flashed from their belts.

"They out of their mind?" asked left.

"We've declared war," said middle. "Looks like Kadish wants everyone to see it."

Haern turned his head so he could watch. Kadish led the way, smiling his red smile. The eye patch hung loose over his face. The Hawks drew their daggers as they neared.

"Where's the rest of ya?" asked middle, stepping closer. He pointed toward the mansion, of which they were in full view. "And did you think to use a bit of stealth? Any guards in there won't care much for a couple of cloaks scouting the place, but you're acting like you're a damn army."

"Who says we aren't?" Kadish asked. "And my men are coming. The question is, where's the Ash Guild? And what about the rest of the little crawly Spiders?"

A bolt struck the ground by their feet, its tip exploding into a puff of thick gray smoke. Both parties turned to see a single man approaching, his dress that of the Ash Guild.

"About time," said Kadish. "Where's your masters?"

The man reloaded his small crossbow but kept it pointed at the ground.

"Waiting for my signal," the Ash scout explained. "Of course, I never expected so many to gather openly in front of the gates of our target."

"Give your signal then," said left. "The sun is almost to the wall. Whatever few guards are left inside have got to be ready for us."

"I'm not to signal until I see someone with authority from the Spider Guild."

Kadish rolled his eye and swore.

"I've got authority, now call for them," said middle, jamming his thumb against his chest.

"Real authority," said the scout.

The Spider Guild members sighed.

"It'll be a moment, then," said middle. "They're coming. Spiders crawl all over the place."

Haern suddenly realized just how vulnerable he was. *Stupid!* he thought. If he had gotten the idea to spy on them from the rooftop, then surely others would as well. He slid away from the edge, started to roll, and then felt a hand clamp over his mouth. The tip of a dagger pressed against his side.

"Don't scream," a feminine voice whispered into his ear. Haern looked up to see Kayla smiling down at him.

"Kayla," Haern said.

"What stupidity brought you here?" she asked. The two met in the center of the roof so that their whispers would not be noticed by the bickering men on the ground.

"I just…I need to do something," he said. He felt his face blush. "I was going to stop them. I wanted to ruin Thren's plans."

Kayla bit her lip and stared. Even with his mask, Haern felt naked. He crossed his arms and looked away.

"I'm to lead this half against the Gemcrofts," she said. "Senke moves against the Connington mansion. There's hundreds of men on either side, Aaron. You can't stop this."

The boy shook his head.

"Not Aaron," he said. "Not now, not ever again. Aaron's dead. I'm Haern now."

Kayla shrugged.

"So be it, Haern. You want out of this life, then get out. You're strong. You're smart. Make a life for yourself in Kinamn, or even in Mordeina if you feel like traveling all the way across the rivers to the other side of the world. But this is Thren's city. Your father's city. Leave, please. You'll only get yourself killed trying to interfere."

Haern shook his head.

"I'm no coward," he said. "And you're wrong. This city belongs to no one. My... Thren's only scared people into thinking that. I can stop them. I can stop the fear."

Kayla stood to her full height and shook her head.

"We're ending this whole stupid war. The Trifect dies tonight. Don't die with it, Haern."

She turned to go, then stopped. One of her throwing daggers whirled through the air, embedding into the wood roof beside Haern's leg.

"In case you need it," she said. He looked up at her, his eyes bloodshot. Kayla stared at him, then crossed her arms and looked away.

"If I tell you something," she said. "Something good, something hopeful, will you leave my operation be?"

Haern tucked the dagger into his belt. It weighed less than a dagger should, and its curve was greater than he liked, but it was vastly better than nothing.

"I promise," he said, not sure if he was lying or not.

"Delysia is alive," Kayla said. Her words struck him like a hammer. "I brought her to the priests of Ashhur. They saved her. Whatever vendetta you carry, whatever guilt, just let it go. Make your new life elsewhere, Haern."

She blew him a kiss and then hopped off the roof, slowing her fall by grabbing hold with her hand for a brief moment. Haern didn't come near to listen to her take charge, didn't look down the streets to where members of the three guilds seemed to be coming out of nowhere. All he could think of was how Delysia had bled in his arms, the arrow piercing her back.

Hearn remembered the phantom image of the girl that had haunted his stay in Karak's temple, of her pleading with him, of the cold fire and her insistence that she had prayed to deaf ears. All lies. The Lion's lies. He felt his anger grow.

"Kayla," he said. "Thank you so much."

He turned and leaped from roof to roof, feeling his heart soaring at the news. Delysia was alive. He couldn't believe it. Delysia was alive. Praise Ashhur, *alive*.

Despite his joy, he knew he couldn't abandon his responsibility. He'd keep his promise, though. Kayla had said Senke was leading the other assault. Hoping he still had time, Haern dropped to the ground and raced toward Leon Connington's estate.

At Kayla's command the three guilds split and surrounded Gemcroft's estate. James and his Ash Guild took the east, Kadish and his Hawks the west. They used no stealth, no subterfuge. Tonight was a night of open power, a display for the whole city to see. The underworld had risen, its teeth were bared, and while the moon crept over the wall, they would taste blood.

"You see them?" asked Veliana, who had insisted she stay with the Spider Guild instead of accompanying her guildmaster. She pointed toward one of the lower windows. Its curtains ruffled and swayed.

"Guards," Kayla said. "There shouldn't be many."

"And if there are?" asked Veliana.

Kayla shrugged.

"Then we have more to kill," she said as she raised her hand. Scouts from both guilds saw her movement and mimicked it. After a count of five she flung down her arm. With the soft sigh of ruffled cloaks and padded feet, the assault began.

Kayla led the front, climbing up ropes that her guildmembers flung over the spikes at the top. She vaulted over, Veliana at her side and keeping up with every movement. Forty of the Spider Guild landed on the front lawn. Once they were gathered together, Kayla charged ahead, her cloak flapping behind her and her hands clutching two of her throwing daggers. During their planning, the one thing they hadn't been able to account for with certainty was the deadliness of Maynard's traps. Her heart in her throat, Kayla dashed across the grass toward the front door, praying she wasn't one of the unlucky ones.

An explosion from behind knocked her to the ground. Rock and dirt rained atop her as several men screamed in pain. Veliana's arms were upon her instantly, tugging her up and pushing her forward.

"Never stop," Veliana shouted as they ran. More explosions rocked the lawn, turning its pristine slopes and gentle curves into a violent assault of fire and stone. Kayla had no idea what magic might be behind them. A few of her guildmembers had rushed ahead of her, and she watched one scream as flame burst upward from a sudden tear in the ground. The force blew him all the way back against the gate. His head snapped violently against the bars. Kayla forced herself to look away. She heard similar explosions of noise and force from other parts of the estate. It seemed the devilish traps completely surrounded the building.

When they were halfway to the front doors, windows on all floors were flung open. Guards with bows and crossbows leaned out, unleashing a deadly barrage. The thieves rolled and ducked, some inadvertently setting off more of the explosions. Smoke billowed to the sky. Kayla flung a dagger, wounding one guard in the shoulder. She saved the rest. The distance was too great.

A stone portico protected them from arrows at the main door. Kayla moved aside as two Spiders knelt underneath it and pulled out their lock-picking instruments.

"They'll have it barred," Veliana shouted.

"One thing at a time," Kayla yelled back.

The rest of the Spider Guild collected underneath the covering, a few stepping out to hurl daggers or fire crossbows. Veliana watched for a moment, then grabbed Kayla's arm.

"Move out, now!" she shouted. "Go through the windows."

"What?" asked Kayla.

"The locks! If the same trap was on the lock..."

It was too late. The doors exploded outward, fire trailing after the shock wave. Kayla rolled along the ground, lucky to have been far enough to the side. Lying on her stomach, she looked up through the smoke and debris to see a great pile of corpses spread out along the steps leading to the door. Fellow members of her guild lay twisted and burned, some with bones poking out from their skin, others still alive and sobbing in pain.

Of her initial forty, only fifteen remained alive and able to fight.

"Shit," Veliana said beside her, resting on her hands and knees. "Hope the others are doing better."

Kayla accepted Veliana's help up. They rushed the doors, which were now wide open. Soldiers with spears braced before the entrance. Compared to the traps, though, they were a welcome relief. Kayla hurled her daggers while two others fired crossbows. The rest of the Spiders dashed between the spears, lashing out with their blades. Only six men had come to guard the front, far too few to hold them off. Once they had broken through, the rest of the guild flooded inside. Kayla stopped at the inner foyer, slumping against a side wall and closing her eyes for a moment.

"We can't hide this," Veliana said, having remained at her side.

"We follow our orders," Kayla said, her eyes still closed.

"Forget your orders. Maynard won't fall for this trap. His

yard is wrecked, his doors broken. Fuck, I wouldn't be surprised if they can see this smoke all the way from the Kensgold."

"We need to find out how the others fared," Kayla said, pushing herself off the wall. "And no matter what, we need to prepare this place for burning."

Screams filled the halls as the Spiders pushed deeper into the mansion. On the far sides, the Hawks and Ashes were certainly doing the same. The two women explored the estate. The occasional body of a guard lay in their path, but more often it was that of a young girl or boy wearing plain clothes. Simple servants, Kayla noted. She tried to steel herself against what she saw. She had known this would happen, she had warned herself plenty, but the carnage was horrific.

They stepped into a bedroom to find two Hawks standing over a young girl who couldn't be any older than twelve. Her clothes were torn, her face bruised. Veliana inhaled sharply.

"Vick?" she hissed, unheard by either. The other man pulled down his pants, and Kayla flung a dagger deep into his back.

"What the *fuck*?" shouted Vick. Kayla twirled another dagger in her hand, her eyes wide with anger.

"Clean and quick," she said. "I made that damn clear before."

"That what you want?" said the Hawk. "Fine. Come here, bitch."

He grabbed the girl, flung her down onto her knees, and then slashed open her throat. The girl cried and gagged as her blood spilled across her dress. Letting go of her hair, Vick laughed as she dropped dead to the carpet.

"Hope you're happy," he said. "She might have had a few more minutes of fun before we did her in."

The dagger stopped its twirl in Kayla's hand. The two stared at one another. Veliana watched, a smirk growing across her face.

"Don't you d—" Vick started to say before Veliana stepped in, drew her own dagger, and thrust it into his chest. His eyes bulged. Veliana grabbed his hair in her hands as she pulled her weapon free.

"You betrayed me," she told him. "Betrayed me, then betrayed your guild to join the Hawks. A shame I don't have the time to make you suffer for it."

He died, Veliana's dagger rammed deep into his throat. Feeling the cold shock creeping through her, Kayla stared at all the blood. The little girl's death haunted her vision. What was the matter with her? She sold information. She spied on men and women in alleys. What could have possessed her to think this was the life for her? To think she was some sort of general, someone to stand beside Thren Felhorn and belong?

The blood spread further. Power, she thought. Is this the power I sought?

"It's brutal, but this is the life we've chosen," Veliana said, putting a hand on her shoulder.

Kayla thought of all the sacrifices she'd already made to put herself in this position. After tonight she would be in Thren's highest graces. She would almost be a queen in power. But when she looked over at Veliana and saw the honest compassion in her eyes, her resolve broke. The woman had fought at her side, pulling her to safety when she should have died at the explosion at the front door. And in return . . .

"Thren wants us to kill you," Kayla whispered.

A shadow seemed to fall over Veliana's face.

"What?" she asked.

"Once the mansion is secure, we're to help the Hawks kill you all," Kayla explained. "Please, you must get out now."

"But we gave in," Veliana said. "We gave him what he wanted."

"Doesn't matter," Kayla said. "James resisted once. He might again. This night is Thren's victory, don't you understand? Not over just the Trifect, but over everyone. He's even planned to kill the king. After tonight, the city is his."

Veliana slammed the door to the bedroom shut and spun to face Kayla.

"We have little time then," she said. "Were your men to wait for a signal?"

Kayla shook her head.

"No, the Hawks were to start it. We just needed to stay out of the way and help if needed."

"Shit," muttered Veliana. "I need to warn James. We need to get him out of here, now!"

"It's too late," Kayla said. "Can't you hear? It's already started."

Veliana paused to listen, the color draining out of her face. Screams had indeed continued. Each had thought at first that they were those of the Gemcroft house guards, or perhaps remaining members of his household. But they were too many for how much time had passed. The Hawks had turned on the Ash, without warning and without mercy.

"You let us walk into this damn trap," Veliana said, closing in on Kayla. "All because of Thren, all because of that stupid egotistical shit. I'll make him pay. I'll . . . his son. Where is his son?"

"Aaron?" Kayla asked as she took a small step backward, her hand resting on her belt of daggers. Veliana drew her own and then pointed one at Kayla's neck.

"You know his plans," Veliana said. "I may not be skilled enough to kill Thren, but I can kill his son. At least I can inflict some measure of pain on that withered heart of his. Now tell me, where is Aaron?"

Kayla hesitated, and that was enough for someone as fast as Veliana. She dodged to one side, avoiding Kayla's thrown dagger, and then delivered a kick to the head. As Kayla collapsed, Veliana fell upon her, her knees on her wrists and her dagger at her throat.

"My guild is dying as we speak," Veliana seethed, her face inches from Kayla's. "I have nothing left to lose, nothing, so do not think I would lie to you now. Tell me, or I'll do to you what was done to me."

Her wounded eye was ugly and red, and Kayla stared at the milky pupil in horror as Veliana's dagger slowly trailed up her neck toward her left eye.

"I sent him away," she said. "He was watching us, so I made him promise to leave us be. He's turned against his father. He wants to stop all this, but he's just a boy. Just a stupid boy."

Veliana left her dagger pressed against Kayla's face as she thought.

"He lied to you," she whispered. "Just like his father, he'll promise one thing and do another. He's at Leon Connington's estate. He must be."

She stood and slowly backed away, watching for the slightest movement on Kayla's part.

"You gave me warning," Veliana said. "For that I'll let you live."

"Aaron has done nothing wrong," Kayla said. "Hate the Spider Guild, and justly so, but he's not his father. He's done nothing wrong."

"Neither did she," Veliana said, pointing at the body of the dead girl. She put her ear against the door, listening. When all was silent, she kicked it open and ran. Kayla rose to her knees, rubbing at her throat where Veliana's knife had pressed. She stared at the bodies around her and wondered how she had fallen so far. All she had wanted was a bit of coin, but Thren had given her a taste of power. He'd hinted at something even greater. Now an ocean of blood swirled across the mansion floor, its guilt on her as much as anyone else. Except Thren.

As if her thoughts had summoned him, Thren Felhorn stepped inside the room and glanced about. Dimly she wondered how much time had passed.

"The Ash Guild is no more," he said, sounding disinterested. He stepped about, seeing the dead Hawks and the young girl. "What is going on here, Kayla? Get off your knees. You aren't some low-rent whore."

"We lost too many," Kayla said. She felt cold inside. Her skin tingled, and she felt certain death awaited her. "We failed you. We can spring no trap here."

Thren tilted his head to one side. He cupped her chin in his hand and forced her to look him in the eye.

"If you failed, it was because of the strength of our opponent and my failure to prepare accordingly. I saw the remnants of the spells on my way inside. Maynard prepared well for us, far better than the others."

Thren nodded toward the carnage.

"You haven't answered my question. What happened here?"

She glanced at the two dead rogues.

"They disobeyed orders," she said. "I made them pay for it."

Thren smiled at her.

"Death for disobedience," he said. "A woman after my own heart."

He kissed her forehead.

"Come with me to the Kensgold. The attack at Leon's has gone smoothly so far, and I've ordered Senke to leave Leon alive so I might give him his deserved punishment. Still, we have much to do before that fight begins. We've struck at the Connington and Gemcroft families, but the Keenans have so far gone unscathed. That changes now."

Thren left the bedroom and headed toward the mansion's exit.

As if lost in a nightmare, Kayla followed.

CHAPTER

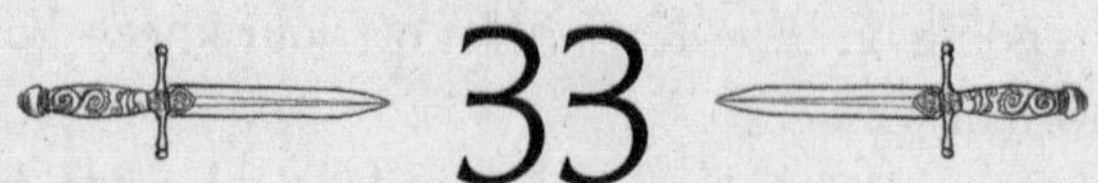

33

The king was in a fouler mood than normal. From the window of a castle tower he had observed the great masses traveling west out of Veldaren, followed by the start of the feasting and celebrations. Gerand was waiting for him in his throne room. Sixteen guards protected His Majesty when he entered.

"It looks like an army gathers at our doorstep," King Vaelor said as he sat on his throne. "And where are my subjects? Shouldn't I have petty squabbles to settle?"

"Most have decided to partake in festivities that transpire every two years rather than wait in line for a ruling they may get on any day," Gerand explained.

"But everyone?" Vaelor wondered. "Surely there's a few level-headed men about somewhere."

"There were a few," Gerand said, clearing his throat. "I sent them away. From everything we know, today should be… interesting, and I felt it best to keep you safe."

King Vaelor rolled his eyes. As if determined to show how brave he was, he dismissed half his retainer of guards, leaving only a paltry eight watching over him. Gerand did his best not to roll his own eyes in return. With the sheer amount of mercenaries gathered outside the walls, the advisor had thought it best to keep the king's day dull. Besides, with all eyes turned to the Kensgold, there was too much risk of a silent dagger striking the other way.

"Safe," the king muttered. "Often you have promised to keep me safe, but where are the results of your promises? What has grown from your comforting words? I was promised the head of Thren Felhorn, yet where is it?"

Gerand coughed and looked at the guards. King Vaelor realized what he wanted and dismissed the remaining eight.

"Don't get any ideas," the king said once they were on the far side of the throne room. He pulled back his robe to reveal his gold sword belted at his hip. Gerand was far from impressed but didn't dare let that show.

"As you must understand," Gerand began, "arranging Thren's murder is no easy feat. Men have wanted him dead for a decade, yet he remains as powerful as ever."

"I want his head," the king said. "Not excuses."

"I am giving you neither," Gerand said. "Only word of what is to come. My men have crawled about the city and spent much. We gained little in return, but all it takes is one whisper, one turncoat, and the whole fortune is worth the coin. And that is what I have: a turncoat."

King Vaelor sat erect in his seat.

"You found a member of his guild to turn against him?" he asked, unable to hide his excitement.

"I cannot say," Gerand insisted. "Surely you understand. I will say nothing of who he or she is, other than that the price was absurdly high. I dare not risk a single whisper reaching Thren. The plans we knew for the Kensgold were but a hoax, and my little bird has informed me of the real plan. If all goes well, I will deliver his head to you on a platter by tomorrow morning."

"Excellent," the king said, slapping his thigh with his hand. "What will I do when you're gone, Gerand?"

The advisor smiled. He had every intention of being around long after King Vaelor was gone, not the reverse.

"A king of your majesty and skill will always find a way to reign," he said.

King Vaelor laughed.

"So true. But what am I to do? With no squabbles, no royal visitors, and no feasts planned, I am sorely pressed for entertainment."

"For that, I have found a solution," Gerand said. He clapped twice, and one of the guards at the throne room's main entrance threw open the doors. Ten girls wearing silks that hid nothing walked into the room, bells jingling from their wrists and ankles.

"Dancers," Gerand said. "Come all the way from Ker. They are known as the Naked Bells, and I have spent a great amount of the crown's coin for their appearance."

Slowly the women began their gyrations.

"Naked Bells?" King Vaelor asked, licking his lips. "Yet I see so much silk."

"Give us time to earn our name," one of the women said, her voice husky and foreign.

The Naked Bells took almost half an hour to fully deserve their name. Gerand watched the dancers with more than a casual interest. Ever since Thren had captured his wife, he'd been worried sick, but he'd also been left to his own devices to satisfy his carnal desires. The exotic women shifted and danced with professional expertise, every movement designed to flaunt a certain curve, emphasize the length of their legs, or bring attention to their lips, breasts, or waists.

Every passing minute saw one of them discard a piece of her silk. The king had watched the entire proceeding with rapt attention. No doubt he would claim two or three to come with him to his bedchambers. The king had no wife, and plenty were unhappy with this fact, but he was still young enough that Gerand had managed to quell most grumblings. Besides, he figured that if worse came to worst, there'd be a handful of bastards to choose from. He watched the naked women dance, the bells on their wrists and ankles jingling, and wondered if one might be the future mother of a king.

One in particular had caught Gerand's eye. Her hair was a deep red, just how he liked. Her breasts were smaller than the others', but he found that attractive as well. Most important, she had been the last to strip completely naked. Or perhaps it was the way the king's eyes lingered on her the longest. Gerand consoled himself by remembering that they were hired to please the king, so please him they would.

No, Gerand thought. *She'll be mine, king or no. I may have a touch of gray in my hair, but I'm far more a man that that stupid brat.*

The Naked Bells' undulations increased in intensity. The bells, all different sizes and pitches, rose into a beautiful chaos of sound. The redhead swirled before King Vaelor, almost within his touch. Out of all of them, only she clutched the bells of her wrists in her hands to stop their ring. Gerand watched, curious as to why. With all the others focusing their noise in a final hurrah, why would she...

And then he saw her fingers twist at a bell, pulling something out from its clapper.

"Stop her!" Gerand shouted, pointing. From the corner a

soldier lowered his crossbow and fired. The bolt struck the redhead in the neck. Her blood splashed across the king's face. The sound of her skull striking the cold stone made Gerand's stomach twist. A thin needle rolled from her dead fingers. The rest of the Naked Bells stepped back, some crying, others staring coldly at the loss of one of their own.

"What is going on here?" the king shouted. Gerand retrieved the pin and held it up for the king to see.

"Do you see the flecks of green?" Gerand asked. "Venom of the hourglass scorpion, I'd wager. It takes several hours to flow through the blood and affect the heart, but once it does, death is inevitable. Someone paid her to kill you."

King Vaelor's face turned a deep shade of red.

"Thren!" he shouted. "It's that bastard Felhorn! I want him dead, do you hear me?"

"I have my plans in motion, Your Majesty."

"Do you know where he is?" the king asked, still shouting.

"Where he is to be, yes," Gerand admitted. "But we've not yet received the signal..."

"Send my soldiers," the king said. "All of them, every man able to hold a sword. He dies tonight, do you understand? Send them. Now!"

"Yes, milord," Gerand said, bowing low.

King Vaelor stomped about, furious and frustrated. At last he pointed to two of the girls, then snapped his fingers.

"Remove their bells," he said. "Search them thoroughly. I won't let that fucker ruin my entertainment, but I won't be stabbed in my own bedchambers either."

Guards neared and undid the leather straps of the bells on their wrists and ankles. The girls reluctantly joined the king in his bedchambers, soldiers following behind with their swords drawn. Once the door was shut, Gerand sighed and turned to the rest.

"I'm sorry," he said. He met the eyes of the guard captain, nodded. Gerand left, not wanting to watch as the remaining guards cut them down and covered the throne room with their beautiful, beautiful corpses.

Senke walked through the halls of the Connington mansion feeling a bit let down. While the doors and windows were thick, the lawn had few traps, and the ones it did have were designed to alert, not kill. The inside was even emptier. By his count, ten soldiers had been left behind as guards. They had died quickly and easily. Other than that, the mansion was vacant.

Gart marched alongside Senke, his mood far more sour.

"No pasty rich people to smash," he grumbled. "This is stupid. I bet Maynard had men left. I should have gone there. Why did Thren make me go here? I wanted head-smashing!"

"Shut up, Gart," Senke said. "You'll still get your chance, remember?"

Gart shrugged.

"Where's Norris?" he asked.

"That I don't know," Senke said. "Him and his Serpents should be setting up the oil for the fires."

The two leaders neared the rows of windows that viewed the front lawn.

"Windows won't open, so we'll focus on holding the doors," Gart said. He pointed outside the gates to the houses on the far side of the road. "We'll have archers there. Once Maynard comes, we squash them in between."

"Simple enough plan," Senke said. "Should work, though.

Did hardly a scratch to the manor, so there's no reason for him to be alarmed."

"He'll be alarmed," Gart said, pointing farther to the east. "Look. Smoke."

Senke lowered his head a little and peered out. Sure enough, a thick plume of smoke rose high from the eastern district.

"That's Maynard's place, all right," Senke said. "Do you think they already set it aflame?"

"I look like a soothsayer?" Gart asked. "Go run and ask if you want answers. I got none but my fists."

"That might explain Thren's delay," Senke muttered.

"What's that?" asked Gart.

"Nothing. Nothing. Let me go check on my men. Stay here and watch for any early arrivals. Try to wait until they're inside to attack. I wouldn't be surprised if Maynard sends someone to check on his home once he sees the smoke from afar. Let them go if possible."

"I'm not an idiot," Gart grumbled.

"Prove it," Senke said as he hurried off. He glanced at the setting sun as he passed by another row of windows. Where was Thren? Why was he so late?

With so many treasures scattered throughout the mansion waiting to be looted, Senke went unnoticed as he walked. He'd already marked his way of escape once the chaos began. It was a slender door that led up to an attic. He'd checked it once, and in the back was a round, dusty window. From there he could reach the roof, and once upon the roof, he could pick any direction he desired to escape. But the plan was worthless without Thren there. Without Thren he'd accomplish nothing.

As he neared the back of the mansion he heard the sound of a scuffle. Curious, Senke pushed open a door leading into a small but well-lit dining hall. One Serpent member lay dead on the floor, another bleeding as he fought a young man with a dirty gray cloak and a torn mask over his face. Senke felt his jaw drop at the sight.

"Impossible," he said.

His voice drew the Serpent's attention for the briefest moment, and that was all the young man needed. He slipped closer, jammed his dagger through ribs, and then slashed to the side. His opponent dead, the boy turned and dropped into a combat stance Senke recognized well, considering he'd taught it to him.

"What are you doing here, Aaron?" Senke asked, not at all fooled by the mask.

"Not Aaron," he said. "I'm Haern. Aaron is dead."

Senke shook his head, hardly able to believe it.

"How many have you killed?" Senke asked as he shut the door.

"Five," said Haern.

"Five?" Senke laughed. "You're out of your mind, Aaron. Sorry. *Haern.* I thought you were with the priests?"

"I escaped," Haern said. He dropped his smaller knives and took a larger pair from the bodies, then tore off one man's cloak and wrapped it around his shoulders. Cleaning the blood off the daggers with the cloak, he tucked them into his belt and tightened the mask over his face. "I've come to stop this, Senke. Will you help me? Or must I kill you too?"

Senke shook his head, torn between horror and hysterics at the boy's audacity.

"I won't help you," he told him. "But I won't stop you either. I'm getting out, Haern. Tonight."

"Out?" asked Haern. "How?"

Senke slumped to his rear.

"I had a feeling Thren's plan was all a lie, so when he told me the new one, I wasn't surprised. So for a rather handsome amount of coin, I sold word of it to the king. In about an hour hundreds of soldiers will surround the estate. If there is a god, Thren will be here when they arrive. As for me, well, there's going to be a big fire and a lot of bodies. No one will bat an eye should I go missing afterward."

The way Haern stood, he clearly had not been prepared to hear of such betrayal from as close a friend as Senke.

"Why would you turn on him?" he asked.

Senke chuckled.

"When I joined the Spider Guild, I was in a bad spot. My son died, all because I couldn't afford for the priests to heal him. My wife blamed it on me, and for good reason. I was lazy. Unreliable. I drank, I slept in alleys, and when I was at my lowest, Thren found me. Something about him, the way he conducts himself, it's both terrifying and inspiring, and it awoke a fire in me that never died. I climbed the ranks, not because I was better, but because I worked harder than anyone else. I gave the guild everything of me, and Thren saw it and rewarded me accordingly. He likes that, Haern, you know that. It's because he's the same way. Nothing matters beyond the narrow focus, the narrow goal, and lately I was watching that goal be crafting you into something terrible. Watching what Thren was doing to you, slowly, methodically killing everything good in his own son..."

He shook his head.

"I used to think all this backstabbing and thieving was just a game. We were all crooks, all worthless scum, so who really cares if we killed each other trying to rob rich men who would rather die than lose a single copper? I thought your father was the best at the game, a man who could have been a god at anything he chose, only he chose a criminal empire to be his legacy.

He would be servant to none, slave to no system, no laws. At times it was fun, the coin was great, the women easy... but this has gone on too long. Whatever charm Thren had, it's slowly died over these past five years. And now to watch as he would deny you a childhood, deny you friends, deny you a *life*..."

Senke rose to his feet, glanced at the door.

"No man could do that to his own son. Only a monster, and I won't be a part of his lair anymore. After this, I'm done. I don't expect much in the way of eternity, but maybe Ashhur will forgive me if I get myself out while there's still time. Looks like I wasn't alone in thinking that too."

Haern's cheeks lifted, and Senke could tell the boy was smiling.

"I survived the priests," he said, clearly proud. "They can't defeat me. No one can."

"Don't get cocky; I could still whup you with one hand..."

He stopped. A dozen men had begun shouting from the main entrance, Gart's voice the loudest.

"Stay here," Senke told Haern. "Lock the door. I'll go see what's going on."

Senke closed the door behind him, waited until he heard Haern lock it, then hurried toward the entrance. He saw a few thieves dashing around the corner, too far ahead for him to ask questions. Gart's shouts were the only ones that he could understand above the throng, and what he heard filled his gut with lead.

"Guards, guards!" shouted Gart. "We got guards to smash!"

Senke dashed through a dining room, turned left down a hallway, then hooked toward the main entrance. Over a hundred thieves lined up along the windows facing the front of the house. Gart towered among them, staring and pointing.

"What is going on here?" Senke shouted.

"Soldiers!" Gart shouted, spinning to greet Senke. "Royal soldiers too! They showed up and started surrounding the place. I count at least five hundred. We got heads to smash, boys, and lots of them!"

While Gart might have been enthused, Senke's face paled. The soldiers had arrived too soon. Thren wasn't even there yet. What was wrong with them? Why had Gerand not waited for his signal?

"We need to delay them," Senke said. "Hold the doors as best we can."

"They got armor," one rogue beside them argued. "Plate mail, for cripes' sake. Helmets, shields, swords...we got daggers and leather. What the fuck you think we can do against that?"

"I expect you to kill them," Senke shouted, a bit of his hardness returning. "Or do you really think they'll let you live if you run out the door with your hands up and your tail between your legs?"

Gart pulled Senke aside and lowered his voice.

"We got a traitor among us," Gart said. "How else did the soldiers come so quick? So who might it be?"

"Not a clue," Senke lied. "We need to hold. Perhaps once the fire is set, we can escape during the commotion."

"Or we'll roast like roaches."

The two leaders stared eye to eye.

"I don't see any other way," Senke said.

"Then we fight," Gart grumbled. "And we hope Thren arrives with enough men to save the day."

"They're coming," several shouted at once. The soldiers rushed through the gates, swarming like metallic ants. They surrounded the complex, this time within the gate instead of without. Most wielded long swords and shields, though some held halberds, spears, and giant mauls. Four carried a thick log with metal handles bolted into the wood.

The men with the log approached the door, a squad of ten protecting them.

"Hold the door," Senke said, taking a step back. "I'll guard the back."

"Better hurry," Gart said. "And you better hope Norris hasn't lost his spine and run!"

Senke had barely left before the surrounding soldiers with mauls smashed in the windows all throughout the lower level. Soldiers poured inside, through far more windows than there were thieves to guard. Senke drew his sword and cut down the first to come near. A second soldier tried to use his shield to block, but Senke rolled atop it, over his head, and then thrust his sword through the shoulder blade. The sounds of battle erupted throughout the mansion.

When he reached the dining hall he found the door open. Haern was gone.

CHAPTER 34

With the first shattering of glass, Haern flung open the door to see the cause. Armored soldiers stood before the windows, swinging enormous mauls that easily bashed through the glass and layered the carpet with shards. Soldiers flowed in through the unguarded windows. He felt torn between relief and worry. Relief because the king's involvement would certainly prevent his father's plans from going as they should. Worry because they'd kill him just as easily as any other member of the thief guilds.

Well, not as easily, he thought with a wry smile. His daggers in hand, he turned right and bolted deeper into the mansion. If there was any hope of escape, he'd try to find it in the back sections. If he was lucky he might slip out through an unwatched window, as he had fleeing Robert Haern's home.

Haern was too fast for the initial wave in the hallway to catch him, but as he burst through the door at the end he found himself in the middle of an armory. Three soldiers approached, their shields leading. Haern rolled to one side, lashing underneath the shield at the closest soldier's ankle. His dagger struck armor and clinked off, doing no damage. When his roll ended he kicked hard, leaping into the very center of the three. They turned on him, but their shields were large and the room small. Haern twirled like a dancer, his daggers punching through creases in armor. He jumped, kicked off a shield, and slammed into the chest of another. As they rolled to the ground Haern's dagger cut into the man's neck once, twice, three times. Blood splattered across his mask.

The other two soldiers, their arms and legs bleeding from several deep cuts, tried to stab Haern as he lay there. Their blades struck air. Haern rolled off and onto his knees, then kicked back. He slid between the remaining two, and this time his daggers found the open spots just above their greaves. To make sure they stayed down, he twisted the daggers when he pulled them out. One dead and two others crumpled to the ground, Haern ran out of the armory and into a corridor.

A man dressed in the garb of the Serpent Guild nearly collided with him. His curved daggers dripped blood.

"Who the fuck are you?" the man had time to ask before Haern lunged. The Serpent was far more skilled than Haern had expected. One curved blade parried his attack, the other slipping downward so Haern might impale himself from his lunge. Twisting his body, Haern angled his knee so that when they struck, he could rebound off and away before getting harmed. When he landed beside the armory door, he had no doubt whom he fought.

"You're Norris," he said.

The guildmaster of the Serpents spat.

"You must be Thren's boy. I'd heard you were getting soft. Did he send you after me, or is this your own stupid ploy?"

"Mine," Haern said, slowly settling into a combat stance. Norris saw this and smirked.

"Think you can handle my cloakdance, boy?" He started swaying, his weapons well hidden. "Come try me."

Norris swirled, his cloak whipping out in chaotic fashion. Haern watched, fascinated. The guildmaster spun faster, faster, his cloak a blur, his hands hidden shadows of death. Waiting. Haern felt like prey mesmerized by the dance of the cobra, though part of it was professional interest. Such a dance, he had to learn it. He had to master such a skill. He stepped forward, then immediately pulled back, a curved dagger slicing just above his head.

Time was not on either of their sides, and both knew it. Haern crouched low, and then lunged left. He hit the wall and then vaulted into the air, his legs flipping high over his head. His daggers thrust downward at the whirl of cloaks, but Norris was not fooled. He batted both aside, pulled out of his dance, and thrust where Haern landed.

Except he didn't land. The corridor was thin enough that Haern's feet pressed flat on the opposite side. His momentum pushed his knees down, and then he kicked. His shoulder rammed Norris in the stomach. One dagger stabbed his chest. The other tore into his groin. Norris collapsed, blood pouring out on his green trousers.

"Always wondered if I could take Thren," he said, his voice labored and in pain. "Can't even kill his damn kid."

Haern stepped close, kicked a dagger out of Norris's hand, and then looped around to do the same to the other.

"My knife or the guards?" he asked.

"A thief to a thief," Norris said, coughing blood.

Haern saluted, then flipped the dagger in his hand and stabbed. Senke entered as he was cleaning off the blade on his cloak.

"There you are!" Senke shouted. "Seems like the whole damn

army is here!" He stopped when he saw the body and realized who it was.

"You killed Norris?" he asked. "Damn. Starting to think you've been holding out on me during our spars."

Crazy as it was, Haern felt embarrassed.

"It's different this way," he said, wishing he could explain. "Practice is practice. This . . . matters. This is real. Now how do we get out of here?"

"Follow me," Senke said. "Going won't be easy. The mansion has a large attic, and from there we can get to the roof."

He smacked Haern on the shoulder.

"No matter what, I'm proud of you," he said.

The two hurried to the end of the corridor and kicked open the door. They were within another dining hall, though smaller and most likely intended for mercenaries and servants. On the far end smoke billowed into the room from underneath the crack of the door. Senke saw this and swore up a storm.

"They've set off the fires?" he wondered aloud. "Well damn it, those stupid cowards. Some of the Serpents must have panicked. We need out, now!"

He pressed his hood over his mouth, then winked at Haern when he saw the boy's mask.

"Almost like you came prepared," he said, chuckling.

Two Serpents came running out the door when they neared. Haern cut down one, Senke the other. Smoke poured in through the open door, and down the hallway they both saw the fires rapidly spreading.

"We can't make it," Haern shouted. Senke knelt and pointed so they could see underneath the smoke.

"You see where the hallway turns?" he asked. "Immediately on your left is a door. It leads up to the attic, and from there we can find a way to safety."

He wiped sweat from his brow as he looked to the fires. "Relative safety," he corrected.

"Let me go first," Haern said. "I'm faster. If the door is blocked by flame, I'll come running."

Senke started to object, but Haern was already dashing down the hall.

The smoke gathered along the ceiling in giant rolling clouds. In each doorway he passed, the fires roared, licking the outsides of their doors, looking like tongues eager to taste more of the building. His eyes stung looking at them. The hallway was unbelievably hot. He wrapped his cloak over his mouth, his mask doing little to keep out the foul air. Cough after cough racked his body. Soon he lost his vision as his eyes watered.

Haern couldn't believe the heat. It didn't seem to matter that his skin touched no fire. The floor warmed his feet. The air sucked at the moisture of his skin, and he felt like a pastry stuck in an oven. He remembered his training, clutched it with all his mind, and forced himself to keep running. Air didn't matter. The heat didn't matter. One foot after the other.

His outstretched hand pressed against the end of the hallway. Feeling a bit of hope, he turned and kept his hand near, occasionally brushing the wall with his fingertips. When he touched a door, he felt like shouting for joy. His fingers found the doorknob, and yet again he wanted to cheer. The doorknob, while not cool, didn't burn to the touch. He flung it open and dashed up the stairs, wishing he could somehow alert Senke to follow. Smoke climbed up with him, and wishing there were another way, he slammed the door shut behind.

The attic was dim, but the few windows let in enough light for him to see. Most were small, but near the back he saw a giant circle of glass that seemed most inviting. Haern could almost imagine the cool air rushing on the outside of it, and he wanted to dive in as if it were water. Piles of discarded armor, old relics of family generations long past, filled the room. Haern weaved about them, all the while wondering when Senke would arrive.

He was halfway to the window when it shattered. A slender woman flew through the shards, landing with a roll along the floor. Haern stared, vaguely recognizing her. She wore the colors of the Ash Guild, but he couldn't place her. She looked about, still struggling to adjust to the darkness. He thought to hide from her, but then he saw her face and knew her name.

"Veliana?" he asked, remembering standing at his father's side as they tried to force her to overthrow her guildmaster and take control.

At the sound of her name the woman spun, her dagger already drawn.

"You're young to be one of the thieves," Veliana said. "What is your name?"

"Haern," he answered. He took a step toward her, still trying to decide if she was dangerous or not. With everyone trying to flee the mansion, it seemed odd someone would try to break in.

Veliana looked a bit disappointed, but then she spotted him standing behind a large crate of wrapped wool. Her whole body tensed. Her mouth curled into a sneer.

"Liar," she said. "You're Thren's child. You think I'd forget a single shred of that moment?"

Haern shook his head.

"Aaron is dead. Leave me be. His sins are mine no more."

Veliana laughed.

"The world doesn't work that way. Change your name, change your face, but the sins are still yours. Your father's killed everyone I've ever cared for. Turn back and die in the fire, or draw your dagger and fight me."

Haern glanced back to the door to the stairs. Smoke had begun pouring thickly through its edges and the crack underneath. Already the heat seeped through the wood floor. Still no sign of Senke, and Haern tried not to think of what had befallen him.

"Don't do this," Haern whispered. The roar of the flames drowned out his words. Veliana lunged, her dagger thrusting straight for his neck. Haern batted it aside with his own, then swept his right foot around in an arc. She leaped over it, her knee ramming forward. His head snapped backward as the knee collided with his face. Blood splattered the inside of his mask.

Staggering, his head still swimming from the smoke and heat, Haern went fully defensive. Veliana's dagger slashed and cut, and despite any openings he might have seen, he refused to try for them. He parried and spun, slowly weaving his way around the piles of junk. The air grew murky and gray from the smoke, much of it starting to pour out the broken window.

"Leave me alone!" he shouted as he crossed his daggers and blocked a vicious downward chop. His elbows shook at the impact, and while he was momentarily distracted by the closeness of her face and the hideousness of her eye, Veliana successfully tripped him with a kick. As he fell he rolled, avoiding her opportunistic strike. He turned and darted through the attic, frantically dashing for the window.

Veliana raced him, her dagger still eager for blood. She reached the window first, but not in enough time to prepare correctly. Haern leaped, slamming his shoulder into hers. As she was pushed back, his daggers curled around her sides, slicing into flesh. Blood spilled down her ribs, across her tunic and pants. Screaming in pain, Veliana whirled. When Haern ducked her high kick, he found a dagger waiting for him low.

He twisted, but not fast enough. The dagger slashed across his shoulder, tearing open a huge gash in his shirt. Blood poured down his arm, the pain terrible, but Haern never let it slow him. His opponent had just scored her first true hit. That was when she was most vulnerable, her confidence soaring with the minor victory.

His foot whirled about him, his left arm flinging his cloak upward to hide his movements. Veliana lost her balance and fell to one knee, letting out a small cry from the harsh landing. Haern's cloak whipped her face, and when she pushed back to see, Haern was there, his fist leading. He punched her throat with all his strength.

Gasping for air, she fell back, holding her dagger out in a meager defense. Haern cut her knuckles to weaken her grip, then slapped the dagger away. Veliana glared with her one good eye as she coughed.

"Aaron is dead," he told her, breathing heavily as his daggers shook in his hands, one of their tips aimed straight for her throat. "Why can't you see that?"

"You're him," Veliana said with a cracking voice. "You can't hide. You're just a coward."

Haern shook his head sadly.

"I'm sorry," he said. "But you're wrong."

He rammed the butt of his dagger against the top of her skull, knocking her out cold. As she slumped to the ground, Haern stuck his head out the window to take a look. A massive crowd gathered about, a mixture of guards, onlookers, and desperate neighbors organizing bucket brigades to ensure the mansion's fire didn't spread. In that chaos he could certainly slip away.

Behind him he heard Veliana moan softly. Haern sighed. At the side of his father he'd left her for dead. He couldn't do so again, not while claiming to be a better person. The fire was already crawling its way up the stairs, its smoke billowing. He had two minutes, maybe three.

Knowing her cloak and colors would condemn her, Haern stripped her down to her undergarments. He searched the crates, holding his cloak over his mouth as he did. Once he found a blanket of sufficient length he dragged it over to Veliana and tied one corner to her wrists. The other half he wrapped around his arm, praying for the best. If Veliana was lucky she'd survive the fall, and those who found her would assume her a frantic house servant fleeing the fire after hiding in the attic. If not, well...

He almost left her for the calm, quiet death from the smoke. Almost.

"We're even," he whispered as he pushed her body out the window. He braced his feet against the wall and held on with all his might. The cloth pulled tight, and he let a bit of it unspool before clamping down again. He nearly went flying out with her, he so badly underestimated the pull. About halfway down she stopped, and he hoped that was close enough. He let go of the cloth, then counted to three before looking.

A couple of onlookers were gathered around her. It appeared someone had caught her. He couldn't hear their voices from so far, but he saw them pointing to her face, and one man beside her shook his head, his look a mixture of anger and pity. Haern sighed. The wounds, blood on her wrists, and tattered clothing told them a story they expected from such a wreckage. Now for his own safety. Haern kicked out a last few shards of glass, stood on the edge of the window, and pulled himself up to the roof.

From there he leaped to a nearby tree, slid down, and vanished amid the mob.

CHAPTER 35

The proceedings bored Torgar tremendously. The sheer amount of revelry around him only worsened his torture. A thousand gallons of alcohol flowed throughout the crowd, the sound of cheers, sex, and fighting roaring for miles, yet he was separated from it all.

"Sit up," Taras whispered next to him. "You're slouching."

Torgar straightened, cracking his back as he did. Sometimes he wondered if boredom was more dangerous than actual combat. Certainly seemed as deadly an opponent. He sat at the incredibly long table set up in the pavilion atop the larger of the two hills chosen for the Kensgold. Members of all three families of the Trifect sat in the hundreds of chairs. He saw ugly cousins, distant relatives, soldiers, and merchants of all kinds. They bickered among themselves, hoping to achieve a better appearance through the sparring of their tongues or the collaborative wealth of their name.

Nonsense, all of it. Torgar knew he could kill every one of them to a man, yet they peered down at him as if their noses were a mile long and he were hard to see. At the head of the table Laurie, Leon, and Maynard talked, sometimes openly, sometimes quietly and hunched together. Taras sat beside his father, listening when it seemed appropriate. Torgar gave the boy credit: he seemed to understand plenty, and he even chipped in once or twice without earning scorn from any of the three. Leon and Maynard seemed to be enjoying themselves, but Laurie was clearly upset. The empty seat beside Torgar was the reason.

Stupid bitch, thought Torgar. *Just had to go running off for her precious walls. Nursing babes are tougher to scare than that broad.*

He might have said it out loud, but he'd been denied the amount of alcohol he'd wanted. Still, his master wanted him at Taras's side, to serve as protection to both the boy and the father. Judging by the haughty grumbling about him, the only danger was from a flying plate of warm food.

"What are they discussing now?" Torgar asked Taras. He tried to whisper, but his deep voice wasn't suited for it.

"They've finished their trade contracts," Taras said, glancing back at the mercenary. "They're discussing the thief guilds now."

"Not much to discuss," Torgar said. "We double up some patrols, hire a few more mercenaries, but it's like swatting at flies buzzing around your horse's ass."

He caught a finely dressed woman in her thirties glaring at him from the opposite side of the table, so he shot her a wink.

"Forgive the color," he said. "My brain is mud and my tongue is blue. I'm only here for my lord."

She sniffed at him and turned toward a lady to her left. They began whispering, each clearly unhappy with his presence. Torgar sighed. By the gods, did he hate being there.

"They're thinking of going to the king," Taras said.

"Good luck with that," Torgar said. "Got a better chance..."

He choked down another colorful comment as a priest of Ashhur walked into the pavilion.

"Who in blazes let him in here?" Torgar asked. Taras, too busy listening to his father discuss bribes, didn't notice. The mercenary captain stood and moved to intercept the priest. The man of the cloth seemed lost amid the sea of people.

"Welcome to our gathering," Torgar said as he grabbed the priest's hand and shook it. The priest, a younger man with neatly trimmed hair and a shadow of growth on his chin, looked thoroughly relieved.

"I must admit, I'm a bit lost," the priest said. "I need to speak with Laurie Keenan, though I don't know his face from the thousand others."

"I'm head of mercenaries for Lord Keenan," Torgar said. "He's busy plotting and planning, so just tell me what you'd tell him and I'll see if it's worth interrupting him for."

The priest didn't ask for proof of his rank or employer or anything. Torgar felt relieved that he'd gotten ahold of the priest first before he blabbed his message to the closest curious Gemcroft relative or Connington sellsword.

"It involves his wife, Madelyn," the priest began.

"Hrm, hold up," Torgar said, pushing his large forefinger into the priest's face. "Not another word. Let's go somewhere with less ears, eh?"

The priest nodded. Torgar led them out one of the side flaps of the tent, nodding at the mercenaries stationed there as they passed.

"What's your name?" Torgar asked as they walked.

"Derek," said the priest. "You may call me Derek."

"Then Derek you are!" said Torgar, laughing in an attempt

to put the man at ease. Leaving the tent didn't seem to help calm him as much as Torgar had hoped. Glancing around at the sheer decadence, Torgar realized why. He wondered how many pillars of Ashhur's faith were being broken even as they spoke.

"Ignore the show," Torgar said, grabbing the priest's shoulders. "Now what is this message about?"

"We found Mrs. Keenan under attack on her way to her estate," Derek began. "We rescued her before she could suffer any real harm. We hoped she'd stay the night in safety at our temple. Many of her guards did. Yet come the morning, it appeared she had run off."

Torgar felt anger bubbling in his chest. While he had been escorting Taras with invitations to the Kensgold, another of his charges had been assaulted in the streets. Since he'd received no word otherwise, he'd assumed Madelyn had made it home safe. But had she actually?

"Why did you take so long to bring us word?" Torgar asked.

"We sent a priest to inform your lord of her staying at our temple." Derek glanced about, his face twitching nervously. "The message never made it to your camp. We recently found out he was murdered. Calan, our high priest, sent members of our order to your estate to see if she were there. She's not. Did she not come here?"

Torgar's look was answer enough.

"Then you must tell your master," Derek insisted. "His wife is missing, and we fear one of the thief guilds were the ones to take her."

"If they did, she may not be alive," Torgar said, sighing. "We've received no demands."

"Actually," Derek said, reaching out a trembling hand, "I think you have."

Within his shaking fingers was a scroll sealed with wax. The wax itself was smooth, showing no insignia. Torgar took it, raising an eyebrow as he did.

"A man in a gray cloak stopped me on the way here," Derek said. "He gave me the scroll and told me to deliver it to whomever I gave my message to. He swore I'd die if I opened it, or even tarried."

He stepped back a little, as if the note might erupt and kill them all. Torgar broke the seal and unrolled it. The message was short and took him little time to read despite his terrible skill at it.

Laurie Keenan,

End the Kensgold. Leave Veldaren tonight. If not, Madelyn dies. Then Taras. Then you.

A Spider.

Torgar rolled up the note and held it so tight the paper crumpled and the wax cracked and fell to the ground in tiny pieces.

"Listen to me, Derek," Torgar said. "Stay here at the Kensgold. They'll kill you on your way back, do you understand?"

"I'm not afraid to die," Derek said, but he certainly looked fearful.

"Scared or not, there's no point in walking back into their trap," the mercenary captain insisted. "But go off and die if you want. I've got more important things to do."

He hurried back into the pavilion, honestly not caring whether or not the priest remained. Laurie was laughing loudly when he arrived, either not noticing or not caring about Torgar's absence.

"Milord," Torgar said, kneeling down beside Laurie's ear. "We need to talk."

"Just a moment," Laurie said, patting the mercenary on the shoulder. "Leon here was just telling a wonderful story about..."

"Now," Torgar insisted. The mood soured immediately. Leon gave him a glare that said in no uncertain terms that he'd be joining Will as game for the gentle touchers if he were Leon's mercenary. Laurie looked at Torgar for a moment, seeing the urgency in his eyes, and then turned to the others.

"A moment, if you will," he said, standing. Taras followed unasked.

"What is so damn important that I must appear subservient to my own mercenary?" Laurie asked once they were outside the tent. In answer Torgar handed him the scroll. Laurie read it, swore, then threw it to the ground and stomped on it with his heel.

"Where's Madelyn?" he asked.

"She never made it home," Torgar explained. He summarized what the priest of Ashhur had told him. When finished, he stepped back and crossed his arms, wondering what his master would do.

"We don't know if she's dead or alive," Laurie said, his face red with anger. "And even if I do what they say, there's no guarantee they'll let her live."

"And the threat on your life, and your son's?"

Laurie glanced at Taras, who had remained quiet.

"I have received a hundred of these every year for the past five," Laurie said. "Why should I treat this one any different?"

Torgar shrugged his shoulders.

"How badly do you want her back?" he asked.

"That's not the point," Laurie said.

"That *is* the point. It's the only damn point. You want to remain powerful in the eyes of the Trifect, then stay. You want to keep your own ego intact, then stay. But if you want her back, then say the word. Pack up all our servants, our food, and our ale, and we go. What will it matter? We've had our feast. You've made your plans."

Laurie looked furious enough to kill. His hand moved to the jeweled dagger hanging from his belt. Torgar refused to move. He'd spoken out of line, but there was one last thing he had to say.

"Give me time," he insisted. "I can find her on my own. I'll bleed these cowards, find where she is, and bring her back safely. Give them what they want. What they ask for is so little. Either way they might kill her, but even a few hours' delay may decide whether I find a prisoner or a corpse."

Laurie drew the dagger. He pointed its blade at Torgar's throat. The hand shook.

"He's right," Taras said. "Either way they'll kill her. This gives us a chance."

The dagger lowered.

"Kneel," Laurie said. Torgar did as told. He didn't even wince when his master grabbed his neck and cut a thin line of blood across his forehead.

"Swear upon your blood," Laurie said, his voice soft and shaking with intensity.

Torgar put his hands to his forehead, feeling the warmth flowing across his palms. After a count of ten, he pulled them back and lifted his hands to the night sky.

"I swear upon my lifeblood that I will bring her back."

Laurie wiped the dagger clean with a cloth and then sheathed it.

"Almost," he said. "But not quite. You'll bring her back *alive*, Torgar. If not, I call your honor false. I call your wisdom foolishness, and my retreat a great jape against my name. If you find her dead, then fall upon your sword, because that death will be far better than the one I give you."

He stormed back into the pavilion, shouting orders. Cries of disappointment followed. The Kensgold was over.

"Let me come with you," Taras said once his father was gone.

"Stay here," Torgar said. "I have enough on my shoulders. I won't have you dying on me while I find your mother."

"I can fight," Taras insisted.

"Follow me outside the camp and I'll kill you myself," Torgar threatened. That seemed to jolt the boy a little. Reluctantly he turned and joined his father in the tent. Torgar shook his head. In truth, he'd have loved to have Taras with him, but the risks were already too great. He would work alone, and he'd work both bloodily and fast.

He swung by the rest of his mercenaries, putting another in charge and informing them of the Kensgold's disbandment. Once that was done he took a horse from Laurie's collection and rode like a demon to the walls of Veldaren. On his way there he rode past a body lying in the grass, its white robes stained crimson with blood.

He'd thought it'd be harder to locate a member of the Spider Guild, but it ended up rather insultingly easy. Torgar caught sight of a gray cloak while riding east through the city. The man was clearly in a hurry, so much so that he wasn't taking any precautions to avoid being followed. Torgar laughed as he rode after him into a narrow alley. The Spider turned at the sound of hoofbeats, but far too late. Torgar leaped off, cracking him atop the head with his fists. The rogue crumpled like an unhooked straw man.

Torgar dragged him farther out of view of the main road,

then pushed him against a wall. He crouched down, pinched the man's nose shut, and then slapped him a few times until he lurched awake.

"Hush now," Torgar said, putting a hand over the man's mouth and then using it to shove him hard against the wall. "I don't want to start cutting pieces off you already."

The Spider paled a little and nodded. Torgar chuckled.

"Good," he said, drawing his sword and resting it across his knees. "You just remember I got this, all right, and things will go well for everyone involved."

"What do you want from me?" the man asked as Torgar removed his hand.

"Your name, first off," Torgar said.

"Tobias."

"Well, Tobias," Torgar said, "now that I know your name, how about I get to know a few more things? For starters, where were you rushing off to in such a big hurry?"

Tobias shut his mouth and purposefully looked away. Torgar rolled his eyes. He struck him with his fist, grabbed his arm, and then buried his sword through the palm. As Tobias screamed, Torgar shoved his hand over his mouth and slammed his head back.

"Listen closely, dumbass," Torgar said. "You ever heard of the Blood Riders? They're stationed out of Ker, carry quite a reputation in the west?"

Tobias's eyes widened at the mention of their name.

"Oh good, you have heard of them," Torgar said. "You know what their favorite method of torture is? They take four of their horses, one for each arm and leg, and then tie a rope securing you from saddle to wrist or ankle. After that, it's off to the races. You should see how much blood can splatter into the air when those ropes pull tight."

Torgar shoved his face into Tobias's and then grinned.

"I used to be a Blood Rider, you goathumper. See my horse over there? I may have only one, but you'd be surprised what I can do with a little bit of rope."

Cold sweat covered Tobias's body. Torgar twisted his sword around a little, shifting bone, and then pulled it out. That done, he removed his hand and asked his question again. This time he got an answer.

"Soldiers attacked us at Leon's place," Tobias said. "I was outside the complex when they came. I hoped to find Thren and warn him."

Torgar glanced east, where a giant plume of smoke stretched to the night sky.

"I think he might already know," Torgar said. "Let's try for something that I wouldn't find out on my own in the next five minutes. Your guildmaster has someone special, very special. Do you know who I'm talking about?"

Tobias's look showed he clearly did.

"Don't ask," the Spider said. "Please, don't ask. Thren will kill me if I tell."

"I'll kill you twice as bad," Torgar growled.

Tobias actually laughed.

"You think you're more frightening than Thren?" he asked. "Go ahead. Use your damn horse. I won't tell."

Torgar sighed. He'd thought for a moment he'd avoided lengthy torture. Oh well. At least it was something he was good at.

All it took was ten minutes. He left Tobias holding his intestines in his hands.

"You're right, Thren may kill you," Torgar said as he mounted his horse. "But you really should have saved us both the trouble."

He rode back to the main street and then hurried east, the clomp of his horse's feet on the dirt a soothing pattern. The directions were simple, the safe house plain and poorly guarded. From what Tobias had told him, Thren didn't have any men to spare on his glorious night. Torgar snorted. Well, he'd play his part in tarnishing that old bastard's glory. So far the smoke seemed focused on the Conningtons' place. Hopefully his own master's mansion had survived intact.

The house appeared the same as any other, with a small door in the front center, no windows, and a slanted roof of wood and clay. Torgar rode a few more houses down to maintain surprise, dismounted, and then tied his horse's reins to the handle of a door. The mercenary captain drew his sword, kissed the blade, and ran. He slammed into the safe house door at full speed, throwing his shoulder into it. The wood cracked and splintered.

"Shit!" Torgar heard a man shout from within. Knowing he had little time, he flung his weight against the door again. It burst open, revealing two men of the Spider Guild standing with their daggers drawn. Madelyn lay slumped in the corner, unmoving. Torgar desperately hoped she wasn't dead. He had no intention of falling on his sword, but by the gods, he didn't want to spend the rest of his days fleeing from Laurie Keenan either.

"Come on, then!" Torgar roared, swinging his sword in a wildly exaggerated arc. "Let's have a fight, eh?"

One of the thieves fell for the bait, lunging inward when Torgar should have been vulnerable. Instead a meaty fist crushed his face, his movement anticipated. When he collapsed, Torgar's long sword pierced through his shoulder and tore free, severing bone and spilling blood across the floor. The remaining man glanced at Madelyn, clearing thinking to use her as a hostage. Torgar never gave him the time. He rushed the man, not at all afraid of his small dagger. He had range, skill, and sheer brute strength.

Accepting a stab to the shoulder, Torgar returned the favor. His sword punched through the Spider's chest and out his back, pinning him to the wall. The mercenary captain grabbed the man's head with his hands, head-butted him, and then twisted violently. When he yanked his sword free, the man fell to the ground dead.

"Gyah," Torgar said, yanking the dagger out of his shoulder and examining it. The blade was serrated, and sure enough he'd felt it. "Mean little prick," he said, tossing the dagger back atop the body. Taking in a deep breath, he turned and lifted Madelyn's body.

She was breathing.

"Must be my lucky night," Torgar said. He stole a long kiss from Madelyn, then exited the home. He untied his reins, slung Madelyn over his shoulders, and then mounted his horse. Madelyn curled in his lap like a child, Torgar snapped the reins and rode back toward Keenan's wagons, hoping to catch up before they gained too much distance from Veldaren.

"Happy fucking Kensgold, Thren," Torgar said as he rode out the city gates and into the night air. "Hope you had as much fun tonight as I have."

CHAPTER

36

Thren had seen the smoke rising as he and Kayla returned from watching the Kensgold to ensure its disbandment. By the time they reached the city, there was no questioning its source. The Connington estate was on fire.

"What would have made the damn fools start so early?" Thren wondered, his voice carrying a hard edge. "Leon isn't anywhere near the city!"

"Perhaps they encountered more resistance than we did at Maynard's?" Kayla asked.

Thren shook his head.

"Whatever the reason, we need to hurry to the Gemcroft estate. If Leon's is already burning, there's little we can do there. Damn it! I had such wonderful plans to make him pay for Will's death. At the very least, I need Maynard to die tonight."

He didn't say why, of course. He'd never admit the danger

hanging over his head from the priests of Karak because they had aided his son.

They ran side by side, both panting from the exertion. When they reached the mansion, he saw a few of the Wolf Guild scattered about, keeping an eye on the roads. Cynric stood in one of the windows of the nearby homes. He cupped his hands to his mouth and howled.

"That man needs his head nailed tighter to his neck," Thren mumbled. The two of them hurried through the door to find the guildmaster waiting.

"We've seen the smoke," Cynric said. "Do you know anything about it? We hoped for a runner or two to clarify, but no one's showed."

"We know as little as you then," Thren said. "Damn. At least the mansion is destroyed. Have you seen anything here?"

"Not a hint of prey," Cynric said. "Rather boring, really. We almost went to join the feast at Leon's. Hopefully you'll remember that when the killing starts. We deserve our share."

Thren left the house, Kayla trailing after him. He walked through the open gate and into the mansion. Kadish was waiting for them.

"I was wondering when you'd return," the man said. "I've been wanting a straight answer about what to do with him."

He pointed to where James Beren lay slumped against a wall, his arms and legs bound tight. His eyes were open, but his mouth was gagged. Thren tilted his head as he thought.

"Is the Ash Guild broken?" he asked.

"We've killed all but a few," Kadish said. "We'll hunt down who we can, but most will just sign on with other guilds, including mine. They're done."

"Good." Thren turned to James and drew his sword. Kneeling down, he removed the gag from his mouth and smiled.

"Do you see what happens when you resist me?" he asked. James nodded, his face bruised and purple. Thren stood and looked to the many members of both the Spider and Hawk Guilds standing about. "Do you all see what happens when you resist me?"

They nodded. In response, Thren turned and rammed his short sword through one of James's eyes. His face locked in a vicious snarl, Thren twisted the blade and then yanked it free. Gore splattered across the floor.

"Do you see now?" he asked them.

He cleaned the blade, sheathed it, and then turned to Kadish.

"Get your men ready," he said. "The Wolf Guild will surround them and cut off any retreat once they're within the outer gate. We'll crush them between us, all of them. We end this tonight!"

Kayla followed him back outside as he walked toward the gate's exit.

"Where are you going now?" she asked.

"To get my son," he said. "The priests should be done with him. I want him to watch our victory."

"But Maynard might be on his way already," Kayla insisted. "We don't have time for you to go looking for him."

Thren snapped to a halt and turned. Something about her words, the way she was trying to stall...

"Why would I need to go looking?" he asked. "Or do you know of some reason he would have left their compound?"

The way Kayla stood there, mouth slightly open, told him all he needed to know. Lies grew and died on her tongue, unable to endure his glare. When she'd joined his guild, he'd seen great promise, someone willing to endure so much for the safety of his son, someone willing to kill and bleed just to join his guild. But now he saw weakness. Now he saw a heart not made for the night.

"Aaron broke out," she said at last. "He resisted their attempts and met with me on the rooftops."

Thren stepped closer toward her. His hand subtly shifted toward the sword strapped to his hip.

"And you never told me this why?" he asked.

"He's dead to you," she said. "He told me so. You'll never see him again."

"Why did you not tell me!" he screamed, not caring that the different guilds were watching.

"Because he deserves better," she whispered. "Better than what you would make him be."

"Better?" asked Thren. "Every living man and woman would soon quake in fear of his name. He would be a killer even greater than I. He was so close to perfect, so close, but now he's gone. Not your place, Kayla. It was never your place."

She dropped to one knee as he swung, drawing daggers free from her belt. They were slender, curved, designed for throwing instead of close melee. Thren knew that, and he kept closer, punching with his swords so that she must twist and parry instead of trying a throw. But despite her skill she was nothing, not to him. Just a girl who threw knives.

One such knife whirled through the air, a single desperate attempt by Kayla. It missed Thren's cheek by a hair's width. And then he was upon her, thrusting his swords through her stomach. She gasped, her hands opening and closing, her dagger belt torn, her daggers clanging off the ground. Her knees buckled, and she fell to her back.

"Doesn't matter," she said, blood dripping down her lips. "He's free of you, Thren. Free..."

Thren stood over her body, his shoulders slumped and his jaw trembling, as he watched her die. Everything was crumbling. The fire at Leon Connington's. His son's betrayal. So far no news had come from the castle about the Naked Bells' attempt on the king, and he still had a chance of killing Maynard Gemcroft. The night wasn't a total loss, not yet.

He returned to the mansion to wait. There was no point in searching for Aaron, not then. When things calmed, he'd scour the city, search under every rock and look into every hole if he must. But not yet.

"What in Karak's name did she do?" Kadish asked when Thren returned.

"She hid things from me," Thren said. "Now see to your men. The Kensgold ended not long ago. They should return within the hour."

Kadish shrugged.

"All right, then. Shame about that bitch, though. She was a cute one."

Remembering how that cuteness had helped corrupt his son, Thren snarled and struck the wall with his fist.

"Or not," Kadish said before going from Hawk to Hawk ensuring their readiness for the ambush.

Maynard Gemcroft knew something was afoot when Laurie disbanded the Kensgold early, but he wasn't sure what exactly. Madelyn's absence was conspicuous, but that wasn't something he could know about for certain. Leon had no shortage of grumblings and complaints, calling Laurie every possible name for a bad host, plus a few more that he probably made up on the spot.

Then they saw the smoke and knew the thief guilds had chosen that night to play. From its direction, he guessed the fire to be at Leon's home. The fat man stood outside the giant pavilion, swearing up a blue storm at the sight.

"They torched my home?" he asked after a minute to compose himself. "Those...those...imbeciles torched my home? I'll gut them all. I'll piss on their heads, rape their ears, feed their pricks to swine, and have *them* rape them too."

"Go to your home, and go well protected," Maynard told him. "The streets are not safe for us, no matter how many soldiers walk with us."

With six hundred armed men at his side, Maynard still felt insecure on his march home. Trailing after the six hundred was a tail of several hundred more, servants and dancers and singers wanting their pay or some beds to rest in. Maynard knew that many more wagons would come throughout the night, carrying whatever remained of his goods to sell, along with a handsome amount of gold. He'd left another two hundred to guard the wagons, but he wasn't worried about theft. It was fire that worried him.

When they reached the mansion, Maynard felt his heart sink. The outer gate was open. All throughout the yard were massive holes from the trap spells he'd had a trio of wizards cast. No bodies remained, though he was certain from the wreckage that many must have died.

"What are your orders?" Maynard's mercenary captain asked him.

"They must have looted while we were gone," Maynard said. "The same probably happened to Leon. Yet why did they not burn it down like his?"

"A trap," the mercenary said. "That is all that makes sense."

Maynard glanced back at the rest of his men. He had the makings of a small army with him. What would they say if he fled, all in fear of a few rogues in his own house? His reputation had already suffered greatly from the war with the thief guilds. Whatever they had planned, he would not back down.

"Take four hundred of your men and scour my home," Maynard ordered. "Leave the rest to protect me and my servants."

"As you wish," said the mercenary captain before turning and relaying the orders in loud, barking yells. Maynard stayed with the remaining two hundred at the gate entrance. He might not run from a trap, but he had no intention of walking into it either.

The mercenaries had reached the door when the first men appeared at the windows of the mansion. Arrows rained down upon them, fired by men of the Hawk and Spider Guilds. Maynard saw this and swore. His mercenaries rushed the door, knowing getting inside would greatly reduce the threat of the archers. Something prevented it, though he could not see what. He heard screams coupled with horrific sounds of battle. Stopped at the door, his mercenaries started to turn and make their way back to the gate.

"Behind!" several shouted. Maynard spun, then felt himself pushed to his knees. Mercenaries stood above him, holding shields high as dozens of arrows rained down. Fear lumped in his throat. Swords rang as men assaulted them from the back. Mailed hands grabbed his shoulders, and under the cover of shields Maynard slowly shifted within the ring of guards.

"We're pressed on both sides," one said.

"They're flooding out of the mansion," said another.

Maynard tried to look but he was surrounded by flesh and armor. He smelled sweat and blood. The air whistled with arrows, followed by the wooden thumps as they hit shields, or screams when they hit something softer.

Stupid, thought Maynard. *Even knowing, I walked right into their trap.*

With attackers on both sides, and archers firing from so many windows, he knew their hope was slim. He pushed aside a soldier, determined to see how dire his situation truly was. As if he had taunted the gods, an arrow sailed through the gap he'd made and slammed into his chest. He collapsed to his knees, his hands clutching the shaft as warm blood flowed across his hands. Around him his mercenaries swore and crowded closer together.

"So stupid," he chuckled. "Oh, Alyssa, if you could only see your father now."

Thren led the initial assault from inside the mansion, feeling like a hundred killings would not quench his bloodlust. He and his men crashed into the first of Maynard's men to reach the door, keeping them bottled up and unable to use their superior numbers to their advantage. The soldiers, frantic to avoid the arrows, were unprepared for the fury of his assault. He knocked aside swords, danced between thrusts, and slashed throat after throat. Bodies piled at the door, and although Kadish and his Hawks stood ready to aid him, Thren needed no help. After the first few the mercenaries had to climb over bodies to reach the door. That momentary loss of solid footing was all it took for a master swordsman like Thren Felhorn.

When Maynard's mercenaries pulled back, Thren signaled the charge. Over a hundred men in cloaks rushed through the windows, slashing with their daggers and swords. Thren nimbly leaped over the bodies, stabbed a soldier in the back, and then shouted to the rest.

"Run, run! Kill them, and Maynard with them!"

He watched the arrows rain down from the Wolf Guild stationed in the houses. The mercenaries had plenty of shields, lessening the effect of the bowmen. No bother. Even though their numbers were equal, Thren had them pressed on both sides. And besides, no one could match him in skill.

Thren lunged into the sea of metal, spinning, cutting, and slashing with a wild rage that filled him with pleasure. This was what he was meant for. He belonged on a field of battle. Perhaps once the city was under his control, he might fulfill his potential, becoming a warrior general of a massive criminal empire.

Thren was pushing his way through the soldiers, making his inevitable approach toward Maynard, when he heard the trumpets call.

Alyssa Gemcroft stood in the center of her troops, Zusa at her side. She'd marched through the city like a returning conqueror, knowing that her father had already returned moments before her. She was done with their quarrel. Her plan was to kneel before Maynard and apologize for following the Kulls' stupidity, and then pay back that stupidity with the heads of Theo and Yoren. Instead she came upon a great battle being waged before her very gates.

"Hurry," she told her mercenaries. "Kill the cloaks! Save my father and I will reward you greatly!"

Beside her a mercenary captain raised a horn to his lips and blew. The clear call rang throughout the city. With a great shout her troops rushed the gates. A few split off into the houses with the archers. Not long after, the barrage of arrows halted. Now crushed between two sides, the Wolf Guild pulled back, turning tail and running in a manner appropriate to their name.

"May I join in?" Zusa asked as the mercenaries turned on the remaining threat within the gates.

"Go right ahead," Alyssa said. Zusa flicked her hair over her shoulder and then dashed into the fray. Alyssa approached, still flanked by ten men. No arrows were being fired, but she felt safer with them there nonetheless. In the middle of the gateway she found her father lying on his side, an arrow in his chest.

"Alyssa?" he said when he saw her. His voice was weak.

Alyssa felt her heart harden at the sight of him. He'd thrown her in the cold cells. He'd insulted her, made her an outcast...

No, she thought. *I did those things myself. With my foolishness. With my pride.*

"Father," she said, kneeling down beside him and wrapping her arms around his neck. Tears welling in her eyes, she kissed his forehead and held him close.

"Daughter," he said, a smile creasing his bloodstained lips. "You were right."

He coughed. More blood spilled across his mouth. The arrow was in his lung, there was little doubt about that.

"No," she said. "Please forgive me. I've come home. I've come back for you, Father, to pledge myself to..."

"Quiet, girl," Maynard said. He relaxed in her arms. "My daughter. My heir."

His voice failed him. His eyes grew distant. He died in her arms, his eyes closed by her fingers, his forehead bathed with her tears. All around them stood Maynard's mercenaries, men of power and influence within the household.

"We heard his words," one of them said. "Give us your orders, Lady Gemcroft."

Alyssa looked up at them as if they should be obvious.

"Slay every last one of them that killed your lord," she said.

Everything was falling apart. Thren fought to the very limits of his skill. Men fell like wheat under a scythe, yet still it was not enough. He watched the Wolf Guild scatter, and in his heart he could not blame them. He'd have done the same thing in their situation.

"Fall back," Thren shouted. Further fighting would only sacrifice whatever good men he had left. The soldiers had grouped together, and their expert formations were far superior to those of men used to attacking from shadows. Even worse, a strange woman in dark wrappings vaulted through his men, slaying them as if they were no more dangerous to her than toys.

They'd left ropes in the back of the mansion just in case they had to make a quick getaway. The last of the Hawks and Spiders turned and fled. In the red haze of his anger, Thren realized he had sent no one in to ignite the fires. The mansion would stand. The failure of it burned in his gut. He'd been so confident of victory he'd never prepared for defeat. So unlike him. So stupid.

The mercenaries gave chase, but they wore heavy armor and carried shields. They slaughtered a dozen that still remained at the ropes, but the rest scattered on the other side of the gate and into the night. Thren led them, wishing so desperately for a way to redo the night.

"Take him," Alyssa said once the guilds were gone and Zusa had returned to her side. Bodies lay everywhere, and the yard stank of battle. Two soldiers lifted Maynard's corpse in their arms. They must have known him well, Alyssa realized, for they showed true sadness at his passing. She shook her head, wishing for a moment of privacy so she might shed her tears. But she was the ruling member of the Gemcroft family and one of the three lords of the Trifect. There was too much to do.

Her father in her escort's arms, she approached the mansion, a lost heir come home.

Home. No matter how sad the moment, the word still felt achingly comfortable in her heart.

EPILOGUE

Deep inside his safe house, Thren talked with two men newly appointed as his advisors. Neither had the strength of Will, the cunning of Kayla, or the skill of Senke. They were sycophants, pure and simple, but he needed them now. He had little else.

Their news was grim. The assassination attempt on the king had failed despite the incredible money he'd paid one of the Naked Bells. The men stationed at Leon Connington's had suffered horrible casualties, eventually setting fire to the mansion before frantically fleeing. Somehow Madelyn Keenan had been found and rescued. His own son was missing, and some one-eyed woman was spreading rumors that she'd killed Aaron and left him to die in the fire at the Connington mansion. Worst of all was his defeat at the Gemcroft estate.

"The priests of Karak have sworn no ill will for the acts of your son against them," one of the sycophants said. "At least Maynard died, and you kept your word to them."

Thren shook his head.

"Get out," he said. The men quickly obeyed. In silence

Thren brooded. His mystique, his prestige, his years and years of respect, had all vanished in a single night. Every aspect of his plan had collapsed. Every single guild in the city had taken massive casualties. Whatever bloody trust he'd earned he'd now lost. The other guilds would start poaching on his territory. The Trifect was already coming down hard, swarming the streets with their troops. Priests of Ashhur roamed the alleys as well, putting a halt to many of his enterprises.

Thren drew a sword and slashed his palm. He raised a clenched fist to the ceiling and bared his teeth.

"This isn't over," he swore. "Not now. Not ever. Not until every lord and lady of the Trifect lies rotting in their grave."

He kissed his fist, tasting the blood on his lips. He had no son. No heir. Death would be his legacy.

The man paced nervously before the wreckage. Despite the massive amount of ash and rubble, he felt certain some juicy remnants still hid within the remains of the Connington estate. The castle guards walked by every so often, but soon they'd switch shifts and he'd have his chance.

He backed away from the gate a bit, slinking farther into the shadows. As he did he felt something sharp poke against his back.

"Spider?" he heard a boy's voice ask.

"Serpent," the man said, his hand slowly dropping to his dagger. "They're all one and the same."

The man whirled, but not fast enough. The dagger flew from the boy's hand. Something sharp pierced his belly. As the pain doubled him over, a blade slashed his face. Through the blood in his eyes he saw a blurry image of a young man standing before him, his face covered by a thin gray cloth. Quiet, unmoving, the young man watched him die, then vanished into the night.

A NOTE FROM THE AUTHOR

So this is a little strange for me. For the first time I get to write a note from the author for a book I already released, and with its own note from the author. But like anyone who has read both the earlier work and this one, I think it's safe to say this is a new book, and therefore deserving of a new note from me to you, dear readers. Oh, and my editor said she loved these little notes I've written for all my books, and encouraged me to write another. So prepare for what will probably be my longest one of these yet.

Where to begin? About two years ago I self-published *A Dance of Cloaks*, with all its warts and in all its glory. It was a significant departure from my earlier works, in both tone and writing style. I feel safe in saying it was a nice step up in terms of quality. Well, that book found an audience, and then found itself a publisher. A real one, I mean. Trust me when I say I didn't quite expect either. Now, I've heard authors say they hate returning to old works (Stephen King refers to it as eating a week-old sandwich, if my memory serves me right). But this was something I'd been wanting to do for a while. That first book had what I'll kindly call growing pains. It was written at a feverish pace, with a complete anything-goes mentality. If I didn't know why a character was doing whatever they were doing, screw it, I'd tie it in later. If plotlines were balls, I was throwing dozens and dozens into the air just to see if I could juggle them all. And the second I thought I was doing all right, I flung one more in for fun.

Well, I'm a bit more under control now, and my wonderful editor Devi can also attest to that (I could probably have convinced her the second book of this series was by a different writer, so great was the improvement). But still this book, which for so many of my readers was a favorite, I wanted another crack at. I wanted to smooth over all those plotlines, to get the timeline firmly under control, to remove the dangling threads I'd left frayed instead of nicely and neatly tying them back into the main story line. With this Orbit release, those growing pains should be gone. The balls should stay nice and high in the air while I'm juggling them.

Have I succeeded? I believe so. This book is better, of that I have no doubt. But if you disagree, and you feel I somehow ruined that original frenetic masterpiece...well, hopefully you'll at least not begrudge me the attempt, right?

Of course, none of this matters to you new readers who have stuck through my ramble thus far. So I'll take yet another step back. Before writing *A Dance of Cloaks* I was busy with my Half-Orcs series. In the second book I introduced Haern the Watcher, who was easily the most popular new character in that book. My father, who spent hours of his time going over it in a hopeless attempt to weed out all my spelling errors and overall stupidity, mentioned to me that of all my characters, the Watcher begged for a novel of his own. My first thought was: uh, but I have no idea what his backstory is. Haern was just supposed to be mysterious, deadly, and basically my ace in the hole if I ever threw the characters into a situation a bit over their heads. My Hermione, if you will. Only male. Wielding swords. And killing people. So not like Hermione at all, but you (hopefully) get my point.

So what story did he have? Well, he was the son of Thren Felhorn, who didn't know his son was still alive... or at least pretended not to. With that beginning I started building, started adding. I took heavy inspiration from Brent Weeks's Night Angel Trilogy, and also read *A Game of Thrones* by George R. R. Martin and felt thoroughly humbled. The world I was building, it was so... empty compared to theirs. I had no important families, no real nobles, no deadly crisscrossing of families. *A Dance of Cloaks* was my chance to change that. My chance to take a tentative step toward learning how to world-build, all while giving a past to a favorite character. Did I have growing pains? Sure. Did I perhaps mistake who was at what mansion during the Bloody Kensgold? Oh yes, yes I did. But I held faith that despite all my faults I was still telling a freaking awesome story people would want to read.

And, thank God, they did.

Obligatory thanks time. Thank you, Dad, for that first spark. Thank you, Michael, for being the most awesome agent a guy like me could ever hope to get. Thank you, Devi, for being as awesome an editor as Michael is an agent. Thank you, Mrs. Patterson, Mrs. Borushaski, and Dr. Joey Brown, for never once making me feel ashamed of telling horror and fantasy stories in your writing classes. Thank you, Sam, for being such a great wife as well as an open ear for all my silly ideas. And a clandestine thank-you to my little super-secret Facebook club, and all the people therein who have helped me so much throughout my entire writing career.

And of course, thank you, dear reader. Despite everything, the good and the bad, I do this for you. In return you've allowed me to live a dream, and to tell the stories I've wanted to tell ever since I was a little kid.

Never in my wildest dreams did I think I could be so blessed.

David Dalglish
March 19, 2013

extras

www.orbitbooks.net

about the author

David Dalglish currently lives in rural Missouri with his wife, Samantha, and daughters Morgan and Katherine. He graduated from Missouri Southern State University in 2006 with a degree in mathematics and currently spends his free time teaching his children the timeless wisdom of Mario jumping on a turtle shell.

Find out more about David Dalglish and other Orbit authors by registering for the free monthly newsletter at www.orbitbooks.net.

if you enjoyed

A DANCE OF CLOAKS

look out for

A DANCE OF BLADES

Shadowdance: Book 2

also by

David Dalglish

Haern watched the ropes fly over the wall, heavy weights on their ends. They clacked against the stone, then settled on the street. The ropes looked like brown snakes in the pale moonlight, appropriately enough given the Serpent Guild controlled them.

For several minutes, nothing. Haern shifted under his well-worn cloak, his exposed hand shivering in the cold while holding an empty bottle. He kept his hood low, and he bobbed his head as if sleeping. When the first Serpent entered the alley from the street, Haern spotted him with ease. The man looked young for such a task, but then two older men arrived, their hands and faces scarred from the brutal life they led. Deep green cloaks fluttered behind them as they rushed past the houses and to the wall where the ropes hung like vines. They tugged each rope twice, giving their signal. Then the older ones grabbed a rope while the younger looped them about a carved inset in the aged stone wall, then tied the weighted ends together.

"Quick and quiet," he heard one of the elder whisper to the younger. "Don't let the crate make a sound when it lands, and the gods help you if you drop it."

Haern let his head bob lower. The three were to his right, little more than twenty feet away. Already he knew their skill was laughable if they had not yet noticed his presence. His right eye peeked from under his hood, his neck twisting slightly to give him a better view. Another Serpent appeared from outside the city, climbing atop the wall and motioning down to the others. Their arm muscles bulging, the older two began pulling on the ropes. Meanwhile the younger steadily took in the slack so it wouldn't get in their way.

Haern coughed as the crate reached the top of the wall. This time the younger heard, and he tensed as if expecting to be shot with an arrow.

"Someone's watching," he whispered to the others.

Haern leaned back, the cloak hiding his grin. About damn time. He let the bottle roll from his limp hand, the sound of glass on stone grating in the silence.

"Just a drunk," said one of them. "Go chase him off."

Haern heard the soft sound of a blade scraping against leather, most likely the young one's belt.

"Get out of here," said the Serpent.

Haern let out a loud, obnoxious snore. A boot kicked his side, but it was weak, hesitant. He shuddered as if waking from a dream.

"Why...why you kick me?" he asked, his hood still low. He had to time it just right, at the exact moment the crate touched ground.

"Beat it!" hissed the young thief. "Now, or I'll gut you!"

Haern looked up into his eyes. He knew shadows danced across his face, but his eyes...the man clearly saw his eyes. His dagger dipped in his hand, and he took a step back. Haern's drunken persona had vanished as if it had never been. No defeat, no inherent feeling of lowliness or shame. Only a calm stare that promised death. As the crate softly thumped to the ground, Haern stood, his intricate gray cloaks falling aside to reveal the two swords sheathed at his hips.

"Shit, it's him!" the thief screamed, turning to run.

Haern felt contempt ripple through him. Such poor training...did the guilds let anyone in now? He took the young man down, making sure no hit was lethal. He needed a message delivered.

"Who?" asked one, turning at the cry.

Haern cut his throat before he could draw his blade. The other yelped and stepped back. His dagger parried the first of Haern's stabs, but he had no concept of positioning. Haern smacked the dagger twice to the right, then slipped his left sword into his belly and twisted. As the thief bled out, Haern looked to the Serpent atop the wall.

"Care to join the fun?" he asked, yanking out his blade and letting the blood drip to the street. "I'm out of players."

Two daggers whirled down at him. He sidestepped one and smacked away the other. Hoping to provoke the man further, Haern kicked the crate. With no other option, the thief turned and fled back down the wall on the other side. Disappointed, Haern sheathed a sword and used the other to pry open the crate. With a loud creak the top came off, revealing three burlap sacks within. He dipped a hand in one, and it came out dripping with gold coins, each one clearly marked with the sigil of the Gemcroft family.

Interesting.

"Please," he heard the young thief beg. He bled from cuts on his arms and legs, most certainly painful, but nothing life-threatening. The worst Haern had done was hamstring him to prevent him from fleeing. "Please, don't kill me. I can't, I can't..."

Haern slung all three bags over his shoulder. With his free hand he pressed the tip of his sword against the young man's throat.

"They'll want to know why you lived," he said.

The man had no response to that, only a pathetic sniffle. Haern shook his head. How far the Serpent Guild had fallen... but all the guilds had fallen since that bloody night five years ago. Thren Felhorn, the legend, had failed in his coup, bringing doom upon the underworld. Thren... his father...

"Tell them you have a message," Haern said. "Tell them I'm watching."

"Who?"

In response Haern took his sword and dipped it in the man's blood.

"They'll know who," he said before vanishing, leaving only a single eye drawn in the dirt as his message, blood for its ink, a sword its quill.

He didn't go far. He had to lug the bags to the rooftops one at a time, but once he was up high his urgency dwindled. The rooftops were his home, had been for years. Following the main road west, he reached the inner markets, still silent and empty. Plunking down the bags, he lay with his eyes closed and waited.

He woke to the sounds of trade. Hunger stirred in his belly, but he ignored it. Hunger, like loneliness and pain, had become a constant companion. He wouldn't call it friend, though.

"May you go to better hands," Haern said to the first sack of gold before stabbing its side. Coins spilled, and he hurled them like rain to the packed streets. Without pause he cut the second and third, flinging them to the suddenly ravenous crowd. They dove and fought as the gold rolled along, bouncing off bodies and plinking into various wooden stalls. Only a few bothered to look up, those who were lame or old and dared not fight the crowd.

"The Watcher!" someone cried. "The Watcher is here!"

The cry put a smile on his lips as Haern fled south, having not kept a single coin.

It had taken five years, but at last Alyssa Gemcroft understood her late father's paranoia. The meal placed before her smelled delicious, spiced pork intermixed with baked apples, but her appetite remained dormant.

"I can have one of the servants taste it, if you'd like," said her closest family advisor, a man named Bertram who had loyally served her father. "I'll even do so myself."

"No," she said, brushing errant strands of her red hair back and tucking them behind her left ear. "That's not necessary. I can afford to skip a meal."

Bertram frowned, and she hated the way he looked at her—like a doting grandfather, or a worried teacher. Just the night before, two servants had died eating their daily rations. Though she'd replaced much of the mansion's food, as well as executed those she thought responsible, the memory lingered in Alyssa's mind. The way the two had retched, their faces turning a horrific shade of purple...

She snapped her fingers, and the many waiting servants rushed to clear the trays away. Despite the rumble in her belly, she felt better with the food gone. At least now she could think without fear of convulsing to death because of some strange toxin. Bertram motioned to a chair beside her, and she gave him permission to sit.

"I know these are not peaceful times," he said, "but we cannot allow fear to control our lives. That is a victory you know the thief guilds have longed for."

"We're approaching the fifth anniversary of the Bloody

Kensgold," Alyssa said, referring to a gathering of the Trifect, the three wealthiest families of merchants, nobles, and power brokers in all of Dezrel. On that night Thren Felhorn had led an uprising of thief guilds against the Trifect, burning down one of their mansions and attempting to annihilate their leaders. He'd failed, and his guild had broken down to a fraction of its former size. On that night Alyssa had assumed control after the death of her father, victim to an arrow as they'd fought to protect their home.

"I know," Bertram said. "Is that what distracts you so? Leon and Laurie have both agreed to delay another Kensgold until this dangerous business is over with."

"And when will that be?" she asked as another servant arrived with a silver cup of wine. "I hide here in my mansion, fearful of my food and scared of every shadow in my bedroom. We cannot defeat the guilds, Bertram. We've broken them, fractured many to pieces, but it's like smashing a puddle with a club. They all come back together, under new names, new leaders."

"The end is approaching," Bertram said. "This is Thren's war, and he champions it with the last of his strength. But he is not so strong, not so young. His Spider Guild is far from the force it used to be. In time the other guilds will see reason and turn against him. Until then, we have only one choice left before us, and that is to endure."

Alyssa closed her eyes and inhaled the scent of the wine. For a moment she wondered if it was poisoned, but she fought the paranoia down. She would not sacrifice such a simple pleasure. She couldn't give the rogues that much of a victory.

Still, when she drank, it was a small sip.

"You told me much the same after the Kensgold," she said, setting down the cup. "As you have every year for the past five. The mercenaries have bled us dry. Our mines to the north no longer produce the yields they were renowned for. The king is too frightened to help us. How long until we eat in rags, without coin for servants and wood for fires?"

"We are on the defensive," Bertram said, accepting his own cup of wine. "Such is our fate for being a large target. But the bloodshed has slowed, you know that as well as I. Be patient. Let us bleed them as they bleed us. The last thing we want is to inflame their passions while we still appear weak and leaderless."

Alyssa felt anger flare in her chest, not only at the insult, but also at its damning familiarity.

"Leaderless?" she asked. "I have protected the Gemcroft name for five years of shadow wars. I've brokered trade agreements, organized mercenaries, bribed nobles, and done everything as well as my father ever did, yet we are *leaderless*? Why is that, Bertram?"

Bertram endured the rant without a shred of emotion on his face, and that only infuriated Alyssa further. Again she felt like a schoolchild before her teacher, and part of her wondered if that was exactly how her advisor viewed her.

"I say this only because the rest of Dezrel believes it," he said when she was finished. "You have no husband, and the only heir to the Gemcroft name is a bastard of unknown heritage."

"Don't talk about Nathaniel that way," she said, her voice turning cold. "Don't you dare speak ill of my son."

Bertram raised his hands and spread his palms.

"I meant no offense, milady. Nathaniel is a good child, smart too. But a lady of your station should be partnered with someone equally influential. You've had many suitors; surely you've taken a liking to one of them?"

Alyssa took another sip of wine, her eyes glancing up at the shadowy corners of the dining hall.

"Leave me," she said. "All of you. We'll speak of this another time."

Bertram stood, bowed, and followed the servants out.

"Come down, Zusa," she told the ceiling. "You know you're always welcome at my table. There's no need for you to skulk and hide."

Clinging like a spider to the wall, Zusa smiled down at her. With deceptive ease she let go, falling headfirst toward the carpet. A deft twist of her arms, a tuck of her knees, and she landed gracefully on her feet, her long cloak billowing behind her. Instead of any normal outfit she wore long strips of cloth wrapped around her body, hiding every inch of skin. Except for above her neck, Alyssa was still pleased to see. Zusa had once belonged to a strict order of Karak, the dark god. Upon her willful exile Zusa had cast aside the cloth from her face, revealing her stunning looks and her beautiful black hair, which she kept cropped short around her neck. Two daggers hung from her belt, wickedly sharp.

"Let me be the one in the shadows," Zusa said, smiling. "That way you are safe, for no assassin can hide beside me."

Alyssa gestured for her friend to sit. Zusa refused, but Alyssa took no offense. It was just one of the skilled lady's many quirks. The woman had rescued her years before from an attempt by a former lover to take over her family line, and then helped protect her estate from Thren's plans. She owed her life to Zusa, so if Zusa wanted to stand instead of sit, she was more than welcome.

"Did you hear everything?" Alyssa asked.

"Everything of worth. The old man is scared. He tries to be the rock in a storm, to survive by doing nothing until it passes."

"Sometimes a sound strategy."

Zusa smirked. "This storm will not pass, not without action. Not with *his* cowardly action. You know what Bertram wants. He wants you bedded and yoked to another man. Then your womanly passions may be safely ignored, and he can rule through your husband."

"Bertram has no desire for power."

Zusa lifted an eyebrow. "Can you know for sure? He is old, but not dead."

Alyssa sighed and drained her cup.

"What should I do?" she asked. She felt tired, lost. She badly missed her son. She'd sent Nathaniel north to Felwood Castle, to be fostered by Lord John Gandrem. John was a good man, and a good friend of the family. More important, he was far away from Veldaren and its guilds of thieves. At least there Nathaniel was safe, and the training he received would help him later in life.

"Bertram's question . . . are there any you have taken a fancy to?" Zusa asked.

Alyssa shrugged.

"Mark Tullen was attractive, though his station is probably lower than Bertram would prefer. At least he was willing to talk to me instead of staring down my blouse. Also, that noble who runs our mines, Arthur something . . ."

"Hadfield," Zusa said.

"That's right. He's pleasant enough, and not ugly . . . little distant, though. Guess that's just a product of being older."

"The older, the less likely to cavort with other women."

"He's more than welcome to," Alyssa said. She stood and turned away, trying to voice a silent fear she'd held on to for years, a fear that had strangled her relationships and kept her unmarried. "But any child we have... that is who will become the Gemcroft heir. Too many will shove Nathaniel aside, deem him unfit, unworthy. I can't do that to him, Zusa. I can't deny him his right. He's my firstborn."

She felt Zusa's arms slip around her. Startled by the uncommon display of emotion, she accepted the hug.

"If your son is strong, he will claim what is his, no matter what the world tries," she said. "Do not be afraid."

"Thank you," Alyssa said, pulling back and smiling. "What would I do without you?"

"May we never find out," Zusa said, bowing low.

Alyssa waved her off, then retreated to her private chambers. She stared out the thick glass window, beyond her mansion's great walls, to the city of Veldaren. She found herself hating the city, hating every dark corner and crevice. Always it conspired against her, waiting with poison and dagger to...

No. She had to stop thinking like that. She had to stop letting the thief guilds control every aspect of her life through force and fear. So she sat at her desk, pulled out an inkwell and a piece of parchment, and paused. She'd sent Nathaniel away to protect him, to be fostered with a good family. Not so long ago her father had done the same with her, and she remembered her anger, her loneliness, and her feelings of betrayal. Gods help her, she'd even sent Nathaniel to the same person she'd been sent to. Once more she understood her father in a way she never had before. He'd hidden her because he loved her, not to get her out of the way as she'd once thought.

Still, how angry she'd been when she returned...

No, she would not let history repeat itself. Her decision made, she dipped the quill in the ink and began writing.

My dear Lord Tullen, she began. *I have a request for you involving my son, Nathaniel...*

CONTINUE THE ADVENTURE

For exclusive news, giveaways and more join us on the official Shadowdance Facebook page.

/SHADOWDANCESERIES